THE CIRCUMSTANTIAL ENEMY

John Richard Bell

Table of Contents

I dedicate this book to my father-in-law, Zlatko Stjepan Muzic whose inspiring true story made this novel possible.

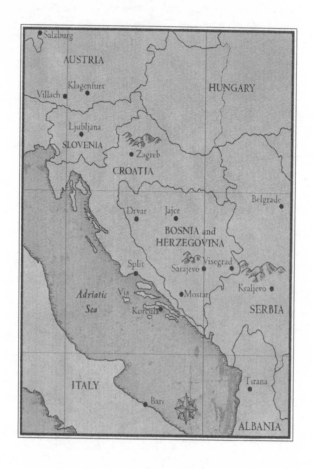

The South Slavic States 1941

Chapter 1

May 1941
Zagreb, Independent State of Croatia

Once the shriek of the steel-wheeled brakes fell silent, Tony Babic squeezed through the partially open doors of the railcar and dashed toward the parks leading to the city center. His frantic strides soon slowed, but not because of breathlessness. The wooded squares' sights, sounds, and smells were messing with a determined mind. The fountains still danced and the vibrant irises and marigolds, always planted with precision, rippled in the wind. He mopped his brow and shifted his duffle from one shoulder to the other, all the while absorbing the wonders around him.

Apart from Wehrmacht vehicles on the street, Zagreb seemed to know nothing of the 12-day invasion. Why would it? This had been Serbia's war, with Belgrade taking the brunt of Hitler's bombs. As Tony considered the notion, his gaze veered to the clusters of leaves that swirled at his ankles and snagged at the cuffs of his uniform. A rumble in the sky and the approach of muddy clouds warned of a downpour. So be it. Whatever the heavens tossed his way could not dampen the thrill of home.

At Zrinjevac, the lower town's most northerly park, he crossed the soggy grass to the east boulevard, his pace quickening at the spectacle of his roofline. He took the tenement's stairs two at a time, heartened by the smell of sauerkraut, fried onions and bacon that surely came from his mother's stove. At door number six, he patted the debris from his overcoat and scrubbed the toes of his boots behind his knees. Side cap adjusted and shoulders back, he knocked, then louder, seconds later. He tried the latch – locked. A painful minute of pacing left little choice but to use his time wisely; he'd get his identity papers stamped at the Defense Ministry.

****

7

The line of soldiers extended beyond the reception area into the hall and down the stairs. Five minutes short of an hour, a pudgy fellow called his name from a cluttered desk at the rear of the office. The desk was twice the size of the twenty facing it, evoking a classroom with a schoolteacher at the head.

As Tony neared, he noticed the patches of darker blue on the uniform. Every insignia of the former Yugoslav state had been removed. Eyes down, the man made notes. Without raising his head, he said, "I'm Captain Skojo of the Croatian Air Force Legion. Give me your papers."

The big fellow took his time scanning Tony's credentials. Finally, he gawked over the spectacles resting on the bridge of his greasy nose. "This says you *were* a second lieutenant, Vlatko Anton Babic." He pushed a disordered batch of papers aside, and an envelope fell to the floor. Tony bent to pick it up.

"Leave it!"

The day had started well, but now Tony's head pounded and his stomach ached.

Skojo placed a sheet of paper on a clipboard and began filling in the blanks. "Why do you sweat, Mr Babic?"

Mister? No, this was not the time or place for a pissing contest. "It's hot in here," Tony said.

"Can't you feel the breeze," Skojo said, gesturing to the window behind him, "or do you have something to hide?" With Tony in his crosshairs, he reached back and closed the window. "Give me your military background."

"It's all there."

"Give it in your own words."

Tony volunteered his training and pilot experience.

"I want specifics on your war involvement."

Tony said he had flown two fighter missions over Belgrade, and one bomber raid at the Albanian border. "Bad weather grounded our fleet for most of the war. Our situation in Kraljevo was the same as the rest of the country."

"Particulars, Mr Babic."

Tony sprinkled a few more breadcrumbs but sidestepped the most haunting hour of his young life.

"And when hostilities ended, where were you?"

"In Visegrad, held by the Germans as a prisoner of war."

Skojo downed what remained of a glass of water he had been cradling. "You'd retreated from Serbia," he said, smacking his lips.

"Yes. They pushed us west."

Smiling for the first time, Skojo leaned back and pulled the window open. "Lieutenant … this war left us with few skilled pilots. Your know-how would be of great value to the new Croat Legion. You're only twenty. Already you have two years in the cockpit."

"My combat record is two days."

The rims of Skojo's specs slipped further down his nose. He removed them and placed them on Tony's papers. "I'm certain you learned plenty in those two days."

Tony felt the sting in his eyes as the seconds elapsed. Evidently, Skojo had no intention of backing off. "Please don't take my silence as disrespectful, Captain … what I learned is painful and personal."

"Does this have to do with your duty as a soldier?"

"I handled myself with dignity as a soldier and an officer."

Skojo wiped the dampness from his face. "Lieutenant Vlatko Babic, I will grant your wish for privacy if you answer my next question honestly. Were you honored to fight for the Serbs?"

"I was not," Tony said, without hesitation.

"Why not?"

This was a second question, but calling Skojo on it would be stupid. "None of us wanted to give our lives for a country not our own."

"Lieutenant, I shall respect your privacy."

Maybe the captain wasn't such a bad guy – maybe intimidation was part of the job.

Skojo waddled to the windowsill, and plopped his ample bottom upon it. "I'll be candid. Germany's giving us self-rule. No one knows how much autonomy the Pavelic government will have under Hitler. But consider the alternative. Stalin's backing the Communists. We can't allow Croatia to suffer the repression of that butcher. Your choice is the Germans or the Reds. We can't count on the Allies for Croat independence. All we got last time was a quarter century of more Serb rule. Your country needs you as a pilot of the Croatian Air Force."

Who was the enemy: the Allies, the Germans, the Communists, or the Serb Royalists? "I just got home, Captain."

"These are urgent times. We must rebuild Croatia's armed forces." Skojo motioned his chin to the closed door of a private office. "Agree to join us, and I will ask Major Schwanitz to appoint you an officer of the Croatian Air Force. Aligning with Germany is our best chance at independence."

In war, there was no such thing as neutrality. Everyone must choose a side. "Do that, Captain." *And let me get the hell out of here.*

****

The high-booted man in the black SS uniform appraised Tony through the slits of his eyes. "Aryan-looking. He is of the Fatherland, Captain Skojo?"

"An able, curly-blonde Croat airman."

SS Major Schwanitz moved closer to Tony. "Sprechen sie Deutsch?"

Tony disclosed a narrow space between his raised forefinger and thumb. "Ich spreche deutsches wenig."

Schwanitz bade a stiff nod to Skojo. Then he marched back to his office, banging the door behind him.

****

A belly full of skewered grilled pork had done little to dilute the alcohol Tony and his best friend had consumed at the tavern. With the local news exhausted, Goran became the inquirer, and the subject predictable.

"I'll tell you this," Tony said, patting the backs of the two empty chairs at his sides, "these will be warmed by female backsides well before this night is over."

"We'll see," Goran said, leaning in. "Tell the story like I was there with you."

Tony couldn't put it off any longer. Thankfully, enough plum brandy and pilsner in him afforded an entertaining account of thrilling chases and narrow escapes, dodging Messerschmitts and guarding the tails of Rado Borcic and Joe Boskovic. This was the brash Tony of old. Behind the facade, of course, was quite another man.

But Goran insisted on more, so Tony ventured further. "Joe was a cocky bugger cut from irregular cloth. He was the eldest of the lot – no one handled a fighter like him, and he let you know it – loved to say he was a better pilot drunk than we were sober." Tony blew cigarette smoke at the ceiling. Then he bowed his head. "Truth is … there are old pilots and bold pilots, but no old bold pilots."

The idiom shook him lucid. Better that he shift to the escape from Serbia. He had enough benign material to captivate Goran for another half hour: the collective decision to retreat; the trek through the forest; his major's expansive knowledge of the wild hills and gorges between Kraljevo and Visegrad on the Drina River in Bosnia.

"When the trucks could go no farther, we ate sandwiches and drank from a stream at the mountain's base before starting up. There was plenty of talk at first. But soon the only sounds were birds, boots on pebbles, and panting ... a lot of panting. My thighs trembled from the weight on my soaking-wet back ... didn't cool off until we reached the mist ..."

At a nearby table, he noticed two fellows pulling out chairs for their girls – just at the right time. Tony gestured with his eyes, and Goran swiveled a quarter turn. "You're drunker than I thought," Goran said, "or you've completely lost your taste in women. Perhaps Roza wasn't as scrumptious as you made out."

Possibly the altitude of the Bosnian hills was as far as he would have to take Goran. "Ah, Roza ..." Tony hugged himself, rocking from side to side. The story he had told many times, but Goran never seemed to tire of it.

Tony closed his eyes. It had been an unusually hot day at the family vineyard. At the time, Rosa was eighteen; he was fifteen. From afar, he had spotted a peasant girl picking grapes alone, her sweat-damp, coal-black tufts straying from beneath a faded red scarf. He remembered trying to get a glimpse of her face as he neared. When she moved to the next vine, the faceless girl stopped him cold. Her weathered, grape-stained blouse, sweated through, clinging to jutting breasts, and an equally flimsy ankle-length gypsy skirt had showed every contour and flexure of strong, smooth buttocks and supple washboard-flat stomach.

Surely she had heard his feet crushing the brittle twigs. Her next movement affirmed his assumption. With the deliberate, unhurried motion of a ballerina stretching at the wall bar, she lowered her basket and arched her back as if to loosen tight muscles. Her breasts, taxing the wet shirt's tenuous restraint, rose heavenward like twin volcanoes. Moments later, she lowered her arms, rotated toward him, and set her hands on her hips as if tendering a challenge.

Tony had felt his chest contract, the tips of his fingers pulsing from a quickened heartbeat. She had cocked her head to one side and eyed him from head to foot. The color of her eyes matched the deep-brown nipples embossing the blouse. Her tongue moistened her plump lips in a circular motion, and her olive cheeks darkened. Speechless and awestruck, he'd stumbled forward, halting four feet from the creature.

Goran was never to know the truth of the 'conquest'. Tony had not bedded Roza; Roza had bedded Tony. Several times over two days in the privacy of a tiny bedroom in the barn, she had tutored him in the ways of love. During their last such wrestling match, Tony's father had entered the barn to fetch a wagon. Josip Babic could not have arrived at a worse time. Roza, at the very gates of heaven, released a round of feral screams. Alarmed, Josip had burst through the door to behold the glistening back and buttocks of a young woman riding her lover in a steeplechase. Her unidentified mount looked to be holding on for dear life.

Josip had slammed the door, and without breaking rhythm, Roza's head turned to see who was there. Horror engulfed Tony, who had craned his neck around her for the same purpose. At the sight of his father, he'd sought to writhe away, but the wild and wailing Roza would not deny herself those final pumps of glory.

Josip had hollered for her to stop, but Roza galloped on for a few more seconds and then, with a last, fragmented moan, dismounted, snatched up the crumpled bedsheet, and covered herself. Meanwhile, Tony, with a pillow over his groin, squirmed to the head of the bed, where he cowered like a yearling before a wolf.

The hand shaking Tony's shoulder brought him back to the tavern. "You've left me," Goran said. "I think I know where you went."

Goran was right. Roza took him as far from Visegrad as he could go.

"Hey, where'd those girls go?"

"To another table. The rest of the story, Tony."

Tony scanned the room, struggling to merge double images into one.

"If it was that bad," Goran said. "You ought to get it out. You'll feel better."

"How would you know?" Tony fumbled for the inside pocket of his jacket. Then, with his eyes locked on Goran, he slapped the table with an open hand. Beneath his palm was a folded piece of notepaper.

Goran snatched it up and began reading:

'Dear Lieutenant Babic,

The kind words in your cablegram were comforting. Ivan was a dutiful soldier for twenty years of war-free service. He was also a loving husband and father. You can imagine how heartbroken we are that he was taken by this brief war.

My daughter and I will be in Zagreb to attend Archbishop Stepinac's May 9 mass for Croat soldiers who died in the war. After the service, we will walk to St Mark's Church for private prayers. This is the church of our marriage and Katarina's baptism.

You wrote that my husband left something for us. Could I impose on you to come to St Mark's so we may retrieve it? Deepest thanks in advance for your consideration,

Maria Kirilenko.'

Goran dabbed his twitching left eye. "What do you have for them?"

Hand shaking, Tony tipped his glass until the last drop of brandy touched his tongue. Then, staring at the empty snifter as he might a confessor, he said, "Major Kirilenko was a selfless man, not the arrogant prick we met at the apprentice trials. Never did he speak of himself. He wanted to know about *you*. 'How are you feeling, soldier?' 'What can I do for you, Lieutenant?' He made you feel special ..." said Tony, now speaking in a whisper.

"I was right next to him ... when he went down ... so fucking pointless. From the start, we made sure the Croat flag was front and center in case we came upon German troops – we didn't want them thinking we were a pack of Serbs. Major Kirilenko and I were together in front when the shot came from the bushes of the riverbank. Then all hell broke loose. His legs gave out and his hat flew off. I ripped open his overcoat ... Blood gushed from his chest. I covered the wound with my hands. His warm blood trickled through my fingers, so I pressed harder. I couldn't stop it."

Tony lowered his head into his hands and slowly his fingers slid up to his brow. "The major gasped, 'No, Tony.' He called me 'Tony'. 'Inside pocket ... for Maria. My pilot badge ...' He used the last of his strength to rip the pin from his tunic. Then he said, 'Katarina'. I felt the last beat of his heart. Katarina was the last word he spoke. I wiped my hands on my coat. I couldn't get all the blood off … It was sticky. The firing stopped when our men raised their hands. I tried to open his fingers for the badge … his grip was so tight, I had to pry each finger back to get it free." He looked up from the empty snifter. "There's your story. Be glad you failed those pilot trials."

Chapter 2

Two women in black emerged from the arched doors of St Mark's. The taller one wore a mesh-veiled narrow-brimmed hat, the other a kerchief. They shaded their brows from the brightness of the sun and squinted at the people congregating in the square below the church steps.

Tony reckoned they would recognize him, if not by the style of his side cap then by the embroidered red and white checkered shield on the breast pocket of his uniform. "That's them," he said to Goran. "I'm hoping your presence will dissuade them from asking too many questions."

"Thank you for coming, Lieutenant Babic," Maria Kirilenko said with a faint smile. Her daughter acknowledged neither.

"Goran and I are very sorry for your loss," Tony said.

"Every seat occupied at the archbishop's mass," Maria Kirilenko said, "and hundreds standing. The Air Force lost 711, seventy-six Croats. My husband was the highest ranked to give his life."

"A brave man, your husband." Tony regretted the way the words rolled off his tongue. Perhaps he should have thought of something else to say – something more insightful and consolatory. With so little sleep, his wits weren't at their sharpest. Still, by now he should have been used to sleepless nights.

"This church holds a warm place in my heart," Maria Kirilenko said, a sliver of joy having swept her face. "I still marvel at those roof tiles. There isn't a structure in Europe that rivals the mosaic."

All four looked up to the south roof and the glittering coats of arms of Croatia and Zagreb.

"An artful masterpiece," Goran said. "Recently refurbished – presuming you consider the nineteenth century recent."

Maria Kirilenko's eyes patiently traversed the church's facade. If it was nostalgia that engaged her, it dissipated the moment she checked her wristwatch. "Please gentlemen; say you will join us for lunch at the Palace Hotel. There we can talk."

Tony was afraid of that.

They strolled through the city's wooded park that bordered a sand-colored four-story building of wrought-iron railings and high-arched window casements. As they entered the hotel's lobby, the aroma of coffee and fresh-baked pastries awakened Tony's appetite. The maître d', a weasel-faced chap with a pencil-thin mustache, took the women's cloaks and led them through the restaurant. Tony abandoned the opulence around him for the lines of the young woman walking ahead of him. None of the tables in the secluded alcove were occupied. Was that intentional?

Peripherally, Katarina's veil rose, but wishing to appear innocuous, Tony took his gaze elsewhere. The sweet smell of femininity remained. On the stroll, he had detected rosebud lips and the faintly cleft chin of a strong jawline behind the veil. Most striking were her eyes. They glistened like polished chestnuts in the sun, but they refused to smile.

How might she look standing atop a lonely hill in a colored frock, its rippling cotton clutching her legs from the shove of the wind, hair wild, eyes cast to the sea, lips parted, and mind heedless of the approaching storm? How long would she mourn? Some women wore black for years. This woman hadn't uttered a word, and yet she exuded potent determination.

When the small talk waned to the brink of discomfort, the major's daughter spoke for the first time, giving Tony his license to study eyes heightened by silky-black brows.

"I understand you brought something for us, Lieutenant."

Though he'd prepared for this, his words eluded him.

"Lieutenant?"

There was no mistaking her firmer voice. "Pardon me, Miss Kirilenko – and please call me Tony."

"I address all soldiers by rank."

"Katarina!" Maria Kirilenko glared at her daughter.

"No, no, Mrs Kirilenko, no offense." Tony told her that he understood. He did not. He handed her a sealed envelope stained by reddish-brown smears. Her eyes welled. "I tried to wipe …" he said. "Sorry for its condition."

He then dug into his pocket for the other item, and held out a fist to Katarina, slowly uncurling his fingers. And there, nestled in the lines of his palm was the major's bronzed pilot badge and the ragged swatch of blue it was fastened to.

Katarina's lips quivered. The moment a tear spilled to her cheek, she snatched up the badge and rushed for the exit.

"Katarina needs me," Maria Kirilenko said, easing her chair away from the table and following her daughter.

"Heartbreaking," Goran said. "She's the image of those textbook illustrations of Aphrodite. Do you remember the beauty mark on Aphrodite's cheek? Katarina's is in the same place."

Twenty minutes later, the women reappeared. The envelope must have contained a long letter.

Maria Kirilenko ordered more coffee as well as rolls and an assortment of sliced meats and cheese. While they waited, Katarina asked Tony to describe his relationship with her father.

Though his mouth was empty, Tony swallowed. Then he dabbed his lips with his napkin. Goran was right: she was beautiful, but so bitter. Tony reversed the linen's fold, returned it to his lap, and turned his head toward Katarina. "The major was my commanding officer."

Seconds passed, and neither Tony nor Katarina shifted their gaze. Finally, she broke the stalemate. "There must be more than that."

Tony fixed his eyes on the pepper mill and delivered an account that was more like a report on troop movements than a luncheon conversation. He gave the facts but not all of them, avoiding heartfelt emotions and the final seconds of Kirilenko's life. Several times Katarina interrupted. He was on trial, a prisoner in the witness box, negotiating minefields planted by a zealous prosecutor hell-bent on destroying him. All the while, his stare never strayed from the pepper grinder, nor did he allow his private sorrow to breach his delivery.

"You haven't mentioned the circumstances of his death," Katarina said.

Tony took an extended sip of coffee. "Everything happened so fast. Your father gave me the letter and the wings before he died."

"You saw my father die?"

"He died quickly and painlessly. Excuse me …" He hurried from the room.

Katarina swiveled in her chair to face Goran. "Your friend tells the story like a newsman. Do *you* know if he was close to my father?"

"Well, uh ... Miss Kirilenko, I, um ..."

"My father loved mentoring young pilots. He maintained the distance of a superior officer, but he was close to many. Was Lieutenant Babic one of them?"

Goran felt fresh dampness around his collar. And that damn eye with its never-ending spasms – without a doubt, she'd see his nervousness. "I don't think so," he said, as though suddenly enlightened. "Tony's not that type of person. I'm his best friend. I cannot say he's even close to me."

"That's odd," Maria Kirilenko said. "His telegram gave the impression that he was very fond of my husband."

Goran's eyelid stepped up its tempo. "Whether he was *close* is another matter."

"Why on earth would he re-enlist?" Katarina asked. "He'll be fighting alongside the savages who killed my father. Has he no conscience?"

"This I can answer with certainty. He loves to fly. Discovery drives him. Other than a bias for Croat nationalism, he's not of political conviction. The Air Force is a means to his adventurous ends. He's naive when it comes to the alliance with Germany. He thinks they're Croatia's saviors."

"And you – what do you think?" At this point, Katarina was on the edge of her chair.

"I don't see it that way."

"Katarina, we are in a public place," Maria Kirilenko said. "You've put Goran in a difficult position. This shall go no further."

Katarina looked to every corner of the alcove. "Who's to hear us?"

"Enough!" Maria Kirilenko said.

"Tell me Goran," Katarina said. "Were you ever interested in a military career?"

"I'm a history teacher. My job is developing young minds. Of course, I would not turn my back on conscription if—" He did a quick double-take. "Here he comes."

When Tony pulled up his chair, Maria Kirilenko said that Katarina would be moving to Zagreb. "She'll live with her aunt and work as a seamstress's apprentice. Katarina enjoys sewing – don't you, dear?"

A faint pink seeped into Katarina's olive complexion.

"Could I impose on the two of you to familiarize her with Zagreb when she arrives?"

"Mother!"

"We can do that, can't we, Tony?" Goran asked.

Tony said nothing. That didn't seem to dissuade Maria Kirilenko from scribbling her daughter's Zagreb address on a piece of paper and tucking it under his side plate.

"We must go," Maria Kirilenko said. "My sister is expecting us."

Once the women were out of the alcove, Tony got up. "That was excruciating."

"You did fine." Goran caught the attention of the passing waiter and asked if they served the wines of Vinograd Kralja.

"Sir, I do not know that vineyard. Is there another wine you'd like me to find?"

"No, no. Two glasses of Kraljevina will do. Make it quick."

"Good idea," Tony said, sitting down. "Two hours walking on egg shells." He brought his elbows to the tabletop and dropped his head into his hands. "They have no idea how difficult that was for me – no idea how much I loved the man. I couldn't talk about that or I'd be crying like baby."

****

In the weeks to come, Goran could not shake Katarina's image. She was always with him – an observer in the classroom, a dinner mate, and a lover in the night when he pleasured himself. Yet, the more he craved her, the more he feared that, like all the others, she would fall into the arms of his friend. This one he would not surrender to Tony's shallow whims.

Goran hiked two flights of stairs to the poorly lit hallway of a tenement building that had seen better days, but was still well kept. At the flat's door, he clamped the flower stems between his knees, combed his hair and mouthed his prologue as might a conscientious thespian. If the aunt answered, he would revert to the back-up line.

The squeaky door opened. The dress of mourning was gone.

"Oh," she said. Katarina retreated by a step and swept back the sleek, ebony locks that rested on her shoulders. "Goran ... I suppose I owe ..."

"Welcome to Zagreb, Katarina. These are for you, bought this morning at our Dolac marketplace. Perhaps I can escort you there at some point.

You will enjoy the wares and the amusing banter between buyers and sellers." Though jittery at first, he had delivered every word of the rehearsed salutation.

Now smiling, her eyes closed as her nose all but touched the petals of the bouquet. "They're beautiful. Oh, but here I stand, keeping you in the hallway – please, come in. I've just finished unpacking."

The sparsely appointed sitting room was clean but dreary, two small windows overlooking a five yard-wide alley connecting the neighboring tenement.

"My aunt's at work. Adela's a dressmaker – the one I can thank for my job with Mr Schwartz. He's a textile wholesaler and owner of the Ilica Street tailor shop."

Goran's father had bought suits there.

"I start Monday, on the upstairs sewing floor. Will you have tea or coffee?"

"Well, I don't want to impose …"

"Don't be silly. I'm so pleased you stopped by. It's strange being in a big city where you don't know anyone. So … tea or coffee?"

He asked for coffee and she fetched a brass mill and a little crock of dark, shiny beans. "In Bosnia we make coffee like the Turks. Here. Start grinding."

Every time Goran thought the task complete, she told him to keep turning the cylinder's long crank. When the beans were fine as snuff, Katarina boiled the powder in a pot of water. Then she poured the steaming tar into tiny cups without handles, adding heaps of sugar.

"Let the dregs settle," she said.

An hour later, when he rose to leave, Katarina inquired of Tony.

"Haven't seen much of him," Goran said.

"I was terribly harsh on him … and not exactly friendly to you, either. I'm really not like that … I was in a sorry state. Could you arrange a coffee klatch for the three of us? I owe Tony an apology."

It had gone so well. Now this. Why didn't he just say that Tony was in Germany or Poland – anywhere but Zagreb? There was no way around it – for the time being. Soon Tony would be gone, fighting a war that would not be short-lived.

****

From a small round table at the Esplanade Hotel's café, Tony saw them enter, Katarina's fingertips tidying a wayward lock of hair jostled by the breeze. She was smiling; her chestnut eyes no longer bespoke anger or disdain. A silver necklace fell below the neckline of a cotton-white blouse under the light green jacket, and the polished black belt on her skirt emphasized a narrow waistline. For a woman, her shoulders were square – like those of a competitive swimmer.

"Good morning, Miss Kirilenko," he said. "Welcome to the greatest city in the world."

"May I call you Tony?" she asked as she sat down at the small round table.

He chuckled. "You can, *Katarina*."

"Thank you for coming," she said. "I want to apologize for my conduct a month ago. I allowed my contempt for the military to spill onto you."

"Apology accepted. You were going through a tough time. Are you enjoying Zagreb?"

"I appreciate your forgiveness. As for Zagreb, I have mixed feelings. I'm happy to live with my aunt. I'm excited about my new job, and—"

"You're a seamstress, no?"

"An apprentice, really."

Goran fidgeted as he peered back and forth between the two – first with his billfold, then his tight-fitting collar, and finally his wristwatch. "It's time—"

"I know little of dressmaking," Tony told her, "but I like dresses, especially on beautiful women." *Actually, I prefer them* off *beautiful women*. Heedless of the amusement this brought to his lips, he held her gaze for an extra beat, and she blushed.

In a surly voice, Goran said, "Katarina works above Schwartz's store near Cellar Ilica."

Goran had gone a sickly pale – Tony reckoned his quip about beautiful women had rattled him. Good thing he hadn't vocalized his thoughts; if she weren't Major Kirilenko's daughter, he'd have her in bed by month's end. He put that thought aside and asked her to explain her mixed feelings about Zagreb.

"You called Zagreb the greatest city in the world. By doing that you've put it in the company of some formidable contenders such as Paris, London and Vienna."

"These cities you know from personal experience?" he asked, aware of the mockery.

"I don't and, I suspect, neither do you."

"*That* will change. But fair enough – point taken. Tell me, though, what's to dislike in Zagreb?"

She craned her neck for a glimpse of the boulevard through the large front window. "Gestapo in the streets, Nazi banners on buildings, hideous armbands and Stars of David on Jews. I'm told the Jews will lose their citizenship and their property – a sign of things to come. Zagreb could become Warsaw, one of the *worst* cities in the world." Her voice retreated to a murmur. "All because of fascist oppression. Croatia will be the Nazi's puppet – it may be already."

Like arguing religion, Tony recognized the futility of political debate.

"The persecution will not stop at the Jews," Goran said. "Pavelic has it in for Serbs as well. One race and one religion is his mantra. Serbs have been seen with blue armbands in the countryside. Supposedly, they're destined for concentration camps that will convert them from Orthodox to Catholic. The worst of it is the fact that the archbishop and the church support that lunatic."

Katarina asked Goran if he thought the non-Catholics of Bosnia and Herzegovina would also face persecution.

"Your lands are under the State of Croatia. That means the Serbs will suffer. Bosnian Moslems might get a reprieve for joining Pavelic against them."

Now looking at Tony, she said, "What do *you* think of this mess?"

"I think we forgot to order coffee," Tony said, signaling for a waiter. He was glad to let the two of them run with the conversation, hoping they would wear out the topic. He didn't like the situation, either. All he wanted was a nation run by Croats, free of Serb rule once and for all. Pavelic's dogma had Serbs in Serbia, Croats in Croatia – not easy in states of mixed ethnicity.

His father had said Archbishop Stepinac feared Communism more than fascism. Stepinac was in a bind, to be sure, and had accepted what he saw as the lesser of competing evils. Josip Babic figured the archbishop had made the right call. Regardless, Tony had made his bed, and now he would sleep in it.

"Tony," she said, "what are your thoughts?"

Oh, she was a tenacious one. "On what?" he asked.

"The oppression, the bigotry, the—"

"Right now, unresolvable," he said. "A soldier's responsibility is to carry out the orders of his superiors."

"I thought as much! Is it any wonder I hate the Army?"

Tony grimaced as though clipped on the back of the head.

Katarina's hand came up to her mouth as though she'd uttered a profanity, and her other hand softly clutched his muscled forearm. "I'm sorry, Tony. That was uncalled for. Please forgive me ... for a second time. Please."

Tony studied her flawlessly manicured hand. Then he moved his arm away to flip open his cigarette case. He offered her a smoke. She shook her head, and he lit one for himself.

"We should leave this dreadful subject," she said. "From the outside, the Esplanade Hotel looks like a palace. We have nothing like it in Sarajevo."

"They built it next to the railway because of the Orient Express," Goran said. "It was known as the traveler's regal resting place."

"The train no longer stops here?" she asked.

"The cancellation is supposedly temporary. I'm guessing until the end of the war."

She swiveled in her chair and leaned towards Tony. "What is it you like most about the city?"

He reckoned she was trying to pacify him by tugging him into safe territory. What the hell, he'd go along with it. He told her of festivals, cafés, taverns and soccer games. Goran, meanwhile, spoke of theaters, galleries and museums. She smiled, the tension gone.

Tony's pictorial account expanded to the countryside around Zagreb – the winemaking to the northeast and his love of the family vineyard.

She admitted to never visiting a vineyard.

"I can fix that," Tony said.

Chapter 3

Dust from the gravel rose above the treetops. A farm hand in the old pickup truck had met the trio at the last stop on the northeast tram route. The horn tooted as it kicked up pebbles on the turn through the vineyard's open gates, stopping at the porch where Josip and Jelena Babic waited. Goran leaped from the cargo compartment and opened the passenger door for Katarina who swung her legs to the side and slid down from the high seat, her checkered frock riding up her slender legs until her toes touched the ground.

With introductions complete, Katarina presented a tin of pastries to Tony's mother. "These were baked this morning by my aunt."

"Sweet of her," Jelena said. "Oh, my, the tin's heavy! She's made enough for every field hand at Vinograd Kralja."

"I'm so happy to be here!" Katarina said. "The hills and valleys are beautiful. So is the vineyard ... It's much bigger than I thought. Tony said it was a 'tiny orchard'."

"Next to some, it is," Josip said.

"Your rows of vines are so evenly placed, like stitching."

"Never counted the rows," Josip said. "But there are 4,223 vines. That's down from last year. We pulled the bad ones early. That should stop the spiteful root worm spreading. Of course, you can never be sure." He scratched at the nape of his neck and pointed to the highest corner of his plot. "Thirty new ones planted up there. Be three years before I get a crop, ten or twelve before prime. Good thing I'm a patient man."

Katarina caught his weak smirk, intended for his wife.

"You'll have no argument from me on your winemaking patience," Jelena said. "As for other chores, I'll hold my tongue." She linked arms with Katarina, and said, "Come with me. You'll want to wash up after that dusty ride."

Josip peered at Tony. "So that's the major's daughter. Your letters said he was short. *She* isn't."

"No, but like him in other ways."

"How so?"

"For starters, she's determined – she's got a point of view on everything and isn't one to hide it. Like him, she's driven by conviction. Smart too."

"Breathtakingly beautiful," added Josip, snickering.

"Goran's already bewitched."

Grinning at Goran, Josip asked if she was aware of his feelings.

"Not yet," he said without making eye contact. "It's still … early."

"He's right, Tata," Tony said. "She'll have to be brought to the trough with care. 'Slow and steady' is my advice."

Josip cupped his hand behind his ear. "Did I hear that right? Tony advocating slow and steady?" He laughed aloud, and Goran joined in. "I'm trying to recall if my son ever looked before he leaped?"

"Okay, Tata, you've had your fun. There must be a task we can help with."

Josip wiped his eyes. "Now that you mention it …" He looked as if a new thought had popped into his head. "I suppose a father shouldn't joke of such things. I'd like my son to be responsible with women. I'd like him to find a nice girl like Katarina, marry, and produce four children, not the other way around – you know, have four children, marry, and look for a nice girl like Katarina."

"Come on, Tata," Tony said, trying not to laugh. "That joke's getting old."

After one last snicker, Josip said the hinges on the barn needed replacing. "Door's a heavy devil. Take it down while I pour us a cool glass of Kraljevina."

With the work complete, Tony began the tour he had promised to Katarina.

"In the winter," he said, "the vines on the trellises are dry, almost black trunks. 'Dead bones,' my father calls them. Once winter's behind us, a green flesh forms … like this." He pulled a wand of new growth toward them. "This cluster will develop over the summer."

"Do you do anything in the winter?" The moment she asked it, she thought the question, silly.

"Not at first. In early March we prune every vine. We have to cut before the buds break. If we don't, there'll be too many unripe clusters. Pruning gives us the right yield for the quality of grapes we're looking for."

"How long before they're picked?"

"No earlier than ninety and no later than a hundred days from flowering. The time to harvest is always a question. We want the grapes at optimal ripeness, but we can't let the frost take them before we do."

The three of them walked to the top of a gentle slope, where she took a moment to view the lovely rounded hills of the neighboring vineyards that huddled between the mountains and the floodplain of the twisting green Sava River.

They came to the barn built into the hillside. "The barn serves many purposes." Tony gave Goran a private wink as he led them inside. "Most importantly, it's a wine cellar. Here we crush and press the grapes. After the juice settles, it's time to ferment and filter. The shaded building is cool – that's important."

Goran told her of the local wine culture and the festive harvest tradition celebrated on St Martin's Day. "On the eleventh of November, the wine is baptized."

Katarina couldn't keep from snickering. "You baptize wine?"

"Folklore," Tony said. "Nobody knows why the growers connect the harvest to St Martin. It might be because the monk died on November 11 – around the time the crop is sampled. Whatever the reason, St Martin's is a good excuse for a party for those who work the fields. For years my grandfather dressed up as St Martin. In a bishop's costume, he cradled a bottle of wine like an infant, whispering away like a priest before christening. The official baptism sets off tambura music, and the party is underway."

"You still do this?" she asked. "I'd love to come if you do."

"It's great fun," Goran said.

Katarina hadn't missed the passion in Tony's voice throughout the tour. Had her mother figured him correctly?

Josip poured wine with a light lunch, and it continued to flow. Katarina stopped at two glasses. Jelena abstained. The men, though not really drunk, were indeed uninhibited.

"You won't have to wait till November," Josip said to Katarina. "We'll celebrate now."

With a glint in his eye, Tony said, "And instead of calling our party St Martin's, we'll name it after his uncouth brother, St Fartin."

Jelena looked aghast as Josip and Goran's chuckles expanded to roars.

"Don't worry, Mother," Tony said, "Tata won't baptize the wine by sitting on it."

This had Katarina trying to contain her giggles.

"Who says we can't re-baptize last year's wine?" Josip said.

Later in the day, sausages of mixed pork and beef sizzled and popped on a grill over the outdoor stone fire pit, giving off the tantalizing smells of meat blended with onions, garlic and spices.

Jelena complemented the cevapcici with bread and a salad of sliced potatoes seasoned with chopped onions, vinegar, oil and black pepper. The field workers joined in, and everyone ate until they could eat no more. Then, in an irreverent mock service, they cheered the cloaked Josip as he performed the ritual. There was more wine, and then, as the evening cooled, most of the workers wandered off to their huts, and the remaining enthusiasts retired into the house.

"Now that's done with," Josip said, "I shall wind the gramophone!"

Tony whispered to Katarina, "Get ready for Croat folk music. He'll start with *Oh, Jelena* – always does."

"I know the song," she said. "An old one played on tamburas."

Although the windows were open, the little sitting room was hot and thick with cigarette and pipe smoke. On the record, a musician plucked out the simple melody on a single string, and the singing started, encouraged by a boisterous Josip.

The moment *Oh Jelena* ended, Josip had the boys push aside the sitting room furniture and roll up the throw rug. While the others clapped to a livelier song, he twirled Jelena in the center of the room.

Tony nudged Goran. "Ask her."

Goran hesitated, so Tony pointed to himself as if to say, if you don't, I will. Goran was up from his chair in a flash.

Katarina raised her arm to accept his hand. She danced smiling, chin up. Every time she twirled to face Tony, she stared at him, and he at her.

Soon, he was the only man who had not danced with Katarina. It would be rude not to ask, so when the gramophone piped out a waltz, he took her right hand in his left and cupped her back. Away they glided, floating about the small space, gazing into each other's eyes as if they were the only ones in the room. His hand slid down her back until his palm reached the curve of her hip. Tiny beads of perspiration sparkled on her seamless brow. He pulled her closer, and her breasts lightly brushed his chest. It wasn't enough.

Her eyes widened and she gave a little gasp when he tightened his hold. He felt her warmth, imagining the glory should the fabric between them magically vanish.

The music stopped, but they danced on until Tony heard the holler.

"Tony! Song's over," one of the hands chanted. He released her and immediately scanned the room for Goran.

By a tall beech near the barn, a man's silhouette stood out in the moonlight. Tony jogged up to him. Goran's glass was empty and he was smoking. Nothing irritated his problematic eye more than cigarette smoke. "What's wrong, Goran?"

Goran took a long drag, coughing twice.

"We've had a splendid day," Tony said. "And now you're sulking? Because I danced with her?"

Goran stamped on the unfinished cigarette. "You never understand, do you? It's *how* you danced with her. You manhandled her. I'm surprised you didn't just screw her right there on the floor in front of your mother and father."

"You're crazy! Jealousy's knocked you off your rails. I've never been anything but a loyal friend to you, and *this* is the shit I get?" The more Tony thought about it, the angrier he became. "If I wanted that filly, she'd be mine like that!" he said, snapping his fingers an inch from Goran's nose.

Goran heaved his glass at a nearby tree and lunged for Tony, who pivoted and stuck out his foot. Goran stumbled over it, and his chest slammed the ground. With venom in his eyes, he jumped to his feet, fists clenched. He charged like a madman but his punch was a wild left haymaker. Tony ducked and countered with a blow to the belly.

Goran dropped to his knees, fighting to breathe.

In a tranquil voice, Tony urged him to stay down. "You don't want to fight me; I'll put you in the hospital."

Goran wheezed for half a minute. Then he touched his lip with his finger. "I'm cut."

"Done swinging?"

Goran nodded.

"Let me take a look," Tony said. Kneeling, Goran tilted his head up to the moonlight.

"Your tooth speared your inside lip. Not deep. It'll heal. Get up – let's make you presentable. There's water in the barn."

When they came to the door they had repaired earlier, Tony said, "Listen to me. I danced with her the way you should have. If you don't hold a woman like that, they don't think you're interested."

"Now she thinks *you're* interested."

Tony wished he could call that back. "Don't blame me for your timidity. I'm not trying to steal her from you." He dipped a clean rag in a bucket of water and squeezed out the excess. "Hold still." He washed the dirt from Goran's chin and rechecked the cut. "Bleeding's near stopped. Comb your hair."

Goran restored the razor part. "How does that look?"

Tony smirked. "No one will know you've scuffled with the pilot trials' wrestling champ."

"Sorry, Tony. I'm in love. I can't think straight. You said I'm crazy – she *makes* me crazy."

Tony grasped Goran's shoulder. "You're suspicious by nature, but this is the worst I've seen you. Get that jealousy under control or you'll never attract a girl like Katarina."

"I don't want a girl *like* Katarina. I want Katarina."

"Yeah, yeah, I know. Let's get back to the party before someone comes looking."

****

Katarina gave a worried glance at the parlor clock. "I really must go," she said. "My aunt will think I've been detained by the Germans."

The man who brought them to the vineyard had dutifully limited himself to just three glasses of wine. Josip told him to forget the trolley stop and he'd run them into the city.

On the way, the three made plans for the next weekend: a hike into the mountains of Slovenia.

"Come for breakfast at eight," she said. "We'll be out the door by nine."

****

On the day of the hike, Katarina's eagerness stalled the moment she opened her door to just one of her new friends.

"What changed his mind?" she asked Goran as they walked to the sofa.

He sat down with a sigh. "Ante Pavelic. He's sent Croat troops to the Eastern Front to help his friends fight the Bolsheviks. Airmen were first to go."

"Tony's in *Russia*?"

"Ultimately. Right now he's on his way to Germany. He gave me the news yesterday."

"How did he seem?" she asked while stacking some magazines on the coffee table.

"Seem?"

"How was he? You know … his state of mind?"

"Probably excited," Goran said, appearing downhearted. "I suppose we're no longer making the trek."

Surmising that he was worried for his friend, she mustered a smile. "Of course we're going! The two of us can manage, can't we?" Despite her disappointment, it gladdened her to see his cloud of gloom disperse.

Chapter 4

July 1941
Greifswald, Germany

An overheated engine explained Tony's evening arrival at the German flight school barracks. He figured the best cots were taken, but that didn't dissuade him from seeking a spot near the rear, ideally in a quiet corner. He entered the barrack like a parched boozer charging through the doors of a tavern. Several outstretched airmen looked up from their newspapers or magazines; the ones who chatted in small clusters peered over but soon went back to their conversations. He hustled down the center aisle, accidentally bumping a red-haired fellow whose back was to him.

"Watch your step," the man said. "Next time, I'll drop you!"

Tony turned to the pair of fiery blue eyes. "Well, well," he said. "Look at what the vultures carried in from that scow in Korcula – the silt of all the worthless fishmongers in the Adriatic."

Like brothers, Tony and Rado Boric embraced, scuffling about the room in a bear hug, oblivious to those who had tucked in for the night.

When they settled, Rado led him to a couple of munitions box stools and a makeshift table. "Housek's also here," Rado said. "He's blown up to the size of a house – we might have to swab him in oil to get him in a cockpit. In Russia we'll have Vinny Rukavina on the ground – all the other techs are German."

Rado's anguish over dogfights and dead friends, confessed in the small hours of those cold nights on the trek to Bosnia's Drina Valley, was still fresh in Tony's mind. Rado had said he was done as a pilot – he would live out his days, fishing. So, why was he here? The explanation was all too familiar.

"It's about controlling my destiny," Rado said. "Better I enroll as a bomber pilot than find myself conscripted to fly fighters. The fighter pilot's life expectancy was less than five days in our last war. I'm assuming you signed on for similar reasons."

31

Two years ago, before any war, Tony had used that rationale, contending that the sky was better than the foxhole – they were hollow words, and he realized it when the remorse of surviving his first dogfight struck. The Messerschmitt pilot had been someone's son, a brother, the husband of a loving wife, the father of a child. The nightly demons had convinced Tony that he hadn't killed a warmonger. He'd killed a man just like himself.

"That's part of it," Tony said, leaning closer to Rado, as if ready to launch into a sermon. "Only those who have flown a plane know the thrill of thundering down the tar, pulling up the nose, and feeling the vibration ease when the wheels leave the ground. A civilian can't possibly imagine the awe of the stars and the glitter of town lights, or the beauty of lakes, forests and snowcapped peaks. Up there you discover virginal domain – frontiers for the taking by this buccaneer of the heavens."

Rado's eyes narrowed, and although Tony's cheeks flushed, he held Rado's gaze.

"Who are you trying to convince," Rado asked, "*me* or *yourself?*"

****

Tony had heard the stories, but they didn't seem real until three months later when he saw the charred shambles from the sky. Ahead of the advancing intruder, the Red Army had demanded that residents burn anything that could be of use to the Germans. Many were ordered to burn their own houses. Those who refused were shot, their properties torched just the same.

Seventy miles southwest of Leningrad, Tony touched Russian soil in his freshly branded Dornier. The hatch opened, and he drew a chilly breath of Russian air.

"Schnell!" A ground staffer pointed to a row of dormitories two hundred yards from the airstrip.

Inside, fifteen pilots of the 5th Wing faced a fidgeting Croat major and a cross-armed, black-booted Luftwaffe colonel clad in a blue-gray, hip-length wool tunic and a peaked cap with the silver-embroidered Luftwaffe eagle. Talk was small until the German gave the major a nod.

In poor German, the Croat stepped forward and introduced himself and his superior. Then, he raised the clipboard that he'd held under his armpit and began reading aloud: "Those who came here by land will vouch for

32

Stalin's brutality. Most Russians welcomed us as liberators. Others, misguided by fear or brainwashed by propaganda fought tooth and nail every step of the way."

His butchered pronunciation aside, Tony was impressed by Major Vicevic's flow. He reckoned him for a career soldier who, like Kirilenko, had languished in the Serb-dominated Yugoslav Air Force. But with the birth of the Croat Air Legion, Vicevic would have been in the right place at the right time. He was now a senior officer, reporting to a German who resembled a recent graduate of Hitler Youth.

Vicevic stroked his graying beard and glanced at the stoic colonel, who peered out over the Croats' heads. "Leningrad is critical to Stalin," Vicevic said. "Our job is to rupture the artery and cut off the blood to his martial muscle. Take Leningrad, and Moscow becomes vulnerable from the rear. There we will suck the last breath out of Stalin."

The words were too eloquent to be his own. Tony reckoned the clipboard script had been authored by a German – maybe Colonel Deichmann himself. Tony's gaze leaped between puppet and puppeteer.

"When war was declared," Vicevic said, "Stalin ordered bunkers and anti-tank ditches around Leningrad. He sent in the Red Army, not to defend the two-and-a-half million residents but to maintain a fortress for Moscow."

The outdated Russian tanks, he explained, had failed to contain the armored Germans, and now Panzer units were within striking distance of the city. "Artillery shelling and bombing began more than a month ago. You will join that attack. Leningrad is on a narrow spit of land between the Gulf of Finland and Lake Lagoda. With our troops to the north and south, and water to the east and west, their only escape is by air or over the lake. You will not bomb residential areas. The infrastructure around the southern outskirts is your target. Cut off their lifeline, they surrender." Like a protégé eager for his mentor's consent, Vicevic glanced back at Deichmann. "You will bomb supply depots, munitions buildings, factories and rail lines coming in and out of Leningrad. Are there questions?"

In Croat, Tony asked when they would fly.

"Sprechen Sie auf Deutsch!" Deichmann's boot came down on the plank floor. "Ich will nicht Kroatisch hören."

Tony understood alright: not only were they to fight for the Germans, they were to speak their language, too. "Schade, Herr Oberst. ["Sorry, Mr Colonel."]

Deichmann's lips tightened as he rocked on his heels.

"Our German friends will groom you for this mission," Vicevic said, ending the pause. "When they are satisfied, you fly."

"Danke, Major Vicevic," Tony said. "Wir können kaum warten." ["We can hardly wait."]

Deichmann puckered, as though unsure whether Tony was flippant or earnest. Vicevic likely didn't wish to find out. He dismissed the Fifth Wing, holding Tony back.

"Deichmann isn't given to humor or tolerance," Vicevic whispered to Tony. "Toying with him was stupid. This is a war of few friends. Men like Deichmann are everywhere."

****

Each day, the Croats received instructions, flight paths, and the location of anti-aircraft defenses. But they remained on the ground, whiling away their time playing cards, writing letters, drinking vodka, and learning Russian from captives of the occupied territory. Rado surmised that Deichmann either shared Hitler's distaste for South Slavs, or he didn't trust them with his precious warplanes. But on their twelfth day on the Eastern Front, fifteen Croat-piloted bombers took to the sky, dropping their payload and avoiding anti-aircraft and a fleet of Russian fighters that arrived too late to fire a shot.

With three million Russians reported dead, Tony thought the invasion was near-complete. It was not to be. The rains of fall transformed dusty roads into muddy slop that devoured horses as well as tanks. Winter brought blizzards of thirty below zero. Trucks remained frozen in the mud, boiler water solidified and engine oil hardened.

Tony's goggles often stuck to his face, fastened by ice. He made sure he never touched metal with his bare hands. Vinny Rukavina wasn't so lucky – ground techs cannot keep planes functional without tools. Ten times a day, he'd come inside to unstick his naked fingers. Vinny even set fires under the engines to warm them, but in the end, nature triumphed. The bombers and the airmen sat idle.

Every Croat officer at the base was ordered to supervise captured Russians – mainly young women used as slave labor to cut trees for

34

firewood and clear the way to the Führer's Promised Land. Their bodies soon withered, and for half a slice of bread, they tendered their skin and bone. To the most callous, rape was a spoil of war. These carnivores wouldn't part with as much as a breadcrumb.

On the days that Tony and Rado led their famished slaves beyond the camp, they requisitioned enough food for double the numbers. The canteen seldom tallied how much food per slave worker was going out.

Some airmen slipped into the hollows of depression at the sight of the vanquished around them. Tales of suffering inside the besieged city came from reconnaissance photographs, escapees sympathetic to the German cause, and Radio Moscow itself. Those who managed to flee Leningrad said that starvation was a far direr threat than Luftwaffe bombs. By Christmas, people were collapsing in the streets, their frozen bodies hidden under fresh snow. Money became worthless. A gorgeous hutch bartered for two slices of bread in September was firewood in December. Traps were laid for anything that moved: at first, stray dogs; then the family cat; and now the rats. Boiling body parts hacked from the dead became more than a rumor.

By candlelight in the warmth of a barrack that smelled like a rugby change room, Tony and his mates engaged in games of rummy. But on one particular evening, with the last hand played, all but two had gathered up their coins and left for their beds. Slouched over the plank table swaying to the music of Radio Moscow, Tony and Rado droned along where they could, looking as though they had no intention of retiring. Seldom did they leave the table with an inch or two of vodka remaining in the bottle.

When the last note of a symphony faded away, the announcer mumbled an introduction to the next piece, a new concerto having to do with the war-torn city of Warsaw. Numbed as he was by the alcohol, Tony hadn't paid much attention until thunderous piano chords in a minor key sent shivers up his back.

When it was over, Rado wiped his wet cheeks with his sleeve. "Heartbreaking," he gasped. "I'll never think of that as the *Warsaw Concerto*. It will always be the *Leningrad Concerto*. I can't clear my mind of them."

"What are you talking about, Rado?"

Rado balanced his cigarette on a heaping ashtray that had been a two-liter kerosene tin in its former life. "The people in that city …" He paused to savor the vodka like he might an aged Bordeaux. "… The ones we're starving to death – murdering."

"Rado, *we're* not—"

"I'm drowning in their horror. Every night, I'm under water, my lungs screaming for air. I wake like a heaving asthmatic. It's my penance, Tony. God wants me to stop. I used to dream of dogfights." He waved his goose-fleshed arm to the north. "Now I see the gaunt faces of emaciated creatures dragging themselves through street rubble of hell frozen over. Their look is the one you see on bedridden elders and the sick who lie shriveled on mattresses reeking of piss and shit, praying that their last breath comes soon. How can God allow it? In a court, he'd be guilty on all counts."

Tony placed his hand over Rado's wrist. "There's nothing we can do."

Rado had not finished. "I long for the Sea of Korcula and the stench of fish guts. I want …" He poured another shot. "I want Angela. I've loved her since I was eleven years old … never told her so." He slouched back in his chair and began tapping his forefinger to the tempo of a string ensemble.

Tony couldn't let it end like this – he couldn't bear to see Rado's pain. "Those who sleep through the night have lost all sorrow. We must go on. It's the only way to get home."

"Is that how you feed your soul?"

Tony poured the last of the vodka. "The same demons pummel me. But I'll not surrender without a fight. I owe it to myself to get out of this place with as much of me intact as possible. I will succeed, because I believe in myself. I *know* and so do you, there is nothing we can do for them. Here, we scrounge grub for the slave girls – each day we leave the canteen with bulging pockets. We could be court-martialed, but we still do it. We demean the bastards who use the girls – a few we've shamed into decency. Protest loudly, they'll shoot us as traitors. Defect to the Russians, we hang."

Rado shrugged. "All this I know."

Tony swirled the rotgut hooch in his mouth and grimaced at the burn in his throat and chest. "You can fight your demons as well as I can mine."

"I'm trying … and I'm sinking."

36

"Try harder." As an afterthought, Tony said, "We ought to put Stalin and Hitler in a hole, just the two of them. Let them duke it out one on one. The war goes to whoever crawls out."

"The devil will crawl out."

"Can't argue that, Rado. Let's hope Deichmann doesn't make us bomb the city itself. That's a moral dilemma neither of us needs."

"Shelling the infrastructure frees up his pilots to level the city. It may be indirect, but make no mistake, we're bombing the people. You're fooling yourself if you don't think so."

There was nothing Tony could say to counter that.

"Moot point anyway," said Rado, slowly shuffling the deck of cards. "When spring comes, I don't think I'll be able to drop another bomb."

Tony unplugged the radio. "Spring's a long way off." Using the table as support, Tony pushed himself up. "Good night." Rather than leave, he crept behind the hunched figure, and through the alcoholic fog he watched Rado open a small notebook to a blank page.

For the second time that night, Tony heard the haunting melody of *Warsaw Concerto*. Rado wrote as he hummed the saddest movement, never pausing, as if the lyrics had come from memory. When he was finished, he let the pencil tumble to the tabletop, and began singing to the theme of the *Warsaw Concerto*.

"Within these walls, we'll never fall while you are there. You bring this blight without the right to take our last son's life. Each time you bomb, he carries on in this despair. Beyond these walls, when you are gone, our last son carries on."

When the bugle introduced the next day, Rado was still at the card table.

****

After a frigid day of woodcutting, Tony noticed two russet draft horses pulling up to the back of the mess hall, where smoke billowed from open-pit fires.

"Check out those beauties," Tony said to Rado.

"Looks like they're dragging a sledge load of boots," Rado said. "Why in hell are they taking boots to the kitchen?"

"Maybe our masters want their cooks in army boots. Maybe they're going to make soup from leather."

"You're revolting."

37

"Depends how hungry you are." He caught Rado's frown and regretted his words – a Leningrader might kill for a bowl of boot-leather broth. "Let's find out."

Hunched in their overcoat collars, they hurried through the snow and wind to the frame building. "What have you there?" Tony asked.

The one tying the reins said, "Red Army boots – warmer than ours and useless to the dead." He jumped onto the sleigh to help his mate, and the two began throwing knee-highs to the ground. The boots thumped on the rock-hard earth as if filled with hardened cement.

Tony looked again at the growing pile on the snow. Then he stepped back. "Jesus Christ!" He turned to Rado, who was wide-eyed and trembling. Indeed, the openings contained solid matter, but not the gray of concrete. The filling was pink. Every boot contained the frozen leg of its previous owner.

The boots had been sawn off at the knees, but Tony knew better than to say so. Strung above the fires or warmed in the mess hall ovens, the dead flesh would thaw so the boots could be slipped free and assigned to needy infantry. What would they do with those legs? Tony thought back to his soup jokes. *God no!*

He tugged on Rado's sleeve, guided him to the barracks, and removed his friend's overcoat. Rado shuffled to his cot and fell into a fetal position.

Chapter 5

January 1942
Zagreb, Independent State of Croatia

It was late afternoon, and the warmth from the Black Eagle's hearth had yet to chase the chill from their ankles.

"Too cold for beer," said Professor Milic, caressing a snifter of brandy. "Here's to the end of oppression." The professor and his young friends raised their glasses.

Milic wore that tired, frumpy plaid blazer, tight around the midriff – the only part of the anatomy that was not thin. Goran had never seen him in anything else. Men wore neckties to appear well-groomed; the effect on the professor was the opposite. Goran thought back to the professor's classroom theatrics. Yes, Milic knew how to be a showman.

"What troubles you, Professor?" asked the rugged one with slanted eyes dwarfed by high Slavic cheekbones and a thick brow. Luka Lipovac's flattened nose made clear that he was no stranger to a back-alley brawl.

Milic heaved a sigh. "Luka, you are a perceptive fellow. Ustasha troopers ... twice they've come to the university, dragging me out of class ... asking questions."

"What do they want?" Goran asked.

"They say I'm leaning too far left. With a dictator like Pavelic, who's a hair to the right of Attila the Hun, it's the truth. Three louts with textbooks for blinders came today. Teaching contrary philosophy is becoming a dangerous profession. Their questions give them away. They know ..." he scanned the room, "... I'm Tito's uncle," he said in a whisper. "A reputable educator cannot avoid stimulating discussion on the war or the ideals of the adversaries. I'll cut back somewhat – I'm not stupid. When I'm with them I play up the persona of a batty old professor."

Luka chuckled. "That can't be difficult."

The professor snarled, but Goran saw through it.

"You're too cheeky for your own good," said Milic. "Glad you weren't one of my students."

"I'd be top of your class, especially in debate."

"With that temper, I think not. If you couldn't win on your wits, you'd do it with your fists." The professor lowered his voice to a hush. "Stalin's asked my nephew to lead an uprising against Hitler and Pavelic in Yugoslavia. A battle cry for freedom is a clever scheme to unify communists against these fascists. It gives those of us not engaged in the war a purpose."

Goran leaned in to the professor. "What do you mean, it gives *us* a purpose?"

Milic swigged his brandy as if it were lager. "A war for liberty is just the shockwave Tito's been looking for – right now, the Soviets are his hope and beacon for power. My friends, we creep toward organized revolt."

"I'm still confused," Goran said. "You say it gives *us* a purpose."

Luka smacked his brow. "Skoda, don't be so fucking dense. Forget the independent Croatian state. We can't live under Pavelic, Hitler or Stalin. With Tito, we get semi-impartial government. In the end, the country may be red. That's better than dead. I'm already in, as a partisan."

"You're a traitor," Goran blurted.

"Say that again," Luka said, "I'll knock your block off! I'm a revolutionary. Stick that in your bourgeoisie pipe and smoke it!"

The professor's bony hand, pasty and spotted by age, clasped Luka's wrist. "You know not the ears in this room. This is a public place. Let your anger erupt so easily and you'll be dead long before you're red."

Goran looked to Rudi, the other tablemate. "Where are you on this?"

"Tell him to go fuck himself, Rudi," Luka said.

"I'll put it this way," Rudi said. "I'm not ready to make that choice, but I respect Luka for his principles. His secret is safe with me."

Goran suddenly felt like the odd man out.

"Stalin's a means to an end," Milic said. "Right now, my nephew needs numbers. Communist values make sense to the persecuted – they see no other way of escape. That makes them ripe for recruitment."

"What of the Chetnik Serb remnants of the Royal Yugoslav Army?" Goran asked. "Won't Britain want *them* as the official resistance?"

"Their leadership is in tatters," the professor said. "The Chetniks fight amongst themselves without a vision for a Serbian federation."

Goran wasn't so sure the Allies would give up on the headstrong Chetniks. He glanced out the window. The snowflakes blowing past the tavern's windows and a street devoid of pedestrians conjured thoughts of Tony on the Eastern Front.

Luka, grimy from his job at the rail yard, swabbed both ears with his finger. "I've been meaning to tell you guys how the railway workers love bullshitting about Tito." He must have seen Milic flinch, because he added "Respectful, of course. He was about forty when he worked there, strong as an ox – a man of action – always direct, always steering clear of Marxist dogma."

"His understanding of human nature," the professor said, "and his convictions make him a great leader."

"Though misguided, you could say that of Hitler," Rudi said.

"Imagine the magnetism it takes to move so many to hideous acts," Milic said. "Two years of war, half a year in Russia, and the worst is yet to come."

"That's why we prefer to dance with the Bolshevik devil," Luka said.

The old man cackled. "Oh, before I forget, Goran, by summer the university may be without Jewish or Serb professors. Last week the Ustashe rounded up six. My department has two vacancies. Indeed, it's a loathsome means of getting in, but now is the time. You'll be a worthy candidate for teaching assistant. Interested?"

****

For now, Eli Schwartz's twenty sewing machines rattled away above the store. Katarina hunched over her workstation, examining the red and white checkerboards of two embroidered Ustasha crests. To the untrained eye, the crests were identical.

"Do you think they'll notice the difference?" The somber voice came from the floor lady standing at Katarina's side.

Katarina looked up at her. "If they have the control patch, the lighter red is easy to see. What else can we do? We're two weeks back-ordered." She pointed to the red on the approved crest. "I'll be glad when this job's over – I prefer dressmaking."

"Don't say that, Katarina. Mr Schwartz's safety depends on this contract. This job keeps him here. The Ustasha think they need a tailor's expertise for this work."

"If you can deal with monotony," Katarina said. "There's nothing to it."

"You and I know that – the customer doesn't. Take these to Mr Schwartz. Ask if we can use the substitute thread."

Katarina hurried down the stairs to a vacant room furnished with a single large cutting table covered in tissue patterns. Against the walls was a wide assortment of garment piles. A second door on a spring led to the storefront. She pushed through it.

"Not now, Katarina."

Katarina stopped and the door banged behind her. Dwarfed by two uniformed men at his sides, a pale and trembling Eli Schwartz peered at her from the cash register counter. The blinds were down, and there was no one else in the store.

"Your Jew whore stays," said the elder Ustasha, a stout man with a jagged red scar running the length of his cheek.

He came out from behind the counter, eyes on the floorboards where Katarina stood. She watched his gaze slither from her ankles to her calf line, knees, and groin, where it momentarily paused, then to her waist. When his eyes rested on her breasts, he scratched his crotch.

"Schwartz, you pick your whores well."

Suddenly cold, Katarina crossed her arms over her bosom and backtracked three steps until her shoulder blades bumped the cutting room door. The trooper edged forward, and she pushed against the door, willing it to open, not daring to show her back, while groping for the doorknob.

"Touch it, and I kill the Jew!" He pulled the Luger pistol from its holster and aimed at the cowering proprietor.

Eli Schwartz extended his quivering fingers. "No, Sergeant, please!"

"Stick the barrel of your gun down his throat, Andro."

"Sergeant, you can't—"

"Do it, Andro! Za dom!"

Andro clicked his boot heels and saluted. "Spremni!"

Katarina had seen the Ustasha version of the Nazis' 'Sieg heil' greeting once before.

Andro raised his pistol. Then, in a whisper that evaded none of them, he said, "This isn't the time for heroism." Eli Schwartz parted his lips and the steel barrel slid between his teeth.

"If he makes one move, kill him." The sergeant replaced his own Luger and returned his gaze to Katarina. "Where's your armband?"

"I ... am not ... Jewish."

The sergeant cocked his head toward Eli Schwartz. "You're that one's whore. That makes you a Jew whore. What's in your hand?"

"Ustasha emblems."

"Give 'em here."

She advanced a half step, watchful of her distance.

"Closer!"

Katarina took another half step, extending her arm to his opened hand. The sergeant seized her by the wrist and yanked her forward, his free hand clasping her lower back, and pulling her against his pelvis. Unable to breathe or scream, she slapped his face. A split second later, his fist slammed her jaw, driving her across the room, where she knocked over a mannequin and crashed into the rim of a display table before tumbling to the floor, moaning. Blood spilled from her mouth in a puddle.

"Please, Sergeant," Andro said. "She's not—"

"Shut up!"

In the tumble, Katarina's smock had ridden high, exposing her thighs. Gaping at the sight, he dropped to one knee, lowered his hand to her head, and removed the kerchief covering her hair. Then he released the pins. Her radiant black hair fell to the hardwood. Through the corner of her eye, she saw him rub a lock between his fingers as if to test its quality. But then he snatched a fistful and dragged her by it toward the cutting room. Certain her hair would rip free from her scalp, she back-pedaled on her heels to keep up.

Once inside the cutting room, he dropped his prey on the floor and shut the door. Then, as though lifting a heavy pot by the side handles, he hauled her up by the hair. Blood continued streaming down her chin.

"An untrained bitch needs to know who is boss." He swiveled his shoulders and unloaded an open-handed blow to the temple. "Take that, you Jew-fucking slut!"

Katarina's head jerked sideways, the blow's impact leaving her stupefied. But within seconds, a primal thought registered through the haze. *The back door.* If only her beaten body would respond.

Grabbing a clump of hair to hold her still, he drove a fist into her jaw. The flesh of her inner cheek mashed against her molars. She tried to cry out. A sharper pain shot through the roof of her skull. The jaw locked. A two-handed push to the chest hurled her at the table's edge, the momentum lifting her off her feet, her back and head bouncing on the oak surface and her limbs dangling to the floor. She was dazed, but not enough to miss his intent.

Ripping the buttons from her bloodied smock, he clawed the brassiere from her chest and flung it aside. Groaning from pain, Katarina cast her eyes to the rear door as he toyed with her, pinching, probing, gnawing, and mumbling vulgarities.

Then he stopped.

Be over, she prayed.

But it was not over – he needed his hands for something else. She couldn't see below the table, but she knew his trousers would be at the rims of his boots, and his woolen underwear at his knees. His hairy thighs touched her knees; then he backed away and stooped to the floor.

Panting on her back, she lifted her head but couldn't make out what he was doing. When he reappeared, she blinked through tears at the knife. The sharp tip of the polished blade came to her throat, and she pleaded for mercy in the only voice left to her: the eyes. In response, he belched the stench of wine and garlic. She found the strength to writhe.

"Stay still or I slit your throat."

Her legs went to rubber as the razor-sharp knife touched the skin of her neck. He showed her the red streak on the steel, and wiped it on her cheek. Then he returned the blade to her throat, his other hand tearing her knickers, and his knees spreading her legs. With each lunge he made, Katarina, who was lying on dress patterns, slid away as if she were on a sheet of slick ice.

He yanked her by the shoulder to bring her closer, but the motion moved her diagonally. At best she expected a punch in the mouth; at worst, a slashed throat. Sweat and spittle showered her battered face.

"Open!" He dropped the blade on the table and fastened his hands on her bare hips.

Through clenched teeth, she whimpered, "No. Please ... no."

He pulled her to him, and she felt the rupture.

"There you are," he sneered. "Beats the old Jew, no?" He turned wild, heaving and grunting like feral hog.

Her fingernails dug into her palms, and she prayed for unconsciousness. Darkness loomed. *I'm going. Thank God.* But at the verge of blackness, Katarina awoke to curled lips and bad teeth. Despite the rapist's crushing weight, all she could think of was the dagger. Where did it fall? Her hands slapped and thrashed at the papers around her.

He laughed. "There you go. I knew it. Sluts like you are good for nothing else." He twisted his neck to the storefront door. "Andro! Get in here! I've a present for you."

Breathless, Katarina scrunched and rummaged through the paper patterns. No longer did she look away. As she probed, she stared with contempt into his delirious eyes. His eyelids closed, and his lips wrinkled. She couldn't allow this animal to spill his foulness inside her.

Her fingers found the smoothness of steel. She pushed the blade around to get at the hilt. She had it ... but her arm was dead.

"Almost there ...," he moaned.

Somehow those words infused her arm with life. She drove the blade deep in his back.

The ramming stopped. He sputtered a muted cough, and slid to the floor, twitching from an altogether different sort of climax from the one he must have expected. Wheezing through her nose, Katarina squirmed off the table and struggled to stand. She found her bearings, steadied herself on the table's edge, and watched the stricken monster move his lips. His cry was no louder than a sparrow's chirp.

Revulsion overcame the urge to escape. Her stomach churned at the awareness of what had happened. Hanging on to the tabletop with both hands, she staggered toward the dying man, stopped a foot short, and bent over. A fresh jolt of pain blasted through her jaw as her clamped teeth parted and a yellow-brown gush splattered his face.

He blinked and puckered his mouth as the slime oozed down his neck and undershirt.

"Rot in it, you filthy pig," she managed to hiss through her teeth.

She heard a rap on the inside door. *The other ...*

Katarina burst through the second door and limped into the snowy laneway. Realizing the other trooper had not followed her, she propped herself against the building and wiped the blood from her chin and throat. Her smock was open, the buttons gone but for one at the waist. She fastened it. Then she hobbled down the secluded alley toward the bustle of Ilica Street, ignoring the tickle on the insides of her thighs.

No, not Ilica – they would look for her there. Wary of passersby and fighting the urge to ask for help, she lumbered down hidden backstreets and cobblestone lanes. With the last of her energy, she climbed the front stairs of Goran's residence. When the door opened, her eyes rolled upward and she collapsed into Goran's arms.

Chapter 6

His father told him to carry her upstairs. "Lay her on your bed. Boil some water. Bring a clean flannel and a towel." Dr Skoda then opened the hall closet, dragged out a dusty black bag, and hurried up to Goran's room.

"She's hypothermic," Dr Skoda said. "Jaw's broken. She needs stitches in her neck to close that gash. Wait downstairs while I examine the rest of her."

Goran perched himself on the second stair from the bottom landing. What kind of man did this? Thirty minutes later, he heard footsteps and sprang to his feet.

"Listen and don't interrupt," his father said. "She's been through hell. I've sedated her and cleaned her wounds. Surgery won't be necessary to mend the jaw. I'll run over to General for the equipment and wire it here. She won't be safe there."

"Why not?"

"She mumbled enough of the story before the drug took hold. The assault happened where she worked. She fought back – stabbed her Ustasha attacker – thinks she killed him. They'll be hunting her."

"What do we do?"

"We keep her here. She's terrified for her aunt, worried they'll find her address. You must alert the aunt right away."

"She *stabbed* the guy?"

"She was raped, Goran … lacerations and bruising in the vaginal area." Goran's gut churned.

"Get to the aunt before they do," Dr Skoda said. "Remove everything from the flat that connects Katarina to friends and family – letters, postcards, that sort of thing. We don't want a trail. Get going! And don't do anything stupid."

****

Goran returned with a bag of loose papers, photos, and letters. "I got there in time, Father. Adela is shaken, but she's a strong woman. I avoided the details."

"Good. I've been to General. A Sergeant Dusan Markovic is a recent admission. I checked his chart: a collapsed lung from a puncture between the ribs. If he steers clear of infection, they'll keep him a day or two. Two uniformed Ustashe were in for a visit, one a captain. I assume he was there to hear how his sergeant ended up with a knife in his back. I stood outside the room, eavesdropping."

"You heard everything?"

"Enough. Markovic said Eli Schwartz stabbed him when he wasn't looking, so he shot him dead. The other one with the captain was at the store too. He corroborated the story."

"They blamed the storekeeper," Goran said.

"It's not as if an Ustasha needs an excuse to murder a Jew. Regardless of motive, he will seek retribution. We have to get her out of Zagreb when she's fit to travel."

****

Professor Milic dozed in his threadbare armchair with the newspaper draped on his chest. High on the back of his chair lounged his scruffy black cat. Kuga had been his wife's pet, and for the ten years since her death, Kuga remained a tender reminder of her.

The banging caused old Kuga to leap from the chair and scamper off. Milic opened his eyes, pushed his fallen specs to the bridge of his nose, and sat upright to get his bearings. Then he swept the paper aside and hobbled toward the bathroom, fighting the buttons on his trousers. The banging did not let up. The bathroom would have to wait. Milic peeked through the small window on the front door.

"You look like you need a whiskey," Milic said, brushing thin strands of gray from his brow.

"Two," said the panting caller. "I cycled here, full clip – went down on the ice, twice."

The professor led Goran to the tiny kitchen table littered with dirty plates and cutlery. The room was cold; he hadn't bothered to light the stove to warm his supper.

"Let me get these out of the way," Milic said. He stacked four plates along with two coffee cups and some knives and forks and placed them on the counter beside a sink high in unwashed wares. What remained, he pushed to the edge of the table.

"What's the problem?" he asked as he plopped himself down.

48

Goran spilled the story of Katarina and Milic hung on every word, scratching his head, raising his brow, and lifting his eyelids. "When Markovic is healthy, he'll interrogate the aunt. If ... *when* he tortures Adela, and *when* she breaks, he'll have Katarina."

Milic fondled his chin, nodding.

"I was thinking ... maybe your nephew ..." Despite the chill in the kitchen, Goran was wet with sweat. "His people might help in some way ..."

Milic's shaky hand poured two glasses of whiskey. "Let's take this one step at a time, my good friend. First, we lay out the facts and consider the options. Problem number one: If the Ustashe get to the aunt, the house of cards tumbles." One hand fiddled with his soup-stained tie while three fingers of the other tapped a rhythm on the rim of his whiskey glass for the better part of a minute. Finally, his hands came together and his fingers meshed.

****

Most of the corridor lights were off. Except for a chorus of snores from the perimeters, the shaded hallways were silent. Sveti Duh General Hospital's night staff completed their paperwork and made their rounds according to the schedules prescribed by the day shift's physicians.

At precisely ten minutes past 3am, two dark-clothed men entered the hospital through a service door. They climbed a rear staircase to the second floor, where they changed into medical smocks and trousers. It didn't matter that neither of them had set foot in the hospital; the one who sent them knew it well – the entrances, exits, staff movements, and the location of room 29: second floor, west wing, two doors from the rear stairwell. If no one was in sight, they could be in that room within seconds.

The scale of this task dwarfed Luka's past assignments. The more seasoned Victor warned him to stay calm. "There's a first time for everyone. Nervousness is good as long as you're prepared. Stay alert, maintain concentration and you succeed." They had reviewed the plan several times since it was hatched just hours ago.

Victor peeked through the crack in the stairwell door. "There's a nurse coming our way." Seconds later, he checked again. "She's in one of the rooms. We hold up till she comes out – see if she's making rounds towards or away from us."

Luka buried his nose in his shirtsleeve.

"Bloody nose or sneeze coming?" Victor asked.

"Can't stand ammonia."

"You won't need your nose. Your eyes and ears will ... Ah, perfect! She's moving away from twenty-nine ... going ... gone into another room. Markovic is next to the window. If he's awake, go for him. Douse him lightly, so he won't be out for long. If he's sleeping, drench the other guy."

Like ghosts, they floated past two doors. The only sounds in room 29 were snores, one guttural and prolonged, the other shallow and fleeting. Inside the doorway, they paused to let their eyes adjust to the darkness.

Luka poured a liberal dose of chloroform onto the rag, walked over to the elderly room-mate, and covered his mouth and nose. The man gave a feeble puff and then relaxed into a deeper slumber.

Luka brought the razor to Markovic's throat.

"Wake up," Victor said, from the other side of the bed.

Markovic stirred.

"Sergeant!"

"Fuck off," muttered Markovic.

"There's a razor at your jugular," Victor said. "Call out, and you're a dead man."

Eyes shot open. Pupils jerked left and right. "Who the fuck are you?"

"Information first," Victor said. "Talk and you'll have no problems. Schwartz's store – who was with you?"

"I've been through that."

"Once more, Sergeant, and make it quick before my friend's touch falters."

Luka applied pressure to the blade.

"Me, the Jew, and Andro – nobody else."

"What is Andro's last name?"

"Vajda."

"A good Ustasha?"

"What you mean, *good* Ustasha?"

"Obedient, dedicated to the principles of cleansing our country of ethnically impure scum," Victor said.

Markovic appeared to be sizing them up. Luka made a deeper indentation in his throat.

"He's soft! No stomach for the job."

"Who killed the Jew?"

"I told Andro to shoot him. He refused. So I had him prop me against the wall so I could do it myself."

Victor turned to Luka. "Do you have a question for Sergeant Markovic?" As Markovic's head rolled towards Luka, Victor drove a hypodermic into his thigh.

"Wha-a-a ...?" The sergeant's eyes closed.

On the landing they removed their whites, wrapped them up, and jogged down the stairs to the outside service door.

"All clear," Victor said. "You learn fast."

****

Goran could wait no longer. He had to catch Milic before he shuffled off to the Black Eagle. While the professor collected his belongings, Goran's bloodshot eyes roamed over the disorder on the desk.

"You look like hell," Milic said, as he secured the buckles on his carrying case. "Sleep with the bottle?"

"I had a couple at Bojana's on the way here. It's been a hard day. What can you tell me?"

"I can tell you that the dead do not interrogate." There was a twinkle in the professor's eye. "Markovic succumbed to a heart attack in his sleep."

"Jesus Christ!" Goran pulled a hankie from his pocket and rubbed his left eye. The twitch was always worse when the virus was awakened. "Andro too?"

"That would raise suspicion. Markovic didn't take care of himself – sixty pounds overweight. A hospital physician signed the death certificate. There won't be an investigation."

"The other guy's still at large?"

"Reprisals don't inspire the men helping you. Their goal is Katarina's safety. Andro disobeyed Markovic's order – treason under Ustasha law. He's either a compassionate man or a coward. We're betting on the former. He'll be shadowed just the same. If I were a man of cards, I'd bet young Andro will let the sleeping dog lie." The professor reached for his jacket.

"If that's true, she may not have to leave Zagreb."

"That's a bad wager," Milic said. "Expect an Ustasha sympathizer to take over Schwartz's business. The workers will ask about her. She

51

disappeared the day Schwartz died. Too many loose ends. We have to get her out of here."

"I was afraid of that ... How?"

"I'll figure that out. If necessary, the partisans will provide safe passage."

"You are officially one of them, aren't you?"

Milic recoiled. "You're looking at me like I'm a criminal."

"I'm sorry, Professor. You know my respect for you. You have always—"

"Goran, I'm an old man. There's just me and old Kuga. I live for my work, my students and these bloody Balkan states. I can't die under the fists of these fascists. My nephew came to me for help. Tito is our country's hope. We need volunteers. A man of your intellect would make a difference, especially when we govern."

"Govern? That's wishful thinking."

"Every great nation started with a leader's compelling vision. The enemy has Hitler and Pavelic; we have Tito. If we don't destroy their demented vision, they'll destroy us."

"But Professor, surely you don't think—"

Milic slammed his hand on the desk. "I'm not finished! Tito's vision is to first rid this country of fascism, and second, to establish an equitable government for all the states within Yugoslavia. If we don't find enough men and women of like mind, he won't stand a chance. We need you, Goran. You'd work alongside Luka and me. Rudi will come over, too."

"Join or not, I'm indebted to the partisans for their help."

"I see reluctance in that sore eye of yours."

Goran stilled the flutter with his pinky. "I suppose you are also a member of the Communist Party."

Milic cleared his throat. "To act as a senior adviser and to influence policy, I have to be. Tito's inner circle is where I can make *my* difference. When the time comes – trust me, it will – I'll be with him at the top, crafting a social and political blueprint. The new Yugoslavia will be the consummate political model for the world. An independent Croat state? Foolish ideology."

"Communist ideology is not?"

Milic gave a world-weary sigh. "Don't expect to find purity in these times, my young friend. A man's risk as a partisan is no greater than his risk as a *Communist* partisan."

Tony had said it, too: there was no neutrality in war. Goran had disagreed with Tony's choice, but that was irrelevant. The professor's call to arms was shocking. Everything was happening much too fast.

"You don't have to join the party to take the oath. My nephew remembers you from your university days. He'd be delighted to have you join his People's Liberation Army."

"He *remembers* me?"

"Indeed – said you were a fine example of Croatia's youth. For those who give of themselves for the revolution they'll be rewards: for those who sit on the fence, a poke in the eye with a sharp stick."

Chapter 7

Sedation and fatigue managed to cradle Katarina through the first hours of sleep. Then, in the days to follow, reeling from wounds her physician was ill-equipped to treat, she slipped in and out of naps, her mind racing and crawling in a bog of numbness, detachment and disbelief. All the while, Dr Skoda refused to leave her side until she drew sustenance though the wire lattice between her teeth. Clear soup, tea, and mashed vegetables mixed with broth and whipped into chowder were all she could ingest.

For three days she lay in the sanctum of Goran's darkened bedroom. Fractured ribs forbade lying on her right side, and the wired jaw forbade rest on the left, and so, on her back, she surveyed the patterns in the wallpaper and the ceiling plaster. The room was austere: a dozen shelves of books and three grainy photos atop the bureau. One picture showed Goran and Tony grinning from ear to ear as do kids posing for photos. The woman in the faded sepia picture beside the boys must have been Goran's mother, and in the third frame, a toddler sat upon an old man's lap.

Staring beyond the whorls of plaster, she reconstructed the muddled composition. The conclusion was always the same. She had thought of her body as precious and had vowed to save it for the man she would marry. A despicable creature had taken it. If she was pregnant, how could she stand the face that would reflect the monstrous sire? She felt damaged – a piece of rotten meat good for nothing but the trash bin. How to go on? She could see only fog, and *he* was out there in it, waiting for her. She could smell him. Would she ever feel safe again?

Into nothingness she slipped, dozing for twenty minutes until the fiend in the Ustasha uniform hauled her back in a sweat, his hands clamped to her hips.

Footsteps. She pulled the bedsheet over her head and lay still, breathing lightly. Even under the covers, she could differentiate the Skodas by the scent of hairdressing – Dr Skoda didn't use the stuff.

"It's just me," Dr Skoda said in a fatherly voice. "I know you're awake. Your aunt is out of danger. She'll come next week."

"Does she know?"

"She knows of the beating, not the … nothing more, and not the stabbing. I assume you wish some things to remain private."

Katarina nodded.

****

Katarina dragged herself from the bed on the fourth day. She turned the doorknob and peeked through the cracked door. All was quiet. In the dressing gown Goran had retrieved from Adela, she crept to the banister of the upper landing, steadied herself, and craned her neck for a glimpse of the downstairs entryway. A minute passed before she put a foot on the first stair. Her steps were slow and wooden as her sweaty palms slid down the polished mahogany banister, mindful to keep a firm grip.

At the bottom landing, she sought a glimmer of familiarity. She'd passed this way but remembered none of it. On one of their outings, Goran had pointed out the two-story dwelling. It had to be one of the most expensive in the city. For a moment, she found solace in the collection of art and the regal furniture, the crystal candelabra, and the lathwork and carvings on the hardwoods. Goran's mother had been gone for twenty years, but Katarina could still feel a woman's touch. From the entryway, she saw a richly framed oil portrait of a woman in the sitting room. The woman looked to be in her twenties, elegantly dressed, and bejeweled as if ready for a night at the opera. She looked so happy. As for her own future, Katarina wondered if she would ever be happy.

A week later, daywear replaced her nightgown. Bruises had lightened to yellow, and the battered eye, which had been swollen shut for several days, functioned as normal. The tenderness in her broken ribs was almost negligible, yet she still flinched from a rare sneeze or cough that could not be suppressed. The wire holding her jaw would come out in a week to ten days.

Goran had said her attacker died of a heart attack. Was this true, or just a fabrication to console? If he *was* dead, it was by her hand. Should she care?

One thing was certain. She couldn't hole up at the apartment forever. But, it was only when Goran approached the subject of escape from Zagreb did she realize how terrifying it would be to walk into the street.

"A friend will escort you from here to the train," he had said. "I will be on board waiting. Luka is a strong brute. He'll guard you with his life. You'll never be alone."

****

Inside the rail car, Goran pressed his cheek against the cold windowpane. He could see enough of the platform to know that most of the seats on the train would be empty. He pulled away to check his watch, leaving a fogged breath spot on the glass. Luka and Katarina were nowhere to be seen, and the train was scheduled to depart in ten minutes. This wasn't the day to count on railway tardiness.

He hadn't wanted Luka anywhere near Katarina. If not for the professor, Goran would never put himself in the crude lout's company. But Milic had been unyielding: this was partisan work; they would do it his way. A scene was to be created in which Luka's girlfriend was leaving town on a solo journey. When she came on board, Goran was to treat her as a stranger. Should there be Ustashe or Gestapo on the car, they were to disembark separately at the next station and catch the next train. And something else: she owed her life to the partisans. Goran was to entice her into their army – Tito's quid pro quo.

"That shouldn't be difficult," Milic had said. "Her hatred for the Ustashe surpasses even ours."

A smartly dressed man with a young woman on his arm stepped away from the ticket office. Goran reckoned he'd worried needlessly until he spotted two uniformed followers. Like hawks eyeing a rabbit on open ground, the Ustasha troopers watched the lovebirds. One of them shouted, and Luka and Katarina stopped. Luka removed a billfold. Katarina opened her purse.

The one holding Katarina's credentials moved his forefinger over the lines as he read. Other than the unrestrained flutter of his eye, Goran sat frozen, his greasy forehead stuck to the glass, watching. Hoping. The trooper questioned, and Goran saw that Luka responded before Katarina had a chance to speak. The Ustasha returned her papers and turned his attention to her escort. Scrolling down the pages of a leather portfolio, he suddenly stiffened. His partner's hand clasped his pistol holster as they both began peppering Luka with questions. Luka had a smirk on his face. Suddenly, he opened his palms as though protesting, and then he broke into laughter.

What in God's name ...? Goran pulled back of the window.

The two high-boots could not bring Luka to seriousness. In contrast, Katarina stood like a statue. The scene was so absurd that the bewildered troopers finally cracked a smile. Luka reacted by tilting his head toward Katarina and moving his hips in lascivious pantomime. Hands waving madly in the air, eyes crossed, he grabbed his crotch, twirled twice, and fell down on the pavers as if struck dead. Then he bounced back to his feet and repeated the parody.

He's crazy.

Townsfolk walked past the spectacle, conspicuous in their determination to pay no attention. During the hilarity, Luka must have asked the troopers something, because one of them gestured with his thumb at the railcar. Arm around his woman's waist, Luka walked her to Goran's coach, whereupon he yanked her close and kissed her lips fervently.

Lecherous bastard!

Despite Goran's rage, when Luka's hands fell to his side, Goran saw this as a way of ending the embrace, but Katarina would not release her grip on his overcoat. Luka then buried his face in the curve of her neck. He must have whispered an instruction, because she abruptly let go of his coat. Luka slapped her backside, gave it a squeeze, and winked at the troopers as she walked toward the carriage. Then he walked away between the chuckling troopers.

****

When the train left the station, Goran scuttled to her seat. "May I join you?" he asked. The professor had told him to wait thirty miles – he hadn't lasted thirty seconds.

The woman who stared blankly at the city buildings gave a gesture of affirmation. Despite his perseverance, Katarina didn't utter a second word until they passed Zagreb's eastern limits.

"I thought I was going to faint," she said. "Luka went into that charade to distract them. They checked our names against lists in a book. He was on the list. A notation said several night calls had been made, but he was never home. They asked why he'd disrespected curfew. He said he was with me – that I suffer from carnal hunger – that I wouldn't let him leave. 'Just look at her,' he said. 'Dog-tired and skinny as a rake.' He caught them off guard. They kept looking at me like I was a ..." She trembled. "I should be used to that. I've felt like one since—"

"Why'd he kiss you like that ... and that lewd slap ...?"

"What do they want with him?" she asked.

"Perhaps they know he's a partisan." Goran's voice barely rose above the rumble of the train.

She heaved a sigh. "Tell me the truth about my attacker."

Goran rubbed both his eyes, though it was only the left that demanded attention. She had given him the perfect segue for raising the professor's business. "I sought the help of partisans to make sure Markovic would never touch you again."

Her hands came to her mouth, and there they remained until Goran neared the finale of his prepared account.

"They forged the death certificate, and your problem went away," he said, delighted with his deliberate delivery.

Next to him was a scarred woman ripe for the proposition. But he would have to bait the hook with care. Gently, he placed his hand on hers. "Katarina, there is a sensitive matter that I must discuss with you."

Her hands formed a ball on her lap. "Is something wrong, Goran?"

"No. It's ... well, I promised I would ask. Those who helped you – those who helped *us* – the partisans want to know if we'll help them rid our country of the fascists. Right now, they are just a rash on Hitler's heel. But with numbers, the rash will spread."

Appearing puzzled, she asked what he was suggesting.

He was ready for this. "For your safety, I owe these men. What they ask is a pittance compared to the risks they took."

"I'm eternally grateful."

"I know. Do you realize how many were involved?"

"Evidently not," she said, now looking out the window.

He would open the gate she'd unlatched. "Professor Milic conceived the plot and masterminded the surveillance and protection of your aunt – two men around the clock for two weeks. Three men worked the intelligence web on Vajda. Aside from that was the death of Markovic. It would be speculation to say how many were involved. I know that two assassins stole into the hospital that night." His voice rose in intensity. "The bastard was dead by morning. A physician prepared the death certificate and expedited the body to the morgue. The doctor was either a partisan or a mercenary. If he was a mercenary, God knows what the professor paid him. The point is moot, though – the doctor risked his career and his life." Goran paused, considering the tale he'd spun and the fact that he was starting to believe his puffery.

Her head was now bowed. "Give me the rest."

"The guy who stuck his neck out for you this morning may be dead or in a rat-infested cell. Luka got you out of harm's way. Count them, Katarina. Milic, three men on Vajda, two watching Adela, two assassins, the doctor, and Luka. Ten."

"You and your father make twelve," she said. "I'm sorry. I was consumed by my own suffering. Why did they do it? They didn't even *know* me."

It was all going to plan. The partisans would bring her to him.

Five signposts later, she said, "What do they want of me?"

"On occasion, they'll ask that you serve as a liaison for their runners. The runners are people who have been driven from their homes. They live in the bush and the mountains."

Her turmoil was obvious. He lifted her chin and kissed her lips ever so gently. When she failed to respond, he withdrew, and said, "They're good men. I suspect nothing will happen until you return to health. We can take the oath in Sarajevo."

"That will make you the enemy of your best friend."

"Yesterday's patriot is today's turncoat," he said.

****

Twenty minutes before Sarajevo, she woke to aching bones from the jostling of the ride. Worse than that, her mind was deluged with unsolvable enigmas. Her fingers raked hair from her face and she turned her head to Goran. He was staring at her.

"Now how do you feel?" he asked as he poured the last of their water into a tin cup.

She managed a feeble smile.

"I'm in love with you," he said.

The smile vanished, and she began digging for a brush in her handbag.

"I love you, Katarina … Do you … have feelings for me?"

She pulled the brush through her shimmering hair and peered out into the black Bosnian night, past the reflection of the man perched on the edge of the seat next to her. Katarina had never been in love, but she

59

knew the difference between *loving* and *being in love*. One loved a mother, a father, a sister or brother. But one *fell* in love with a man. To love a man was to want all of that man: mind, body, heart and soul.

The train stopped and the doors opened. Unexpectedly, Goran's lips were on hers. She went rigid, and then twisted away, her fingernails digging into the handbag on her lap.

"I'm sorry," he said. "I've wanted to do that for so long."

She didn't know what to say.

He said, "I can't live without you. I'll come to Sarajevo every month."

But she had already gathered her bag and was almost at the exit door.

****

The explanation was plausible, but Maria Kirilenko wasn't fooled. She knew Katarina's moods and manners too well. On her daughter's second night in Sarajevo, Maria was awakened by soft whimpering.

In the little woman's arms, between sobs, Katarina told snippets of what had happened. By dawn, Maria had it all: the beating and the rape; the knifing of the attacker; his murder; her convalescence; the escape, and the price for it. As the tale unfolded, Maria had fought the urge to vent her horror in unbridled wailing. But no, she would not let her anguish devolve onto her daughter. She edged the conversation toward Katarina's obligation to the partisans and a workable course of action.

"We will support those who helped you," Maria Kirilenko said. "Runners and fugitives are welcome in our home." Then she asked about Goran. "He's smitten."

"Don't worry, Mama, I'm not ready for marriage. Not after this."

"Foolish is the woman who compromises her independence during war. Walk carefully while I nurse you back to good health."

Chapter 8

When the savage winter receded, the shelling resumed. Following an afternoon of rail bombing, Tony completed flight log entries in the cockpit while a crewman helped with the canopy. He looked down, and there on the ground, gazing up was the perturbed mug of Captain Housek.

"Lieutenant, we need to talk," Housek said. "Not here. The officers' lounge."

The euphemism for the dingy, one-room log shack still amused Tony. The lounge was a haven for an officer to blow smoke and nip vodka amid the comradeship of his partners in war. No matter how cold the outside temperatures, the lounge stayed toasty warm, thanks to 'Ursie', the potbelly stove.

Tony made small talk as they walked, but he saw that Housek was in no mood for chitchat. On the farthest table, a half-full bottle of vodka had been left by last night's patrons. Housek grabbed it and filled two shot glasses.

"I want no bullshit, Babic. What's with Borcic? Fucking guy hasn't hit a rail line yet."

"What makes you think that?"

"Not much I don't know." Housek raised his vodka to Tony. "This loosens tongues. Borcic flies wide of the targets. He wastes bombs on open fields or drops zilch, claiming the bays jam and the hinges lock. Bullshit! Our mechanics find nothing wrong. I think he's gone over."

Tony picked at the stubble under his chin. Aside from suspecting Rado's loyalties, Housek had it right. "He hasn't defected. His mind's gone unhinged."

Housek slammed his now-empty shot glass on the tabletop. "Lost his fucking nerve?" He looked back at the collection of tipsy Germans who remained engrossed in their own conversations "He's on his way to a court-martial."

61

"You can't, Captain."

"Damn nits." Housek began scratching the back of his head like a hound with a bad case of fleas. "He's put me in a hell of a bind."

"He's sick," Tony said.

"Cowardice isn't an illness. Borcic's sabotaging the operation – he commits treason every time he flies. Deichmann will hang me by the balls if I ignore it. "

"A German court-martial is a death sentence," said Tony. "You don't want that on your conscience. There must be another way."

Housek rose slightly, and moved closer to Tony. "Tell me what *you'd* do in my shoes."

"Rado's an abstainer." Tony felt the dampness under his armpits. "I'll admit it was stupid to think this could continue. I'd hoped we'd be home before word got out." He paused to unzip his flight suit to the waist. "Reassign him. Make him my radio-gunner. Radio-gunners don't pinpoint targets or drop bombs."

Housek downed his vodka. "This is an ugly place to wage war. It's survival of the fittest. Borcic's not fit. We both know it. He threatens *my* survival."

"Give him to me, Captain. All he has to do is operate the radio and watch my backside as dorsal gunner."

"I think Vicevic knows. He could be watching me. If I do nothing, I'm an accomplice. You know what that means."

Tony shook his head. "Stuff like this takes time to move up the ladder. When did you hear of it?"

"Last night."

"Okay, so last night you got the goods," Tony said with finality. "Tomorrow you move a weary pilot to radio-gunner and promote an apprentice to pilot."

By now, Housek was tapping the table with the bottom of his glass. "It's a demotion – a blow to a pilot's ego."

"Rado has no ego."

Housek sat in silence under Tony's stare. But a thought must have come into his mind, because his frown dissipated and his pudgy cheeks suddenly glowed scarlet. "You want me to put my neck on the chopping block for Borcic. That risk requires a reward."

Damn it, Housek. Isn't a man's life enough of a reward? "Okay, Captain. I'll bite. What's on your mind?"

Housek whistled air through his teeth. "The Russian steno ... Machine-gun Olga. You have a way with her."

"Not the way you suggest."

Having lost her family to a bomb, and terrified of being mistaken for a Jew, Olga had devised an audacious survival plan: she had positioned herself to Deichmann as a stalwart anti-Communist with linguistic and typing skills. One look at her, and Deichmann didn't even bother to verify her assertion. By the time his troops reached Leningrad, her ineptitude was known. Undeterred, she pushed the keys with two fingers and picked up German through daily exchanges with Deichmann's cohorts. Behind her back, she was known as 'Machine-gun Olga', not for the brisk rat-a-tat of the Underwood but for the tempo with which her naked hips reputedly slapped the officers' bellies during the long nights in the frigid wasteland.

"I want her," Housek said, his brow wet. "One pop is all."

Olga wasn't a whore – she fucked to live. Tony would love to shove that down his throat. But he didn't dare rile Housek when he needed him most. "Olga's verboten – she bangs for Deichmann and his inner circle."

"You mean his *'in her'* circle, don't you?"

Tony fashioned the required chuckle. "If she snitches, you can kiss your balls good-bye."

"She's got a thing for you, Babic. You can get her to keep her mouth shut."

Housek had fallen to the lowest rung: a piece of ass for a man's life. The Eastern Front was awfully good at leeching out virtue. Tony's best bet was to buy time. He suggested they present the radio-gunner option to Rado. There was no point in approaching Olga if Rado refused. Besides, that would eliminate the hazard of Olga squealing to Deichmann.

"And if Borcic agrees?" Housek asked.

Tony felt his leg snagged in his own trap. "Then, for a minute anyway," he said with another forged snicker, "the war won't seem so bad to you."

"One pop," Housek said, drooling with lust." But if there's trouble in your plane, Borcic won't be the only one court-martialed."

Housek hovered over the shapely woman typing out the court-martial. Olga hammered away, flinging the carriage arm to the right at the command of the return bell. When finished, she whipped the sheet from the machine and handed it to him.

"Hope I not make too many mistakes," she said in German.

Rather than check her work, Housek checked Olga. She couldn't be any older than seventeen.

"Vhat wrong, Captain? You have fever?"

"Daydreaming, that's all." He now looked over the summons. "Not a word to anyone, understand?"

"Olga used to secrets."

He lowered his eyes to her breasts. "I'm sure you are."

Seemingly unfazed by the insinuation, Olga inserted fresh paper into the Underwood and Housek bade her farewell. Into the chilly downpour he walked, raising his overcoat collar above his ears and dodging the mud puddles blocking his path to the officers' lounge. Nodding to the Germans huddling around Ursie, he scooted to the table he had shared with Tony.

A blast of rain followed Rado through the door. An irate German yelled at him to slam it shut, but Rado closed it slowly and gently. He brushed the rain from his trench coat and meandered towards Housek. Rado's trembling fingers went for the filled shot glass that Housek had used as the document's paper weight.

"Christ, Borcic. The way you're hand's shaking, you could jerk off in ten seconds flat. Are you bone cold, shit jumpy, or just pissing yourself at the prospect of the day's first drink?" He studied Rado's smirk, deeming it contrived.

"I'm all of that, Captain." Rado downed the vodka in one chug. As he read, his fingertips stroked the rough grain of the tabletop. "So, you're court-martialing me."

Housek lit a cigarette, adding another cloud to the bluish-gray haze in the room. "What do you have to say for yourself?"

Rado said there was more vodka in Russia than guns.

"We're doing our best to reduce the inventory, Lieutenant. Now, stop dicking around. We're not talking about revoking your postal privileges."

"Captain, each day we're here, we lose a piece of our souls. Think of it as shaving slices of salami. One slice doesn't make a difference. But eventually the salami's gone." He motioned north. "Those starving people are taking one slice at a time."

Rado's eerie calmness angered Housek. "This is *war,* for Christ sake! War brings out the worst in men. Look around – this shit-hole verifies it."

"War can also bring out the *best* in men. Most soldiers aren't vicious and cruel, nor do they rape and murder."

Housek held up his hand. "Whoa, Lieutenant, you're getting way too philosophical."

"Call me a coward; call me a traitor. Call me what you like in this writ. I'm worn out. I won't drop another bomb. If that means a court-martial, so be it."

"Stop your sniveling – it's embarrassing." Housek glanced over at the Germans, fearful they would see the tears streaming down Rado's cheeks. "And don't be so fucking idealistic. I can't send you up knowing you're sabotaging the mission. Drop the bombs where you're supposed to, the court-martial goes away. Will you?"

"No."

"You'd rather dangle from a rope or fall to a firing squad. This is not smart, soldier. Not smart at all."

"Suffering begets wisdom."

"Cut the shit!" This crack had several Germans looking their way. Housek gave an abbreviated, casual salute. It was time to play his last card. "Vicevic hasn't seen the papers. Step down as pilot and take the dorsal position in Babic's plane. Ride as radio-gunner and you escape court-martial. Can you do that till we're out of here?"

Rado peered at the document, remaining silent.

"I won't strip your second lieutenant's stripe. But to maintain protocol, Babic will move up to first lieutenant."

"Will he have me?"

"Kissed my boots at the suggestion."

"How much longer will we be here, Captain?"

"Reject this, and you'll be here for the rest of your life." Housek waved the paper at Rado. "Can I feed this to Ursie?"

****

Just when it looked as though the war on the Eastern Front would drag on forever, the Croats' role ended. Tony was returning to Croatia to battle a new army of 150,000 in red star hats. His wheels touched the Zagreb tarmac, and two of his three airmen echoed his cheer. After kissing his St Christopher medal, he craned his neck for a glimpse of Rado. Like a man sedated, Rado had floated through the necessary rudiments in Tony's dorsal hatch for six months, not once pressing the trigger.

"Rado?"

His radioman was cradling his head in his hands. Tony removed his cap and headset. He could hear muffled whimpers that rose to howls, sending shivers up Tony's spine.

A night with the Babic family and Rado was off to Split for the three-week leave – after that, a four-month posting in Mostar under Tony's safekeeping. They were to reunite with Housek as members of the new Third Bomber Wing, stationed at the Sarajevo-Rajlovac airfield. The uncertainty of their parting left Tony wondering whether Rado would report at all.

Plagued by ominous forebodings, Tony approached leave as if it were his last hours on earth. He had plenty to do and plenty to see in a short time. From Josip and Jelena he learned about the escalating conflict within Yugoslavia between the Nazi-sponsored Ustashe and Tito's rebels.

"What choice do the fascists give the persecuted?" Josip asked his son. "Wait to be annihilated, or join the partisans? Serbia's almost free of German control, and Bosnia weakens. Unless there's an increase in ground forces, Croatia isn't far behind."

Tony wasn't interested. He needed a break before his turmoil would return – this time bombing Yugoslav partisans in his own country. Until then, apart from relaxing with his parents, he kept to himself. Alone, he climbed hazardous rocky crags, ignoring warning markers. Harmless jostles on the soccer pitch turned into quarrels and fistfights. He drank and chased women like a man possessed. Whereas his past womanizing had reflected self-imposed restraints – his women had to be young, beautiful, and unmarried – now he didn't much care.

****

On his nineteenth day in Zagreb, a throbbing head ended an all-too-short sleep. Pulling the comforter over his chilled shoulders, Tony replayed the previous night's events.

Fifteen years his senior, the woman had been nothing more than warm blubber. At the nightclub he had stalked her, and there he had made the 'kill'. The frau of the Gestapo captain got what she deserved. But as sordid and wicked as he made her out to be, Tony could not smother the pangs of self-reproach. *You don't take another man's wife.* Irrespective of the shallow vanity it took to parade his wife like a trinket, the SS HauptsturmFührer had trusted Tony. The headache was penance for his deceit.

He had felt similar remorse on other head-thumping mornings. Every time he spiked himself with liquor he took leave of his morals. In Russia, righteousness had prevailed. He had never touched a woman there, though he couldn't deny mulling over a romp with Olga. But that would have been mostly about rubbing the noses of his German masters in their own shit. Tony had loathed going to her on Housek's behalf. He had considered the options, in the end deciding to give Olga the straight goods in the hope she would find compassion. Indeed, she had typed the court-martial document herself, so she knew he wasn't lying. He'd told her she held a good man's life in her hands. By servicing Housek, she could save that life.

The bright beam slanting between the curtains of his room failed to impede the image of Olga staring up like a child listening to a disgraced father asking her to steal. He had stammered through the appeal, and Olga, feeling his angst, had stopped him.

"No, Tony. No need you be sorry," she had said. "Olga do this for Schweinhunds many times – why I not do for Housek one time? And you, too, Tony, if you want …"

Olga was a fighter and a survivor. Regardless of her beauty and her willingness, he would not dishonor her.

So why his revolting behavior here in Zagreb? Was it simply that here, unlike in the ice and snow of Leningrad and the soot over Belgrade, he was not in a fight for his life?

With the pillow wedged under his neck, he contemplated his remaining days of leave. He had spent ten minutes with Goran on arrival, but had yet to make a night of it on the town. Apparently, Katarina had gone to back to Sarajevo. That puzzled him because Goran had said they were in love and planning to marry after the war. Why live two hundred miles apart? Tonight he meant to find out.

****

They were to meet at Cellar Ilica. Firstly, Tony would retrieve his modest Foreign Service benefit from the Ministry of Defense. He could go there in civvies, but he felt duty bound to wear his dress uniform with his latest stripe. If Goran hadn't left the university, he'd stop by and the two of them could walk to the bar together.

At the university, Tony asked a group of students gathered at a bulletin board to direct him to Assistant Professor Skoda's classroom. They didn't know Skoda, but they knew Milic. Tony jogged up the stairs to the second-floor corridor where his saw a gathering of men in conversation by the classroom door. Goran had described Milic well.

"Professor Skoda!" Tony said. The six gazed at the well-groomed soldier coming their way.

Goran seemed taken aback. "Tony," he said. "I thought we were meeting at the tavern."

"I had some time on my hands. Hope I haven't interrupted anything."

"Not at all," the old man said, limping forward with his hand extended. "I'm Professor Milic. You must be Tony Babic. Goran speaks of you often. I'm surprised we've never met."

"Three years in the service might explain why our paths haven't crossed," Tony said.

Goran made the introductions. His colleagues were civil, except for one.

"So you're Babic." Luka's dismissive acknowledgement contrasted the professor's graciousness. Tony offered his hand, but Luka would not take it.

"You must be an orphan, Mr Lipovac, for if you had a mother or father, they would have taught you respect for a soldier of your country."

Luka took a step forward, his hands clasped into fists. "My country? Don't be so sure. I see what country you fight for, Herr Babic."

Suddenly, Milic was between them. "Run along, Luka. You've got an errand to complete. This is silly."

Luka lumbered down the hallway, and then slowed, looking back over his shoulder.

"Go!" the professor said, and within seconds, Luka was heading down the stairs. "Don't mind him, Lieutenant. Uniforms bring out the worst in Luka. He wasn't a well-behaved adolescent, if you know what I mean."

"He'd better watch himself. Mouth off like that to the Gestapo, and he'll be a *dead* orphan." Tony's disposition brightened. "Any of you care to join Luka and me at the Ilica?"

"I'm sorry, we cannot," Milic said. "We have a ticklish academic matter to resolve. Do you mind if we keep Goran for five minutes?"

As soon as the door of the lecture hall closed, Milic turned to Goran. "This is a splendid opportunity. In your friend, we have a connection to the enemy. Where will he be stationed?"

"First Mostar, then Sarajevo."

"Do you know any particulars of his mission?"

"No."

"Find out."

Chapter 9

June 1943
Zagreb, Independent State of Croatia

In its infancy, Professor Milic's dabs of general advice were his link to the partisans. By the spring of 1943, he had become Tito's most valued political strategist. Seldom did an academic get the chance to transform classroom rhetoric into policy, and though Milic was invigorated by the prospect of creating social change, the hours and the stress had taken their toll.

Tonight, Luka had come over for an update on partisan progress. The devoted freedom fighter, a brute of a man with razor-sharp wits, reminded Milic of his nephew at a similar age. That might explain why Tito had taken an immediate liking to Luka, later suggesting that Milic mentor the up-and-comer, test him in situations of conflict, smooth the rough edges and cool his temper.

"Here's where we stand," the weary professor said, stoking a waning fire. He traced the military setbacks brought on by Hitler's reinforcements, but said the Germans couldn't sustain it. "They'll need their troops elsewhere. They're going down in Russia, and the North African surrender has cut their numbers by two hundred and seventy-five thousand." He noticed the corners of Luka's lips lift. "Britain is soon to realize Yugoslavia's monarchy cannot be restored."

"Can't wait to see the end of those bastard Chetniks," Luka said.

"With them out of the way, we're the bona fide resistance – the only army capable of driving out Hitler. The Allies will end up giving us the arms Stalin didn't."

"You really think so?"

"It's very promising. The Russians are pushing back, tooth and nail. The Americans are adding troops and planes in Europe. Tito wants to help that along by substantially improving intelligence within Yugoslavia. Our current network stinks. He's thinking that many of us have connections in the government and the Croat army. That's an untapped resource. With a little ingenuity, we can infiltrate the enemy. I want your help in compromising the Croat Air Force."

"Say the word and tell me how."

"Do you remember Goran's pal, Tony Babic."

Luka cracked his knuckles. "Sure do. I'd love to knock that gloat off his pretty face."

Milic cackled. "Rubbed you the wrong way – I thought you were going to punch him one. You've matured since then, no?"

"Guys like him think they can parade around Zagreb demanding respect 'cause they're nationalists. They think they're different from Nazis and Ustashe – they're not. Sleep with barbarians, you are one." A loud crack in the fireplace sent a glowing ember onto the rug. Luka scooped it up with callused fingers and lobbed it back. "If he survives the war, I'll hunt him down like the rest of them."

"When the war's over, you're on your own. In the meantime, I want no personal vendettas. The party comes first. Goran was supposed to dig up details on Babic's Mostar assignment."

"Months ago."

"I was hoping to secure flight intelligence and alert our comrades in the hills to the targets and the timing of raids. He came up with nothing. We need a better link to Babic. Don't misconstrue; I'm not questioning Goran's loyalty. He's just not suited for this work. He said Babic's mission was selective bombing of mountain hideouts. What good is that? We need dates, locations and numbers of aircraft." The professor scooped up Kuga, who had been rubbing against his ankle. "We have liaisons at the bases in Zagreb, Banja Luka and Mostar. Babic's now in Sarajevo; we don't have a connection there."

"What have you got in mind, professor?"

"Think on it. Call it a test. Prove to me that my counsel hasn't been for naught."

Luka tossed two more birch logs into the glowing hearth. Then he clapped his hands together. "We need a comrade in Sarajevo who can get what we want from any airman. We have a striking one: Skoda's woman."

Milic smiled. "It's time we called in our chits on Miss Kirilenko. She knew Babic in Zagreb. I want her to get reacquainted with him. His weakness is the ladies. From what I've heard, she has the necessary assets to get what we want."

"A year ago she was in a bad way," Luka said. "She's beautiful, though – no question there. Whether she'll be able—"

"She'll have no choice!" Milic was bushed. Some days he was so tired he nodded off in the lecture hall. And now, with the partisans closing in on his dream, he feared he might not make it to the end.

"Where does Skoda fit?"

"I cannot risk Goran's involvement," Milic lamented. "His jealousy transcends his loyalty. Of course, based on our friendship, I must bring him into this at some stage. You're to be the go-between."

The smile on Luka's unshaven mug exposed his crooked teeth.

"First, convince Miss Kirilenko to accept the task. Second, suggest she conceive a means to meet Babic. From there, she's to build trust. Suggest a romantic affiliation, but approach that delicately. Her job is to uncover particulars of the Legion's flight missions. We need to know when they fly, where they fly, and for what purpose. If she has to sleep with him to find out, so be it – it's a small price for the life we saved."

Still smiling, Luka said, "If she'd sleep with me, I'd tell her anything she wanted to know."

"Precisely what I'm counting on with Babic," Milic said with a chuckle that became a bout of coughing. He reached for the glass of water at his side.

"Hell of a cough you got there, Professor."

The professor's shirtsleeve muffled the last of his hacking. "I can't seem to shake this damn thing."

"And if Katarina says no?"

"She won't. What moral harm can come from intelligence that will save innocents from bombs? Your demeanor must be empathetic, compassionate and persuasive. Given her debt, a soft sell should suffice. You are well-positioned to make the case. You put her on that train."

"And if that don't work?"

"You step up the persuasion."

"Not sure what you mean, Professor."

Milic's eyelids near closed. "Should she resist and should you exhaust all means of gentle inducement, threaten her with the aunt's safety – even her mother – though that shouldn't be necessary."

"I'm good at scaring the crap out of guys, but women? Not so sure I—
"

"If you weren't the best man for the job, I'd have picked another."

****

Sarajevo's workday was drawing to a close. Across the street from the tailor shop where Katarina worked, a tall, burly tradesman with a shaggy mustache, high cheekbones and rumpled clothes slouched against the brick wall between the butcher shop and the barber.

In this city of mosques and minarets, Luka was but one enemy within a disparate assembly of combatants. Allied with the fascists, militant Moslems attacked the Chetniks while Croat Ustashe continued their quest to cleanse Bosnia and Herzegovina of Serbs, Jews and Gypsies. The partisans, lacking any homeland allies, battled anyone in a uniform. The Chetniks battled everyone.

Katarina emerged from the shop wearing a wispy summer frock that rippled in the breeze. Luka licked his lips, placed his thumb and forefinger over his curled tongue, and gave a sharp whistle. Her head jerked his way. He stepped out from the shade of the awning, tipping the peak of his woolly newsboy cap and beckoning her with a loose wrist. She slowed at the road's edge, glancing left and right with the air of someone about to commit an infraction. Good – always wise to check for troopers.

The last time he saw Katarina she was skeletal. Now she looked exquisite. *Luscious,* he said to himself as she approached – too much woman for Skoda. What could she possibly see in the guy?

"Luka …?"

"Yup, it's me, Miss Kirilenko."

Checking the street again, she turned back to him, taking a half-step closer. Then she rushed forward, hooking her arms around his neck. The contact and her scent conjured memories of their parting embrace at the rail station. His revolutionary intensity withered, replaced by ardor of a different sort. His rough palms clasped her lower back.

Seconds later, her chin edged up his brawny chest. "You've grown a mustache and you've let your hair grow."

The spell broken, Luka's arms fell to his sides. "All part of the peasant look," he said, shrugging his shoulders. "Like our leader, I got a bunch of disguises."

73

"You've been in my prayers."

"Not sure I deserve your prayers, Miss Kirilenko. Others guys helped, too, you know. Guys that—"

"But no one had your courage. Now, if you please, no more 'Miss Kirilenko'. I'm Katarina to you."

Milic had been right. The soft approach would do it.

****

They wanted classified information. To settle her account, Katarina would have to steal and to bear false witness. She abhorred that aspect of the restitution. She also feared that once they had their bite, their hunger would not subside. In war, the rules changed. She had acknowledged that her reckoning would be in the currency of the creditor's choice, but for the first time since taking the partisan oath, she realized that her role was far more than a vague promise of help.

Why had the professor kept Goran out of this? A friend of Milic *and* Tony, Goran came to Sarajevo a couple of days every month. Wouldn't he be the perfect liaison between Zagreb and Sarajevo? Apparently not – they wanted Goran in the dark, and Luka as the conduit.

Three days after Italy's surrender, Katarina rode the Saturday morning tram to the city's eastern perimeter. She got off in the suburb of Rajlovac, home of the Sarajevo airfield, and spent the day walking the flagstone streets, browsing the shops and observing the comings and goings of the townsfolk, in particular the men in Air Force uniforms.

Sunday afternoon she repeated the routine, on her stroll noticing a hand-lettered sports poster glued to a storefront window. As she read, her heartbeat quickened – a soccer match slated for September 18 between the Third Bomber Wing of the Air Force and the Infantry's Second Mountain Brigade. *Three weeks from now.* She figured Tony would be on the team.

For two weeks she grappled with the complexities of her plan. The night before the match, she tucked herself into bed, and visualized the sequence for the following day. Her imagined journey began with the morning tram and ended the instant she parted from Tony in the evening.

She had asked Luka if she could extract the intelligence from any of the airmen, but he had been adamant: they wanted it from Tony Babic. By one o'clock, she had mentally rehearsed every contingency. Now, if only she could sleep ...

The outside breeze and the moonlight drew silhouettes of dancing leaves on the ceiling. Apart from the intermittent swish of the wind through the maple's branches and the ticking of the bedside clock, the night was still. Her mind strayed from the task but not from the target of her deceit. Ever since Tony's departure from Zagreb, she had searched the papers for reports on the war in Russia, wondering whether his emotional armor had been dented or torn, whether he had come to his senses on the absurdity of war, the injustice of racial repression, and the evil of Hitler and Pavelic.

Tony was a mystery – a man of conflicting character and motive. The day they first met, she had detested him, though she later regretted tarring him with the same brush as the institution he represented. Then, making amends over coffee at the Esplanade, they had bickered about the country's political strife. But later, at the vineyard, he was another person: warm, kind and exuberant. Waltzing in his arms, she had felt the magnetism, two dreamers oblivious to the world around them. And now he was the enemy. What kind of man would she find tomorrow?

****

She walked the dry field early, looking for the best place to bump into Tony after the game. As the hour neared game time, she crossed the road, and hiked up a wooded hillside, where she could watch the teams and spectators arrive.

She heard the rumble of truck engines. A line of six troop carriers and a command car turned off from the road and stopped at different points around the field. Armed soldiers piled out of the trucks – perhaps a hundred of them. Players made easy sniper targets – venues such as these were ripe for Tito to cause havoc. Katarina had sent word of her planned encounter via a runner, but who could say whether Luka had received the message.

The enthusiastic and the elderly arrived early, some of them carrying three-legged wooden stools and putting them just outside the powdered line of play. Black-veiled Moslem women strolled behind husbands attired in baggy breeches and fez hats. In contrast, many of the Catholic women wore bright red kerchiefs and shawls. Once a suitable crowd assembled, Katarina left the seclusion of the hill to blend in.

The rear doors of two Air Force trucks swung open, and a dozen men in soccer garb jumped to the ground. Katarina lifted her heels for a

75

glimpse of their faces. Where was he? Nine, ten, eleven … twelve … A driver closed the truck doors, and her heart sank – Tony was not on the team. It had always been a possibility.

Then a muscular arm pushed the passenger door open. Her heart raced. A player had been chatting with one of the drivers. With his back to her, he trotted to the Third Wing's bench. He was sun-bronzed and looked as though he had been on a holiday. Perhaps Russia hadn't been as bad as she thought. He jumped, stretched his legs and did some stunts, kicking the ball in the air from behind his back and catching it on the back of his neck. Then, slowly, the ball rolled down his spine, only to be bumped back up by his heel. The crowd clapped. Tony grinned and pulled the next stunt from his bag of tricks.

He's such a show-off – in the middle of a war, without a care in the world.

****

Katarina had not intended to view the game, but to plot the rendezvous. It didn't work out that way. From the opening whistle, she cheered for the curly-blond striker with the dazzling speed and ball control. He had a knack for taking a pass in his own zone, beginning with a dribble, faking a pass or two, dribbling some more with a defender hanging on, and charging the opponent's goal. Once in scoring range, he dragged two more shadows and punched the ball to an open team-mate for a shot on goal.

As the game was coming to an end, Katarina hurried from the end zone corner to a spot near the trucks. She hoped her snug-fitting suit would catch his eye – now to cast the hook. She applied lipstick, unfastened the pins holding her hair in a bun, and brushed it out.

At the final whistle, the Air Legion's players rushed to the goal. Some piled onto their goalie. Others slapped backs and raised their fists to the sky. The ritual complete, they shook hands with the losing team and jogged to the sidelines. The crowd dispersed, and disappointed infantry guards left as players collected their belongings and headed for the trucks.

Here he comes.

When Tony was in range she stepped into the path he would take, unintentionally catching the eye of an Air Force player several strides ahead of him.

"Say you're waiting for me," he said in a hopeful voice.

She gave a cheerful side-to-side headshake.

"Then who?"

"Don't fret," Katarina said, pausing long enough for her mark to notice. "I'm not meeting an infantryman."

Tony stopped. "Katarina ...? What are you doing here?"

"What am *I* doing here," she said, with her hand on her hip, feigning surprise. "I live here."

"Uh ... just surprised to see you, I guess."

"I came to watch. Congratulations, by the way."

As they spoke, other players hopped up onto the trucks. One of them shouted, "Let's go, Casanova. Celebration's at the base."

Tony called to the driver. "Wait a minute, Blaz." To Katarina he said, "I have to ride with the team. I'm free after that. Have dinner with me."

"I can't stay that late."

"You must."

Katarina grinned as she brushed her hair back. "Isn't that a little presumptuous?"

"There's so much to talk about. How long's it been? Two years? Please."

"I'll stay until the dinner hour. Shall I meet you at the gates of the base?"

"You know the way?"

"N-no," she stuttered. "I ... assumed it wasn't far."

Tony seized her hand. "Blaz, we have company." He stepped aside to reveal his passenger. "Surely we can squeeze her in between us."

****

Dinner for four had never been part of Katarina's plan. But Rado and Vinny Rukavina had insisted on meeting their former major's daughter. A glass of wine in the Moslem quarter soon eased her angst. The eatery, large enough to seat twenty in a pinch, had colorfully patterned walls, a ceiling fan and Bosnian folk music playing over a gramophone.

The yarns and recollections from the three airmen flowed right along with the wine. She couldn't help giggling at their vivid animations. Tony shared a wrestling story in which Major Kirilenko, then a lieutenant at the pilot trials, had set him up against a brute that outweighed him by a hundred pounds.

"You should have seen that gorilla," Tony said. "I just knew the major had it in for me."

"Why would he do such a thing?" Katarina asked. "It's so unlike him."

"Not in the role of commander. I came to learn that his methods depended on the student, the situation and the lesson he wished to instill. I asked him many times why he did that to me. I waited more than a year for the answer."

Katarina's eyebrows rose. "And ...?"

"Well ... this part isn't so funny. He wanted *me* to figure it out for myself. And like I said, it took a while. When I finally got it, I was drunk, standing next to your father and relieving myself in the latrine."

Rado and Vinny giggled at Tony's admission.

Through her own snickers, Katarina managed to say, "Don't keep me in suspense."

"He thought me brash and cocky."

"There's a shock," chided Rado.

"Did you disagree with his assessment?" she asked.

"Good question," Tony said, between sips of wine. "The major wanted to teach me humility."

"To be fair, he's learned some humility," Rado said. "Sadly, not enough."

"I whipped the big oaf," Tony said, "so, the major's caper backfired. But there was something he liked in me – whatever it was got me into pilot school. Without him, I'd still be in the machine shop."

Katarina wondered if an adventurer could ever be chained to a lathe. Already, he had opened up to her. And now, she would have to work him, pick him like ripened fruit – peel the skin, gouge out the stone and hand it over to Luka. *What have I become?*

With the base's curfew approaching, Vinny and Rado bade their goodnights and Tony escorted Katarina to her home in Sarajevo's Croat district. On the rocking tram, he asked of her relationship, giving her the impression that he thought she and Goran were on the road to matrimony.

"Oh no," she said, "Goran's a close friend."

Then he asked of her hasty flight from Zagreb. She had planned for this question and had prepared a response. But another thought crossed her mind. She opened her mouth to reply, just as the tram rounded a curve, jostling them both. She clasped the back of the seat ahead of her and then said, "Tony … can I trust you?"

"Sure."

"Promise what I tell you will remain a secret?"

Appearing mystified, he said, "Yes, of course."

"If the circumstances of my departure from Zagreb fall into the wrong hands, I will be persecuted."

"Your secret's safe."

"Would you trust me with information that might harm you?"

"Sure."

"We'll see …"

"What's that supposed to mean?"

"One day I'll find out," she said. "We didn't get off to a good start in Zagreb. Now I feel we are closer. I just don't want to be disappointed."

"You won't be."

"Okay. I'll trust you … " She told a fabricated version that excluded most of the truth including the rape and the stabbing. After that, she explained, remaining in Zagreb had been too dangerous. She planned on returning when it was safe to do so – if ever.

In the light of the moon, they walked two blocks from the trolley line to a tiny stucco house diminished by the maple.

"This is where I live. Would you like to come in? My mother seldom retires before ten."

"I'd love to," he said, "but even if I make the last trolley, I've busted curfew. That's a problem." He laughed. "But it's not a violation punishable by death. This breach has been worth it."

She smiled. "I enjoyed having Vinny and Rado along … Will I see you again?"

"I'm flying for the next six days."

"Where to?" she asked in a voice of casualness, trying not to sound anxious or desperate. By chance, she might glean something useful.

"I'd be court-martialed if I told you."

She gave a faint grin. "So much for trust."

"It's not that I don't trust you – I can't break my oath. Surely you understand."

"I was interested, that's all. When will I see you again?"

"Next Sunday's a free day."

"I have plans … But I can change them. We can walk the city or hike the hills."

"Let's hike."

She said she'd attend early mass. "Can you be here at ten?"

"I'll be thinking about it all week." He put his hands on her shoulders and pecked her cheek.

Chapter 10

Katarina used her spare time volunteering at an overcrowded orphanage for Orthodox children of Serb parents butchered in Ustasha concentration camps. Today, she whipped through her dishwashing chores. She had to dash off to the market, but the constraint of time would not preclude her from partaking in the most gratifying duty a woman could bestow on a frightened orphan – she held them in her arms, stroking scrawny backs, combing matted hair, wiping runny noses, kissing sallow cheeks, and whispering motherly compassion.

Sarajevo's Baščaršija market was crowded and chaotic, yet Katarina was no longer in a hurry. All that was left to add to her wicker basket were green beans and a large tomato.

As she inspected a tomato, she heard a familiar growl from behind. "Don't turn around. I pass, you follow, twenty paces back."

The strapping man in the newsboy's cap brushed past her and she trailed him to a shady lane wide enough for a sidecar motorbike. He veered into another lane, and from there he ducked behind a heap of boxes into the recessed rear doorway of a boarding house. Seconds later, she slid beside him.

"You meet up with him?" Luka's eyes were cold.

She forced a weak smile and said, "Yes."

"How'd you do?"

"There was a complication. I had less than an hour with him alone … He wouldn't say where he was flying."

"Tito near died in the Sutjeska raid," Luka said. "No idea the Germans were onto him. We're at the turning point. Right now, intelligence is as important as guns. We need details. Damn soon. How are you going to get it? What's your plan?"

"I'm seeing him Sunday."

"That's too fu- … too damn long."

"Luka, he's on duty."

"Is he on duty at night?"

She wouldn't answer that.

"Okay, okay," Luka said. "Here's why it's urgent: Churchill's dumped the Chetniks. He's going with us. That means guns, clothes and food will come by boat from Italy. We want to make sure those boats get here."

"I don't understand."

"We don't want the Croat Air Force bombing the shit outta ... uh, sorry ... sinking the boats. We need flight schedules. If we have times and dates, we avoid the bombs. No sailor needs to die. Get us something, Katarina. And get it before the Politburo loses patience."

"What's 'losing patience' supposed to mean?"

He said nothing, as though somewhere else. Something was on his mind – Katarina saw it in his eyes. She repeated her question.

"You have ways to get the information. A beautiful woman holds a sharp blade. In the heat of passion a beautiful woman can extract a man's deepest secrets."

"Eloquent words, Luka – in my case, hurtful. They're not your words ... a professor's, I suspect."

"Comrades of the Liberation Army make sacrifices. That includes you. Some loving in return for weapons is a bargain."

"Tell your professor ... I'll use other means."

"Do whatever you have to. I don't want to see your family hurt."

He was gone before she shook herself lucid. Steadying herself against the doorway, she watched a rat scamper over a mound of garbage from an overturned trash can, while pondering the threat and the lewd suggestion. *Okay Tony, do what you want with me, but first ...* The notion was preposterous. He'd know she was the enemy's whore. With time, she might develop a relationship to cement his faith in her. If she could do that, she might cajole crumbs of intelligence. But that could take months.

****

All week, Tony envisioned the hike with Katarina in the foothills of the Dinaric Alps. Climbing had been a medium of escape. To ease his soul in those early days after Russia, he had hiked solo to the Sljeme Peak of Medvednica Mountain near Zagreb. When ascending a steep windblown crag, his mind was consumed by the next notch or edge for a finger or toe to lodge itself. This left no room in his mind for withered Russian girls or corrupt officers – no room for his past.

Though he had yet to understand his enigmatic tour guide, there was little doubt that he was chipping away the shards of ice from her impenetrable shield. The ambiguity would clear. It was just a matter of time.

They set out under a balmy October sky, with unusually warm breezes swirling through the hills around Sarajevo. Steps from the top of the grassy rock outcropping overlooking the city, Tony reached for Katarina's hand. She latched on and scampered over the last rungs of jagged rock. He peered into her eyes, and she responded with a sheepish look.

"Anything wrong, Katarina?"

"I should unpack the lunch."

"Yes … of course," he said, pulling the blanket from his rucksack. His eyes followed her with a hunger unrelated to the lunch of liverwurst, crusty bread and sliced apples.

On the perch of a private world, they drank Grasevina from a wineskin and surveyed a tranquil city tucked beneath verdant hills clad in pine and larch and emerald grass. Without the drone of aircraft engines, distant artillery blasts, or billowing smoke columns, the only threat to their serenity was the twitter of wrens and the rustle of leaves swept by gentle gusts.

"This is how the world should be," Katarina said, taking a soft, gift-wrapped package from her bag. "And this … is for you."

He broke the seal and pulled away the tissue paper she'd used to wrap four white handkerchiefs.

"Look at the corners, Vlatko Anton Babic." She had embroidered 'VAB' in dark red.

"I love that it was you who made them." He laid the gift aside and leaned over to kiss the beauty mark on her cheek. Expecting her to turn her head to accommodate, she held her ground and locked her eyes on his. The warmth of her breath was irresistible. Clasping her to him by the small of her back, he pressed his lips to hers and lowered her to the blanket.

****

For fifteen minutes her head had been bowed in the shadowed pew of the church. Luka had said he would come at ten – after all she had been through, it would be a cruel injustice if he didn't show.

Heavy footsteps put those wonderings to rest. Luka halted at the pew where she knelt. He crouched, crossed himself and slid across the polished oak. She passed him the notepaper and watched his grimy fingers unfold it over an opened prayer book.

"This scribble," he said, "don't look like a flight plan."

"Flight plans are issued each morning," she said. Tony had said that he was never certain of any route until then: weather changes and adjustments are made. "It's impossible to get an official plan. This is a weekly itinerary – made sparingly for first lieutenants and above. It isn't final, but endpoints rarely change. This gives Tony's destination every day of the week except Sunday." She pointed to the first column. "Today he's patrolling the knolls around Tuzia. Tomorrow he flies the Sutjeska district. These numbers correspond with each day of flight. I think they're coordinates."

"You wrote this?"

"Yes."

"How'd you—?"

"You wanted it; I got it. How I got it isn't your concern." That the information was now in partisan hands might explain her rising fearlessness. She preferred that rationale to the other: that she was too numbed by self-contempt to care anymore.

"You did good, Katarina."

"This gives you *where* he flies. And here – see here?" She fingered the Friday and Saturday columns. "There's a change. These flights were underlined on the original. He's supposed to patrol the Adriatic between Vis and Bari. He takes off at six each morning."

Luka puckered his lips and released a soft, prolonged whistle. "I know what they're up to."

Perhaps this would satisfy them. Perhaps they'd leave her alone.

"I've got to get this to Milic." He peeled back a sock, folding the itinerary into a small square and tucking it under his arch. "This Sunday, meet him again." He pulled up the sock and tied the lace. "Whatever you did to get this, do it again."

****

Luka sprinted east of Baščaršija, slowing a block from the shoe repair storefront to survey the street's nooks and crannies. Nothing looked out of place.

"Are my grandfather's shoes finished?" he asked the leather-smocked man buffing a boot.

"Black or brown?" the shoemaker asked, without looking up.

"One's black; the other's brown."

The shoemaker gestured to a curtained doorway. "In there. Behind another curtain is a door. The telephone's inside."

What if the professor wasn't home? Use the usual liaisons, or board a train for Zagreb? The train would cost him a day. By the third ring, he'd decided on the regular runner.

A bout of ill health had triggered the professor's sabbatical. Luka figured it was the strain of party demands. The professor, reluctant to reduce his teaching load, had taken on too much for a man his age. Constantly fatigued, he couldn't get over the chronic cough. His doctor had suggested a break. Luka was shocked that Milic had finally agreed.

A muffled hack came from the other end of the line.

"You okay, Professor?"

"Is this my rugged friend?" Milic gasped between coughs.

"I'm your rugged friend." Wary of wiretapping, Luka would choose his words carefully. "I have it. Gives us today till Sunday, times and dates," he said, failing miserably at containing his excitement. "What do I do with it?"

"I will ring back."

Twelve minutes later, the receiver was against Luka's ear ahead of the bell hammer completing the ring.

"You're the runner," Milic said, "from beginning to end. I'll give you a telephone number. Dial immediately after I hang up. They'll tell you where to go." He dictated the number and repeated it. "Now, listen carefully."

****

Two hours past sundown, Luka was at the hillside encampment expecting to find Tito. Instead, two partisan fighters no older than fourteen handed him the reins of a horse. After an hour of uphill trekking in the dark, the three riders came to a thick stand of tall pines. His guides ducked under the branches and pushed onward. Another ten minutes of slaps and scratches by the interweaving boughs, and they came upon a clearing and a row of armed sentries.

"It's the Stipic boys," a guard said. "Lower your rifles."

The horses were secured in a small paddock, and one of the brothers gave Luka his final instructions. "That brush slope behind the sentries – a thousand feet up it is the cave. He's there." He shone his flashlight on a narrow footpath. "Here, take the light."

Outside the cave, he found a sturdily built man with a red star side cap sitting on a munitions crate facing a rebel half his age. A larger crate between them served as the table for the chessboard. Wrapped in a long woolen overcoat, Tito calmly blew a puff of pipe smoke as he advanced his knight to within striking distance of his rival's king. "Check." Tito glanced over at Luka, who waited at a respectful distance. "The runner over there wants to see me," Tito said to his opponent. "Rethink your strategy while I'm gone."

He sauntered over to Luka. "Good to see you. You bring tidings?"

Under the flicker of candlelight, Tito perused the flight schedule while Luka explained.

"Hold it, Luka. You're saying Hitler's onto it?"

"Whether he is or isn't, a Croat bomber's going to be over the Adriatic on Friday and Saturday. Why else would they fly between Vis and Bari? For weeks they've pounded the mountains. This Friday, six in the morning, there's a change to sea patrol. Flight path's way too coincidental. They think the supplies are going to Vis."

"So *you* think."

As if missing the mild reprimand, Luka said, "I'm thinking they got it from intelligence or guesswork."

Tito slipped the paper into his inside coat pocket. "Our intelligence is improving. Your network is worth its weight in gold. Is there more?"

"Yeah. Schedules aren't supposed to be fixed, but my source says they rarely change."

"I'll not forget your good work."

Chapter 11

October 1943
Sarajevo Air Base

After the usual checks from the cockpit, Tony pulled on his gloves and adjusted his leather cap with the built-in headphones. When his three crewmen were strapped in, he swung the nose of the Dornier bomber into the gentle breeze and roared between two rows of ignited flares into the darkness.

As he climbed, the gray dawn began to seep in, and the scenery below coalesced as Captain Housek had described: a scattering of local fishing boats hugging the craggy Dalmatians. Beyond the islands spread the vast, shimmering Adriatic, its emerald beauty unblemished by any sign of man. But for the drone of the dual engines, all was peaceful.

"Your kind of flight, Rado," Tony said into the headset's mouthpiece.

"Are you bored already?" Rado asked from behind.

"I can't say a peek at the Italian coast hasn't crossed my mind."

"Not a good idea, Tony. Twenty miles from shore is our no-fly zone."

At the prescribed surveillance coordinates, Tony shielded his eyes from the dazzling brilliance in the southeast and made the curl north of Bari on the heel of Italy's boot. Perhaps it was the tranquility in the sky that evoked the image of Katarina. His heartbeat quickened at the thought of seeing her again on Sunday.

Suddenly, Rado hollered, "Dots to the northwest! Our altitude, eight o'clock."

Tony looked back over his left shoulder. "*Shit!* You see three, Rado?"

"Four. Not ours from there."

"Better be. Spitfires or Hurricanes will be on us in minutes." Tony's first instinct was cloud cover where he could hide for hours, knowing the fighters wouldn't go in blind and risk colliding with him or each other. Today, there wasn't a puff of white anywhere, or a hope of outrunning fighters. He might press the Dornier to 265 miles per hour, but to do that he'd have to be at 13,000 feet – he'd waste precious time in the climb.

Lighten the load by dropping the bombs? That would make little difference. Fighters had so much more to work with – top speeds of 350 to 400 miles per hour.

He powered full throttle for Albania to the east. "Ready the guns. No one fires until I give the order."

A minute later, the sleek lines and elliptical wings of the RAF were in view. Soon he would see the red, white, and blue bull's-eyes of four grayish-brown camouflaged Spitfires, the fastest birds known to man. He knew of the Brylcreem Boys by reputation and had mocked their nickname. Now the story wasn't so funny – nor was the lethal mix of skill, speed and firepower.

"Coming up on us," Tony said. The Spitfires had lowered their altitude, wary of exposing their bellies. "Any second now ... Make sure you don't—"

The Dornier shuddered as Browning machine guns peppered it. When the last Spitfire zipped past, Tony checked the instrument panel. Everything seemed in order. None of the crew took a hit. He eased the control column forward and dived while the attackers regrouped and followed, a quarter mile back. Then, at just 200 feet from the rippling sea, he pulled up and leveled, negating an underside assault.

Three hundred yards from his tail and closing, they launched a second assault. A slug sliced Tony's left biceps. *Jesus ... what to do?* "If we don't return fire, they might leave us be." So far, the strategy had proved futile. *Maybe they think we're out of ammo.* If that thought crossed their minds, they might relax their guard and show their bellies. *Don't be stupid.* He ransacked his bag of tricks – empty. One more attack and they'd have to bail, but no chance, this close to the water.

Tony couldn't keep from thinking that this day would be his last – at twenty-two his life at an end. His hand groped for the medal at his chest, trembling fingers running down the fine chain. At the end he felt the embossment of his father's St Christopher medal. His thumb and forefinger pinched it tightly.

"Okay, this is it!" he said. "When in range, we fire. You hear me, Rado? I need you to fire. Can you do that? Rado! Rado, God damn it! ... Rado-o-o-o ..."

From above, the Spitfires zoomed in like rockets. Tony had four shooters and eight guns. He and Rado manned three each. The gunners in the nose and the ventral hatch operated the other two. Having frozen under Russian attack on the Eastern Front, Rado's guns had been quiet for a year.

"I need you, Rado. Need you more than ever. What are you doing back there?"

For seasoned fighter pilots, the Brylcreem Boys had chosen a reckless line by coming in with vulnerable undersides. If they had wagered that the beleaguered bomber with the silent guns couldn't defend itself, the most important law of air combat had just swung in Tony's favor – the element of surprise.

"Wait for my order. Need you, Rado. Need you to fire." Sparks came from the lead Spitfire. "Let them have it!"

The guns clattered, and bright threads of tracer fire leaped the gap between the Dornier and its attackers. Shards of lead and aircraft skin ripped through Tony's flight suit. Glass splinters stung his face, and a blast of cold swept the cockpit through fresh holes in the canopy.

The storm ended as fast as it had begun. Feeling the loss of power, Tony scanned the altimeter and airspeed dials. Smoke gushed from the starboard engine. Rudder control was sluggish. He opened the throttle and pulled the stick to raise the nose, ignoring the warm, widening crimson on his coveralls above the right knee.

The moment the pain registered, a voice in his head told him to forget the leg. *Keep your wits on the fight. Nothing else matters.*

"Two down," Rado said. "A smoking third is fleeing west. One unharmed. I took some shrapnel …"

"You fired," Tony said, "and you nailed them." But the elation was fleeting. Outside, a healthy fighter, hell-bent on retribution, recoiled in safe airspace. Inside, two gunners lay dead or disabled, and the starboard engine coughed and sputtered like an engine sucking fumes instead of gas.

"That guy's going to take his time working on us from below," Tony said. "And we're down to one engine. I have to get us higher or the parachutes won't catch."

They would either splatter on a bedrock sea or find themselves prisoners in their own plane when it smacked the water. Tony crept to 1,350 feet – still risky for a jump. Another hundred and they'd be safe. Meanwhile, the Spitfire completed a wide loop and positioned itself for attack. Having witnessed the carnage of his fleet, the Brit would proceed warily.

"We're at fourteen hundred," Tony said. "But now the good engine's smoking. Rado, we have to bail or we're going down with her. Unhook. I'll release the hatch and then roll her upside down. Push out when I have her steady." He yanked the release lever, pulled a second time, a third, a fourth. "Handle must be clogged with shrapnel." Eyes on the Spitfire, he gave a two-handed tug with all his strength. "Stuck!" He reared his head to Rado, who had climbed out of his seat, his back now lodged against the canopy roof.

From a squat position, Rado straightened his legs, let out a raucous grunt, and slammed his shoulder blades against the cage. It didn't budge. He kept at it, and on his fifth hoist, the hatch moved. On the next heave, it sprang loose, catching a wall of air and soaring through the slipstream, followed by Rado, wrenched from the cockpit and tossed between twin tail fins. Seconds later, Rado oscillated downward under an inflated canopy.

Tony eased the shuddering beast upside down, amending the trim tabs to keep the nose up. But the plane *was* falling – already a good seventy-five feet lower than Rado. The slipstream was the problem. To get free at 175 miles an hour, he would need tremendous force to push through the pressure binding him to the cockpit – more strength than he had in one good leg. It didn't matter; the Spitfire would end his quandary. He tore off the oxygen mask and headset umbilical. *Lord in heaven, here he comes.*

The Spitfire whizzed by like a rocket, its guns silent. Tony thought he was dreaming. Had he been spared? Not yet. He still had to free himself from an inverted plane, but how? He propped himself up by the arms, bent his good leg, and pressed his toes against the seat. The wounded leg was like a haunch of beef. The good one pushed him into fresh air but the slipstream shoved him back. Grabbing the control column to avert the death dive, he tried again, this time stooping lower, his injured arm clutching the seat back, the other steadying the stick. He let go, extending his arms and pushing with the good leg. This time the air snatched his head and shoulders and whipped him from the cockpit. The instant he was free, he pulled the ripcord handle. Then came the glorious *whoomph* of inflated silk that yanked the harness straps into his armpits.

Thanking God for the pain, he watched the bomber plummet toward the sea with half his crew inside. On impact it exploded. It was over – two Spitfires and one Dornier destroyed, one smoking Spitfire in retreat, one still lurking in the sky.

As the sea loomed beneath him, he speculated how cold it would be. He had paid attention to the flight school lessons on survival in the elements, particularly the premise that frigid waters triggered cold immersion response starting with an irrepressible gasping reflex and ending with cardiac arrest or paralysis.

Though he had willed himself to resist panic, the moment he broke the surface, his lungs deflated in a desperate gasp – the water was so cold, he couldn't suppress the urge. Flailing wildly, he dipped under, lungs already screaming for oxygen. The more he thrashed, the more they cried. Down he went. After a few seconds, he slowed his arms and came up, suddenly aware of the saltwater, which felt like white-hot pokers in his raw wounds.

The life preserver was in tatters from shrapnel – no point pulling the inflation chord. In a frantic search, he looked in every direction for Rado and land. Neither came to view – only palls of smoke from the Dornier and the two Spitfires. High above, the victor circled.

"Rado! Where are you?" Tony's shouts vied with the engine of the aircraft above. Better to save his breath until the noise faded. Rado was out there, though perhaps miles away.

The Brit waggled his wings in salute on a western course. Then he veered southwest. Tony figured the western line was a courtesy, showing him the closest land; the southwest line represented the homeward route. Perhaps the dogfights and their aftermath hadn't extinguished the ethic of honor and fair play after all.

He checked his watch – stopped at 0735. For several minutes, he screamed and whistled for Rado, finally tossing his goggles in frustration. He kept his leather cap to conserve body heat and offer protection from the sun should his day last that long.

Treading water, he appraised his injuries: bullet wounds in the left arm, thigh and calf, shrapnel cuts and scratches everywhere. A kick of the good leg brought his nose above the surface. Through the stinging he blinked at the vista of a vibrant azure numerator and a rippling blue-gray denominator.

Keep moving. All you can do. In a still, cold, infinite sea, Tony moved his arms and kicked his leg in a rough sidestroke in the direction signaled by a merciful enemy. But the cold soon sapped his strength. His teeth chattered, and his swimming degenerated into floating on his back while feebly sculling away from the morning sun. The bleeding slowed – perhaps the saltwater was sealing as well as cleaning his wounds. With any luck, the saltwater's buoyancy might keep him afloat for a few hours. He yearned to hear the drone of a plane, the purr of a boat, or even the whimper of a human. But apart from the slap of his hand on water, all was silent as he inched toward the emptiness.

As the hours ticked by, his skin chafed from the incessant rub of the flight suit and all feeling in the injured leg had gone. He couldn't let that happen to the wounded arm; if he didn't keep it moving, it would seize up and become just more drag. The pain he could endure, but not the fear of descending into the blackness. His only choice was to feed his mind with hope. These were busy waters – surely a skiff or steamer would come by.

He still had the Luger, and while he had the strength he could end the misery at any moment, though he mustn't leave it too long. Would the pistol still fire? He took it from its holster and placed it on his chest, careful not to let it slip from his fingers. Barrel to the sky, he fired, shattering the peace. That left eight rounds. He listened for a reply. Nothing. He cast his thoughts to land, secured the Luger, rolled over and began a breaststroke.

Just as the merciless sun began to sink from its zenith Tony slipped into despondency. His chapped lips stung, and his throat felt scalded by the devil's own brew. When the first dreaded shiver came, it brought terror with it, for this was the sign of falling body temperature. The skin of his hands was white. His muscles howled from exhaustion, and fresh welts from the flight suit stung like an attack from angered wasps. There was no point in extending the misery.

He labored to draw the Luger to his temple. The images of everyone he had ever loved appeared in his mind's eye as the wrinkled skin of his forefinger touched the trigger. He closed his eyes, increased the pressure, and whispered two prayers through cold-numbed lips. The first prayer was for his family, the second for himself. He mouthed *amen* and twisted his head in every direction one last time. No speck of land anywhere. He squeezed the trigger.

A deafening crack shattered the silence. At the last instant, the muzzle had drifted aside. The gunshot stunned him sober. Seconds ago, finality made sense. Now it defied logic.

In shock ... mind's playing games. Forget the pain. Think of something nice.

As the ring in his right ear subsided, he thought of Katarina. How his heart had fluttered when their lips melded. Willing the sea air to replicate her fragrance, he closed his eyes and inhaled. His dying fingers caressed the current as though it were supple skin.

On that idyllic perch above Sarajevo, he had contained a voracious urge. He couldn't remember ever wanting another woman as much. There had been others as voluptuous and as beautiful, but none as captivating. Beyond the superficial, Katarina was a woman of inner substance and morality, her values passed on by the incomparable Major Kirilenko. Tony had embraced her with passion and vigor, but her somber eyes had stilled his ambition. To use the major's daughter for his own pleasure ... well, it was unfathomable. Alone in the cold, he mourned the fact that he would never see her again.

He slipped below and gagged on brine. One weak kick and his head broke the surface. He expelled a mouthful of water and gasped another breath.

Think of something else. Pass the time ...

The game board of last wishes came into his mind. Hours had passed since he thought of the man he loved like a brother. Rado had watched out for Tony during Germany's invasion of Yugoslavia. In the first months of Leningrad, the mentorship continued. Then winter came, and Rado had gone down in flames on that grave night when they'd listened to *Warsaw Concerto*. The wound was as fatal as a bayonet through the heart. Rado wouldn't risk hurting anyone with his bombs. Yet this morning, Rado had pressed the triggers. He wouldn't end a life to save his own; he had killed to spare Tony.

Take me. Save him.

The next exhalation dipped Tony under, and again he gagged. And again the will to live pushed him to the surface. Another hour, and the retreating sun would slip below the horizon. Tony's appointment with the Grim Reaper would come sooner. Submerged erect, arms extended straight out from the shoulders, and heels together, he resembled a rigid cross. Only his hands moved, sculling just enough to keep his nose out of the water. His skin was raw from almost ten hours of chafing. A compassionate death by gunshot was now impossible, for the Luger was too heavy to lift. His mind no longer would function beyond holding him to the primal mandate to breathe.

Tony's eyelids felt as if they were joined by glue. He didn't care; he had seen enough. But that hum … was it ringing in the ears from his failed suicide? His eyelids flickered, but he would have to use his fingers to break the bond, and he hadn't the strength to raise his hand out of the water.

The monotone grew louder. Was this the sound one heard when passing to the next world? He dipped his face beneath the surface to dissolve the glue that held his eyelids fast. One seal broke, and he took one last peep through the slit before leaving this world. Then the shadow fell over him.

The shadow was not his Maker's, and the hum was not the music of the angels.

Arms hauled him up, and his heels bounced over the gunwales as two men jabbered away in a language he couldn't place. They dragged him beside another body – alive or dead, he couldn't say. They slipped a life preserver under his neck and covered him with blankets. He caught a glimpse of the other man's boots – German-issued? Then his head slid off the vest and came to rest within inches of an owl-eyed expression. Tony's mouth opened, but he hadn't the strength to scream.

Chapter 12

October 1943
Bari, Italy

Hospital attendants cut away the enemy officer's flight suit. Lieutenant Vlatko Anton Babic's waterlogged soldier book had already been deciphered. They had his mug shot, height, weight, rank, duties, birthplace and parental information – all recorded, dried out and placed in a manila envelope on a string around the prisoner's neck.

Medics pumped him with morphine and sulfonamide antibiotics to dull the pain and ward off infection. But the blood had flowed freely until the salt water cleansed and sealed the wounds; the usual symptoms of infection – redness, heat, swelling and pus – were absent.

Corpselike, he lay on a cot in a corridor. The envelope on his chest also contained his St Christopher medal and a zinc dog tag identifying unit, number and blood type. Hurried staff flew passed him without a glance, and sometimes a nurse or medic stopped long enough to peruse the contents, only to discover that the cadaverous patient was the enemy. Tending to soldiers wounded by the likes of the injured prisoner became the greater urgency.

Six weeks ago, the medical facility at Bari suffered heavy shelling and was almost destroyed. Floating in and out of consciousness, Tony knew none of that. For two days he lay naked, weak and stinking of urine under a moth-eaten blanket. When conscious, he longed for water, thinking it cruel that he'd survived the sea and would die of thirst in a hospital. Body sores and blisters like second-degree burns were in the first phase of scabbing. Those beneath the bandages stuck to their dressings so that his slightest movement pulled away fragile membranes of coagulation. Blood leached to the bed sheets, the healing process starting anew.

The bullet to the arm had passed through cleanly, and the one lodged in the left calf would not be difficult to extract. The challenge was the slug imbedded between muscle and bone above the knee. Slugs are removed when easy to do so – when the risk of further damage was low. In Tony's case, the danger wasn't low, but if the slug was not removed, its presence would impede tissue repair and likely cause nerve damage. With infection at bay, the over-worked surgeon let the thigh wound be, choosing to remove the slug from the calf and moving on to more pressing matters – saving lives and limbs of Allies.

****

For Tony, the past days had been hazy. How long since they pulled him from the sea? And that Red Cross nurse that changed his dressings – fancy thinking she was Katarina. It must have been the morphine. The mind was playing him up. Could the dead man next to him on the floorboards of the rescue boat also have been an apparition?

Four days at Bari, and Tony was transported to the Santa Marta POW hospital in Catania, Sicily, where authorities either hadn't read the Geneva Convention's medical code of conduct, chose to ignore it, or simply were overwhelmed by the task of treating so many with so little. Hygiene was appalling, food and fresh gauze scarce, and staff levels low. Add to that a rash of malaria spread by mosquitoes from the marshlands which had left a trail of dead POWs and sick medics. Prisoners changed their own bandages, applied ointments and scrounged chow. Infection, not wounds became the killer.

The cots in Tony's ward were so close together that the wider nurses had to sidle between them to treat the patients. Now that it was October, the ward's four windows remained closed to retain heat. They also retained the stench of excrement, urine, body odor, ammonia and infection. Tony wasn't sure which was worse – shivering in the cold, clean air or retching from the foulness he breathed.

The muscles of his swollen left leg had atrophied, and the puffiness encasing the knee had yet to recede. A young doctor, reputedly the best of an exhausted lot, eventually took out the slug, removed the dead tissue, and ordered that the gash be left without sutures or bandage in the hope that bleeding from an exposed wound would cleanse it.

But the bleeding stopped, and the skin surrounding the incision became red and feverish. By morning, red streaks ran beyond the swelling zone and a yellow discharge collected inside the opening. The smell made Tony gag. A dutiful nurse swabbed the pus with antiseptic, but her efforts were futile – the tissue was rotting.

If the infection wasn't stamped out, gangrene would take the leg. Tony's body had rejected the antibiotic sulfa drugs. Penicillin was the answer, but an army short on the miracle drug would not waste it on the enemy. Santa Marta hadn't seen a new vial in two weeks.

Thankfully, there was no shortage of morphine. A generous shot lulled Tony to sleep, but by three in the morning, chills, fever and an entourage of dead men disrupted his slumber. The young Messerschmitt pilot he'd killed over Belgrade and the lanky red-haired fisherman from Korcula stood watch at his bedside, and in a crescent behind them, Major Kirilenko and all the others he'd met along the deadly way.

The delirium lasted three days. It was a tingling that startled him awake. The throb in the leg was gone, but what the hell was that itch? The knee felt as if it were hooked to a hundred hairline strands of low-voltage current. He started to shake. Was this how it felt? *Christ, no!* The bastards had promised not to amputate. He'd given countless warnings, but the staff made it clear he may have to trade the leg for his life. Tony had said he wouldn't make that trade.

He couldn't bring himself to raise his head and look. So instead, he studied the map of russet stains in the ceiling, following the contours as if the water lines were the shores of Dalmatian islands on the Adriatic Sea. He traced every cove, isthmus and peninsula connected by dust-laden cobwebs draping the dangling light bulbs.

Damn itching.

Perspiration from his chest trickled down the furrow of his abdominal muscles to his navel. *Let there be two.* He squinted down his sopping chest. The bedsheet tented at the end of the cot. *Wiggle them.* The tent moved where his right foot should be. To see the left, he would have to sit up.

"Jesus Christ! Help! Help me-e-e-e-e-e!"

The man in the next cot asked what was wrong.

"Get them off! Get them off me!" Dozens of cream-colored maggots slithered and squirmed in the flesh in and around the uncovered wound. Tony whipped his head to his left and a stream of vomit splattered the floor and the legs of the next cot.

"Those grubs," said his roommate, "are your best chance of saving that leg. They love rotting flesh – won't bother with the healthy stuff. Feed them well."

****

The little critters did their job, and three weeks later, four MP's lifted Tony onto a stretcher and transported him to the airstrip. He was bound for Algiers to join the remnants of Field Marshal Rommel's elite Afrika Korps, a once strong army. Having shed forty pounds in five weeks, the German infantry first lieutenant's uniform that he wore hung like a rag. He hadn't weighed 145 since he was 13 years old.

An olive-drab truck with a canvas cover bed carried him from the North African airfield to a detention center enclosed by miles of barbed wire strung around telephone poles. Once the healthier prisoners were led inside the gates, MPs lifted Tony from the cargo box. He propped a crutch under his left armpit and looked past the barbed wire to a sea of pup tents, a few wood shanties and thousands of dejected faces. The day's downpour had left the horde of drenched prisoners in a sea of muck. With no particular place to go, they shuffled aimlessly through the mud between islands of silt.

A guard frisked Tony for contraband, then handed him a blanket.

"Wohin gehe ich?" Tony asked.

The guard didn't speak German, but he must have been familiar with the question. He pointed with his rifle in the direction of the gloom-ridden scene.

Tony limped into the stockade, shivering from the damp and cold. Still, these shakes were mild compared to the chills and spasms he had suffered in the hospital when his morphine line went dry.

He could feel their eyes on him as he struggled to hold his balance. Some wore bandages; many limped. Most were baked a desert brown by the hot sun. No one offered a helping hand. With the day fading, Tony would need a dry place to sleep before the chill reached his bones. He poked his head through the flaps of a large tent packed with mounds of mud around the base.

"You don't belong here," a lodger said. "Out!"

Where was he to go? "Anywhere but here" seemed the answer. He limped to the next tent, a four-man, and then another after that – every tent inhabited by mean-eyed prisoners. Five shelters later, he came upon a tent that might accommodate twelve. A foul odor from the floor of russet silt made him gag and cough. Make do or go on? He remembered passing some empty oil drums and stacks of lumber. An hour later, he collapsed on five timber planks supported by two horizontal drums that he'd dragged inside.

By dawn, the rain that pelted the porous canopy during the night had passed. Tony lay on the splintery boards pondering what to do and where to go. He willed his aching body into a sitting position and his boot splashed the silt. The movement sent a lightning bolt through the rigid knee of the injured leg.

Despite the predicament, Tony would not allow himself to lose hope. Yesterday was the first day he noticed mobility in the leg. He pulled himself up on the crutch and limped into the wasteland. Under a heavy GI watch, a long queue of tattered uniforms clutched empty plates. He asked where he might find one.

The prisoner behind him pointed to a storage tent a hundred yards away. "Hurry or you won't eat," he said.

"Save my place?" Tony asked.

"You must be joking."

Tony returned with a dish and spoon gripped in his free hand, expecting another twenty minutes until breakfast. Though his eyes were riveted on the lineup, he couldn't avoid a barefoot fellow thrashing through the mud with such delight that one might think he had struck gold. The treasures clutched in his hands were two steaming shoes. Some laughed, but most looked away from the degradation. Seemingly, this fellow would rather eat out of his shoes than waste time getting a plate from the supply tent.

The slop man spooned a sticky brown glop onto Tony's dish. Tony brought it to his nose and turned aside. Something was off. He wanted to dump the slop on his plate into the slop beneath his feet, but that would be stupid. Holding his breath, he raised the plate to his chin, and shoveled the rancid gruel into his mouth. *No food, no strength.* He would consume whatever they gave him. But, the heaving began before he could get it all down.

With nothing left in his belly to vomit, he tottered on the crutch, wiped his chin, and hobbled to the queue for another try. He might be back at the head of the line in time for lunch if there was anything to be had.

"Wasser! Wasser da drüben!" The shout had come from the gates. From army trucks, GIs began unloading five-gallon jerry cans of drinking water. Tony stayed in the slop line. This time he would eat slower. But now he felt a different sort of churning in his gut. If he didn't leave the queue, he would soil himself. He limped to the latrine huts. Like so many others who didn't or couldn't wait their turn, he relieved himself in the open.

****

On his way to the medical tent, two GIs snatched three buttons from his uniform. Keepsakes, he figured. Later he would learn that daggers, pistols and medals were cherished souvenirs.

A GI interpreter who spoke passable German met him inside. The man said his mother and father had immigrated to Milwaukee from Hamburg when he was twelve. Before soldiering, he had worked on the line at Pabst Brewing. Tony had never heard of Milwaukee or Pabst. The thought of sipping beer brought the first smile to his face since he flew out of Sarajevo.

With the Pabst guy at his side, Tony was fingerprinted, photographed and interviewed by a US intelligence man. The official asked if Germany could still win the war. Tony said he didn't know a thing about military strategy or any sort of scientific or industrial secrets. Was Tony aware of the fate of those who refused to answer questions? No, he didn't know that, either. In Bari he had divulged the purpose of the mission that rendered him a half-cripple and killed his flight crew. He repeated that story.

Spies? No, he had never met a spy; at least, he didn't think so. The intelligence man tapped his pen on the plank desk, presumably satisfied.

To the doctor, Tony described his wounds and their treatment. Pushed for corresponding timelines, he said to the Pabst man, "Tell him I was out of it for days. I remember being shot down on the eighth of October – I'll never forget that date. The surgery on this leg was done at Santa Marta."

The doctor scribbled on a War Department form. To the interpreter he said, "Take this and translate," as he waved on the next prisoner.

The Pabst man scanned the form and then said, "Here's the deal, Vlatko. First off, you've got a bad case of malnutrition."

"Have you tried the food?" Tony asked.

The Pabst man laughed and looked back. "Hey, Doc, Vlatko hates the food." The doctor paid no attention.

"I've seen the crap they feed you," the Pabst man said. "Sure as hell ain't from Grandma's crock. Never mind. You're out of here in a couple days – food's better where you're going."

"Where is that?"

"The US of A. It's your lucky day."

He had heard about luck from the Bari interrogators. "Yes please, more fucking luck."

His interpreter appeared perplexed, but quickly shook it off. "There's hundreds behind you, Vlatko. We have to get a move on. Report says the wop doc did a good job on you. You're to exercise – won't get better till you do. Do leg squats and you get fit faster. As many as you can."

"My leg won't bend."

"Hey, Doc, Vlatko says he can't squat."

Without looking up from a throat opened by a wooden tongue depressor, the physician said that he would demonstrate. He put the stick down, faced Tony, and lowered himself into a crouch while issuing instructions.

"Doc says your leg bends no more than twelve degrees. Each day you bend it a little farther. Exercise two to three hours a day. You should get a degree or two a day. The leg will be at right angles in six weeks. Work hard and you should be able to do a full squat in three months – six months, you're good as new. Doc says sit on a chair with a weight on the foot. You can wrap some stones in a rag. Swing the foot up and down like this. That builds these muscles."

He pinched Tony's quadriceps.

"Ouch!"

"Still sore, huh? The speed of heeling is up to you. I have to translate for that guy over there. Good luck, Vlatko."

"Tanks you, Herr Pabst," Tony said in the language he must learn as soon as possible.

****

Another line, another destination – Tony and a thousand others boarded boxcars for Casablanca, on Morocco's northwest coast. The Red Cross paperback tucked under the belt of his trousers felt like a billfold of money. It arrived yesterday, and he had studied it until nightfall. Once he found his spot on the boxcar's floor he would open it to the page he had bookmarked. If *Basic English for Germans* had been *Basic English for*

101

Croats, he would be further along, for he spoke German far better than he could read or write it.

Nine hours of jostling ended a third of the way to Casablanca. The POWs filed from the cars to a recently erected enclosure in Oran. A couple of wishful GIs frisked them for souvenirs, but by now the pickings were slim – the quality stuff was already in the hands of their countrymen stationed in Algiers. The food was edible and the helpings more plentiful than Tony had expected. His spirits rose. He was out of Algiers, the prognosis for the leg was good, and he was learning English. Though the ride lacked comfort, he had enough light to read. He couldn't think of a better way to pass the time.

****

At the crack of dawn, Tony's back was up against another boxcar wall. He opened *Basic English* and steadied it on his right knee, maneuvering the pages to catch the swatches of light peeking through the sideboards. Now and then he practiced his English on anyone who was game. Leg squats were out of the question – a man with a crutch did not stand in a moving boxcar. With each passing hour, the ache in his back and spine grew. No matter how he arranged himself on the floor or postured his back, the thin flesh on his bones would not absorb the pounding of a railcar with bad shock absorbers.

After four days of this misery, they came upon the shambles of Casablanca. If a building had escaped German bombs, Tony hadn't seen it. Near the docks, the prisoners made their way over the rubble to an embarkation holding tank encircled by loops of sharp wire. This would be Tony's home until he boarded a ship for America.

Chapter 13

Goran sought solace in the bottle in the weeks following the scuffle in the professor's sitting room. The bastards had kept him out of it – they'd snared his best friend and used the love of his life to set the trap. To his father, he explained the broken hand as the consequence of an unprovoked brawl at Cellar Ilica, not a fist intended for Luka that landed on an unforgiving hardwood floor. Goran could see the repugnance in his father in the argument that followed. It wasn't the first time Dr Skoda had called him a liar and a drunk. Goran didn't much care. He steered clear of his father – when the doctor was home, Goran was either at the university or spending his pay at the city's cheaper and more miserable bars. At the end of a boozy night, he either tottered home like a lonely vagrant or paid for a street woman's services. His life of stimulating academics, an enthralling woman, and the camaraderie of bright political minds had collapsed like a building battered by bombs. He had always feared that his friend would steal his woman; it was small comfort knowing that the transgression had cost Tony his life.

They all had betrayed him. Political ambition explained the deception of Milic, Luka and Rudi, but Katarina's actions – purportedly to pay her dues – were abhorrent. She had lowered herself to the status of a whore. All those months deflecting his advances, contending that intimacy was a gift saved for marriage, had been cheap talk – she had let Tony do as he pleased. Worse yet, she probably liked it.

****

The professor's snoops had kept him posted on Goran's regression. Milic could not let another day pass without trying to reach out to him. Several minutes pounding on lavish oak, and finally he heard fumbling at the lock. The door cracked open. An unkempt man squinted out at him.

Wheezing from the walk, Milic elbowed the door another couple of inches for a better view of the unshaven, open-robed zombie that reeked of alcohol.

"Might an old man come in to rest his tired bones?"

"Why are you here?" Though drunk, Goran was far from incoherent.

To save you from yourself. Milic pushed through the door and shuffled to the study with Goran trailing. A bottle of cheap whiskey was open, but Goran didn't offer him a drink.

"You're a fool," Milic said after catching his breath. "You realize that, don't you?"

"I realize I was a fool to trust a pack of sewer rats."

"We've been friends a long time. I am here to help. Let me."

"Friends do not deceive friends."

"Are you so intoxicated by booze and hatred that you won't listen to a friendly voice of wisdom and reason?"

Goran preserved his pout and shrugged his shoulders.

Milic began his sermon, as was his way, with the larger strife: the partisan campaign that came above all else. Whatever it took to expel the fascists and terminate the Chetniks was worth the sacrifice. He then restated his own role in the brain trust, and the fact he would be a potent figure in the new government. Those who gave of themselves for the revolution would reap post-war rewards: Luka and Rudi – Goran, too, until this setback.

"I don't need you after the war," Goran said. "My family has more money than I can piss away in two lifetimes."

"Don't be so sure. We'll use the riches of his adversaries to rebuild this country. You wouldn't want Tito taking yours, would you?"

A glimmer of sobriety seemed to creep into Goran's bleary gaze. "Suppose not."

With that affirmation, Milic maneuvered around to the cause of Goran's misery. If Goran didn't come to his senses, he would lose Katarina forever. Tony Babic was out of the way, a casualty of war. Milic urged Goran to give Katarina the sad story and convince her that she hadn't committed a wicked sin: that she had, in fact, been morally correct in helping the anti-fascists. But under no circumstance was Goran to pry into how she wheedled that flight itinerary. That minefield, he must avoid.

"Follow this advice, and your relationship with Miss Kirilenko is salvageable."

"Rather late, wouldn't you say? You turned Katarina into a whore. You'll want to use her for another airman and another after that. That's why you came. Admit it."

"You're being ridiculous! For the time being, Miss Kirilenko isn't needed. And frankly, based on what happened to Babic and his crew as a result of her information, I doubt she'd consent. Miss Kirilenko is a good woman who will have to bear the weight of four deaths. Be there for her. Console her and you reassemble the shattered pieces of your life. She can still be yours."

Milic watched Goran amble to the picture window overlooking Tomislav Square. "Stop sulking and pull yourself out of this rut. Re-establish yourself with Miss Kirilenko. Dump that poisonous rotgut into the sink and hop on the water cart. I need you sober to discuss partisan developments."

Goran turned from the window. "I don't want Luka near her. Promise me that."

Milic sighed. "You just can't help yourself, can you?"

"Promise me."

"I'll do better than that," Milic said. "The Ustashe have issued a warrant for Luka's arrest. He'll remain with Tito at our Bosnian headquarters. Like it or not, Luka will be a force in the new Yugoslavia. He's not someone you want to cross. You enlisted with the partisans but put off joining the party. For your own good, do it now. Then clean yourself up, get on a train, and spend two or three days in Sarajevo."

****

Later that day, a cablegram for Goran arrived from Katarina. Giving her the distressing news of Tony's finish would be unnecessary.

When they met in Sarajevo, Goran went along with the pretense, feigning shock and grief at the outset and finding cruel pleasure in watching her writhe as she unraveled the conspiracy that ended his friend's life.

"According to a friend at the Sarajevo base, he's officially missing in action," Katarina said. "My trickery was disgraceful ... I don't know how I'll ever get over it."

The scene was unfolding as Milic had predicted. Goran offered his condolences, but there was still a minefield in his path. He could not resist charging into it. "How did you wangle the flight plan?"

Her lips quivered in silence.

You let him fuck you. That's what you did. You traded your body. At this moment, he hated the woman he would always love. She didn't answer, so he posed the question again. When she blinked, he knew he had drawn her back to the present.

"Please Goran, spare me the shame."

Eying her lovingly, he said, "I understand, my darling." But when he turned away, his eyes burned with contempt.

****

From every corner of the country, partisan delegates converged on the Bosnian town of Jajce to attend the second convention of the Anti-Fascist Council of the National Liberation of Yugoslavia. The venue would allow Tito to establish a government-in-waiting. Equally important was the message it would send Britain and America. The fact that the convention was held in the middle of the Independent State of Croatia would impress the Allies. As for Hitler and Pavelic, this was Tito's wily way of rubbing their fascist faces in Croatian dirt.

Milic and Rudi journeyed together by rail and then by truck, finally reuniting with Luka, who had been helping senior party echelon organize the conference. When the vast gathering ended, Rudi and Milic bade an early morning farewell to Luka, who would remain in Jajce. By dusk they were in Zagreb where they found the professor's front door ajar, the lock broken and the jamb splintered.

"Just a minute, Professor," Rudi said. "Someone might be inside. I'll go in first. Wait here."

Ignoring the warning, Milic followed Rudi inside. Broken glass, papers and books lay scattered everywhere, drawers and cabinets emptied.

"He's gone," Rudi said.

"You mean *they've* gone. This isn't the mess of a lone bandit, Rudi. I wonder what they've taken ... " Milic held his nose. "That stench – it smells like burnt hair." The source of the smell lay on the fireplace grate. Heedless of the loose papers strewn over the armchair, Milic flopped down onto it.

"How could they ... something so vile?"

Rudi, who had been checking the kitchen, put a hand on the professor's shoulder.

"This is the malice of vengeful people," Milic said. "They haven't been gone long. A few embers are glowing." He pushed himself up from the chair and kicked back the rug. The two floorboards that hid his papers appeared untouched.

"On the porch!" Rudi said. He pulled back the carpet as four blue uniforms stormed the sitting room.

"Are you Milic?" the Ustasha sergeant said.

"*You* did this?" The professor asked.

"Answer me. Are you Professor Zarko Milic?"

"I am."

The sergeant turned to Rudi. "And you?"

"Rudi Stutz. I am the professor's student."

"A student, eh? More like a dissident Communist collaborator."

To shift the attention from Rudi, the professor again asked if they'd caused the disorder.

The sergeant broke into a laugh. "That cat of yours was an excellent host – frisky little bugger amused us while we searched. We tried like hell to catch him – chased him all over the house. He was way too quick so I gave my boys an incentive. Willi here nailed him in the back – paralyzed his hind legs. But those front paws kept right on pedaling, dragging the rest of him like a sleigh on snow. He didn't make a peep. Brave little bugger."

Pale and trembling, Milic collapsed into his chair, and threw his head back in a blank stare.

"He pedaled around till he ran out of steam," the sergeant said. "He looked up at us with sad green eyes. Willi here felt so sorry for him, so he put him out of his misery and tossed him in the fire."

Milic shook as though in toxic shock. "You'll roast in hell! What's the matter with you people? No Jews or Serbs to murder, so you resort to house pets?"

"You'll be in hell before us." The Ustasha sergeant shook a handwritten paper in the professor's face. "You're guilty of treason against the Independent State of Croatia." He read a passage aloud: "'While the fascists vacillate, the socialist winds blow through the corridors of Tito's aspiration. The lids of their caskets are closing. Within a year we shall ship the dead to the devil's doorstep, where retribution can go on until the end of time.' Need I read more, or confirm your handwriting?"

As a rule, the old man had been meticulous with his private papers. Those destined for posterity he stored in the floorboards under the rug; everything else, he burned. This entry was the latest account of Tito's campaign. One day he planned to publish a memoir of this era in Yugoslav history. The page must have slipped from his lap and fallen under the armchair when he dozed off. He'd checked the house before he left; his fatigued mind was not as sharp lately.

"Look up Rudi Stutz in the dossier," the sergeant said.

"No Stutz on the A list," Willi said. "Milic is here ... leftist professor of history at—"

"I know that! Check B and C for Stutz."

"Not on B. On the C list, let me see ... Stricevic, Stulic, Stutz. Stutz, Rudi ... clerk, Zagreb City Hall."

"Well, well, well," the sergeant said. "One stone for two blackbirds is good hunting."

Milic held up his open hand. "It is I you want. Let the student go. He is neither a Communist nor a partisan."

"He's not a student! He's a city clerk."

"A city clerk and a night student," Milic said.

"What's in it for me if I release him?"

The professor had feared this day might come. They had tolerated his eccentricities and diverted their energies to the tasks of racial cleansing and other repression. But now, with Hitler fading and Tito rising, they were frantic. Milic could not escape this most difficult, most definitive moment of his life. The time had come for a man of virtue to stand by his convictions, even though those convictions might cost him his life.

"Free Rudi and I will confess," Milic said.

"No, Professor!" Rudi said. "You can't—"

The sergeant moved within a foot of Milic. "Are you a partisan and a member of the Communist Party?"

"I am."

"He's lying to protect me. He's not—"

A rifle cracked the side of Rudi's head, and he slumped to the floor.

Milic had considered the probability of these thugs knowing his connection to Tito or his standing in the party. Were they in the know or just low-level Ustashe making routine raids from blacklists of anti-fascist sympathizers? If they suspected they had harpooned a whale, the professor's interrogation in the dungeons would be merciless. He might endure the torture for hours, even days. His heart would remain strong; it was his mind that would falter. The Ustashe seldom let a man die until he talked.

"This old coot," the sergeant said, "preaches leftist propaganda to the state's youth. That makes him dangerous. Drag them both outside."

Willi led the professor to a back corner of the house and tied his hands behind his back. "Stand there. Make a move and we kill the clerk."

Five yards in front of the professor, three Ustashe formed a line. Standing in the corner, the professor resembled a vagrant in his shabby jacket, spotted brown tie and rumpled trousers. He drew in his stomach and lifted his chin. Though his eyes welled, his defiant stare remained on his executioners.

"Hold it," the sergeant said. "I want Stutz to see this. Fill that bucket and douse him."

The cold splash revived Rudi. A trooper propped him against the trunk of a young tree.

"Stutz! This is the consequence of treason."

"My God, you can't. Please don't!"

In a calm voice, Milic said, "It's all right, Rudi. I'm ready to go. I didn't have much time. And now, with Kuga gone—"

"Shut up, traitor!" the sergeant said. "Ustashe, ready your guns ... aim ... fire!"

Three gunshots merged into one.

Rudi hung his head and wept. The muzzle of a Luger touched the soft flesh under his chin. Gently the sergeant raised the pistol, lifting Rudi's gaze to his. Then the barrel moved to the center of the forehead, where it rested. The sergeant pulled the gun away, grinned at the circular imprint on the skin, and pulled the trigger.

Chapter 14

December 1943
Casablanca, Morocco

Tony broke out of a Rado daydream, scratching at the lice on his scalp. He'd come to terms with his friend's demise – Rado's death had not been his fault – but the guilt of surviving continued to claw at his emotions. From his bed, he looked up at the dusty, cobwebbed canvas, and for the first time he acknowledged that he would not come out of this war as strong as he went into it. At twenty-two, Tony was no longer young.

Exercise time. He swung his legs over the cot, and a shiver shot up his spine when his bare feet touched the cold earth. He reached down for the pouch of sand and placed it over his foot. Three hundred leg raises from a sitting position might get him through four pages of *Basic English.* Tony used the hours of the day to keep his wits sharp and to contest the monotony of incarceration. But he couldn't spend the entire day reading a book on English and exercising a stubborn leg.

His regimen ended at seventy-eight lifts when a POW threw open the flaps of the big tent. "Schnell! Das Schiff ist hier!"

Beyond the wharves and quays of the sprawling dockside, a massive, snow-white three-funneled ocean liner entered the harbor. Someone in the exuberant crowd of POWs said it was the *Empress of Scotland,* now a transatlantic carrier of troops from Canada and the United States.

****

Naked but for his crutch, Tony shuffled through the footbaths and icy sprays of the delousing tent. Shaking from the cold, he retrieved his fumigated garments and joined his final queue in North Africa. This one led to the deck of the *Empress.*

With a gathering of officers, Tony awaited his on-board duties. One by one, they clicked their heels and stiff-arm saluted the captain. Tony saluted conventionally.

"What is this, Lieutenant? You disrespect the Führer by refusing to utter 'Sieg heil' to a superior officer of the Reich?"

"Captain, I'm not a Nazi."

"You are a Slavic dog impersonating an officer of the Reich." To his staff, the captain said, "Confine him to solitary. Four days on bread and water."

On the floor of a steamy eight-by-eight cell next to the engine room was a soiled mattress slightly thicker than a plush rug, and an empty lard bucket toilet. Tony stripped to his skivvies, but that didn't cool the room or dampen the hiss and growl of boilers and turbines.

In the morning, two MPs came by. The big husky one with the crew-cut pinched his nose. "Diesel and shit makes a nasty mix, Jimmy. Like a furnace in here. He whipped off his hat and mopped his crew-cut. "Let's get— Holy cow, a jailbird! The Krauts are supposed to report infractions."

"Good day, misters." The smiling, drenched prisoner sat up on the mattress.

"Guy's banged up pretty good," said Jimmy, the shorter of the two. "What's your name, soldier?"

"Vlatko Babic ... Tony ... I not Kraut. I Kroatische. That mean Croat."

Jimmy tapped the bars of the cell. "Why are you in jail?"

Tony guessed his meaning. "I not Nazi. I not say 'Sieg heil' to captain."

"Show us your papers."

Tony scratched the back of his head, trying to make sense of those four words.

Jimmy unfolded an imaginary paper, and Tony dug into his pocket for the Algiers document.

While Jimmy read the document, the one with his nose buried in a handkerchief backed up to the doorway.

"Don't be squeamish, Al. We're 'bout done. Any guy who won't kiss Nazi ass is in for a rough ride. This skinny bugger's as hot as a pig on a spit. He's got a busted leg and probably hasn't eaten since Casablanca. Let's put him with the Wops."

Jimmy and Al helped Tony up four flights of stairs to a cluttered deck of POWs. The climb tired him and his first whiff of wintry air made him gasp. Steps later, he stumbled, and the big guy caught him by the waist.

"Take it easy, Vlatko," Al said. "You're short of breath. Breathe slowly. We're heading along the starboard deck."

At the first funnel, they went down another stairwell to the ship's hold, stepping over the ledge of a cargo door into a freight compartment crammed with thirty cots in a space that might comfortably sleep twelve.

"Italianos, relax," Jimmy said to Tony's new roommates. "Vlatko, that cot over there, the one not messed up – that's for you." He pointed at the cot, and then back at Tony. "You sleep there." Then he tossed him a red and white pack of cigarettes.

Tony caught the pack in one hand and studied the bull's-eye design. "Lucky ... Strike."

"Yep, American smokes. English magazines and newspapers are over there, on that table. Read 'em, okay, Vlatko?"

Tony's eyes glistened. "Tank you for cot and Lucky Strike."

****

Though Tony couldn't speak the language, he was glad to join the Italians rather than dwell in a cabin with a pack of Nazi officers. On the voyage he'd strengthen the leg, improve his English, and fortify his famished body with canned C-rations. Every meal included meat, and he gladly wolfed it down with beans, with potato hash, and with vegetables in a stew, ending the feast by wiping the last drops of gravy out of the can with his finger.

Daily visits by Jimmy and Al became as regular as canned meat at dinners. Tony deluged them with questions: "How you say dis? Vhat is dat?" The MPs patiently corrected his errors but weren't above a good laugh at his expense.

One afternoon, they sat on Tony's cot listening to him read from a book on English pronunciation.

"No, Vlatko," Jimmy said. "It's *wood,* not *vood.* You live with *Wops,* not *vops.* Round your lips as if you're saying '*you.*' Watch." Slowly, Jimmy mouthed "you," and Tony mimicked him more or less correctly.

"The 'W' ..." Jimmy placed his forefinger under the letter in the alphabet table in the book. "When 'W' begins a word, round your lips. Like this: *w-w-w-wood.*"

Tony placed his hand on the only table in the dorm. "Is this made of wood?"

Jimmy nodded. "Very good."

Al bore a wily look. "Vlatko, can you say 'fuck'?"

"Vhat is 'fuck'?"

The MPs howled. Tony presumed he had made a joke, though he hadn't a clue why they laughed.

"Not '*vhat* is fuck' – '*what* is fuck.'" Big Al jumped up and pumped his hips in vulgar pantomime.

Tony slapped his brow. "Many words for this in Croat. We say 'pizda,' 'jebati,' 'zajabati.'"

"America, too," Jimmy said. "'Fuck' can be a good or bad word. You fuck a woman – that's good. On the other hand, if a guy's giving you a bad time, like those prick Nazis, you tell 'em to fuck off!"

Tony peered at Al. "Fuck off, Al."

The howls returned, and Al, weakened by the hilarity, shook his head. "Shit, Vlatko, don't … tell *me* to fuck off! Save that for the Krauts."

Tony, now stoked by the humor he'd created, wasn't finished. "The place this ship go … Norfuck … Is dis where people go fuck in de north?"

"You got me again." Al said. "At this rate, you'll be the English teacher and the comedian at the Fritz Ritz."

"Vhat is Fritz Ritz?"

"More lessons tomorrow, Vlatko," Jimmy said. "We have rounds to make. Tomorrow, you tell us how you got shot; we tell you about America."

****

On the second day of January 1944, every prisoner hung over the rails gaping at the coast and Norfolk's harbor. Joyous or resentful, their view of America depended on the reputation and innuendo garnered from newspapers, movies, and word of mouth.

Aside from the thieves who had snatched his buttons, the Americans had treated Tony with dignity. Down the gangplank he limped in a body fifteen pounds heavier than when he left Africa. One step short of the dock, he tossed his crutch into the Atlantic.

After delousing, Tony reclaimed his disinfected uniform and presented his papers, photograph and serial number 6WG-1759 to a youthful chap in a pressed beige uniform, side cap and tie. He would be interned at a camp in district 6, wherever that was. Aware that 'W' stood for 'War Department', and 'G' for 'Germany', Tony smiled, and in English enquired if 'G' could be changed to 'C' – for 'Croatia'.

The deskman pointed to the railcars. "That's your train."

The coaches looked new – nothing like the rickety boxcars in Africa. A man with coal-black skin, wearing a railroad uniform, was placing step stools at their doorways. This was how prisoners were treated in America? There must be a catch.

He boarded a heated coach with upholstered bench seats, two bathrooms and large windows. Every window seat was taken so he chose a place next to a hulk of a man with three stripes on his sleeve. The fellow said his name was Bo Zick. His accent was unmistakable.

"Sergeant, you're shaking the hand of First Lieutenant Tony Babic of the Croat Air Force Legion. Already you forget military protocol?"

"Sorry. Figured you for a blue-eye, Lieutenant – that's why you didn't get a salute." Bo motioned to the POWs on the bench facing them. "That's Hermann Vogler. He says he's Czech because he lived there before moving back to Munich, but to me he's just Hermann the German. The guy next to him is a Pole – a beanpole, you might say. He's Ladders Lipinski."

Tony asked the Pole if he'd heard his name correctly.

"You sure did," Bo said. "Ladders was a house painter. Hermann the German tuned pianos. He doesn't say much – won't even tell us how he got into the army. Sure as hell didn't volunteer, did you, Hermann?"

Hermann didn't look back from the window.

"Ladders went from painting houses to painting swastikas on the tails of planes and commandants." Bo's smile revealed two sizable gaps in his teeth.

"Stuff it, Bo!" Ladders said.

"Keep your paint in the can, Ladders. Ladders can be sensitive, Lieutenant. Me, I used to be a boxer – before that, a book-keeper."

No doubt he talked too much, but Tony couldn't help warming to Bo. The man's history was on his face. Scar lines weaved through the wild eyebrows. His nose had been broken enough times that it had no real shape, and his ears were swollen and misshapen enough to resemble dried apricots. This fellow working with figures all day at a desk seemed incomprehensible.

"Oh, yeah," Bo said, "I forgot to add gambling to my résumé."

"You consider gambling a *job*?" Tony asked.

"Anything that makes money is a job – if you lose money, it's a habit. Gambling became a job when I started putting money on my bouts.

Every time I lost the fight, I won the bet. Figure that, will you? I soon got better at gambling than boxing. In the army I plied both trades – built a pretty good nest egg."

"How'd you manage that?" Ladders asked.

"Now *you're* teasing *me*. You build a string of wins, at least three in a row. You tell everyone your next opponent doesn't stand a chance. Then you bet a whack of money on the guy. America is the land of plenty – plenty for you, plenty for me."

"You can't make money in prison," Ladders said.

"If you use your head, there's a way." Bo removed his cap and massaged a three-inch furrow at the side of his hairless skull. "Not many Germans in this car. You don't suppose they separated us, do you?"

Ladders' head rotated on his slender neck like a periscope. "I don't think so. Hermann's German ... Hans is up there, and Werner and Rolf are behind us."

"Two months of captivity," Tony said, "and I saw only one example of segregation. Two MPs kept me from the Nazis on the *Empress*."

"Did the Nazis—" Bo halted in mid-sentence.

One of three MPs with submachine guns called them to attention, and a middle-aged civilian in a gray pinstriped suit climbed aboard. He said his name was Feinstein, an interpreter for the War Department.

"Guy's a Jew," Bo whispered. "Already, they shit in the Germans' nest."

"Shut up," Hermann said.

"Sorry Hermann, that slipped past my internal censor – too many hits in the head."

Tony had expected Bo, a sergeant, to reprimand the corporal. But, his attention went right back to Feinstein the moment he began reading from a dossier:

"'Prisoners of war are subject to the laws, regulations and orders in force in the military of the detaining nation. Acts of insubordination shall render prisoners liable to the measures prescribed by such regulations, except as otherwise provided in this chapter."

He removed the spectacles. "As prisoners, you can expect fair and humane treatment from this compassionate nation. You are going to Camp Graham, near Rockford, Illinois. Under no circumstances will you enter any other coach. Stay seated at all times. Raise your hand if you need the restroom. The train makes as few stops as possible." Feinstein held up the booklet from which he had read. "This is the Geneva Convention as it relates to prisoners of war. The articles, over a hundred of them, will be circulated here and posted inside the camp so you'll know your rights. To alleviate concerns you may have, I will summarize the articles pertaining to camp life."

Bo eased forward and released a loud fart. Several men snickered.

Feinstein put his specs back on and turned a page: "'Article twenty-five. POW quarters must meet the same standards as those of the captor.'" He looked up. "'Article twenty-six. Food will be in quantity, quality, and variety to keep POWs in good health. Article twenty-eight. Tobacco is permitted.'"

"Das ist gut," Bo said.

"Prisoners are to wear uniforms in the camp. You're still soldiers. Act with military decorum. Salute captors of higher rank and always salute the camp commander. Inside the camp, we expect courtesy. And we expect it here." He lowered the dossier, frowning at Bo.

Feinstein read seven more articles. "The rest you can read for yourselves."

****

At every opportunity, Tony practiced his English on a congenial guard, asking what he might expect to find at Camp Graham. The guard, who had endured six months of tedious rail duty, seemed happy to oblige. With a capacity of 4,800, Camp Graham was one of many POW stockades scattered throughout America. POWs would live in one of four separate compounds, each containing twenty-four barracks of fifty prisoners apiece. Graham was on a 250-acre farm field enclosed by two concentric ten-foot-high chain-link fences eight feet apart and topped with barbed wire. Eight watchtowers equipped with searchlights and machine guns were in place to dissuade prisoners from taking leave.

The base had hot shower and laundry facilities, a chapel, and a soccer pitch inside a recreational field. The guard estimated the sports ground at around twenty-five acres. Each compound contained four mess buildings with kitchens, four latrines, an infirmary, a postal exchange, a workshop and a recreation hall. The compounds were individually fenced and segregated by German or Italian nationality.

Order within the stockade was the responsibility of the incarcerated. Military hierarchy prevailed. The guard hadn't heard of any problems. American officers and NCOs rarely came inside other than for inspections and special events, such as soccer matches and theatrical or musical performances.

The place sounded like a summer camp, although Tony didn't like the notion of prisoners in charge of prisoners; that seemed too much like animals running a zoo. He had already witnessed the contemptuous treatment of non-Nazis by senior officers trained in the discipline of the Third Reich.

Thirty-five hours and a thousand miles of rolling landscape, cornfields and roadways ended at a city of tar-papered barracks in the farmlands. For Tony, the passage invoked images of the train journey he had made in 1939 to the pilot apprentice trials – not that the sights remotely resembled the Croatian countryside. This was winter, and the lands were soothing white, not dusty brown. America was rich – autos everywhere and so many houses, mostly of wood, not stone or brick. He had seen towering city skylines; even the smaller towns had dozens of tall buildings as opposed to the scattering of shanties, a church and a school that passed for a village back home.

Seemingly undeterred by the driving blizzard, armed soldiers escorted fifty-two Italians to Compound D and ushered the remaining 287 prisoners to Compound C's auditorium, where they were searched for unauthorized goods and currency. No one had as much as a nickel.

Open corrugated boxes along the wall contained denims and wool trousers, gloves, shirts, shoes, socks, undies, coats and jackets. Tony picked up a dark blue shirt with 'POW' in white on the back. Matching trousers carried the same lettering on the front thighs.

"Testing one, two, three," came over the speakers. The POWs stopped what they were doing and looked up at an elevated stage.

Camp commander Colonel Thomas Manning, formerly retired, was a grandfatherly sort with a silver military hair-cut and a leathery complexion. He reminded Tony of the old man who owned the orchard next to Vinograd Kralja. Through a German-speaking GI, Manning offered the usual platitudes about an atmosphere of mutual respect. Nobody liked imprisonment, he said, but he promised to do his best to make it as tolerable as possible. He outlined the most important regulations: infractions and punishment; facility maintenance and care; medical inspections; letter frequency and content. "Then there's this matter of remuneration," he said. You're entitled to a monthly stipend, paid by check upon release." Manning disclosed the rates by rank.

Bo flashed a jack-o-lantern grin. "See what I mean, Lieutenant? Twenty dollars a month! We might leave with a thousand bucks in our pockets. Imagine what that buys in Croatia."

"Sergeant, I'd have to stay four years to earn that much. There must be a better way." He winked, and Bo's grin expanded.

"Non-negotiable canteen coupons are the camp currency," Manning said. "You get a week's supply at a time. A day's value of fifteen cents buys a package of cigarettes. You can earn extra by participating in work parties inside and outside the camp. Use your coupons for toiletries, books, magazines, candy. You won't need them for breakfast, lunch or dinner – that's on the house." The old man paused, ostensibly looking for a reaction. Some of the POWs gave a giggle upon translation.

"Clothing stenciled 'POW' is for jobs outside the camp – roadwork and farm duty when the weather improves. Rockford's factories also need labor. The coupon wage is ten cents an hour. Officers and NCOs aren't required to do this work. If they so choose, they may work as supervisors. Camp Graham is also an academic institute. There's much to learn in our classrooms – trades, history and language. Take the opportunity and you will prosper when this war ends. Stay out of trouble, work hard, and listen to your camp leaders."

Manning looked to his left, and two grim-faced Germans in smartly pressed SS uniforms clicked the heels of their shiny high boots and walked onto the stage. The fine hairs on the back of Tony's neck sprung to attention.

Chapter 15

January 1944
Rockford, Illinois

SS Major Helmut Mauer's steely eyes bored into the *Drahtpost* newspaper as he spooned the last of his cornflakes between thin lips. He then finished the dregs of his coffee, pushed away the paper, and glared at the receding darkness through the mess hall window.

"Ugh!" he groaned. "Why do I drink this swill, Herr Colonel?"

"To prompt Heimatland memories," said Colonel Wolfgang von Arnim through the wad of toast and jam puffing his cheek. "Have faith, Major. With the invasion will come the arabicas of Hamburg."

Arnim was the younger brother of the general who had replaced Rommel in Africa. Mauer reckoned the surname explained how a dumpy man five inches under mandatory officer height became a member of the SS. The error in discipline bothered him almost as much as the Lagersprecher allowing six months of inactivity and gluttony to stretch his tunic to the limit. Tall and wiry Mauer also ate well, but never gained weight.

"Our armies will come, Herr Colonel. Of this I am certain. But I shall not depart this soil until two personal objectives are completed."

"Those objectives, Major?"

"Retribution upon every camp traitor, even those whose loyalty I have forced. That fulfilled, I shall fish the Fox River."

"Diverse goals," Arnim said.

"One is capture and kill, the other is capture and release. The method sets them apart, Herr Colonel."

Arnim's brow lifted. "You still tie the knots, Helmut?"

Mauer liked it when Arnim used his first name. Seldom was the prisoner's spokesman, the Lagersprecher, this informal. "The knot, Herr Colonel, is the weakest union between the fisherman and the catch. The wrong choice of knot can punish. You must tie with the correct lubrication and pressure to make perfect. I like to trim ..." He noticed

Arnim eyeing a band of Nazis at another table. "I am sorry ... to you this is uninteresting."

His attention restored, Arnim said, "Your skill with the knots has many uses. Does today's *Drahtpost* please you?"

"Our methods are subtle and effective." Mauer's forefinger underscored the date on the cover page. "The '44' after January ... Otto has styled the fours and drawn the lines very close to resemble the swastika."

"I see the lightning lines of the SS."

"A clever dual strategy, Herr Colonel," Mauer re-opened the *Drahtpost* to sports. "We crushed Compound B in table tennis. Friday we play those useless Italians."

Arnim grimaced. "Useless at table tennis, but not soccer."

Mauer hadn't wanted to discuss soccer. "Snow or sleet, we practice every day. We improve tremendously. Of course, Italy has De Luca. You know of this challenge."

"The Rockford papers call the match 'an event that cannot be missed'." Arnim opened his palms as though bewildered. "How do people in that grimy little town spend their days?"

"Making furniture and auto parts," Mauer said, derisively. "School sports stimulate their miserable lives."

"To these peasants, our match is professional. Manning has ordered timber for bleachers. The US Army will attend. So will guards, POWs, and the public – some from as far away as Chicago. Losing is impossible."

Mauer hadn't heard about the bleachers or the flood of spectators.

Without a miracle, losing was probable. The Italians had three players from highly regarded clubs, and the captain of the 1938 World Cup champions.

"Do not be concerned, Herr Colonel. We have until April. From the three hundred arrivals I expect two or three to replace our weakest. Germany shall prevail."

"Make certain of it."

****

Mauer's troop goose-stepped to the barracks of the new arrivals. The SS Major planned to process two barracks and a hundred men before work duty began. Within two days he would have a list of those on his side –

the side of Hitler. Then he would cement their belief in the Reich and in Nazi leadership in the camp. The ambivalent and the resisters would be dealt with by other means. To Mauer's thinking, the policy of relegating camp control to men like himself and Arnim was idiotic. Provided they didn't bring attention to their motives, they could run Graham as they pleased.

"Heil Hitler!" Twenty Nazis, including Mauer, barged into the rectangular bunkhouse comprising a grand room with a bedroom for two officers at the rear and a cast-iron heater in the center. Heels clicked to attention. Half of the inmates responded by raising their arms in the Hitler salute. Counting Mauer's troop of Nazis, seventy men crowded the bunkhouse 15 – 48 of them stood rigid at the foot locker next to the end of his cot.

Stern-faced, Mauer pointed to the wall closest to the door. "Friends of the Reich shall step over there. There is a form for you to register your allegiance to Adolf Hitler. Read the oath, Sergeant Burger."

The brutish-looking sergeant half shouted, "I swear to thee, Adolf Hitler as Führer and chancellor of the German Reich, loyalty and bravery. I vow to support the Nazi Party, to support thee and my superiors whom thou shall appoint. I give you obedience unto death, so help me God." The reference to Nazism had been a recent Mauer addition.

Eleven men who saluted with a stiff arm signed their names. Mauer crossed his arms on his narrow chest, and glared at the others. "Now is the time of reckoning. The wise shall take this opportunity." Like radar scanning the skies, the hollow-cheeked major surveyed the internees. Three more joined the believers. Still, thirty percent was not a ratio that would please Arnim or the Führer.

"You … little mouse …" Mauer approached a small, thin-haired man. "Look at me!"

The man flinched.

"Germans don't cringe like cowards," Mauer said.

Without expression, the man said he was Czech.

"State your name!"

"Hermann Vogler."

"You are *Corporal* Hermann Vogler! *Corporal* Vogler, you are of Bavarian speech."

In monotone, Hermann said, "Major, I am from Bavaria but—"

"Corporal Vogler, you are a liar. Get over there and align yourself with soldiers of the Third Reich. Sign the allegiance, and I overlook this indiscretion."

Mauer saw Hermann's eyes glance up at his cap. "I see your fascination with the death's head and crossbones. It is a warning to our enemies. Are you an enemy?"

Mauer waited several seconds but Hermann did not reply. "I see," Mauer said. "In you, Vogler, we have a liar *and* a coward. I shall deal with you later." To Sergeant Burger, he whispered, "Note the location of his cot: west wall, third from the north." To the prisoners, he hollered, "Where is your barrack leader?"

A trooper scurried down the rows of cots and pounded on the officers' door.

A blond man in briefs and undershirt, with shaving cream on his chin, stuck his head through the gap in the door.

"You are barrack leader?" Mauer asked.

"Not by choice, sir," Tony said, wiping the foam away with a towel.

Mauer caught the accent and the cynicism, and then searching for any hint of trepidation, detected none. Finally, he stiff-armed and shouted, "Heil Hitler!"

The barrack leader's hand came to his temple in a brisk traditional salute. "Sir, I am not an officer of the Wehrmacht. I am First Lieutenant Tony Babic, Croat Air Legion. This infantry uniform was issued by a prisoner-of-war hospital."

Always one for patience and fact-finding, Mauer took a moment to assess the man and the situation. "Your German is good," he said in Serbo-Croat. "I know a little of the language from my days in Belgrade. We did you Croats a favor – there are now fewer Serbs on this earth." He left the sentence hanging, all the while measuring Tony's reaction. "Any Serbs in this worthless lot?"

"Sir, last night this lot arrived from Norfolk. I request that you withhold judgment until they settle in."

Several POWs took a deep breath, but Mauer remained calm. "I am Major Mauer of the Waffen-SS. In this stalag you obey my orders and leave the requests to me. Sergeant, make your list. We have still to profile barrack 16."

Mauer took it upon himself to interrogate the blue-eyed barrack leader who could pass for a poster German. He reckoned the customary Nazi mantra of lockstep order would not be effective with this one, but there were many ways to skin a cat ... or a rat.

Tony answered all of his questions, concluding with a wish for an independent Croatia but refusing to embrace Nazism.

"I see, I see ..." Mauer nodded as though the rebuff of Nazism hadn't registered. "You have sacrificed for us," he said, expecting some elaboration from Tony.

"This is true, Major."

"You say you played soccer for Zagreb. Gradjanski or Concordia?" The question seemed to lighten Tony's demeanor.

"I was on Concordia's practice roster. If not for the war I'd have been on the 1940 squad."

"These past four years ... how much have you played?"

"I've kept it up, Major. Of course, I haven't booted a ball since taking two slugs in the leg. There will always be pain, but there's no reason to think I won't play again."

"When?"

"I don't know."

"I shall have Doctor Armstrong examine you. Are you a forward?"

"Striker. Since I was four, every coach had me at center. I was very fast and goals came easy."

Mauer smiled inwardly. The creator had made a mistake – this one would have made a superb German. "Very well, Lieutenant. I wish you success with your rehabilitation." He looked at Bo, then at Burger. "The big oaf is yours, Sergeant."

When the Nazis left for barrack 16, Tony hurried outside to the snow-dusted lane separating the barracks with Bo close behind. The only Americans in sight were high in the towers.

"What do you make of that, Lieutenant?"

"Bo, this isn't America. This is the Third Reich."

****

The main meal was served at midday – today the German cooks had prepared potato soup, pig's knuckles, wurst, and sauerkraut. Tonight, Mauer and Arnim ate a supper of scrambled eggs and lightly fried tomatoes. Arnim wanted to hear about the new arrival of POWs.

"I was dissatisfied, Herr Colonel – not discouraged."

Arnim stuffed a tomato slice into his mouth. "Explain." As he chewed, puffy, pink jowls spilled over his collar.

"Fewer Nazis with each shipment, Herr Colonel. I recommend the Holy Ghost ..."

"How many sessions?" Arnim picked with his little fingernail at a tomato seed stuck in his teeth.

"Two courts will be sufficient for word of mouth to do the rest."

"Tell me of your progress with soccer recruitment."

"There is good news." The news was always good when Mauer responded to Arnim's unease. "We have a Croat lieutenant who played for Zagreb Concordia."

Arnim stopped chewing. "A Slav? Are you mad?"

"Pale blue eyes, yellow hair – no one could look more Aryan, Herr Colonel. Yes, there is Slav accent in his German, but he is fluent. I recommend we watch his play. He could be useful."

"The Slav agrees to represent the Reich?"

"Indeed." The misrepresentation was necessary. And anyway, Mauer had a repertoire of tactics for enlisting cooperation.

****

During the night, the Lager Gestapo nudged Hermann Vogler awake with the barrel of a Luger facsimile.

"Not a sound, Vogler," said one of Mauer's henchmen. "Come with us."

They blindfolded the barefoot prisoner and herded him through the snow to storehouse 3, the supply hut shielded from the views of the west and north towers.

Inside, Arnim waited at a table in front of a red, white, and black swastika banner pinned to the wall. A statuesque Mauer stood next to him in buffed leather boots, fists resting on his hips. His expression was as dour as the gray uniform that boasted a Knight's Cross at the throat, two Iron Crosses at the chest, and a circular SS belt buckle. Inwardly, he was smiling. The seated assembly facing him was going to see him at this best. He asked that the blindfolds be removed.

The prisoners' expressions were as he expected. First, their eyes widened in shock, then came the fright, and finally the panic of tremors and sweat. Mauer snapped to attention, launched a straight arm, and hailed the Führer. The congregation replicated the tribute, and Arnim slammed a camp-carved gavel down on the desktop planks.

"The defendants," Arnim said, "are not to speak of the proceedings of this court." He looked at the six men cowering before him in their nightwear. "You are Germans who have retracted your allegiance to the Führer. The charge is treason. Who speaks for Ernst Schultz, Heinz Schmidt, Hermann Vogler, Gerhard Busch, Christoph Schreiber and Wilhelm Stocker?"

The accused turned their heads to the assembly of Nazis, but the room remained silent.

"Then you defend yourself or plead guilty. Treason is punishable by death. Who wishes to speak?"

Mauer saw Hermann Vogler pull his shoulders back and take a breath. When Hermann stood up, Mauer smelled defiance. Had he misjudged the little mouse's resolve?

Hermann said the charges were preposterous. "I fought bravely until my capture in Italy. Never did I disobey an order. Never did I flee from battle. I was conscripted in Czechoslovakia, reported for duty and served honorably. I killed for Germany. I am not a traitor." He sat down.

"Remain standing!" Mauer said, mortified at having selected an insolent defendant for the war court. The meek were easy converts. They returned to their barracks as Nazis – their bunkmates caught on.

Leather gloves loose in his hand, Mauer strutted like a peacock in front of the defendants. "A man seldom goes to war as a deserter, Corporal. You claim you weren't a turncoat in the field, yet here you refuse to give of yourself for the Führer. This evidence is irrefutable."

"A good German is not necessarily a Nazi," Herman said, without the slightest flutter in his voice. Again, Hermann sat.

This time, Mauer's gloves struck Hermann's cheek. "You repulsive little worm! Get up!" Under a torrent of back and forth leather slaps, the little man remained seated, eyes closed. Enraged, Mauer belted him across the head with his free hand.

"Enough!" Arnim said, striking the gavel. "I declare Corporal Vogler guilty of treason. The Lager Gestapo will remove him."

Two of the remaining five declared loyalty to Hitler, and were returned to their bunkhouse. The three holdouts trailed Hermann to the latrines, where they were roped to chairs.

Mauer circled them, checking the knots. After draping his tunic over a stack of boxes, he handed his peaked hat and gloves to a guard and rolled up his shirtsleeves.

"You look thirsty," Mauer said to the prisoners. "Tormento de toca shall quench your thirst. And no, this is not a Spanish cocktail." He seized a handful of Hermann's hair, wrenched it back, and pushed the nozzle of a metal funnel deep into his throat. His victim gagged. Mauer yanked it out and tossed it to Burger as Hermann coughed blood; the funnel's sharp edges would have scratched the tender lining of his throat. Mauer's arms remained folded until the hacking subsided. Blood trickled from the corner of Hermann's mouth and down his chin.

"Now for some water. I shall pour every drop from that four-gallon bucket down the cone into your throat. Resist and you choke. Accept the laws of gravity or drown. Water fills your stomach, then your intestines. I stop pouring when your hand goes up. That is when you are ready to reaffirm your faith in the Führer. Fail to do this and the flow continues. Organs expand. Visceral tissues convulse." Mauer waved a sheet of paper like a flag. "Sign this form and you avoid the pain."

Three holdouts signed. Hermann spat more blood.

"Return these three," Mauer said. "Sergeant Burger, perhaps you would like to assist in the art of persuasion."

All day the urge had been building in Mauer. Thankfully there was a holdout. Thankfully it was the runt.

****

Dr Armstrong looked young enough to be in medical school. Tony greeted him and pointed to the man still in bed.

Armstrong stooped over the cot. "Glad you speak English, Lieutenant Babic. Tell him to roll on his back."

Hermann didn't budge. Armstrong pulled up the nightshirt and pressed his fingers to the abdomen. Hermann groaned. "He's sore down there. Don't see any bruises – must be internal. I'm going to press gently. Tell him I want to know where it hurts."

"Corporal not talk," Tony said.

"He can't or won't?"

"English mistake … Corporal cannot talk."

Armstrong continued palpating the stomach and abdomen. Hermann's face twisted with each probe. "Tell him I'm done down there. Open your mouth, Corporal – like this," he said, opening his own mouth wide.

Hermann's jaw lowered, and Armstrong inserted the wooden tongue depressor, flicked on his penlight, and peeked down the throat. "Good grief!"

"What wrong?" Tony asked.

Armstrong hesitated, and then said, "A serious case of strep throat."

"What mean strep?"

"Bad throat infection." Armstrong grabbed himself by the throat. "Lymph glands are swollen. Tonsils and throat are as red as a batch of ripe strawberries." He raised the forefinger of one hand and four fingers on the other. "Have him take one pill four times a day for a week. That should clear it up. Understand? One pill at breakfast, one at lunch, supper and bedtime." He tossed Tony the pill bottle. "I'll write a note excusing him from work duty."

"I understand," Tony said.

"By the way," Armstrong said. "Aren't you the guy who wants me to look at your leg?"

"Major Mauer wants that."

"What's the matter with *his* leg?" Armstrong chortled. "Just kidding – show me the knee."

Tony dropped his trousers, and Armstrong manipulated the wounded area.

"Nasty scar, Lieutenant. Looks like you've done a good job rebuilding the quadriceps ... these." Armstrong pinched the skin.

"Leg raises help pass time ... and a book on English."

"At least a couple more weeks before you're fit to play," Armstrong said.

So that was it: Mauer wanted him for soccer.

When Armstrong left, Tony called a barrack meeting. "Hermann's in a bad way," he said. "The doctor says throat infection. Throat infections don't cripple a man – at least, not overnight." He looked at Hermann, who was taking shallow breaths. "Did any of you hear him cry out in the night?"

A few heads shook. The rest answered with blank stares.

"Okay, did anyone see anything strange?"

Not a word.

Chapter 16

The blizzard that whitened the tar paper on the barracks peppered the two cowering Croats trudging between the waist-high snowdrifts. For all but a few men smoking in barrack doorways, the stockade was an austere wasteland. Shouting over the wind proved fruitless; Tony would save his words for the canteen.

He thought of Rado, wondering how long the gash in his heart would ooze grief. Perhaps an affable prison mate like Bo would prove to be a useful diversion.

"I'll buy the Schlitz," he said to Bo at the counter.

The storekeeper plunked two bottles down and Tony counted out fifty-five cents in coupons. "That should cover the beers and a pack of Camels, Hans." Turning to Bo, he said, "I can't believe I'm in a prison camp buying beer with *their* money."

"The Nazis call it coddling – a plot to take down fascism."

In a wordless toast at a table, they clanked bottles and took blissful gulps of beer.

Tony cupped the bottle in his hand, peering at the label. "Unless I've read it wrong, this beer made Milwaukee famous. How can a beer do that?"

Bo took another swig. "Don't know and don't care. A shame it's three-point-two – weaker than piss."

"Then drink piss. It's free. Beer was ten cents when Graham opened. They had to double the price because they couldn't keep it in stock. Now it's almost two days' pay. They can't want us drinking much. Is there a better way to spend their money?"

Bo's scarred brow arced. "Sure is. Be my partner in business."

"Hah! What kind of business?"

"Actually, two businesses."

"You're kidding."

Bo's wide grin waned. "They're unrelated, but one feeds the other. Together they generate big cash."

Tony gave a skeptical head shake, but he was curious what Bo had in mind.

Bo grabbed the package of smokes that Tony had balanced on the top of his beer bottle. "For these, you paid fifteen coupon cents. My idea is to buy a bunch of smokes to sell outside the camp. When we leave for work duty, we bring them with us and sell them for seven cents – real money, Tony. You can carry two packs in your pockets. The guards don't give a shit. More than that goes in the crotch – they won't touch you there."

Bo swigged his beer, presumably waiting for Tony to do the math.

"Okay, Bo. Say we cut back on other goodies and buy thirty packs a week and get seven cents each; that's two dollars and ten cents – *if* we sell them and *if* we're not caught. That would be a haul … *if* I went along with your scheme."

"You're thinking small-time. What are the Yanks going to do if they catch you? They'll take the cash; that's it. You were a fighter pilot, for Christ's sake! This is kid's play. The big idea is using our guys to buy the fags. That would give us an inventory from twenty, maybe thirty buyers. Not thirty packs a week – *five or six hundred*. We sell for them and take a cut for putting our nuts on the block."

"Nuts on the block? That sounds like risk."

"Nah, it's a scam to take forty percent. They get sixty. Everybody's happy. You and I make twenty bucks a week."

"What makes you think they want real money?"

"Everybody's going home. Most think life will be harsh. Uncle Sam's cash will be a godsend. As soon as we get enough cash from the sale of smokes, we open the Lucky Buck bookmaking business."

Tony hiked his eyebrows.

Bo had reckoned that soccer, boxing and table tennis would draw the most bets. He admitted that they'd need a lot of coupons to build a balanced treasury of cash and coupons, but twenty-five cents for a coupon dollar would take care of that. They'd start small and build to the main events for the big paydays.

"I know nothing about business," Tony said. Though he admired Bo's ingenuity, he could not envision the potential. How the hell would they keep from going broke?

Bo said they'd play the odds. "Take the big soccer game – assume we peg Germany's chances of beating Italy at one in four. That means for every dollar bet on the Krauts, we pay out four dollars if they win. If too much money's on Germany, we adjust the odds to make betting on them less attractive.

Tony was lost, but he wouldn't say so.

"The objective," Bo said, "is to manage risk so you have funds to pay, no matter who wins. Now, once a guy makes a bet, he gets the odds we promised. Changed odds are for new bets. Yep, it's a heap of administration, but I can handle it. I'm good with figures. So, how do we make money?"

"You're a mind reader."

"We take a seven percent handling fee on the payouts. There'll be times we lose money because we didn't balance the odds. Other times we'll be ahead. That's why we need a rainy-day fund. But seven percent is chicken feed. No one should go into a business with that rate of return."

"I'm completely lost."

Bo gave his best jack-o-lantern smile. "You're forgetting my other … uh, talent. In this business, that skill will be used sparingly – for the jackpots."

Tony couldn't hold back his chuckle. "You may be good at rigging fights, but explain how you rig soccer matches."

"That's where *you* come in. Play in the big game and we have an advantage."

"I'll not throw a game. I may go along with your cigarette scheme, but that's all. We came here to discuss Hermann. All you've talked about is making money."

The bruiser's head dropped ever so slightly.

Bo said the ardent Nazis were bunked in barracks 1 to 4 and 19 through 22. "The rest of us are sandwiched in the middle. Eight barracks is 400, give or take. They've converted sixty-two of the guys who came with us from Norfolk. Some were already that way; the others were scared enough to piss themselves. Those here the longest say the Nazis know everything. They read every letter in and out. They threaten to smuggle names of their enemies to Heinrich Himmler, who's vowed to punish their families in Germany. Some call it fear-mongering. Who knows for sure?"

"Hermann's strep throat was at the hand of the Holy Ghost," Tony said. "Two of ours were awake when the Lager Gestapo took him. We have to defend our barrack from these barbarians."

"How?"

Tony downed the last of his beer and pushed the bottle to the side. "If you like *my* idea, I'll call a meeting of the men."

****

In daylight, Graham was a bustling place, with plenty to ease the boredom. Tony spread his time between classroom study, paid supervisory duty, movies, soccer and the library. He attended Sunday morning worship more for spirituality than for the theological doctrines of a chaplain unsympathetic to Nazi order. Either way, the chapel was a sanctuary.

Accompanying POWs to external jobs at every opportunity padded his wallet to the tune of eighty coupon cents per day. Never in his life had he earned so much doing so little. With so many young Americans overseas, Rockford's food-processing plants needed labor. Tony's favorite task had him overseeing POWs working on the assembly line of the Quaker Oats pet food factory. The half-hour all-you-can-eat hot lunch also wasn't hard to take.

Colonel Manning was on record saying that out-of-camp duty reduced the frustrations of captivity, which led to depression, despondency and anarchy. A breakdown in order or morale wasn't going to happen on his watch – of this he assured his superiors and the local citizens.

Major Kirilenko had ingrained in Tony the ethic of seeing to the welfare of every soldier under his command. Tony had wanted none of this in America, but recent events demanded that he fulfill the obligation. The little Czech-German had disgraced Mauer in the presence of subordinates at the war court. That night, five others sang before a drop of water touched their throats. Hermann drank three gallons, and still he would not submit. Shattering his resolve became Mauer's obsession.

By March, the Holy Ghost had visited barrack 15 four times, abducting Hermann on three of those occasions. Most recently they had dumped him on the snowy barrack steps an hour before reveille, and there he had lain like a dead man, his neck raw from rope burn.

This was the fork in the road. Tony called a meeting of the barrack. "We have to do something," he said. "I'm suggesting guard duty from lights-out till bugle call." Everyone nodded.

The watch started immediately, with two-hour rotations of sentries equipped with sports whistles at the windows. On the third night of the watch, a whistle blast had every man out of bed. Four thugs entered the barracks with baseball bats. They came to a halt the moment an outer searchlight illuminated forty-two inmates with handmade clubs.

"You shall regret this," one of the intruders said. "We will return with an army."

By this point, Mauer had coaxed as many Germans as he could from Tony's barrack. Those who converted transferred to pro-Nazi housing; Hungarians, Czechs and Poles replaced them. Yet, the resistance did not end the tyranny. Every night, stones peppered the roof, bats smashed windows and tar paper was torn from the exterior walls. Out of sentry view, a fire started under a corner of the structure. Ladders, having seen the glow, blew the whistle and grabbed two pails of piss to douse the flames. The buckets had begun not as a fire precaution but to preclude nocturnal visits to the latrines.

At best, the plan had been a stop-gap measure. Tony would work on a longer-term strategy, but first he had to determine a realistic outcome. He could not stamp out every Nazi at Graham. Safeguarding barrack 15 until the end of the war? That was possible if he did battle on the terms that suited his resources, not his enemy's. Gang warfare was foolhardy – the Nazis were masters at using the tools of oppression, violence and terror. Tony would opt for a passive war using softer weapons – negotiation, deal making and propaganda.

****

Opened in May of 1943, Graham was the first camp with a POW graveyard. A death from natural causes occurred in July. Then, in August, a man was discovered dangling from a noose in the latrines of the Afrika Korps internees, a signed suicide note in his pocket. By February 1944, the number of gravestones had swelled to nine.

An American plant worker overheard two POWs discussing the suicides. The eavesdropper was a neighbor of a cub journalist for the *Rockford Morning Star*. Enticed by the potential of a story, the reporter snooped around Graham, posing questions from outside the fence. The prisoners gave him enough to pester Colonel Manning for an interview. Manning had consented, confident that his stature and fatherly style would satisfy the youngster and defuse the gossip,

Bobby Rose came into Manning's office as might a schoolboy sent to the headmaster for some infraction. But once Bobby Rose opened his mouth, it was the fatherly one who recoiled. As Manning hemmed and hawed, Bobby Rose strode about the office like a seasoned attorney pelting an ill-equipped witness with damning questions.

Manning said Graham's casualty rate was no greater than the average camp, but he had misjudged the person before him. Bobby Rose had done his homework. War Department records showed 102 POW deaths in the nation as of December 31, 1943 – less than one casualty per prison camp. Bobby Rose had Manning backed into a corner.

The consequence appeared in the *Star*'s February 28 issue:

'GRAHAM POW DEATHS HIGHEST IN NATION by Bobbie Rose
Camp Graham has the highest POW death rate of any camp in America. Asked why the incidence exceeds one man per month, camp commander Colonel Manning said, "This isn't unusual. Despite complete adherence to Geneva Convention protocol, incarcerated men become despondent."

Since May, one POW died of natural causes, two drowned and six perished by suicidal hangings. The two incidents of drowning were said to be accidental. This reporter asked how a man can drown in a camp that doesn't have a pond, a lake or a swimming pool. But Colonel Manning says a person can drown in two inches of water.'

Manning feared that the article would bring an inquest by the Provost Marshal General's Office. He could lose his operational rank and find himself back in the Eau Claire bungalow he and his wife of forty-two years bought upon retirement to Wisconsin. When the war broke out, the army had called on the retired colonel to head a prisoner-of-war camp. That beat pulling weeds, trimming hedges, shoveling snow, and repeating stories of the Great War to the gray-hairs at the town's library. This war had given him a new beginning.

The death rates had to be arrested. He told Arnim to calm the prisoners. No more suicides, or Arnim and Mauer would find themselves at Camp

Alva, the Nazi outpost in Oklahoma that housed the most treacherous agitators.

****

As it turned out, *The Rockford Star* article failed to trigger an investigation. Vigilante patrols persisted, but none of the barracks were violated. The threat of violence was enough to sustain the undertow of fear, and though the night court lay dormant, Tony cautioned his men not to be fooled by the lull in the storm.

For distraction, he put his mind to sports and business. The partners needed one or two American workers per factory to act as middlemen between cigarette buyer and seller. While the POWs worked the lines and operated machines, Tony sized up the civilians, striking up conversations and establishing cordial relationships. Every approach, every casual remark, had been rehearsed. He would deviate when necessary and execute the planned adjustment.

"Get to know the man," Bo had said. "Pour the concrete. Let it set. Add to the foundation. Understand his patriotism. Make sure he won't betray you. If you read him wrong, he'll squeal and the venture's dead."

The target had to believe that the transaction, though covert, did not threaten American security. The resale of cigarettes was a harmless scheme by which penniless POWs might come up with pocket change to buy a pair of stockings for their girl when the war ended – when they could rejoice in democratic freedom. They weren't dealing in stolen goods. The cigarettes were purchased with coupons earned from work in American factories, fields and orchards at the paltry wage of ten cents an hour. No one got rich selling a pack of smokes for under a dime. It might take six months for a POW to make fifty cents – what harm could come of that?

This was the sympathy card, the humble face of the proposition. Beyond emotion, they needed logic to seal the deal. The logic was value – brand-name smokes at half price. If a pack-a-day smoker saved seven cents a pack, he could put two dollars a month in the cookie jar. On top of that – and this was where the enterprising nature of man came into play – if a middleman charged an extra penny or two on every pack he sold, his earnings could triple. That carrot, when necessary, was saved for the pitch's finale.

By April, Tony and Bo had partners in six factories. They set their prices at eight cents for middleman on purchases of less than sixty packs; quantities exceeding sixty packs got a one-cent discount. The middleman could choose Pall Mall, Lucky Strike, Chesterfield or Camels. Their network consisted of thirty-four POW suppliers, ten factory middlemen and five salesmen. Over the course of a day at the factory, a salesman collected cigarettes from the POWs and delivered them to the American middleman. At week's end, Bo and Tony disbursed the proceeds.

In a country where the average monthly wage was $200, Tony and Bo grossed $15.14 in their first week of operations, $25.22 in the second, and $47.60 in the third.

Bo handed Tony a note as they walked into their room. "Look at this. I've worked the numbers – we're miles ahead of expectations – thirty-four bucks in profit. That's enough to kick-start Lucky Buck."

Tony flopped on the bed and his head sank into the pillow. "Think we can keep it up?"

"We have to guard against a spike in demand – Canteen Hans could get wise. Right now we've got thirty-four guys buying two packs a day. In a month we'll have sixty. We need to increase our supply in small bites. We don't want Hans raising the red flag."

"I'll leave that to you, Bo. I need to put in time exercising a wobbly left leg."

****

Tony's leg survived the matches of Compound C's house league, though it was stiff and sore by the second half. The German coaches observed from a distance. Knowing that Tony wasn't physically capable of helping Germany at this stage, Mauer convinced Manning to delay the German-Italian match until mid-May, when the snow was sure to be gone.

One Saturday, as Tony laid out his gear for practice, he heard footsteps outside his room, then a faint knock. The door was sufficiently ajar to catch a glimpse of the caller.

"Door's open, Ladders."

Ladders ducked under the door joist.

"Feeling all right?" Tony asked. "You look like you've seen a ghost – sorry, poor choice of words."

"Sergeant Burger is here. Major Mauer wishes to see you."

Tony stiffened. The name put him on instant alert. Nonetheless, he chuckled and laced his boots as though about to embark on a Sunday stroll. "So, the mutt from hell wants to see me, does he? Now, what do you suppose the devil's lapdog wants of a Croat?" Tony wondered whether his bravado had fooled Ladders. "Mauer's goon wants to escort me?"

"Yes – and three others."

****

Mauer was alone at a bench table for ten in the Nazi mess hall, in front of him an assortment of wooden spools of thread, and some loose catgut monofilament. Like a watchmaker examining the intricate workings of a timepiece, he hung his head over a thread clasped between skeletal fingers, and with precision, he looped and threaded a complex knot, then another.

"Herr Major," Burger said. "I have the Slav for you."

If Mauer saw Tony, it was peripherally. "Sit down, Lieutenant. I finish the nail knot ... then you."

Tony lifted his leg over the bench across from Mauer, watching him pull the thread through a loop.

"Do you fly fish, Lieutenant?"

His calmness had Tony clasping his hands together to ensure his fingers would not tremble. "I haven't had the pleasure, Major."

"Striking, cold-blooded beings ... river trout," Mauer said, hardly moving his lips. "So beautiful, I can't bring myself to kill them, even though I love their flavor. On this line I have the Albright knot. It comes after the arbor knot at the reel. The arbor secures the backing. The Albright connects the fly to the backing. This is the nail knot. It connects the leader to the fly line."

"Do you miss fishing, Major?"

"The answer is obvious. You know that." Mauer glanced up. His colorless, thin lips curled into a bare grin.

Tony writhed inwardly. Had the monster seen his fear?

"Manning promised some hours at the Fox River this summer," Mauer said. This is now impossible. He is shitting himself over the Jew's column. So why, you ask, do I tie knots if I cannot fish? It is a pastime. You see my fastidiousness. I tie with patience and precision." Mauer dipped the thread into a saucer of water, and then he eased the line tight.

"My favorite stream is sixty miles east of Strasbourg, in Alsace. Perhaps you shall be my guest after the Allies surrender."

The thought of surrender must have wrenched Mauer from his bliss, for he bolted upright, swept his work aside, and picked up a string that looked like industrial twine. Looping and threading, his fingers moved at the speed of a sidewalk trickster handling cards. In seconds, he had woven the end of the string into a slipknot with neatly bound coils. His dark eyes bored into Tony as he raised the twine and held it out. A miniature five-coil hangman's noose dangled at Tony's nose.

"Don't be afraid, Lieutenant. This is for rats. I sedate them. When they come to, the noose is snug around their neck. They squirm, it tightens." He tossed the twine aside and called for coffee.

Tony tried to look unperturbed. This was the last man on earth to whom he could show weakness.

"Two matters involving you shall be resolved." Mauer said. "First, you shall play for the Reich on the thirteenth of May."

Tony detested the thought, though he had already acquiesced to Bo, purportedly for business reasons. His prime motive for playing was to remain on cordial terms with Mauer and keep the Nazis at bay. This wasn't war; it was a game.

"Is something on your mind, Lieutenant?"

Tony scratched the back of his neck, summoning what he hoped would pass for nonchalance. "Major ... I appreciate your confidence in me. The leg is almost like new. I'm sure I'd be your best player ... if I accepted your invitation."

Mauer's eyes went cold, and a tinge of pink erased the sallowness in his cheeks.

Tony's heart hammered. "Major, from what I hear, the only one I cannot outplay is the professional."

Perhaps it was the reality that composed Mauer, for he slouched back in his chair and sighed. "De Luca is the problem. Why do you say *if* you play for us?"

The poker game was on – now for the bluff. "I will accept your invitation – under two conditions."

"Gott im Himmel! This is not an invitation. This is an order!" Mauer's fingernails raked back the stray locks of coal-black hair from his ashen forehead.

"My condition is modest."

Mauer cracked the knuckles of both fists. Through clenched teeth, he finally said, "You know not whom you deal with."

"If you will allow me …"

"Select your words carefully."

"The night raids on barrack 15, Major – they are to be suspended."

"Impossible!" The slam of Mauer's palm sent spools of thread rolling across the table. Two bounced on the floor.

"Then I can't help you win the game."

Hands on the tabletop, Mauer rose slightly. "You greatly underestimate me."

Tony didn't wince as he had when Mauer swung the noose in front of his eyes. If the man wasn't desperate, he would have ordered a dose of Holy Ghost justice regardless of Arnim's moratorium. Barrack 15's night watch could dissuade a small mob, but a major assault would be devastating.

Eyes glaring daggers, Mauer sank back onto the bench. Picking up a thread, he fiddled with it like a Greek toying with worry beads. The pinkness in his cheeks dissipated. "I shall do this," he said in a whisper. "Your barrack shall be off limits to night patrol until the game. The arrangement shall continue if, and only if, Germany triumphs. A loss … well, I leave the ramifications of that to your imagination. Acceptable?"

Mauer had ceded ground. "Quite," Tony said in a state of near-shock. But when he rose to leave, Mauer's forefinger motioned downward.

"You are not dismissed. What is your second condition?"

Oh, what the hell … "I wish to be compensated for—"

"No one is paid to play! Are Ustashe the only honorable Slavs in your pathetic country?"

Let it go or … "I'm not asking to be paid to play. I'm asking to be compensated for my contribution to the win. I'm asking two weeks' pay for each goal I score. If I score two or three, Germany wins."

"You are as arrogant as you are corrupt. Where do I find thirty dollars in tickets?"

"I'll take Yankee dollars if you prefer."

"Shut up! You shall receive canteen tickets in the sum of five dollars per goal and ten dollars for the win. You must score. No goal, no money. No win, no money."

"I accept, Major."

"Then we have a pact, provided you respect secrecy. One leak and your barrack will suffer the wrath of the Lager Gestapo. I shall use you as an example."

"Yes, Major." Tony got up.

Mauer pointed at Tony's empty chair, and when Tony was seated, he said, "Your bookie operation is verboten."

Oh my God. "Like tying flies," Tony said, "Lucky Buck is a hobby. My NCO and I run it for fun. We don't make much, and sometimes we lose money when the odds aren't right. We take a commission – a handling fee on winnings – just seven percent."

"Ja, this I know. If you wish to stay in business, you shall reduce that commission. A portion shall now be paid as a royalty."

"What is a royalty?"

"A royalty gives you the right to operate. This is not a deal with the Nazis. This is a deal with me."

"I already have a partner."

"You and that Slavic oaf get four percent. I get three."

"Major, you're asking for more than me and Sergeant Zick. We're doing all the work."

"You fail to appreciate my influence. How would you like to advertise Lucky Buck to 5,000 prisoners? The *Drahtpost* can post odds and announce results. Use it as you wish. Otto Renziehausen is the publisher. Give him the information; he makes your advertising, even a weekly flyer for you to be delivered to every barrack, including the Italians'. With publicity like this, your hobby will be a business. Fail to accept this generous offer ... I report the illegal activity to Colonel Manning. If *I* sanction Lucky Buck in the *Drahtpost,* Manning will not stop it. I shall tell him it is a harmless game that keeps prisoners from trouble."

How would Bo handle this? Tony's fingers drummed the table. Mauer would be the conduit to spread the word – more bets, more profit. They had never counted on their seven percent commission generating big money; they were going to strike it rich on a couple of rigged boxing bouts. Mauer was offering security insurance – at least until May 13. If he was as greedy as Tony suspected, he wouldn't jeopardize a gravy train by bullying barrack 15.

"It's a deal, Major."

"One more thing, Lieutenant."

Oh God, now what?

"For the soccer game, you are to set the odds favoring Italy to win."

"I don't understand. Italy *is* favored to win."

"Ja, they have De Luca. A bet on Germany shall yield a fine return."

"If Germany wins."

"You said De Luca is the only player better than you. This is why I agree to bonus money."

"Yes Major, but I can't *guarantee* a win. Anything can happen out there."

"And if De Luca does not play?"

"That would help." Tony was getting used to surprises.

"Expect a wager from me on Germany."

Chapter 17

April 1944
Drvar, Bosnia

German air raids on Jajce forced Tito to relocate partisan headquarters to a hideout less detectable from the air. The camouflaged cave above Drvar had kept the Politburo safe until the spring runoff rendered it unlivable. When the thaw came, the inner circle had made their way down the valley to a village hiding place.

With the cave's pathways once again dry, Luka and Tito sat on the porch of the wood shack built into the rock opening. As they snapped kindling on their knees and tossed it onto a pile, Luka raised the subject that had pestered him, day and night. He could not rest until the murders of Rudi and the professor were avenged. Determining the identity of the executioners was easy – how and when they should pay for their crime presented the challenge. A bullet in the head was too humane.

The plot hatched soon after the Nazis draped a swastika banner over the bronze shoulders of the mounted horseman, Josip Jelacic, in Zagreb's main square. The newspaper's depiction of this revolting sight showed the freshly cloaked general extending his sword on behalf of the Nazis. The papers said the red, white and black cape had been affixed in the night. No one had dared remove it and Luka, so incensed by the sacrilege, had come 125 miles to tear it down himself.

As he laid out his plan for revenge, Tito had nodded, chuckled and slapped his knee. But by the time the intricacies of the scheme were fully disclosed, Tito had stopped breaking branches.

Sensing doubt, Luka said, "What's wrong, Marshal?"

"Sure you want to do this?"

"Don't you love the twist?"

"Yes, it has a certain ironic brilliance. But it won't be easy. If they catch you, you're dead. And it won't be quick."

Luka said he was ready for the unexpected.

"If it works," said Tito, "you'll have Hitler and Pavelic livid. Our warriors are tired; they need a lift. This caper's akin to my walking up to Ustasha troopers in disguise."

Luka laughed. Tito was coming around – he was sure of it. "You wanted a match and they gave you one."

"I yapped with them for twenty minutes. The tale spread like wildfire. One little trick is all it takes. Now the story is legendary. Your caper might trump it. It won't make the Croat papers – they'll suppress it – elsewhere, perhaps. Sure you have the manpower?"

"I need seven guys. I got six. I'm going to get Goran Skoda. He was your uncle's student. You met us at the same time, back in '41, the professor's house."

"Nervous fellow?"

"Yeah, that's Skoda."

"Are you sure he's the type for this sort of work?"

****

Goran pushed through the university's exit doors, but before he could mount his bicycle, a hand clutched his shoulder from behind with more force than necessary. Goran jerked his head around to face a well-groomed bearded man in an open trench coat, blue pinstriped slacks, perfectly knotted necktie and a stylish fedora.

"How you doing, comrade?" Luka asked. If not for the guttural rasp, Goran would not have recognized him.

"Keep your voice down," Goran said, eyes darting in every direction as though searching for Ustasha uniforms. "Why are you in Zagreb?"

"Why don't you shake the hand of an old friend? It's been months."

"Oh … yes … Sorry. I am pleased to see you." Goran let his hand go limp on the second pump, yet his old friend held him with an iron grip.

"Your fucking eye looks like shit, Skoda – all red and swollen shut. From the left you look like a Chinaman – been on the wrong end of a knuckle?" At last, he released his hold.

"I have a medical condition," Goran said, absently wiping his palm on his pant leg. "It flares up two or three times a year. Why are you here?"

"Unfinished business." Luka hawked loudly and spat at the bicycle spokes, where the glob hung suspended. "Comrade, we need to talk."

Goran glanced over his shoulder. "This is not a good time for me … I have an engagement."

"Shitty for me, too – matter of fact, fucking dangerous. I'm up to twenty-four on the Ustasha shit list. Done awfully good at pissing off Pavelic, no? Sooner we deal with our business, sooner I'm out of here."

"The Eagle has become a Gestapo favorite" Goran said. "The other taverns aren't much safer. Anyone can be a plainclothes policeman. Let me think."

"Make it fast. They nab me here, you got some explaining to do."

Goran made another quick scan of their surroundings. "I'll go inside alone. Meet me in room 23. That office used to be the professor's."

"You got a twenty-second head start."

Minutes later, Luka sat on the desk peering down at Goran in the chair. "I'm here to avenge the deaths of Rudi and the professor. Tito loves my plan. He's given us two days to get it done."

"What are you talking about? I can't be of any help finding the assassins."

Luka gave him a wily smirk. "You don't have to – I know who they are."

"How can you be sure?" Goran said as he gnawed the end of a pencil.

"We have our ways. You remember Andro Vajda?"

"The Ustasha at Schwartz's store, the one you tailed. He's one of them?"

"Shit, no! Vajda coughed up the names. You found us a hell of a great contact." Luka gazed down at the papers neatly stacked on Goran's desk, and began rearranging them as though interested in their content. "He's been real useful. Tito's overjoyed we infiltrated the Zagreb Ustashe. Vajda's in our pocket. When the war's over and we round up the bastards for slaughter, our spies get pardoned." He picked up a small pile of essays. "Going to pass these guys?"

Goran wiped the inflamed eye with a handkerchief. "What is it you want from me?"

"Two hours of your time." Luka handed him the sleeve of a matchbox. "One in the morning, come to the address written inside – a warehouse three blocks east of Jelacic Square. Wear dark stuff. You're out past curfew, so you don't want to get stopped. Look edgy, and a harmless question becomes an inquisition. Don't be late."

****

144

Goran finished his last brandy of the night. Three drinks bestowed bravery; any more made you stupid. He walked past the portrait of his mother to the front window where he leaned on the sill and stared out at the drizzle sprinkling the square's darkened boulevards. To broaden his view of the rail station's block-long facade, he flattened his cheek against the partly-misted pane. Except for the occasional passing umbrella or motor car, the quarter was desolate.

As he stepped back, the sights faded, and his eyes focused on the rivulets of mist worming their way down the glass. What in God's name did that lunatic have in store for him? Katarina had warned of this, saying it was only a matter of time before Luka demanded his pound of flesh. Well, Katarina had given more than her share: she had given four airmen.

Life without Tony had not been as bleak as he'd expected. Ostensibly elated by news of Tony's resurrection and incarceration in America, Goran fretted over the ramifications. Though Josip had asked him to inform Katarina of the good news, he had not done so.

Goran recalled the professor's counsel: when the partisans finally took control, Luka would assume a position of power; he would not make a kind enemy. Though bolstered by arms and supplies from Bari, the partisan army was currently at an impasse with German and Croat forces. Nonetheless, on a broader scale, according to international war analysts, Hitler's day of reckoning drew ever nearer. Goran had heeded Milic's advice and taken the party oath. Unlike Tony, he would be fully entrenched with the victors.

In charcoal trousers, black cap and a navy windbreaker, he hovered in the open doorway waiting for the square to clear. It was twenty-five minutes past midnight; he couldn't wait much longer. A lone lorry labored up the east boulevard from the south. The instant he saw the tail lights, he scampered down the steps into the drizzle, and darted to the east side's glistening pavement. Like a feral cat, he cut behind the tenement blocks where secluded laneways meandered to the upper town. At Jurisic Street he rested, but not for long – he dare not be late.

At two minutes to one, he rapped on the heavy-planked double door of the old warehouse. A steel rod slammed back from the inside, and a ray of light escaped as the door creaked open.

A rough-looking fellow blocked the light. "Who are you?" he said. His breath smelled of sardines.

Goran took a step back. "Goran Skoda ... a friend of Luka ... Luka Lipovac."

The door creaked wider. "Come in. I'm Victor."

Goran squeezed through the opening to a crude, dimly lit office.

"Follow me. He's in the knackers' yard."

They walked toward the mumble of voices in a dark corner. Four men peered up at the shadows in the rafters. What were they looking at? Ten steps later, Goran gasped. Blood dripped from deep gashes to the throats of three corpses hanging by their feet from the beams. He felt his throat contracting.

Luka sauntered over. Grinning, he squeezed Goran's shoulder. "Sorry you didn't get to cut their throats. That pleasure was mine. You should have seen their eyes – the size of hardboiled eggs. These are the cocksuckers who murdered our friends."

Through the trembling fingers covering his mouth, Goran said, "Wh- what do you want from me?"

Luka pointed up to the middle corpse, the only victim with hands bound behind his back. "That little lump of shit is the sergeant. We drain him. We cut him down. We get him ready for the show."

When the sergeant's blood slowed to a drop every three or four seconds, Luka told them to take him down easy. "I want his uniform clean." To an accomplice in a newsboy's hat, he said, "Chop up the other two. Start with the saw and cleaver. Grind up what you can and mix what's left in the tubs of pork waste. They're in the cooler. Then scrub the area and get your pretty ass outta here. Meet me at the same place, okay?"

Only upon seeing the figure respond with a wink did Goran realize the hacker was a woman. Tall and stocky with a dusky Mediterranean complexion, Ella wore a man's sweater and loose-fitting breeches. The newsboy's hat kept her hair from her broad shoulders. Though her jawline was mannish, she was striking. Ella typified the thousands of women living in the forests with the men of Tito's army. Probably like most Slavic peasant women before the war – docile and domesticated, cooking and cleaning for her family, submitting to the whims of a boorish husband – now she was preparing to chop up two corpses.

Victor untied the rope while two of his companions supported the body at the small of the back, taking care to keep the uniform above the puddles of blood on the floor.

"Good job, comrades," Luka said. "Lay him face up on the big cutting table."

Arms at his side, the Ustasha sergeant looked like a cadaver ready for storage on a morgue slab.

Luka hopped up onto the table, and the woman passed him a brace and bit. Standing upright and straddling the corpse's trunk, he brought the foot-long bit down to the center of the ribcage, six inches below the chin. The inch-and-a-half-diameter tip rested on fabric. But Luka wasn't ready to rotate the handle. The frightening glare on his face chilled Goran to his core. Katarina had been right: liberators became perpetrators.

"Get over here, Skoda. This prick ordered the killing. Now it's *his* turn to get screwed. Come watch. Don't be bashful."

As Goran inched forward, Luka bent over the body and applied weight to the polished round wood hand-piece at the brace's top. He cranked clockwise. The cutting and grinding of bone sounded like the carving of soft wood. Within a minute, the sharp bit had bored through the chest and out the spine.

"How's that, Sarge?" Now cranking counter-clockwise, Luka pulled out the crimson-coated steel. "Cover him in that blanket and toss him in the wheelbarrow. Skoda and I will carry one ladder, Victor and Vlado on the other." He then nodded to a big, powerfully built man with arms as thick as Goran's legs. "Wheelbarrow's yours, Nick."

"In the name of God, Luka!" Goran said. "Isn't this enough?"

"The square's three blocks away," Luka said. "We're going to move carefully. I lead; you follow. When we get to the plaza's outskirts we hide against the café on Vlaska's northeast corner. Nick gets a five-minute rest. Then we go. We have to move fast, 'cause we're wide open in the plaza, in plain view. Once we're at the monument we can finish the job in two and a half minutes."

At that point Luka glanced over at Victor. He paused, and then said, "Victor. You look restless."

Luka had surpassed Victor in the partisan pecking order, yet he had not lost respect for the man who taught him the killing arts. Victor motioned with his head for a private moment, and together, they stepped away.

"Your friend's not up to it," Victor said. "If he's not shaking like a leaf, he's ready to shit his pants. He makes it dangerous for the rest of us. The mission is at risk. Leave him here with Ella."

Luka hooked an arm around Victor's neck and pulled him close. "A long time ago you told me there's a first time for everyone. You remember where?"

"Sveti Duh Hospital. Another Ustasha sergeant. Back then, you were ready. Your friend isn't."

"Hey, have I ever botched an assignment?"

"That's not—"

"Go along with me on this. Will you do that, Victor?"

"You're the boss."

Dampened by the drizzle, they reached the edge of Jelacic Square at twenty past two. During the short break to restore Nick's strength, two armored patrols passed five minutes apart.

"We wait for another," Luka said. "Next patrol should be in four or five minutes. If that's the case, we have a pattern. To be safe, we have three minutes in the plaza. If they spot us, run like rabbits in every direction. But don't jump the gun – wait for my word. Got it, Skoda?"

"They have rifles and a machine gun on the truck's roof," Goran said. "How can you have a footrace against that? Running left, right or center doesn't much matter – they'll pick us off like pigeons."

"Don't be stupid," Luka said. "It's dark, misty and rainy. No moon. Even with the big torch, they'll have trouble taking aim. When you take off, don't run in a straight line. On foot they'll go in a pack after one guy – three or four of 'em. That's all those Leichter Panzerspähwagens can carry."

Goran couldn't stop shaking. This was a nightmare. No, much worse – one wakes from a nightmare. "What do we do if someone wanders onto the square?"

"Christ, man! Take a fucking look! Nobody's here. Uniforms show, you freeze or drop to the ground. All we'll get is a drunk or two who've busted curfew. Forget 'em – they'll be scared sober and scamper off when they see what we're up to. Do as you're told and never—"

"I hear engines," Vlado said. "See the headlights? Coming from Praska Street."

A motorbike and sidecar with a rotating searchlight preceded the Panzerspähwagen. The vehicles turned left from Praska onto Ilica and motored along the plaza's southern boundary. When the taillights disappeared in the mist, Luka scanned the periphery of the vacant square commanded by Josip Jelacic and his majestic stallion.

Suddenly, he grabbed the front of the ladder and yanked Goran onto the cobblestone street. Victor and Vlado trailed, followed by Nick who galloped like a rhino behind the wheelbarrow. Twenty seconds later, they were at the monument. Goran and Luka raised their ladder at the side of the stone pedestal.

"Put it against his neck," Luka told Goran.

"Whose neck?"

"The horse's, you idiot!"

Victor and Vlado positioned their ladder at the front of the monument, against the stallion's muzzle, and at a right angle to the side ladder. Victor turned over the body. With it lying on its belly in the wheelbarrow, he and Luka tucked their fingers under a rope bound to the chest just beneath his armpits. Goran and Vlado gripped the sergeant's belt at his waist, and together the four pallbearers lifted, climbing the rungs in unison with the corpse suspended between the two ladders.

The trouble came at the top where they tried to raise the dead man above the outstretched bronze sword of General Jelacic. The sword's tip was too far away, nullifying any leverage. The ladders would need to be reset.

Luka checked his watch. "Almost two minutes."

"No," Goran said. "There isn't time. They'll be back any second. We—"

"Then we hurry," Victor said.

They lowered the body and adjusted the ladders.

"Two and a half minutes," Luka said.

Cargo in hand, they climbed a second time. Even with leverage on their side, fitting a button-size hole in the chest of a 150-pound man over the point of an extended saber fifteen feet in the air would not be easy. Luka and Victor pulled; Nick and Goran pushed.

From below, Nick said, "He's like a ton of jelly. Goran and Vlado! Move to the outside of the rungs." Nick straddled both ladders. Once his feet shared the same rungs as the rear men, he placed his palms on the sergeant's buttocks and took some of the weight.

"That's better," Victor said. "Now we have the height, we can twist him into place. Lift his butt … steady … no, that won't work. Swing him the other way. Yeah, that's better. Now back him up a little. All but there …" They made a few more alterations, and Victor said the words Goran longed to hear. "Tip's in the hole. Slide him down the blade, all the way to the hilt."

The sword snagged.

"Careful!" Victor said. "The sword will break if it isn't at the right angle. Lower him an inch."

"It's supposed to be tight," Luka said. "Aha. That feels right. That's it, don't you think, Victor?"

"Perfect."

Luka giggled. "Take his weight and pull him down. The sword ought to slice through the hole. He should slip down easy."

They tugged the torso all the way to the general's fist. The victim's head and shoulders slouched forward to the right of the horse's mane. Arms and feet dangled limply. The masterful statue of General Jelacic now rode into battle looking like a medieval knight with his impaled foe.

"Four minutes," Luka said. "Give me the cap." Vlado whipped the Ustasha cap from his own head and passed it up. "You didn't look so good in that," Luka said as he returned it to the rightful owner. "Okay, down we go. Grab everything."

They had picked up but one ladder when a beam illuminated Jurisic Street.

"Drop it!" Luka said. "Duck behind the monument!"

The patrol van reached the square and slowed.

"Should we run?" Goran asked.

"Stay fucking still or *I'll* kill you right here. From Jurisic the body's hidden by the horse. They won't see it unless they turn their heads when they pass."

"They're sure to do that." Goran said.

"The eye weakens to familiarity. It's the same statue they've seen a thousand times … All right, here they come. If they stop and get out, spread out and run like hell."

The truck maintained its speed and passed the statue, the red taillights fading away in the fog.

Blushing with excitement, Luka gazed upward. "This awaits the rest of your lot. I'll crucify every fucking one of you. In ten minutes a comrade is going to snap the picture. It will make tomorrow's papers. The old man will remember all of you for this. Let's go – I got one more body to screw before sunrise."

They bolted for the shadowy exit of Vlaska Street, dumped the ladders and the wheelbarrow in a laneway and went their separate ways.

Chapter 18

April 1944
Rockford, Illinois

After the first *Drahtpost* ad for Lucky Buck, the traffic flow through barrack 15 was so hectic that the rumor mill had Chicago prostitutes holed up in the back room. The partners began with betting lines on table tennis and boxing only. They would post the odds on the soccer match closer to game day.

Neither thought it right that strangers traipsed through the bunkhouse without regard for peace and quiet. Tony would go to Mauer and request a workplace, perhaps the post office or a reserved table in one of the mess halls for a few hours a day. He had to see Mauer anyway – the royalty was due. Bo suggested paying in coupons, but Tony said they would be nuts to mess with a creature like Mauer.

The meeting could not have gone better.

"You know, Bo, forty-two cents in cash and a buck-eighty in coupons isn't much, but it was enough to make Mauer's eyes pop. I dumped the loot on the table and he pounced on it like he'd laid a royal flush at Monte Carlo. Mauer's given us the storehouse by number two mess to conduct business. He wants to know when we're going to publish the soccer line. I said you were the odds-maker. Of course, he was quick to tell me that I'm supposed to tell you what to do."

"To properly set the odds," Bo said, "I'm going to need a hundred percent honesty from you. No bravado, okay?"

"What are you getting at?"

"How good's the leg and how good are you?"

From a sitting position on his bed, Tony raised his left knee and straightened it six times. "Not what it used to be, but good enough."

"You didn't answer the second part of my question."

"I'm no match for De Luca, and no worse than their three club players."

"What're the odds of beating them?"

"Not good, maybe forty-sixty."

"Would you bet four bucks on Germany to make six?"

Tony shook his head.

"How about thirty-seventy?"

"Bo, there's something you ought to know."

Bo hurried to the door and whipped it open. A quick peek left and right, and he slammed it shut. "What?"

"De Luca won't be playing. I got it from the lapdog."

"Not playing? How would Mauer—?"

"Don't ask," Tony said, shifting his weight on the bed.

"Our silent partner's earning his cut. Can you win?"

"You never know. With a hot goalie …"

"Win and you won't have to sabotage the match."

"I told you—"

Bo laughed. "I'm yanking your bad leg. Here's how we do it. We publish a blurb about you starring for Zagreb; we quote you saying you can run rings around De Luca. That'll piss off the Wops. We go out at even. They'll love those odds and flood us with cash. With so many Germans, we'll need those bets to manage risk."

"Don't forget Mauer," Tony said. "He wants to bet on Germany when the odds favor Italy."

"No problem. Nearer game day, we adjust the odds to favor the Wops. Make sure he holds his bet till the end. By that time we'll have more dough on the Wops so when you guys win, the payout's small and the profit's big."

"Promise me you'll keep enough cash to cover us if we lose."

"There'll be plenty. This is the big payday. Lose and we take a break until the championship boxing match in June. We'll make wads on that. It's a sure thing because I'm favored."

Tony wondered if the big guy was getting caught up in the gambler's rush. "I don't like using the soccer game for the jackpot. It isn't like fixing a fight – anything can happen with twenty-two guys on the field."

****

Bo never cared if his mouth was full – even with cheeks bloated like a hamster's he would yammer on about matters as trivial as ice cream viscosity or as cryptic as homosexuality in a POW camp. Today the self-anointed windbag was ranting about boxing champ Joe Louis's habit of dropping the left glove after a jab. Bo was in mid-sentence when he fell silent, wearing the look of a man just fleeced. Tony thought a slice of dry potato might have lodged in his windpipe.

All of a sudden, Bo began patting his pockets. As it turned out, he wasn't checking for money or a pocket watch. Heaving a sigh of relief, he pulled the Lucky Buck leaflet from his back pocket. Then he unfolded the flyer, and madly scratched out the scribbled sums and penciled in new ones. When finished, he peered at Tony, shook his head, and scuttled from the mess hall.

The issue bothering Bo would have to wait. Tony wasn't going to miss the Monday night movie.

A half hour before lights-out, he found Bo on his cot, the blanket pulled over his head. Strange – Bo hated retiring early. Most nights he wouldn't even lie down until the room went black.

"Good movie tonight," Tony said. "Andy Hardy was trying to be a big man by hiring a looker as his secretary. He … What's wrong, Bo?"

Bo let out a deep breath but didn't emerge from the improvised pup tent.

"If it's Lucky Buck, I have a right to know," Tony said.

Bo turned from his right side to his left. "I've let you down. Pains me to tell you … stupid … unnecessary." Bo pulled off the blanket and swung his feet down to the floor. "It's out of control. This week we've taken in so much dough, I'm out of places to hide it. I've got bills in clothes linings. Friday, I nailed four more two-by-fours to the corner joists." He looked up at his slapdash carpentry. "Coins and coupons stuffed behind 'em."

With twice-a-day soccer practice, Tony had entrusted the week's transactions to Bo.

"There's too much on the Wops, Tony. Everyone says De Luca's gonna wipe the field with you and Schroeder. They can't resist fifty-fifty odds."

"Change the odds."

"Yeah, I know I made that sound easy. Trouble is we've got only four days to promote bets on the Krauts." Bo pulled out the flyer from under the pillow. "This is where we stand: win and we're rich; lose and we're dead. We need another hundred on Germany."

"Give it here." The last three lines were all that mattered.

	Italian Win	German Win
Profit	*($120.40)*	*$143.84*
Opening Treasury	*$100.20*	*$100.20*
Closing Treasury	*($ 20.20)*	*$244.04*

"Bo, you're a great bookkeeper but a lousy gambler. How could you let this happen?"

"I got blindsided by the fever – making a hundred smackers on one hit. I put off doing the math. When I did, I realized the shit we're in."

Not wanting to let him off easy, Tony said, "You had a hunch. You've looked sick since Thursday. You should have said something when there was still time to do something."

"I can post new odds at breakfast, but most of the money's in and a big change will piss off a lot of guys. Think Mauer can get more Wops to sit out?"

Tony rubbed his eyes. "I don't know. If he bribed De Luca, he can bribe others. If he's threatened De Luca, I can't sic him on another. No one deserves that."

"Think he got to De Luca through the Yanks?"

"How would I know? His line on De Luca not playing could be bullshit. Ever think that?"

"No sleep for me tonight," Bo said. "Maybe it's best we close the bets and cut Mauer an irresistible one-off deal – Italy favored five to two. Ten bucks on Germany halves our deficit and pays fifteen bucks profit on a ten-buck bet."

"I hate seeing the bastard advantaged."

"If you guys lose, makes no difference. 'Course, if the game goes the other way, then we make a fortune."

Tony sighed. "That's the kind of thinking that got us into this trouble in the first place."

****

"Are we prepared?" Arnim asked Mauer.

In less than a week, the chronic stitch in Mauer's side would be gone. "Ja, Herr Colonel. The Slav takes center forward in a defensive role. Covering De Luca frees Schroeder on the wing."

"A hound in the lineup does not please me. I must trust you on his worth. He is not a supporter of the Reich, and yet, you convinced him to play."

"Babic believes in money, Herr Colonel. He runs the bookie shop you have seen in the *Drahtpost*. When one understands a man's motives, the means of persuasion are incidental."

"These affairs I leave to you. The bookie shop is the subject of my appointment with Colonel Manning. You were to pacify him. Lieutenant Dixon suggests otherwise. I suspect Manning will demand termination."

Mauer's chin puckered. "May I accompany you to safeguard our interests?" he said through clenched teeth.

"There is a problem?"

"There is not a problem, Herr Colonel."

****

The inaugural Lucky Buck advertisement had required explanation. Arnim, who wasn't interested in issues extraneous to the Nazi cause, appointed Mauer as his designee. Mauer compared Lucky Buck to Wednesday night bingo: an innocuous diversion for POWs. If the army permitted a prisoner to enjoy a night of bingo for two coupon cents, what harm could come from wagering two cents on boxing or table tennis? Manning had bought it.

But subsequent publicity drove the betting into the spotlight. Keen to raise the stakes, Mauer promoted Lucky Buck to the prison guard network via a couple of free spirits who had promised to keep it under wraps. But word spread. Family members and civilian friends wanted in on the action, and soon Lucky Buck's tentacles had wormed their way into the camp commander's office. Having barely escaped an investigation after Bobby Rose's critique, Manning could ill afford the scandal of a bookie operation in his camp.

Mauer and Arnim found Manning at his desk, head down and fists clutching a pencil.

"This has gone too far!" Manning said. "You two will have me strung up by my clusters." He looked more like a frail old man croaking orders in a convalescent home than a colonel of the United States Army.

"What bothers you, Colonel?" Arnim asked in heavily accented English. His command of the language was not as good as Mauer's.

"Lucky Buck! My son-in-law asked me to place a bet for him. So did the deputy mayor, for crying out loud! Everyone knows of the bookie ring. I can't have it. A call from Bobby Rose, and … Close it today! MPs will accompany you and confiscate the money."

"Colonel," Mauer said in a compassionate voice. "There is reason—"

"Helmut, I don't want your explanations! Close it! And for the love of Pete, sit down!"

Arnim sank into the chair, tugging his ill-fitting tunic that strained every button. Mauer remained standing.

"Please, Colonel, hear me out," Mauer said.

"Make it quick."

"Lagersprecher and I agree with you. Lucky Buck stops. Those responsible will be punished. But it is foolish to stop it before the game is over."

"Today, Helmut. I should have stopped it when I first learned of it."

"The reporter would agree. He is clever. Lucky Buck has been in *Drahtpost* every week for a month. He has you … how you say … by the clusters? You approved Lucky Buck."

"On your errant advice!" The pencil snapped, and Manning flung the pieces at the coat-rack.

"You need a plan," Mauer said.

"You have one?" Arnim asked Mauer.

"An idea, Herr Colonel. Colonel Manning needs proof of an investigation. Make it from first *Drahtpost* advertisement of Lucky Buck."

"Are you suggesting a phony paper trail?" Manning asked.

As though he hadn't heard the question, Mauer turned to Arnim. "Colonel Manning tells staff he is getting evidence to make arrest. He says Lucky Buck harmless at first, not now. When investigation is over, he stops crooked business, punishes bookies. We support story and Colonel Manning."

"It won't fly," Manning said. "I can have the names of the bookies in two minutes."

"Stop Lucky Buck now, you anger thousands."

"*Thousands?* My God! How big has this become?"

"Winners will be mad if you stop Lucky Buck from paying. Let bookies pay winners; then make arrest. Punish. No one will blame you for coupon bets on table tennis. But when you hear of cash bets, you make investigation and you stop it."

"Das ist überzeugend!" Arnim said, smiling.

"Colonel von Arnim says the argument is convincing," Mauer said to Manning. "I get names for you. Give them two days to pay winners … then make arrest. Stop now … you have riot."

Manning flicked open his stainless steel Zippo lighter. "I don't like it."

Mauer said he and Arnim would help plan the raid. "Plan now, make raid later. We make plan for newspapers. Everything shall be in place for you."

Manning puffed away in the awkward silence.

****

Tony closed the betting office but didn't leave. When the pale, grim-faced bettor arrived, he handed Tony an envelope marked 'Germany'.

"Two to five," Mauer said.

"Those odds are only for you, Major."

Behind the makeshift counter of stacked footlockers, Tony tallied seventeen one dollar bills and a five – not one coupon. He opened the record book, inked the entry, and duplicated the particulars on a signed customer stub.

"Show this when you collect. Good day, Major."

Mauer stowed the stub. Then he slid a second envelope across the metal.

Tony glared at the word 'Italy' that had been penciled on the front.

"What are you waiting for, Lieutenant? It isn't laced with cyanide."

Tony broke the seal: three crisp banknotes bearing Andrew Jackson's likeness. "Sixty dollars is a substantial wager, Major. Who is it from?"

"The investor wishes to remain anonymous. The odds for this bet remain at even, I presume?"

"Yes … but, Major, I need a name for the receipt."

"No, you don't."

Tony's armpits were as sticky as cotton candy. "Major, we operate by process and discipline. I can't take a bet without a name. By rights, I should not even be taking *this* bet. Officially bets are closed."

"Then make it official. Sign *your* name."

"I cannot—"

"Then make the receipt out to me!"

Tony bent over the records and completed the transaction. "There you are." He handed over the receipt.

"You forgot to wish me luck," Mauer said, snatching the receipt and heading for the door.

Mauer's first bet had made Lucky Buck solvent. Then came the grenade. Head spinning, Tony left the office fretting over an Italian win and speculating on the mystery bettor's identity. Why hadn't Mauer given the name or names? Sixty dollars suggested a pooling of bets. But what if … No, it couldn't be. For one thing, Mauer wouldn't have that much money. Second, a staunch Nazi would never desert the Reich. If De Luca played, the profit would be sixty dollars for sure. That made Mauer plausible as the anonymous bettor. But with De Luca in the lineup, twenty-two dollars on the German team made no sense.

The quandary would have to wait. In fifteen minutes, he was to be on the field for a final practice. The inconsistency would be tackled with Bo when they stuffed eighty-two Yankee dollars into newly fashioned hideaways.

****

In the American officers' mess hall, four long tables draped in white and set for thirty awaited players, coaches and trainers on the eve of the game. Nazi and Italian flag centerpieces designated the teams' seating. Manning, Arnim, Mauer two Italian officers were to dine at the head table, under the watchful eye of twenty military police standing at parade rest.

Tony paid little attention to the pretentious blather of head table diners. As he chewed the succulent roast beef, he watched Mauer's black eyes roving the room. Mauer calmly sliced his meat, chewing longer than everyone else and wearing a contemplative expression, as if seeking the origin of some obscure seasoning. Like the Americans, he placed his knife on the plate before lifting his fork. He ate in the same calculating way that he ruled. The sixty bucks on Italy and twenty-two on Germany remained a mystery. Had Mauer duped him? Would De Luca play?

An MP hurried into the room with a bottle of champagne. He handed it to Mauer who popped the cork, dousing the chatter.

"Now that I have your attention," he said, in German. "I shall apologize for the tardiness of this delivery. Securing champagne on short notice can be taxing, but the Reich has ways."

The Germans chuckled. Manning appeared shocked at the translation. The Italian interpreter didn't even bother translating.

While an MP poured for the head table, Mauer called the team captains forward. He had arranged for two extra flutes at his place setting. One he handed to Karl Schroeder, the other to Roberto de Luca.

Manning, who appeared calm, proposed the toast. Schroeder, De Luca and those at the head table sipped their bubbly while the rest of the players, all on their feet, tipped glasses of ginger ale.

As they drank, Tony weighed the difference that De Luca would make to the game's outcome. The Germans had designated Tony as De Luca's shadow, responsible for keeping the star forward off the score sheet. Through the chain-linked fence, he and Karl Schroeder had watched the Italians practice, studying formations and plays and developing profiles of every player's strengths and weaknesses. The team was fast, nimble, experienced and well-coached. A zone defense had the best chance of beating them.

****

Saturday turned out to be one of the warmest May days ever recorded in Rockford. The sunshine, the event and the rivalry stoked everyone. But the bleachers, built to hold nine thousand, couldn't handle the overflow created by the enthusiasm for the match. Game-day stragglers would be forced to stand cheek by jowl in the end zones. For security, a south bleacher pen of chain-link mesh and barbed wire would separate POWs from the rest. Within that pen, another cage was there to protect the Italians.

By ten o'clock, the prisoners, many of them in T-shirts, were seated at their designated sections – all but one of them. In the dim barrack light, Mauer buttoned a blue shirt stenciled with 'POW'. The hat pulled low on his forehead was not the peaked visor cap of the SS. He had told Arnim he would be fifteen to twenty minutes late for the game – said he had felt sick in the night, probably from "something off" at dinner. One or two more trips to the latrines, and he would meet the colonel in the stands.

Up in the watchtowers, every sentry's gaze was directed to the soccer field. The distraction allowed Mauer to dash out the door and scoot between the rows of barracks to the storehouse where he had handed Tony eighty-two dollars. He opened eighteen footlockers, one after another – all empty. Muttering profanities, he went through the stacks of bed linens on the shelves, checking every blanket, sheet and pillowcase. The ceiling and walls were clean – no insulation or inner boards where one might bore holes to stash loot. What about the floorboards? With a pocket-knife he tested every groove of 200 square feet of flooring.

Having wasted precious minutes, he left the shack in a shambles and dashed down the narrow lane between barracks, feeling the heat that radiated from tarpaper baked by the sun. At the corner of barrack 15, he peered up at the only visible watchtower. The sentry's back was to him. Inside, he scanned perfectly made beds, shirts hung on rafters and pinups on the wall.

Tony's infantry uniform and overcoat hung on a beam in the officer's quarters. Mauer patted down the garments, checking all the hems. At the cuffs and edges of the coats, he saw the loose threads. He worked his fingers into the openings but found nothing.

A tunic and another overcoat were draped on a hanger on the other side of the room. He would check these, too, once he finished rummaging Tony's footlocker. He flipped through the pages of books, newspapers and magazines, and checked work clothes, underwear, socks and shoes. Senior Nazis reportedly used shoe heels to conceal messages or cyanide capsules – why not money? He twisted the heels and pried with his knife – immovable.

He separated letters, dumped a deck of playing cards on the bed, and looked inside packages of Lucky Strikes. At the bottom of the trunk, beneath a chessboard, he found the Lucky Buck betting book. The pages contained more than a hundred soccer entries. He didn't have time to total the wagers; his guess, five hundred dollars.

Under one mattress Mauer found several thick bundles wrapped in craft paper. He tore back the wrapping of one package, then the others. Canteen tickets – more than a thousand of them. Into his empty knapsack they went. Where was the cash?

The storehouse he had left in shambles, but this room had to appear untouched. He tidied the beds, then the footlocker, before scampering to Bo's trunk to check the clothes, cigarettes, magazines, a punching speed bag and a pair of boxing gloves. Slipping his hand into a glove, he felt paper. The glove contained dollar bills, twenty of them. Twenty-four more had been hidden in the other glove.

Still, the find was paltry – the Slavs had taken nearly three hundred dollars. He checked the hour: ten minutes past eleven. The game was under way. Through open windows, he could hear the dull hum of the crowd and the intermittent *oohs* and *ahs*. No matter – money trumped time. If he needed another forty-five minutes to steal every cent from Tony and Bo, so be it.

He circled, scanning the floor, the walls, the ceiling. The bedroom was identical to his: 240 square feet with two cots, two footlockers and two night tables. But something was peculiar, something out of place. What could it be? He dropped to his knees and started in one corner with the blade. Ten minutes into the task, he found a loose slat under Bo's bed. A thunderous roar came from the field – someone had scored a goal and Mauer edged up a two-foot board.

Four cloth bags of coins had been lodged between the joists. He removed one bag and hefted it in the palm of his hand – perhaps four pounds. Stowing the bags with the coupons in his knapsack, he returned to all fours, trembling with excitement. But that was it – the only loose plank in the entire floor. Where was the rest of the money? In the overhead lights ... the beams ... behind the washbasin?

His eyes fell on the pinups that adorned one wall: Rita Hayworth, Betty Grable, Jane Russell and Carole Landis. Landis's sultry splendor reminded him of the Jew in Minsk. He had held her delicate neck too tightly while forcing himself on her. By the time he was done, her lush lips had turned blue. By dying, she had stolen his pleasure. The blunder had taught him to pay more attention during the breath sport. The timing of climax must be close, but never after the last beat of the heart.

The thought wrenched him back to his purpose. Plucking the bottom pins from the pinups, he looked behind the movie stars' pretty bottoms. Nothing seemed amiss with the wallboard.

With nowhere else to look, he hoisted the heavy bag of loot and went back to the main bunkhouse. But before departing, Mauer spread two packets of coupons between the mattress and the springs of a cot on the west wall. After re-tucking the covers, he was out the door and hustling back to his barrack. With the contents of the heist safely stored, he shed the disguise and dressed in his SS uniform.

Mauer quickstepped to the bleacher occupied by Arnim. He plunked himself down on the spare seat and checked the big clock. They must be into the second half.

"Helmut, you *are* here. You're soaking from sweat. Is it the heat, or are you sick?"

"Stomach poisoning, Herr Colonel. Just like De Luca." A thunderous roar all but drowned out his words. The German goalkeeper had failed to clear, and the charging Italian winger buried the ball in the top corner of the net. With a half-hour left to play, the game was tied.

Chapter 19

During the night, medics had hurried to the barrack of a man suffering from convulsions and reeking of excrement. Having diagnosed an acute case of food poisoning, Dr Armstrong had attached a hydration IV and confined Roberto de Luca to the infirmary for twenty-four hours.

This turn of events had Karl Schroeder so elated that he questioned the wisdom of the zone defense. But Tony argued for sticking with the zone – even without De Luca, the Italians were long in firepower. Schroeder acquiesced. They would play it safe and wait for the break.

The opening came early. Schroeder broke clear and scored on Tony's pinpoint pass. Then the Italians tied it and with minutes remaining, Tony headed a high ball, faked out two defenders, and fired a bullet past the sprawling goalkeeper. With the one-goal advantage, Germany tightened the defense, and at the final whistle Tony pumped his fists and leaped in the air. He was back in Zagreb – the golden boy of the city league who had dominated the field, outmaneuvered challengers, netted goals and beamed with pride. This match he had not dominated, but his goal and assist had made the difference. The fans knew it, and so did Rockford's sports press.

Relishing the success of a contest that exhilarated so many and that went off without a hitch, Manning consented to post-game interviews, ostensibly to bolster a public image tainted by *The Rockford Star*.

Blackened with muck from yesterday's downpour, the elated trio of Tony, Schroeder and goalkeeper Heinrich Felgen sat on a bleacher bench four steps above the gathering of news columnists and photographers.

"I want to begin," Manning said to the reporters, "by thanking you for the news coverage leading up to the game. Today you witnessed a stellar example of Geneva Convention humanity. Considering national rivalries, don't you think the prisoners were well behaved and orderly?" He paused, as if expecting a response, but the reporters appeared as though they couldn't care less.

"These three are available for questions. Number nine, to your left, is Lieutenant Babic. He speaks English – learned it right here at Graham. In the middle is team captain Corporal Schroeder. On his right is Private Felgen, the acrobat who made that remarkable dive to avert the tying goal."

Cameras flashed, and the writers all talked at once.

Manning raised an open palm. "Hold it, fellows! Lieutenant Babic's English isn't *that* good. One at a time. Speak slowly." He nodded to a cigar-chomping man in a tired sport jacket.

"Joe Wilton, the *Telegraph.*" Joe Wilton put his foot on the first step of the bleacher. "As the underdog, this win must come as a surprise. How surprising was it?"

"What is 'underdog'?" Tony asked.

Wilton removed his cigar. "Let's see … how can I put it? Simplest way's to say most folks 'round here were counting on the Italians winning. They were the favorites – that made you guys the underdogs."

Of course, Tony knew all about favorites and underdogs. He posed the question to buy some time to construct a reply. "Italians have good players. We happy to win."

"Happy their top player took sick?" Wilton had a crafty grin on his face.

Tony didn't change his expression, nor did he respond.

"That's a question, Private Felgen," Wilton said.

"My name Babic. Ugly one is Felgen." Tony gave the goalie a tap on the back of the head, and the pressmen snickered.

"I'll re-word the question," Wilton said. "Do you think you'd have won with De Luca out there?"

"Out where? Where is De Luca?"

The assembly laughed when Tony looked left and right, mimicking a search.

"With De Luca playing," Wilton said.

Tony translated for his mates and in German, Schroeder said, "Tell him we're sorry De Luca's sick."

Tony repeated Schroeder's response in English.

"You still haven't answered the question."

Another huddle was pointless. "Yes, we still win," Tony said. "We make plan for De Luca."

After several questions and answers on the strategy, a curly-haired reporter in a short-sleeved white shirt stepped forward.

165

"Make it brief, Mr Rose, and stick to sports," Manning said.

Bobby Rose grinned at Manning and then turned to the players. "Does this victory represent a proud moment for Nazi Germany?"

Tony translated, and Schroeder's smile dissolved. Felgen dropped his head so low that he looked like he had lost something under the bleachers. Tony stared passively at Bobby Rose. For a cub reporter, the guy was an incisive exploratory journalist.

"I'll put it this way," Bobby Rose said. "Is this more than a sports victory for Germany?"

Tony looked puzzled. "I not understand."

"Let me reword the question. I am—"

"Please, Mr Rose," Manning said, stepping in front of the players. "This is not—"

"Colonel, I am asking if this conquest is a political statement." He reset his gaze on the players. "Is it?"

Again, the prisoners huddled. Schroeder said, "If we're not careful, this could land us in a pile of dog shit."

"I know the dog," Tony said. "Why don't I just say the win is a proud moment for the team? That can't hurt."

The goalkeeper warned that the questioner was Bobby Rose, not some sports reporter.

The reporters had seemed content to wait it out until Bobby Rose broke the silence. "This *was* more than a game, wasn't it? Was it retribution for the Italian surrender?"

Manning, looking gray, came between the players and the gallery, apparently ready to terminate the interview. Before he opened his mouth, a *Chicago Tribune* reporter said he was sent to cover sports, not politics. He wanted more on the winning goal, and he asked if the play was a pre-planned maneuver.

Delighted by the respite, Tony said, "I strip ball from midfielder, but no one up with me. I dribble past defense, say prayer, close eyes and kick. Hope for the best, as you say." He flashed a row of pearly white teeth.

The reporters laughed – even a smirk from Manning. Then, someone asked about the players' soccer careers before the war.

Tony said that Schroeder had captained the Hamburg team in the North German league, and goalkeeping happened to be a Felgen sideline. He had been an accomplished gymnast.

"Me? In Croatia I play on Zagreb Concordia practice squad."

Joe Wilton asked why a German would be playing soccer in Croatia.

"That question, easy … I am Croat. Croats live in Croatia."

"Sounds to me like the Germans couldn't win on their own," quipped Bobby Rose.

To that, Joe Wilton said, "You mean Hitler slipped in a ringer?"

A pasty-white Manning threw up his hands. "Again, you're mixing sport with politics. MPs, escort the prisoners to their compound."

****

At the next day's breakfast, the Nazis reveled in the most thrilling moments of the match, including Mauer, whose dour countenance masked his inner euphoria. He had been the rainmaker, the one who masterminded the win that would halt Arnim's nagging. Moreover, the outcome had proved financially lucrative.

"Herr Major, which play impressed you most?" asked a Lieutenant.

Mauer looked up from his cereal. "Which one impressed *you*?"

"Felgen's last save. His dive buried them."

"Extraordinary reflexes," Mauer said. "For me, the best play was our first goal." *The one I didn't see.* "Schroeder could smell it. He and Felgen were our best players." Mauer was pleased by his cohorts' political savvy. No one had mentioned the Slav.

Then, as if it had fallen from the ceiling, *The Rockford Star* landed on Mauer's bowl. The paper had been folded to display the heading, 'CROAT WINS IT FOR THE GERMANS' and a photo of Tony booting the ball past the sprawling goalkeeper. Mauer sprang to his feet and swung around with his fist cocked.

"Have you seen this?" Arnim growled, ignoring those who had sprung to attention and saluted. He slid past Mauer and slammed his fist on the story, breaking the bowl and a plate into pieces. The room hushed. "This … I did not want! You let that hound to steal our glory."

Mauer seethed at the boorish intrusion and the unjust accusation. He had laced De Luca's champagne. He had recruited the Slav to seal the win. He had pushed the game into May to let Babic's leg heal. He had engineered *all of it* for this contemptuous prick.

"You tainted the victory," Arnim said, "by disregarding the most important reason for the win: Aryan superiority. Do you remember that, or has your mind gone to mush? Months of training, ruined. Get out of my sight!"

"Herr Colonel, please—"

"Leave now, or be demoted to captain!" Arnim swept the remnants of Mauer's breakfast to the floor.

The eye of every Nazi followed Mauer's march to the exit.

The victory was bittersweet: Germany had won, but a non-German had determined the outcome. And the press made sure everyone knew it. Yes, Mauer had gone against Arnim's wish for a team of Aryan bluebloods. But bastardizing the dream had been the lesser evil. Everything had gone according to plan until Babic shot off his big mouth. Mauer's first instinct was to beat Tony to a pulp. But by the time he reached his barrack, reason advised otherwise. His plan was already in place. With Lucky Buck soon to be ashes, Babic was of no further use. Mauer would collect his winnings and return barrack 15 to the Lager Gestapo's night list.

To Mauer, the sin of publicly demeaning a senior officer of the Waffen-SS was reprehensible. That left him with two choices: he could let time heal his shattered pride; or be the first to find Arnim dangling from a rafter.

Money was the priority. Mauer had pilfered $45.00 in notes, $28.34 in coin, and 32 coupon dollars, give or take a few cents. Add to the heist his winnings of $33.00 and $7.00 in royalties, and he had amassed $145.00. But eating him was the knowledge that his windfall could have been four times that amount.

****

As a reward for good behavior in the bleachers, Manning relaxed restrictions on beer consumption. Financed by an abundance of coupons, Tony and Bo bought countless rounds for their bunkhouse buddies. Drink enough 3.2 beer, and it was possible to dull most pain but not the throb of a waking headache.

Tony, who had slept the night on his back, rolled over to face his roommate who was lacing his boot. "Bo, we must have spent twenty-five bucks last night," he said, in a voice that was hoarse.

"Not like we're short of coupons," Bo said. "Besides, they won't do us any good back home ... You kicked their butts yesterday."

"That match brought back memories. I want this war over with. I want to try out for Concordia – bet I could make it."

"Not so fast. We've got more money to make here."

"A great distraction, I'll admit. But you know, Bo, that game made me homesick. When I get back, there's a girl to look up ... she lives in Sarajevo."

"You never mentioned that one. Is she anything like the tigress that took your virginity?"

"Nothing like Roza ... I met her three years ago ... at first, she couldn't stand me." A glazed look came over him as though a vision had entranced him. "I kissed her once – just once – and lately I can't get her out of my head. My brain's been cluttered with all that war shit. Maybe that's why I didn't think of her ... It's not that I've put those horrors behind me. Anyway, I'm going to look her up."

"She could be married with kids."

"Could be ... trouble is, she's my best friend's girl. Someday I'll tell you about her father – a remarkable man – my CO in Serbia." Tony sat up, rubbing moist eyes. "Shall we skip breakfast and go through the accounts? We need to settle up with the winners."

Bo stacked the footlockers beneath the four-by-four ceiling rafter that ran the length of the room. Standing on them, with the beam at eye level, he used a screwdriver to lift the wood slats covering the trough he had carved into the top of the beam.

Tony craned his neck to the rafter. "We need three hundred and six dollars and forty cents to pay thirty-two cash clients."

"I'm guessing those guys represent a couple hundred," Bo said. "Glad we made 'em pool their dough. The bookkeeping would have driven me nuts."

"You're already nuts. Bring down two seventy-five. We can use the bills in your gloves and the coins in the floor to make up the rest."

Bo tossed the money on Tony's cot. Then, after putting the two footlockers back, he slithered on his stomach to the loose floorboard beneath his bed.

"Jesus! A thief's been here!"

Bo scampered from under the bed and dug for the boxing gloves in his trunk. When his hands came out empty, he hurled them against the wall. Meanwhile, Tony checked the mattresses. It could have been worse. If the burglar had discovered the main safe in the rafters, they were sunk.

"Did we have any coin up there?" Tony asked. "We don't want to pay in paper."

"Maybe ten bucks in quarters and dimes – just coupons behind the new two-by-fours and thousands more buried outside."

"Funny the thief didn't notice those two-by-fours – they serve no structural purpose."

"I hate to say it," Bo said, his thumb motioning to the door. "They know when we come and go. Never underestimate the thirst for cash."

"Hard to believe the thief is one of ours. Someone's seventy-five bucks richer and loaded down with enough coupons to last three years. Keep an eye out for a big spender."

They wrapped thirty-two packets of cash, totaling $306.40, and sixty-eight packets of coupons valued at $190.52. Tony was about to grab the record book when the door swung open, banging against the inner wall and vibrating on its hinges.

Mauer was alone. "Out of here, Zick."

Bo jumped to attention, saluted, and then looked to Tony. Tony nodded, and Bo left, closing the door behind him.

"Is there a problem, Major? I thought you'd be—"

"You made a grave error. You told the press you were Croat. This was a German team. Arnim did not want you on the team. I convinced him otherwise."

"The right decision, Major – I helped—"

"Give me my money."

Tony picked up the parcel marked 'Mauer – $37.69'. "You're owed your original bet of twenty-two dollars plus thirty-three dollars in winnings, less handling fee and my soccer bonus. May I have your receipt?"

Mauer's eyes roamed the room as he dug into his pocket for the receipt. "You pay in cash. I pay in coupons."

"You are quite right." Tony pulled a stack of greenbacks from his pocket and counted out fifteen notes. "Here you are. Please sign the book to certify payment." His fingernail marked the spot. Mauer didn't move, seeming awestruck by the sheaf of bills in Tony's hand. "Major?"

"Ja, ja." He scribbled his initials and reached into his tunic pocket. "Here is your bonus."

"Major, if I may? The sixty dollars on Italy – can you tell me who made the bet?"

"This alarmed you," Mauer said. "The money was from the American officers' club. I encouraged them."

"May I ask why?"

"Use your head, Lieutenant. This I did to raise the stakes and hedge my bet. Italy wins? I get three percent of the payout."

"There was four hundred and twenty dollars on Italy." Tony calculated in his head. "You would have made over twelve dollars."

"What is my royalty from the German win?"

"We took in two hundred and forty-eight dollars. Three per cent times two hundred is six dollars. Three times forty-eight is another dollar forty-four. Your royalty will be roughly seven dollars and fifty cents."

"I want it now."

Rile Mauer by insisting they stick with the schedule? Not a chance. Tony peeled off eight singles from the bundle. "I won't bother with the coins. The game was very profitable. Thank you for your help."

Mauer's eyelids narrowed to slits. "You offer a gratuity to a Wehrmacht superior?"

Tony raised his palms. "No insult intended." But, he realized that he had caught Mauer between pride and his gluttony.

Gluttony won. Mauer snatched the money and stormed off.

****

The raid came two days later. MPs marshaled barrack 15's prisoners to the chain-link fence. When the ransacking of lockers, cots and clothing was complete, the inmates were returned – all but three. Tony, Bo, and Hermann were shackled and marched to the guardhouse between the compounds and the American garrison.

The Americans had the evidence: Lucky Buck's record book, eight dollar bills confiscated from the pockets of the barrack leader and his NCO, and hundreds of coupons discovered under the enlisted man's mattress.

When the prisoners were alone, Bo said, "Hermann, those coupons under your mattress belong to us."

"You can't think I stole them."

Bo paced four steps forward and three steps back. "What do you expect us to think? If *you* aren't the thief, who is? And why would the thief want you to have eight coupon bucks and none for nobody else?"

Herman backed away from the bars and sat with his head slumped in his hands. "The Nazis are out to frame their whipping boy."

"Who's going to part with eight coupon dollars to make it look like you were a partner in Lucky Buck?" Tony asked. "The betting shop's a petty crime. I'm surprised we were even arrested. Our operation's been in the *Drahtpost* for weeks, and no one deemed it unlawful till now. At most, we'll lose two weeks' of beer privileges and movies."

"That's not what bothers me, Lieutenant. It's the dishonor. This is Mauer's work."

Tony knew of Mauer's contempt for Hermann, but giving up coupons just to frame the guy didn't gel. Bo had thought the robbery an inside job. But if the thief was on the inside, why implicate one of Bo's friends? The damned thing was convoluted. As much as Tony tried to deny it, the evidence pointed to the little man with the lion's heart.

****

As senior officer and barrack leader, Tony's sentence was five days in the guardhouse on bread and water for operating a business for profit in a prison camp; Bo's punishment was three days; Hermann got a day.

Once Bo was released, the jailhouse was quiet. With no one to talk to, Tony thought back to the contents of his father's last letter, the one delivered the day after he agreed to play for Germany. Its time of arrival wasn't by chance; the postmark gave it away. Barrack 15's in-bound and out-bound correspondence had been suspended since mid-February. The resumption of mail must have been Mauer's means of reminding them who held the power at Graham.

Tony had to find a way to cope with the political divergence in the camp – figure out how to conceal his motives, how to beat the system, get ahead of the game, and outwit the thief, the Nazis and Manning, too. If that required manipulation, then so be it. Defiance had many faces. Tony had gone along with Bo on the moneymaking schemes to better himself financially. He could live with fixing a few fights.

A diet of doughy white bread had him longing for a heaping plate of meat and potatoes. Upon release he would go directly to the mess hall. But when he left his jail cell on his fifth day of confinement, he decided that a growling stomach would have to wait.

He charged through the door of Barrack 15, went down on one knee and spread his arms like the singer Al Jolson. "I'm back!" he crooned. The dozen men sitting about gave a lackluster response. An air of sobriety hung over the room.

"What's wrong?" he asked. When no one answered, he walked over to Ladders, who was polishing a shoe with unusual care. "Let's have it."

The buffing stopped. "You need to see Bo, Lieutenant."

Tony found Bo on his bed reading *Police Gazette*. He had a welt over one eye – not unusual for a boxer. Tony cocked his head toward the bunkhouse. "Those guys look like they just came back from a funeral."

"The funeral was yesterday ... Hermann's."

Tony dropped onto his cot and raked back his hair. "I can't believe ..." Tony was now rubbing his eyes.

"They had the casket draped in a swastika banner," Bo said. "Imagine the hypocrisy. I get chills thinking about it."

Tony shook his head in dismay. "Of all the goddamn – how'd Hermann die?"

"The night before I got out of jail, he missed curfew. The men thought it strange because he was so punctual. Someone said he must have escaped. But Hermann wasn't the type, right? Sure, he was scared of the Lager Gestapo, but *escape*? No way. Our guys waited till midnight. Then Ladders organized a search. Ten of ours snuck into the grounds, figuring a war court, but the building was dark. They searched every storehouse, then the latrines. He was in the shower room nearest our barrack, hanging from a rafter, with a suicide note in his pocket. Ladders took it. I've read it over and over – it makes no sense. Hermann's handwriting, but his words aren't what you'd expect. Look, I never read anything he wrote, but most people write like they talk, don't they?"

"You think he was forced."

"You remember what he said in the guardhouse? That stuff about how he couldn't live a dishonored life? I hear it over and over in my head."

"Where's the note?"

Bo had it in his hip pocket:

173

Mein Kampf mit der Aufsicht ist zu unerträglich geworden. Mein
Alternative ist eine Flucht. Ich kann nicht fliehen, Tod ist mein
Überleben. Männer warten auf den Frieden, wenn der Krieg
enden. Ich werde darauf nicht warten. Die Zeit meiner
Ruhe ist in meiner Wahl. Heute ist das. Hermann Vogler'

"Mein Kampf, my ass," Tony said. "Hermann would never write that."
He read the note again as he sauntered about the room. At the window,
he peered out to the walkway between the buildings. "It doesn't sound
right – that stuff about his intolerable fight with supervision, and death
being his only escape. I don't know what to make of it. You can say a
suicidal man is irrational or off his rocker. That's one explanation ...
How'd he hang himself?"

"A rope looped over a rafter. A bench was knocked over on the floor
beneath him. Ladders reckoned Hermann stood on it and kicked it
away."

"Was his neck broken?"

"Don't know."

"No sign of the seventy-five bucks?"

"You got that right, Tony."

Tony turned from the window. "Didn't he say that life as a thief wasn't
worth living?"

"Pretty much his words."

"He's so full of shame and so despondent from the thievery that he
kills himself? He goes to that extreme, but doesn't feel guilty enough to
give the money back. This is the man who suffered three Holy Ghost
tortures without breaking. It doesn't add up. We're going to get to the
bottom of this, God damn it! Get Ladders in here."

Ladders came in without the usual bounce in his stride. "Bo says you
want to hear about the suicide note—"

"First, Corporal Lipinski, I want your recollection from the time
Corporal Vogler missed curfew – every detail."

Ladders filled in the missing particulars from Bo's account. As he
described finding the body, Tony said, "What kind of rope?"

"A normal rope."

"Describe a 'normal rope', Corporal."

Ladders massaged his throat. "The rope ... yes, of course ... it looked like the type you see on a winch or pulley."

"How thick?"

"Lieutenant, I didn't pay much attention to it." Ladders' chin quivered. "I was looking at Hermann ... the expression on his face."

"Stick with the rope, Corporal. How thick?"

"Maybe a half inch. No more."

"Describe the knot."

"I can't remember the knot."

"Think, Corporal Lipinski! Did the knot look like a hangman's noose or a makeshift slip knot?"

"A hangman's noose." Ladders looked as shocked as Tony by the sudden recollection. "Yes, a neatly tied hangman's noose."

"How many coils? Think carefully, Corporal."

"I saw the coils ... yes, for a second. I was holding Hermann up – you know, taking his weight while the others untied the rope from the beam."

"Two coils? Ten?"

"Somewhere in between."

"Closer to two or closer to ten? This is important, Corporal."

Ladders closed his eyes. "I think five, maybe six."

"Now we're getting somewhere. Who has the rope?"

"The MPs took it with the body."

"Describe Corporal Vogler. Any bruises, cuts, grazes, odd marks? Were his clothes torn? Did he look like he struggled?"

"I was so horrified by the look on his face, I thought I was going to black out. I'll never forget it. Maybe it was just me, but I saw the look of defiance. Not anger, not rage, not fear or contentment. Defiance, Lieutenant, plain and simple. His lips and tongue were blue. The tip poked out. His eyes were open, his skin, white."

"No marks of violence?"

"None that I could see."

"Did you check his hands and fingernails?"

"No. My mind was on the note."

"At ease," Tony said. He looked over at Bo, hunched on a footlocker, smoking. "Any questions, Bo?"

Bo asked Ladders how he discovered the note.

"When I wrapped my arms around him I saw it in his shirt pocket. As soon as we lowered him I took it and slipped it into mine."

"You were very observant given the situation," Tony said. "And smart to conceal that note. Why'd you do that?"

"To protect Hermann. I wanted to be the first to read it. I could always give it up later, and I did, to Bo, the next morning."

"You think Hermann killed himself?"

"I thought so until I read the note. Now I'm not so sure. He wasn't himself after he got out of the slammer. I think he was upset about the raid and jail – certainly not despondent."

"If it was murder," Tony said, "who killed him?"

"He said the Holy Ghost was out to get him. But proving it was them is another matter. And even if you solve the mystery, Lieutenant, how do you take them on? Try and you're next."

"Ladders, the tragic death of Hermann is a great loss to all of us. He was a very brave man. I was honored to know him these past five months. At some point I will inform his family that he was a soldier of – no, a *human being* – of the highest distinction."

Ladders' eyes widened.

"Is there more, Ladders?"

"Yes. Hermann was very fond of you, sir. He said you were beyond your years – a fine example of an officer at such a young age."

Tony felt his throat constrict.

When the door closed, Bo asked Tony what, if anything, was he was going to do

"I'm going to sleep on it. But you better brace yourself. What's on my mind makes the German's V-2 Rocket seem like a firecracker."

176

Chapter 20

April 1944
Sarajevo, Independent State of Croatia

Six months after the ambush, Katarina heard the news. Vinny Rukavina said he didn't know the extent of Tony's injuries – only that Josip Babic had informed Captain Housek that Tony was safe and well in a prisoner-of-war camp in America.

Despite her elation, there was a niggling uncertainty that she could not shake – a month had passed since Captain Housek received Josip's news. Yet, a week ago when Goran came for a visit, he had said nothing of it, speaking as though Tony was still missing. Should she cable Goran? No, she would take a few days to think on it. But this did not dissuade her from seeking Tony's US coordinates from Josip.

A fortnight later, the cablegram from Zagreb only added to her confusion:

'Pleased Goran told you of Tony. Send mail to Vlatko Babic 6WG1759, POW Camp Graham, Rockford, Illinois, c/o G.P.O. Box 20 New York – Josip Babic.'

Her two-year relationship with Goran now teetered on wooden stilts infested with termites. He considered her his fiancée, the love of his life, but in her mind he was a fixture of obligation and atonement. Forever grateful that he had been there in her darkest moments, she had prolonged the liaison but had drawn the line at physical intimacy, invoking the 'not before marriage' doctrine of chastity. On the rare occasions that she had weakened to his perseverance, the image of the Ustasha attacker threw her into a convulsive abyss before Goran could remove a stitch of her armor.

Maria Kirilenko had urged her to end the charade, arguing that it would be over if Tony were alive. That situation was no longer hypothetical. Moreover, Goran had given her every reason to break all ties – keeping Tony's survival from her was indefensible. She had tried to love him.

Suspecting that he knew the truth, his suffering had begun to manifest itself in jealous rage.

She worked at several drafts, settling on the shortest version:

'Dear Goran,

I am eternally thankful for what you did for me in Zagreb. However, after months of tribulation, I can no longer mislead you into believing that one day I will be your wife. Our relationship holds no future. I believe it is best we not see each other for the time being. I am sorry for misleading you. Please understand.

A friend always,

Katarina'

Her quivering hand reached for a clean sheet of notepaper. On that page, she began a second letter, this one to the man she loved:

'Dear Tony,

When you didn't come for dinner that Saturday in October, I knew something was wrong. Every day after that – for six months now – I lit a candle for you and said the same prayer. I asked our Lord and Savior to spare your life. Until you are home, I will continue to light a candle. The flame will burn for as long as it takes – years, if necessary.

Our picnic in the Sarajevo hills is fresh in my mind. Up there in the clean air, away from the war, you were the man I remembered from Vinograd Kralja. That man was the Tony I long for. No matter how hard I try to suppress my feelings, I cannot deny them. I know this comes as a shock. Other than the vineyard and our moments together in Sarajevo, I was not very nice to you. It is hard to explain. That juvenile behavior had to do with my father and the life of a soldier's daughter. I blamed the army for stealing him from me. I am over that. My heart has opened.

As I write these words, I feel myself in your arms, as I did on that day in the mountains. Am I being silly? I've never thought of myself as silly, but maybe love makes me this way. You are my first love, and you will be my last. When a woman believes that the man she loves is dead, she regrets never having told him of her love. The moment you went missing, I knew. Do you have feelings for me? Am I silly to think your desire for me on the picnic blanket was more than male yearning?

As for life in Sarajevo, I continue working as a seamstress in repair and restoration. The work is difficult and the hours long, but it puts food on the table. My mother works with me from the house. I worry for her. She is very thin. In my spare time, I volunteer at an orphanage. The little ones brighten my day, but when I leave them, their eyes sadden, and so do mine. Some call me 'Mama'. One day.

Goran came last month. He has asked me to be his wife many times and I have evaded the question. I should have dealt with this long ago. I didn't want to hurt him. He has been so kind.

Before concluding, I wish to express my condolences for the loss of your friends. I know how close you were to Rado, and I feel privileged to have met him, though it was but once. The depth of my sorrow is more than you will ever know.

My address is on the envelope. Come back to me, Tony.

With love,

Katarina'

She mailed one of the letters, and tore the other into little pieces.

****

Six months ago, the Führer had sent bombers to wipe out the partisans' Jajce headquarters, and Tito along with it. But warning of the raid had come from Luka, through an agent in Zagreb. How long would it take for the Germans to discover Tito's cave hideout above Drvar – more importantly, when would they mount an attack? The agent's assignment was to find out.

While in Zagreb settling the score for the murders of Rudi and Milic, Luka had connected with the copper-skinned woman who adeptly deployed a lengthy repertoire of skills to advance the partisan cause. A remarkable espionage resource, the Chameleon could live for days in the woods without food or just as easily as paint her face and lounge in a posh hotel room before a lust-crazed enemy whose throat she planned to slit.

Ella's current assignment began with an orchestrated lobby encounter at the Esplanade Hotel. Colonel Christoph Schwanitz, the second most powerful German in Zagreb, likely figured her for a high-class lady of the evening. He would soon discover the contrary: she would portray a simple woman who craved the decorated breastplate and power of his uniform. She towered over Schwanitz by four inches, but what of it? Within ten days, she was his mistress.

Because he insisted that they converse in his language, months of cozy encounters improved Ella's German. She asked for little, explaining at the outset that he need not shower her with jewels or silk stockings. She led him to believe that she valued the safety of his companionship. For this, she promised to worship him like a God, fuck him brainless, and endure his boring stories that droned on into the quiet hours of the night. He spoke of his wife and children in Berlin and bragged of countless Wehrmacht triumphs, on occasion venturing beyond the benign into precious morsels pertaining to Hitler's war on her comrades. Through it all, Ella's russet eyes beamed in wonderment at the revolting little man.

She cooed about how she had never met another like him. "Tell me more, Christoph," she would plead. A calculated blend of questions, most of them naive and one or two of a leading nature, followed the flattery.

"You have met Hitler?" she would ask. "Oh, you have not. Then how do you know what he is like? Does he care about people like me? He won't leave us to the Russians, will he, Christoph? He won't do that, will he?"

The Chameleon kept up her blandishments until Schwanitz's eyelids drooped. And while he snored, she would rummage through his briefcase dossier, his pockets and his billfold.

****

Luka moved along the well-trodden path by the river and then hiked between the crags and cliffs leading to the hideout. Halfway up a steep slope, with Drvar at his rear, he came to the familiar rock crevice. Three flights of wooden stairs would bring him to the stick-and-leaf-camouflaged house at the cave's mouth.

Though dusk had yet to descend, Tito's secretary's desk was in the shadows. Zdenka, the student from Belgrade had two oil lamps to brighten her workplace, but only one was lit. Seemingly unaware of Luka's stare, the slender girl drummed away at the keys of her typewriter. She was sleeping with Tito, and Luka knew it. The image of the poker-faced girl, naked and panting and begging the Old Man to keep up his pace, brought a wily grin to his face. Still wearing it, he said he wanted to see Tito.

She removed her side cap and scratched her head, shaven to make the lice easier to get at. "Marshal Tito is in conference. Are you expected?"

Luka did not have an appointment. "He'll want to see me."

"What is your name?"

Before Luka could answer, a drowsy member of the Politburo stepped from the war room into the foyer. Having met Milovan Djilas but once, Luka was certain that Djilas wouldn't remember him, but the instant Tito's confidant spotted him perched on the corner of Zdenka's desk, he beamed and extended his hand.

"Congratulations, Luka!" he said, giving Luka an enthusiastic shake. "Suppose you've come to see the boss. They're wrapping up – five hours I've been in there. I'm beat, and the Old Man's still in second gear. That job you pulled in Zagreb – extraordinary!"

"Try hoisting a dead hippo on the point of a sword," Luka said. "I was lucky the damn thing didn't bust." Luka glanced at Zdenka, who continued typing as though not hearing a word.

"I can imagine," Djilas said. "Has Zdenka told the Old Man you're here?"

She rose from the desk and went into the war room, returning with four Politburo members. Every one of them was at least fifteen years Tito's junior. "He will see you now," she said to Luka.

Through the open door, he could see the huge map of Yugoslavia pinned to the wall. Scored with arrows, circles and squares, it presumably represented the partisan army's latest battle plan. Curtains of parachute silk covered the windows on the adjoining wall. For a frame structure built into a hole in a mountain, the war room was an impressive abode.

Having gained some muscle and looking nowhere near his years, Tito scooted from behind his desk. "My, oh, my!" he said. "How the hell did you spike an Ustasha in the heart of Zagreb?" He didn't give Luka a chance to respond. "I know you used the night, but what astounded me most was they let it be. Pavelic was in Berlin and didn't get word till the next afternoon. Word has it the Ustashe had a tough time getting down a granite-stiff body. They had to use a winch attached to a tank!"

"Really?"

"Okay, that's a bit far-fetched. More like six troopers on the roof of a truck."

"Yeah, I was real happy with the outcome. Sure got the headlines we wanted."

"Churchill, Stalin, Roosevelt – they all saw the photo." Tito opened a drawer, and one by one, he dropped three newspapers on the olive-drab US Army blanket covering his five plank timber desk. "*The Washington Post* and the *Times* of New York and London make powerful statements. They also make you the latest hero of our people. You've done Uncle Zarko proud."

Luka credited the professor for his rise in the partisan army. He had loved Milic like the father he never knew – the father who died in the last days of the First World War. Tito's reference invoked a mix of sadness, humility and fury in his rising star. Luka lowered his eyes, sighed, and clenched his fists. But he held his tongue. The professor would have been proud of that as well.

"Luka, there are two issues we ought to discuss. The pending German assault on the cave ... Have you anything from the Chameleon?"

"The raids will be any day. Hitler wants you in the worst way."

"The little shit better be quick because he's running out of time. So there's nothing more specific, then."

The higher pitch indicated that Tito's assertion was purely rhetorical. Luka shook his head.

"Very well ... issue number two. With the end near, we're shifting attention to the prospect and challenge of post-war rule. We've come a long way, Luka. We cannot screw it up when we take over. We'll need to control every anti-Communist faction in the country." He walked over to the map and fingered a territory circled by several deep blue lines. "I want to go beyond the reckoning of the Chetniks. Can you believe they still whine to Churchill? It's vital we stamp out every opponent, be they individuals or political groups." He rested his back against the map. "Do you know Marko Rankovic?"

"I know him by reputation. He's the guy who survived the Gestapo clubbing."

"Rankovic knows you – also by reputation. Every council member knows Luka Lipovac." Tito picked up the *Washington Post,* opened to the Jelacic monument photo. "Because of *this,* you're in demand. Rankovic was the resolute-looking Serb who left the office before you came in. He has no love for Croats. You and I are exceptions. I've slated him to head the intelligence agency from Belgrade. He'll need a loyalist in Zagreb. You."

Luka rocked on the balls of his feet, gloating.

"As leader of the secret police, he'll monitor every objector, interrogating, jailing and executing as necessary. You'll lead Zagreb's interior division of counter-intelligence, and you'll have a free hand to punish every enemy – the list is long, I assure you. No one will forget the fact that Croatia supported the fascists."

Luka said he'd like to start with Christoph Schwanitz."

"You ought to be considerate in this regard," Tito said.

Luka could not hide his perplexity because Tito had just alluded to iron-fisted retribution. *"Considerate?* You can't be—"

Tito laughed. "Don't you think the Chameleon's earned that privilege?"

****

At daybreak, the howl of aircraft and thunder of bombs had the partisan cabinet peering from their mountain refuge to the valley. Smoke rose from the town. Soon they would smell the destruction of Drvar. Luka, standing several feet back of the leaders, looked up at the busy sky. He had yet to see Tito. Had the boss slipped away in the night? But no, here was Tito, casually stepping from the veranda onto the pebbled landing.

Djilas gestured to the Junkers 52 squadrons zooming into the valley, disgorging paratroopers. "The bombers and fighters have served their purpose, Marshal. Those paratroopers will organize the ascent."

"They know what they're doing," Tito said, appearing unruffled by the implications.

No one asked for instructions. Luka figured Tito would give them when he was good and ready.

Tito's quiet appraisal lasted thirty seconds. "I've been on the radio," he said. "Our Sixth Division's six miles away. The cadet school's at the river. I'm counting on them holding the line till the Sixth Division shows – should be nine to nine-thirty."

"Too late," Rankovic said. He pointed to a squadron of Junkers towing transport gliders. "Those birds carry infantry."

The gliders landed wherever they could. A few crash-landed, but most set down smoothly, releasing soldiers with machine guns. Within ninety minutes, the town must have fallen, because the climb began. Other than the topographic barriers and the route by the river, the path was open. The entire partisan leadership and support staff might have a forty-five-minute head start on the commandos.

Never one to be stubborn or emotional in these predicaments, Tito ordered everyone into civvies. They had five minutes to gather one bag of belongings and report to the war room.

Those who arrived early found him standing over an open trapdoor in the floor. "This is our way out," he said. "Luka and Boris will help you down."

The two strongmen braced themselves on opposite sides of the open square. Each held a thick rope by which to lower their comrades to the shallow riverbed.

"You're first, Marshal," Rankovic said.

This was the prudent decision: Tito first, then the Politburo, then the two secretaries, and finally the foot soldiers. Luka looped the bowline under Tito's arms.

Once the last member of the Politburo was out, Luka took charge. "Hurry up, Zdenka!" he said. Grabbing her slender waist, he pulled her to the edge. "Don't look down, and you won't be scared." He tightened the rope and lowered her while his partner harnessed the other woman.

Twenty-five minutes after Tito's exit, it was Luka's turn. The last escapee knotted the rope to the handle of the office door and shimmied down to the water like a circus performer descending from the high wire. He left the dangling rope and jogged across the stream to join the others beneath the green veil of orchards and forest.

Chapter 21

May 1944
Rockford, Illinois

Mindful of the hour, Tony marked the particulars of each packed and bound pallet of marmalade. In a couple of minutes, the Americans would leave for coffee break. Tony was glad to see that the months of tedious watching had lulled the guards into complacency. The two MPs near Tony's checking station paid scant attention to the prisoners, preferring to play cribbage, leaf through car magazines, and 'shoot the breeze', as the Americans often said. At this moment, they were absorbed in penny-a-game cribbage, and none of the pegs had reached the skunk line. Barring a phenomenal hand to accelerate the game's finale, they would not be distracted for another five to ten minutes.

A loud buzzer cut through the factory hum. The conveyor belt stopped, and Tony fell in behind the procession of American workers headed for the cafeteria. Once the MPs were out of sight, he veered off and scampered between pallets of jams and jellies to the shipping-and-receiving office by the transport doors. Nine minutes from now, the shipper and his crew would return from their coffee break. He stole into the office, dialed zero, and dropped to the floor behind the desk so he wouldn't be seen through the window facing the loading dock.

The operator connected him. A perky female voice said, *"Rockford Morning Star.* How may I direct your call?"

"I like speak to Bobby Rose."

"May I inform Mr Rose who is calling?"

"Tony Babic. I from Camp Graham." While he waited, he eyed the shipper's street clothes hung over a hook. They just might fit. He had money – his back denim pocket was sewn over a ten-dollar bill. He could be out the transport door in less than a minute.

"Bobby Rose here."

"My name Tony Babic. You remember me? Prisoner of war who score winning goal."

The newsman chuckled. "I'm amazed you have telephone privileges. Only in America."

"I not at Graham. Sycamore Canning. Not have long to talk." It took him fifty seconds to read the text.

"Okay, Tony. You want me to ring Manning at nine tomorrow. I'll do that. If I get through and hear what I think I'm going to hear, you'll make the front page. If Manning denies the assertion, I'll threaten to be at the gates, pronto! If he sloughs me off, I'll come out anyway to check things out."

"Thank you, Bobby Rose."

"Hope this works for you, Tony. I smell a rat in that nest."

"Many rats." Tony hung up and snuck back to the packing line, undetected.

The next morning, all hell broke loose. A hundred feet from four MPs at the fence by the vehicle reception station, a charging Tony hollered, "Prisoner riot! Riot in Barrack 15." He latched on to the chain-links. "Come fast! Tell Colonel Manning you have big trouble."

The startled guards shaded their eyes from the blinding sun. "Might be a brawl," one said.

"Send guards, worse than brawl," Tony said, shaking the fence. He spun a half turn and sprinted back up the lane to a barrack with windows boarded from the inside. Half-inch openings between the planks admitted ample daylight for the inmates to see outside, but were small enough to impede tear gas grenades.

"We're under way," Tony said. "Anyone with second thoughts, speak now. There's still time to walk out of here." He roved the room, making eye contact with each of them. "Guess you want to stay. Nail the two-by-sixes to the doorjambs."

The minutes of silence seemed endless, and the main room warmed up – not enough to make them break a sweat. But Tony smelled the sweat.

"Boots on gravel," Bo said.

The handle rattled. "Military Police! Open up!"

The next sound was a rifle butt against the door. "You're in violation of camp rules! Open or we break in!"

Inches from the boarded door, Tony shouted back in English. "We obey Geneva Convention! This is a political protest! We make hunger strike until complaint heard! Starve if necessary." He had written and memorized his opening salvo.

Through the slits in the window planks, the strikers watched the MPs scamper off, probably to seek the counsel of a superior.

"That's step one," Tony said. "It might be an hour before we hear from them again."

The MPs were back in half that time. "Lieutenant Dixon here! Come out with your hands up."

"Lieutenant Dixon, this is Lieutenant Babic. We not come out. We not make complaint to you. We make complaint to officer of Provost Marshal General."

In a voice suggesting exasperation, Dixon said, "You leave us no choice but to bust through this door."

A swarm of prisoners around Tony backed away from the entry area.

"That, big mistake. Army look bad, not follow Geneva Convention. You tell Colonel Manning. Better you safe than sorry," Tony said, giving a hopeful thumbs-up to the men. But he knew that if Dixon rammed the door, they were done.

****

At first Manning had vacillated, asking the caller for a minute to tie up some loose ends. Having been hoodwinked by Bobby Rose in the past, he needed to collect his thoughts. If the call was about that suicide, the little bugger wouldn't let go until he had answers. Better he handle him sooner than later.

"Has there been another hanging, Colonel?"

Out of the gate, Bobby Rose had him on the defensive. "Sadly, yes, a suicide last week. Mr Rose, we have five thou—"

"Does the hunger strike have anything to do with the alleged suicide?"

"What are you talking about?"

"There's a protest right under your nose, and you don't know it? You've got POWs who won't eat until someone from the PMG's office hears their grievance. Geneva gives them unrestricted rights to apply to a representative of the protecting power regarding complaints on the conditions of captivity."

The smart-ass had read the captivity articles of the Convention. "How … did you hear of the strike?"

"I have my contacts. The protesters say Corporal Vogler was lynched by the Nazis. You've got a rash of terrorism in your camp. Are you aware of that, Colonel?"

Manning didn't respond.

"Colonel? What are you going to do about Nazi violence?"

What was Manning going to do? He was going to tell Bobby Rose that this was *none of his goddamned business*! But he didn't. He said, "This is Army business!" and slammed down the receiver.

Expecting Bobby Rose and maybe a photographer to be on their way, Manning motored to the mayhem. A couple of hundred POWs were milling around barrack 15, including Arnim and Mauer. Manning called the Lagersprecher over, and Mauer came along.

"Troublemakers inside, Colonel Manning," Mauer said. "We shall deal with them."

"No, you won't." Manning gripped the top of the jeep's window and pulled himself upright. "Lieutenant Dixon! Clear the crowd. I don't give a shit where they go, long as it's not here!"

A perplexed-looking Arnim peered back and forth between Manning, Mauer and the mob. Mauer translated, and then added, "I fear the protest has to do with us."

Arnim replied in German. "Ask Manning if … no, *tell* Manning we stay. The Convention entitles us to be present in cases of protest and arrest."

Mauer made the case, but Manning was having none of it. "Article 78 entitles prisoners to make grievances through their representatives or directly. Your help, they don't want. Leave this to me."

When the stockade cleared, he tapped on the barred door. "This is Colonel Manning. Why do you protest?"

"Good morning, Colonel," Tony said. "Boards come down only when PMG official meet with us."

Manning figured as much. "I'll see what I can do."

"One more thing," Tony said. "If guards leave at twenty-two hundred hours like always, Nazis break in and kill us."

Manning groaned. He should have known it would come to this – that someone would make a stand.

****

The men of barrack 15 had prepared for the strike with six piss buckets behind a draped bedsheet, and a week's supply of water and Coca-Cola. With luck, they wouldn't need it all.

By midday, the stifling bunkhouse reeked of cigarette and pipe smoke. The protesters peeped through the gaps at guards pounding stakes and roping off a 'No Entry' zone. The hours passed with books and games, but as the heat and humidity permeated, so did the tension.

At supper hour, Bo strode down the center aisle, carrying a cardboard box on his shoulder. "Chow time! Come an' git it!" he bellowed in a Yankee dialect. "This may be a hunger strike, but everyone gets a three-course meal. Tonight's menu is chocolate bars, hard candy and peanuts. Don't gobble it up too fast, or you'll be shitting all night long. We don't want those pails overflowing. The stink will drive us out before the PMG ever gets in."

Tony sensed the overall edginess. Hopefully, an official would show up on the strike's second day. Had he misjudged the action's impact? Would the Provost Marshal General's Office care a fig for forty-two guys in one slammer when they had hundreds of camps and 400,000 prisoners to worry about?

"Must be ninety in here," Bo said. "Think it's safe to remove the odd plank to get a breeze?"

Tony scratched his head. "We don't want a tear gas canister in here." Of course, if Manning wanted them out, all he had to do was break down the door. "I think we've got the old guy by the balls. He'll stick to protocol. Two bucks says Bobby Rose is out there bugging the shit out of him. I wish I'd thought of Bobby Rose sooner – I could have saved Hermann." Tony toweled his face and swigged a mouthful of warm cola. "Take down one board from each window."

By nightfall, four portable searchlights and three dozen armed guards surrounded the building. The scene was as quiet as a vacant raft on a calm sea.

****

At 06:30, the lights were already on in Manning's office. The weary colonel had spent the night worrying that Washington would call for his head on a stick. Yesterday he had made a slew of calls for information on Colonel Bruce Widrington of the Provost Marshal General's Office. Widrington was well-regarded, fair, bright, cooperative and no-nonsense.

189

As for how Manning might handle himself, he had weighed the consequences of three options: back the Nazis, the protesters, or neither? No matter how he sliced the pie, he was knee-deep in pectin. The uprising was in *his* camp, under *his* watch. This second day of protest might be his last as an active colonel in the US Army.

DC was an hour ahead of Illinois. Widrington was already in the air. From Chicago's Douglas Field, an army vehicle would bring him ninety-five miles west, putting his arrival at around 1030.

The *Star* lay folded in Manning's in-basket. He opened it to the front page and the grinning mug of a handsome prisoner in a soccer jersey:

'HUNGER STRIKE AT GRAHAM by Bobby Rose

Yesterday, forty-two prisoners of war boarded themselves in a barrack to protest Nazi repression at Camp Graham. They refuse to eat or come out until their grievances are heard by the War Department.

The hunger strike and sit-in comes days after the death of another prisoner. The strikers say the death was a Nazi lynching and not suicide. They claim fanatic Nazi elements are responsible for several violent camp deaths. This is the seventh hanging in a year and the tenth fatality at Graham. One man died of natural causes, two drowned and seven perished by rope.

POW Tony Babic, spokesman for the protesters, said, "We are a barrack of Non-German democrats. We are Croats, Poles, Hungarians, Slovenes and Czechs who were dragged into the war by the Germans. We deplore Nazism. We protest the terror inflicted on us and ask that every non-German be relocated to a Nazi-free camp."

Those who attended Camp Graham's exciting soccer match may remember Babic as the player who scored the winning goal in the 2-1 German victory. Asked why a Croat would play for the Germans, Babic said he had no problem with Germans. "It is the Nazis I detest. There is a difference, you know."

Three months ago the Star *reported an alarming incidence of prisoner fatalities. Commanding Officer Colonel Thomas Manning said the death rates were within the norms of prison camps in this country. Figures from the War Department fail to corroborate this contention. The* Star *estimates the fatality incidence at Graham to be five times the US average.*

190

*An official of the Provost Marshal General's Office is expected to meet
with the protesters.'*

"Shit!" Manning shouted. "Shit, shit, *shit!*"

****

The lanky, well-groomed fellow with the trimmed reddish-brown
mustache and boyish freckles looked remarkably fresh after a five-hour
journey, most of it in a commercial airliner. Widrington established
meeting parameters and explained his role in circumstances such as
these, adding that he and Manning would tackle the issue as teammates.
Would the camp commander mind if they got on a 'first-name' basis?

Hell no. With a little luck, he just might get through this mess after all.

"All right," Widrington said. "Item one: I'm not meeting the protesters
until I have the facts. Let's start with you. I've read today's *Chicago
Tribune*. They must have picked up the story from the Associated Press
newswire."

Manning stiffened.

"No doubt," Widrington said, "this will generate a great deal of public
interest. Doesn't mean we can't tack and jibe our way through the storm.
Start with the casualties, Tom. Go back to the first incident – the soldier
who died from natural causes."

Manning folded his hands and swallowed. "When the camp opened, I
was—"

"Hold that thought, Tom. I need you to get the chief medical officer
over here with the files on the deceased: medical exams, death
certificates, coroner's reports."

Manning reached for the pencil holder and accidentally tipped it over,
scattering pencils all over his desk. As he scooped them up, he described
Doctor Armstrong's credentials.

"Call him."

Manning retrieved the last pencil, and then dialed.

"Doc, I'm with Colonel Widrington of the PMGO ... Yes, that's right,
the strike. He wants the files on every deceased POW." Manning pressed
the phone to his ear. The other ear turned red. "Of course I do! Doc—"
He turned his swivel chair to face the window, his back to Widrington.
"I'm aware of that ... He wants every one of them."

Manning covered the receiver with his palm and turned his head to Widrington. "He'll need some time to locate the files."

"Tell him we're racing the clock. He's got ten minutes."

"The colonel wants you here right away. Bring as many files as you can."

"All of them," Widrington said.

After hanging up, Manning said, "Bruce, that *Tribune* article ... it is one journalist's opinion."

"Once a paper's on the newsstands, his opinion is the public's opinion. All right, Tom, back to when the camp opened. Take me through it."

****

Dr Armstrong brought in four folders – six were missing – an infirmary break-in.

"I assume you knew of this, Tom."

Manning offered a sheepish nod.

Widrington responded with one of those 'why the hell didn't you say so in the first place' expressions? "Have you apprehended the perpetrator?" he asked

"The thief is likely a POW," Manning said, placing his bet.

"The suspect is the person or persons incriminated by the information," Widrington said. "Someone was out to destroy evidence. Could that someone be one of ours?"

The inference deepened the ruts across Manning's weathered brow.

According to the death certificate in the first file, a 46-year-old sergeant died of a heart attack. He had been forty-five pounds overweight, with a history of high blood pressure. The file seemed in order. Two dossiers contained information on POWs who died by their own hand in the latrines. Both used a rope, and both left suicide notes. They were in good health and there was no indication of a struggle. 'Death by suicidal suffocation' had been written on the death certificates.

Widrington flipped through the folder of the latest casualty, the one that had triggered the protest. The coroner's report said 'suspected suicide' by suffocation. Corporal Hermann Vogler had not left a suicide note.

Widrington picked up a second paper from the file. "Doctor, this report dated January 7, 1944 ... you diagnosed Corporal Vogler with strep throat. You wrote: 'Internal abrasions in the upper windpipe and tonsils' but you didn't indicate the cause."

The flush-faced physician said he didn't know the cause.

"Are abrasions symptoms of strep throat or are we looking at a case of bad dentistry?"

Manning caught the sarcasm. Speculating Widrington's next question, he asked Armstrong why he diagnosed strep throat.

"To be honest, Colonel, I was unsure of the affliction. Vogler's throat was red and swollen. A foreign object had been down there. I asked; he denied."

"Did you check his rectum?" Widrington asked.

"No."

"Ever consider that whatever went down his throat might also have gone up his ass?" Widrington began reading aloud. "'Tenderness in the stomach and abdominal area' – what caused that?"

"I couldn't be sure."

"Related to the throat?"

"I don't think so."

"Was he beaten?"

"No signs. I prescribed medication for strep throat and checked him a week later. He was recovering nicely, so I gave the condition no further thought."

Widrington began tapping a pencil on the table as if it were a drumstick. "They didn't steal this file."

"Corporal Vogler was alive when the other files went missing."

"Yes, of course. He died on the seventeenth of May. All right, Doctor, go through the missing files by memory."

"That won't be easy."

"Do your best."

An hour before sunset, Widrington was finished with Armstrong. Three hours later he seemed ready to wrap it up. Manning sure as hell was ready to call it a day.

"Seems those hungry boys in the boarded barrack have a legitimate beef," Widrington said. Those suicides look like murder. That how you see it, Tom?"

"There's no proof, but with six files missing—"

"Six files *stolen*. Tom, I have to ask … Why in the hell didn't you shut them down? You've got an epidemic of vigilante violence here. The evidence was staring you in the face six months ago."

Manning took a deep breath and exhaled. "The evidence was circumstantial."

"Ten deaths in twelve months, six files stolen, three of the dead with lacerations down their throats – and forty-two hunger strikers telling you so. Why didn't you come down on them?"

Manning heaved another sigh. "When I came here in '42 I was told to make security my priority. They said what went on in the prisoner stockade was the enemy's business."

"Not murder. Early in the war, we allowed the enemy to discipline themselves – no longer. Widrington sorted through a hoard of briefcase papers. "Here – Lieutenant Colonel Leon Jaworski's January bulletin. You must have read it. 'Camp commanders are to make immediate searches of perpetrators. Confiscate the clubs and the weapons. If the attacks are during the night, be there to apprehend the violators.'"

Manning had read it but wouldn't admit it. By the time Jaworski's bulletin arrived, the graveyard population had expanded to eight. Then along came Bobby Rose.

Widrington explained the options in the morning. Manning was to retire forthwith or endure an inquiry, not the way to end an illustrious career. Manning, argued that the evidence was in stolen files, likely destroyed.

"This doesn't create a cold case," countered Widrington. "Interviews will unearth witnesses and bring charges. In an inquiry, we'll make deals with the ones who come forward. Even those of the Lager Gestapo can beat the rap if they sell out the ringleaders. The truth will come out, and the trial or trials will be long and debilitating. Do you really want that?"

With 80,000 Americans in German camps, Widrington knew that a trial at this time would not be in America's best interest. It wasn't as if Graham's Nazis had murdered GIs. They'd slain their own. Moreover, Hitler was volatile and delusional. Risk the safety of 80,000 for a handful of Nazi assassins? No way.

Once Manning had gathered his belongings and said his goodbyes, Widrington went into damage control.

****

Mauer and Arnim had been dressing for dinner when a troop of MPs entered their quarters.

"I bring orders from Colonel Widrington, interim camp commander," Lieutenant Dixon said.

Mauer ceased buttoning his tunic and began pelting Dixon with a stream of questions.

"Major!" Arnim said. "Let lieutenant read orders."

"Thank you, Colonel," Dixon said. "At twenty-three hundred hours, ninety-four prisoners are to be packed for transfer to another camp. They will assemble outside their barracks and be ready to march under guard to the inspection station." He raised his eyes. "Both of you are on the transfer list."

"Give me that list!" Mauer said. Dixon's sergeant complied and Mauer skimmed through the names. "We shall meet your new commandant."

"No you won't. My orders are to take all ninety-four by force if necessary. There will be serious consequences for disorder. This is how the two of you avoid a murder trial. We have the evidence. Colonel Widrington is offering a way out."

Mauer and Arnim exchanged glances, and then debated their choices in rapid-fire German.

Finally, Arnim said, "We not make trouble, Lieutenant."

Dixon returned to the script. "Everyone will be searched for contraband before boarding buses. Transferees are permitted two duffel bags of personal items."

"Babic's protest," Arnim muttered in German. "He is the swine behind our expulsion and Manning's retirement."

Choosing to ignore the remark, Mauer asked where they would be moved.

"Colonel Widrington didn't state your destination."

Arnim frowned, and then looked directly into Mauer's black eyes. "You reap what you sow."

Mauer felt the rising rage. He couldn't deny it; the Lagersprecher was right. With Babic, they had won the battle and lost the war. If they were destined for Camp Alva, he would tumble in the pecking order. Even more devastating was the matter of his money – how would he get it out? He asked if they could take canteen coupons.

"A two-week supply," Dixon said. "More than that, spend them in the canteen, but don't forget the two-duffel maximum. I'll leave you to pack."

Mauer owned fishing books, a radio and a camera. He didn't care for much else. It was the money he wanted – it amounted to five months' pay. The moment Arnim left for supper, Mauer began stitching bills into the linings of his clothes. Arnim would be gone for an hour – ample time to conceal eighty-two dollars in notes. Coins were the problem. He was loath to leave even a nickel behind. With any luck, they would search senior officers less rigorously than enlisted men.

He tore out the guts of his Philco radio and loaded the casing with nickels, dimes and quarters. If they didn't lift the radio and feel its weight, he would be all right. The remaining coin and coupons could be stored at the bottom of the duffels. He had replaced the last screw on the back of the Philco just as Arnim returned.

"The men in the mess wish to see you, Major. You have explaining to do."

"Explaining?"

"Why we are moving. Your man Babic. Many questions." The long knives were out, it seemed.

Mauer smelled a rat; Arnim was too composed. "I have explained myself to you, Herr Colonel. This is sufficient." Mauer lived by the ethic of eliminating an enemy before he eliminated you. Once he had dealt with the more pressing matter, he would devise a means to eliminate Arnim.

****

The postmaster handed Mauer the key to the post room. In the bags of impounded mail, he found eight letters addressed to Tony Babic. When he'd finished reading the one from Sarajevo, he said, "Babic and a Russian bitch, how fucking sweet."

He tore off the address and stuffed it in his pocket. Then he held the flame of a match under the corner of Katarina's admission of love.

****

As a last act of audacity, the Nazis goose-stepped to the inspection station. The dampness under Mauer's armpits had nothing to do with the warmth of the night. Fifty yards from the gates, he gazed at the standing silhouette in Colonel Manning's office window. Under Widrington, life at Graham would be trying. The transfer was in his best interest: no investigation, no trial. If only the bastard had given more notice, Mauer could have had a fail-safe scheme to take his money with him.

At the checkpoint, a sentry pointed to his duffel bags.

Appearing indifferent, Mauer said, "Nothing of interest."

"My orders are to check every bag."

Mauer tendered one of the duffels.

"Both!" The guard began burrowing into the contents, suddenly stopping.

In a private room, in Mauer's presence, they dumped out the contents of both bags on a long table. Out tumbled clothes … and coins. Most were caught by rumpled shirts and trousers; some rolled across the floor. A pile of coupons fell like wet leaves on top of the heap.

An MP picked up the radio and tossed it in the air, catching it in both hands. "This must have lead circuits." He lobbed it once more but made no effort to catch it. The radio hit the concrete floor and shattered, sending coins all over the room.

"Okay, Major, spread your legs and raise your arms."

"This is an insult to a senior officer of the SS."

"You could be the fucking Führer for all I care. Spread 'em or we will."

Two guards patted him down. "Sleeves feel funny," said one.

Resistance was futile. Mauer removed every stitch of clothing. In a prisoner-of-war camp, the naked major had accumulated a hundred eighty-eight dollars in cash. And in the camp it stayed.

Chapter 22

"Lieutenant Babic, my name is Colonel Widrington. I'm here to discuss your grievance."

"We take boards down, Colonel, "Tony said. "Meet in my office." He winked at the men.

Using a makeshift crowbar, they wrenched the cross boards from the door, and six MPs with guns in shiny leather holsters entered, trailed by Widrington, the only one that did not grimace at the stench of human waste, body odor and cigarette smoke.

The prisoners saluted, after which Tony introduced himself as a lieutenant of the Croatian Air Force. "Please come to back room. Smell not like this."

Away from the others, Widrington apologized for the distress caused by the Nazis, and expressed regret that those responsible would not face a military court.

"They are murderers, Colonel. Nazis—"

Widrington raised his hand. "Tony," he said calmly, "allow me to finish."

Widrington admitted that murders had likely been committed. How many, he couldn't say. Medical files had been stolen and destroyed. If there was to be a trial, the government would be forced to appoint an accomplished attorney to defend the accused. Circumstantial evidence would not bring a conviction.

"This is how it's done in America," Widrington said. "People are innocent until proven guilty. A guilty verdict requires an open-and-shut case."

The terminology was confusing, but Tony got the drift. The murderers were going to get away with it.

"Our attorneys can make a strong case but the problem is pinpointing the killers. Me? I'd hang 'em all, but that's not the way the system works. So here's what I've done: I've relocated the radicals. Arnim, Mauer, Burger, and ninety-one others – shipped out last night. They're off to the Alcatraz of prison camps, in Oklahoma. This annuls your relocation demands."

"What means 'Alcraz' and 'nulls'?"

"Don't worry about Alcatraz. It's just slang. 'Annul' means moving you guys is no longer necessary. I've eliminated your problem. However, I'm still going to grant your wish. Within three weeks you and your men will be spending the rest of the war in a peaceful compound."

Mauer, Arnim and Burger getting away with murder made Tony's blood boil, but there was nothing he could do about it – the decision was made, and they were gone, out of his life forever.

"Men work hard for coupons, Colonel. Can they take them to new camp?"

"I'll make sure of it."

"I end strike. One thing more … " In Tony's mind, none of this would have happened under diligent leadership. Ninety-four Nazis gone meant three hundred left. It could start again. "Colonel Manning do very bad job. He—"

"I'm taking over. Lieutenant, you're a courageous young man. I wish you the best." Widrington put out his hand, and Tony shook it.

****

Widrington invited Bobby Rose to the camp, and they met in what had been Manning's office.

"Colonel Manning served his country well – forty years of exemplary duty," Widrington said. "Regrettably, his last year was plagued by ill health. You understand me, don't you, Mr Rose?"

"That depends. Your cooperation regarding Nazi terror and the hunger strike will determine where the 'retired' colonel fits into my story."

"Mr Rose, I'll be candid. When we invade Europe, we fear Hitler will be as ruthless with American POWs as he is with the Jews." Suspecting that Bobby Rose was Jewish, Widrington said the Nazis' slaughter of Jews is understated. "To limit the atrocities, we must liberate concentration camps as soon as possible. This brings me to you. Sensationalize your scoop in this little corner of America, and the Associated Press latches on to it. The story travels to every city on earth, including Berlin. That may be good for you, Mr Rose, but not so good for 80,000 American POWs."

"You'll have to do better than that."

199

Widrington eyed Bobby Rose as might a prosecutor weighing the honesty of a witness. Had the young man's journalistic principles ever conflicted with his personal ethics? Not likely. This story was internationally gift-wrapped.

Widrington hunched forward. "Charging two or three Nazis with murder … conducting a trial, finding them guilty and sentencing them with death makes for a series of marvelous stories, doesn't it?"

The sudden change in Bobby Rose's stoic expression gave Widrington his answer.

"At this moment in Yugoslavia," Widrington said, "Hitler threatens to take a hundred lives for every German killed. Call it blackmail. Call it insanity. Call it what you like. It makes our situation at Graham rather thorny."

"I'm the son of Jewish immigrants," Bobby Rose said. "We owe our lives to this country. But there will be a story. Give me the truth and trust my discretion."

Widrington distrusted reporters. Like criminal attorneys, they lived by a different rule book. Bobby Rose had uncovered murder, intimidation and conspiracy on the watch of a colonel of the United States Army. Manning had served up a feast of explosive headlines. Widrington had to defuse the bomb. He must give a little to get a lot, firstly admitting that Nazi intimidation occurred in many POW camps. Segregation was the answer and the PMG was on it. After generalizing on re-education, he was ready to steer his discourse to the local conundrum and hopefully corral Bobby Rose into self-censorship.

"I'll trust you to do right by those the story places in peril," Widrington said. "We suspect some victims were so traumatized by the Nazis here at Graham that they took their own lives. As for the others, a long trial with circumstantial evidence will prove counterproductive. We've relocated the fanatics to Camp Alva in Oklahoma – ninety-four left yesterday."

"What? I've been parked outside those gates for three days."

Widrington stroked his ginger mustache. "You weren't there at midnight."

"Smart move, Colonel."

"Alva is reserved for the most extreme Nazi leaders and Gestapo agents. For all intents and purposes, they're in jail." A penitentiary Alva was not – Widrington had stretched the point. He had also neglected to mention the stolen medical files. "I'm also delighted to tell you that the hunger strike has come to a satisfactory conclusion. The strikers will be heading south."

Widrington paused and peered at Bobby Rose, speculating if any of this would influence the desired outcome. "I've been a soldier for more than twenty-five years. In that time, I've become a pretty good judge of character. You strike me as a humane individual; that's why I've been candid. I wish to make two requests of you."

"Colonel, you can make ten requests, but I can't promise to comply."

"This is all I ask. Number one: please don't sensationalize this story. Number two: please don't tarnish Colonel Manning's reputation."

"This *is* a sensational story, Colonel."

"It doesn't have to be."

The story appeared on page 2 of the *Rockford Star* and page 6 of the *Chicago Tribune:*

'POW STRIKE ENDS AT CAMP GRAHAM by Bobby Rose
In its fourth day, the War Department settled the grievances of 42 hunger-striking non-German POWs at Rockford's Camp Graham. Colonel Bruce Widrington of the Provost Marshal General's Office said, "After a thorough investigation we accepted the prisoners' complaints of Nazi violence against certain prisoners."

Regarding the high death rates at Graham, Colonel Widrington said, "The rates are higher than the average POW camp. We attribute this to raised levels of anxiety. The troublemakers, 94 of them, have been relocated to a camp designed for ardent Nazis in Oklahoma."

He said there was insufficient evidence to support charges of murder. Colonel Widrington became interim commander of Camp Graham upon the retirement of 64-year-old Colonel Thomas G. Manning.'
****

The inch-long incision in the seam of the deflated boxing speed bag worked flawlessly: Tony and Bo had folded and stuffed in every bill except a fiver and twelve singles. Looking over Bo's shoulder, Tony asked if they should make the hole bigger to cram in the last of their riches.

"Let's not," Bo said. The swelling in his face had receded, but the brownish-yellow bruising beneath both eyes look frightful. "The ball looks perfectly inflated. That's what we want." He had taken to folding the last few crimped greenbacks over the point of a nail file and pushing them, one by one, through the puncture until they disappeared.

Bo squeezed the seams together, and Tony sutured the incision with a needle and thread. The bag of dollars must have weighed three or four pounds. Bo backed up to the wall and tossed it to Tony.

"That catch won't do," Bo said. "Snag it like it's full of air."

The money ball went back and forth until it appeared as though they were playing catch with a feather weight. The loot was safe, provided the checkpoint guards didn't handle the bag.

Three days earlier, a right hook had sent the heavily favored sergeant to the canvas in the fourth round of the championship bout. The mother lode of winnings boosted Lucky Buck's treasury to $518 in cash, and a $122 dollars in coupons. Thirty-two dollars in loose change would stay behind. The entrepreneurs had offered attractive incentives to those willing to trade paper for coin, without much luck. Either there wasn't enough paper in the camp or the prisoners foresaw the same problem when their time came to leave.

They gathered their belongings on an auspicious date: June 6, 1944, the day the Allies landed on the beaches of Normandy. Tony and Bo were last in the queue. Marching double file, they moved slowly toward the guards and the Dobermans. Those ahead passed through with no trouble; the inspectors might be relaxed by the time Tony and Bo reached the checkpoint.

"Next!" a guard said.

Bo offered his kit bag to one MP, and then opened his arms to another. Tony's left hand held a camera and his duffel; the speed bag was in his right. They had rehearsed the handoff in their room, practicing all sorts of maneuvers depending on guard position and circumstance. The time had come to perform the sleight of hand.

The MP nodded to Tony.

Tony offered the duffel. The instant the MP's fingers touched it, Tony let the camera slip from his hand. The doctored camera casing, brittle as eggshell, splintered into pieces on the asphalt.

The MPs looked to the ground, and the speed bag was in the air. Tony dropped to his knees and howled, "Jesus Christus! Gott verdammt es! Ten-buck camera, kaput! Impossible fix. You grab bag. Jerk camera loose." He remained on all fours, picking up pieces and bemoaning misfortune.

Meanwhile, Bo, having caught the speed bag with one hand, held it against his hip, like a quarterback shielding the football from a defender. He sauntered to the end of the line as the guards converged on Tony. The one clutching Tony's duffel said, "Soldier, you have to get up. My partner's gonna pat you down while I check your stuff."

"Hold that man!" The shout came from the administration building. Lieutenant Dixon walked briskly towards the checkpoint.

Tony froze. Was that a smile on Dixon's face?

"I have a package for you, Lieutenant Babic."

"Is it mail?"

"Sort of. The new postmaster found hundreds of letters. We have to sort and screen. Anything for your troop, we'll forward to Ralston. Oops, you didn't hear it from me, okay? Your new home's in Louisiana, near the thriving metropolis of Ralston, population 7,000. POWs are half of that." He gave Tony a manila package.

Tony sank onto the vacant railcar seat next to Bo. The sender had included a note:

'Thanks for trusting me, Tony. You broke the story wide open. The savages had to be stopped. You did it.

I am enclosing a memento of your time in Rockford. They won't tell me where you are going, so you might want to write me when you get there. I have an ulterior motive. A journalist is a curious beast. Your experiences might make for another story.

Bobby Rose.'

"Man, oh, man," Bo said. "Look at all these news articles."

Tony handed him several that were paper-clipped together. "These are soccer stories. And these are on the strike ... and this one ... Bobby Rose's first article on Graham. The Yanks call it the 'tip of the iceberg'. That means much more lies below the surface. He's included clippings from other locals and the *Chicago Tribune*."

"Hell of a souvenir, Tony. One day you'll show your grandchildren. Tell them what old Gramps was up to in '44."

When the train reached cruising speed, they eased back in their cushioned seats, watching telephone poles go by, the wires held by green insulators on horizontal timbers. The sights beyond were less familiar – not the America they had seen on the rails to Rockford. Back then, the northeast tip of Illinois, along the shores of Lake Michigan, had been carpeted in white. Now all was green.

Click-clacking over the rail joints, the Illinois Central carried them past towns, cornfields, orchards and hog farms. The size of America was impossible to comprehend, and Tony never tired of the vast mosaic of lakes, rivers, woods and valleys. The idle hours in the night, he used for habitual reflections – ruminations about loved ones at home and those lost in the war. He had traveled from the other side of the world, and he was still alive despite overwhelming odds: eleven hours in a frigid sea, three bullets in the body, filthy hospital wards, a love affair with morphine and the pain of the abrupt breakup, the squalor of Algiers and Oran, and the murderous Nazis at Rockford.

Now, with luck, he would live out the rest of the war amid the tranquility of a benevolent Louisiana camp. The respite might be six months, a year at most. Then home. Should he expect a chaotic, war-torn country, a Stalinist puppet state, or an independent, democratic Croatia? The future was beyond his control. Although he lamented the tragic demise of Hermann Vogler, he could not help feeling the euphoria of a camp life free of brutality. He looked down the endless row of telephone poles, imagining the checkpoint scene where Dixon's MPs had fleeced Mauer of his money. He snickered at the image of Mauer's face contorted in rage. Then he laughed loud and long.

Chapter 23

June 1944
Ralston, Louisiana

Fifty miles south of Arkansas, in northern Louisiana, lay Ralston, a town surrounded by low rolling hills, scattered pines and cotton fields. Shortly after admittance, Tony found himself in the office of camp commander Captain Henry Hobson II. Hobson was hunched over his desk with a watchmaker's glass to his eye. The severe center part that split his salt-and-pepper hair made him looked like a grown-up Alfalfa, the kid Tony had seen in the Our Gang films at Graham.

Floor-to-ceiling shelves laden with books and neatly arranged trophies lined one wall of the office; a cleanly brushed blackboard and eight framed certificates covered most of another. Apart from a small American flag fluttering in the breeze from a humming fan, and framed photos of President Roosevelt and General Eisenhower, the office looked more like the den of a college dean than one of a career militarist.

Appearing cool and comfortable in a starched, long-sleeved khaki shirt that looked spanking new, Alfalfa raised his head to the perspiring prisoner and grinned. Then he adjusted the knot in his tie. As Tony neared, he realized that the sickly-sweet scent that invaded his nostrils was not hair cream but cologne – a ghastly cheap one.

Tony saluted. The grinning CO, who looked to be about fifty, returned the gesture.

"Hello Loot. Colonel Widrington's told me all about *you*. Hear you speak a dang good line of *Anglais*."

Hobson's drawl had Tony guessing, yet he deciphered enough to get the gist. "Good day, Captain. Very hot day, no?"

"To you it must feel like the Devil's steam bath. I'm used to humidity, of course, being raised in Savannah. Here we're ninety to a hundred through September. It can get hotter than an orgy of mice in a thick sock. Tonight might drop down to seventy if we're lucky."

Tony hadn't the foggiest idea what Hobson was talking about – had it to do with the temperature? Yes, that was it. "Rockford not hot like this," Tony said.

"Rockford's colder than Digger Darrel, Ralston's undertaker. I'd freeze my tail up there … Sit yourself over there." He extended his arm to a clean worktable. "When you came in, you must have thought I was blind as a bat. I'm not. I was checking out a 1910 George Washington two-cent stamp that's never been used."

"Stamp too old to put on letter?"

"Hah! That's a good one. Not too old – too costly. A collector's gonna pay at least a fifty for one so rare. This one's gonna enrich that silverware collection." With a thumb and two straight fingers, Hobson mimicked a gun and aimed at the trophies on the bookshelf. He released the imaginary hammer.

"Someone pay fifty cents for a two-cent stamp?"

Hobson slapped his thigh. "Not fifty *cents*. Fifty *bucks*! Sounds crazy, I know. We're a crazy bunch. Stamp collecting's like screwing – once you start, you can't stop. How 'bout a coffee, Loot? Do you like your coffee the way you like your women?"

"Sorry, Captain, I not understand."

"How do you like your women? Black? White? Sweet? I'm asking how you want your coffee made."

It was too hot for coffee, but Tony said, "I like coffee black."

"You're a rascal, you are. I'm gonna have to keep an eye on you. Relax, Loot, I'm joshing. Let me get serious and tell you about Camp Ralston. We've got twenty-eight hundred here, another thousand on the way – Frogs, Romanians, Wops, Czechs, Polaks and Slavs like you in the non-Kraut compound – compound number one. Krauts live in the other compounds. We've got a theater, woodwork shop, tennis courts, a library, loads of sports equipment, even a beer garden."

Tony smiled. "Not have beer garden at Graham." He was starting to get used to the dialect.

"The Army agreed to a beer garden because of the heat. Falstaff comes up from New Orleans. Three-point-two's the best we can do. Hah!"

And thus it went for the next hour. Hobson went over the camp rules, which mirrored those of Graham.

For a prison-of-war camp, Ralston seemed ideal. Cotton and cane needed harvesting, and plenty of open space discouraged escape. To avoid sticking out, a runaway would have to make it all the way to Shreveport, seventy miles east.

"Here, there are no factories," Hobson said. "Prisoners work the roads and the plantations. You won't do any of that. You and I will spend a heap of time together." He leaned closer and his eyes grew larger. "Loot, you're my new camp spokesman."

Tony pulled back, blinking erratically. "Me, Lagersprecher?"

"You should be happier than a tick on a fat dog's neck. First lieutenant's the top gun here. You speak English. You're a young buck, but Widrington thinks you're up to the task. There's only one condition, Loot: I don't want you gawking at my wife. Your predecessor messed with her. I had him shot."

Tony's jaw dropped.

"Hah. Got you again, Loot. I didn't kill the guy." Hobson's broad smile expanded, revealing his top row of even teeth, but for one. "I slapped his marbles between two bricks, that's all."

Another joke. What to make of Captain Henry Hobson II?

****

Weeks later, the mail confiscated by the Nazis arrived at Ralston. Tony's father described the dismal state of the family wine business. Vinograd Kralja had lost most of its Zagreb cafés, and Josip had resorted to selling door to door – a bottle here, one or two there. Aside from this, the Babics were well. But nothing came from Goran and this troubled Tony.

The mornings settled into peacefulness once the work crews departed on trucks and buses for the plantations. On this muggy morning, a hundred squawking starlings seemed determined to extinguish any hope of serenity. Fifteen minutes to eight, and already the mercury was above eighty – the poor devils in the steamy fields would be down to drenched undershirts or bare skin. Meanwhile, Tony puffed a cigarette on the shaded bunkhouse porch as he peered down the dirt road to the guardhouse. Today he would be supervising yard work at the Hobson residence.

The liberties accorded the Lagersprecher included a jeep and driver to get him around the 500-acre camp and beyond. He could visit any compound anytime, provided he was with his authorized driver, Corporal Billy 'Slim' Metcalf.

Bo stepped from the bunkhouse onto the porch and gave a loud fart by way of greeting. "Tony, we should get back into business."

Tony blew smoke into the cloudless sky. Then he said, "We've been through this. It's not worth the effort. No factories ... and field workers poor as dirt."

Bo didn't dispute that. He was thinking of Lucky Buck as a hobby to earn some extra coupons.

"For a hobby," Tony said, "you don't need me."

"I do. You have the connections, the run of the camp, access to 3,000 guys. My latest idea's a dandy. I want to put those god-awful cockroaches to work. Introducing ... drum roll, please ... the Lucky Buck Führer Derbies!"

"What the ...?

"Cockroach races! We put little dabs of colored paint on their backs so you know which one your money's on. All we have to do is dump them at one end of a long gutter and put a flashlight on their asses. They hate light – that's why they run like hell at the flick of a switch. First roach to the end wins. I've got some great runners – Rudolph Hitler, Bony Parts, Six-Leg Winnie, Messy Lenny, Uncle Joe, Uncle Sam, the Desert Fuck, Mister—"

"Okay Bo, I get it. Six-Leg Winnie is Churchill. The Desert Fuck is Rommel. Bony Parts and Messy Lenny? Who are they?"

"Napoleon and Mussolini."

Tony half laughed. "And Rudolph Hitler?"

"The Führer's long-lost brother – the kinder of the Hitler boys."

"These Führer Derbies ... are they games of chance?"

"Not likely – though I haven't quite figured how to stack the deck."

But you will. Hearing the rev of an engine, Tony craned his neck to the rising plume of brown dust 200 yards away. The disorderly flock of starlings moved to a quieter perch.

"Looks like your taxicab," Bo said. "Bet you a buck Slim has no license."

The jeep pulled up to the porch. "All set to go, Loot?" The constantly moving toothpick on Slim's tongue failed to hamper his delivery.

In Croatian, Bo said, "I'm expecting a full report on the captain's wife."

Rumors about Pinky Hobson were rampant among the POWs and Tony's curiosity had gotten the better of him.

Slim rode the clutch through the gates. Then, stuffing his cap between his chubby thighs, he gunned the gas pedal and wrestled the gearshift straight into third. The Army truck carrying the POW work crew loomed ahead, and Slim rode up to within six feet of its bumper before veering left and zipping past with his fist on the horn. He didn't ease off the accelerator until he came to the freshly-painted 'Welcome to Ralston' sign. Three blocks later, Ralston's main street, with its town hall, general store, movie house, gas station, bank, two churches and a school, was in his rearview mirror.

"Hank the Deuce rents the place," Slim shouted, glancing between the road and Tony. The toothpick twirled and jumped as if with a life of its own.

The engine was noisy, but Tony had heard him fine. "What means 'Hank the Deuce'?" Tony asked, in an equally loud holler.

"'Hank' is short for 'Henry,' like 'Loot' is short for 'Lieutenant'. Ace is one in cards, right? Well, deuce is two. Instead of saying Henry Hobson the Second, we say Hank the Deuce. He's one for nicknames, but he wouldn't want one for himself."

Slim was as amusing as the explanation. "The Dupree Manor is the most expensive home in the Ralston area," he said. "The owner lives in Baton Rouge now – folks say he kept the house for sentimental reasons. Edmond Dupree's bank account sure didn't need rent money."

Slim allowed the jeep's wheels to drift to the soft shoulder. He yanked left, forcing Tony right. "Sorry 'bout that, Loot. We're back on tar. So how'd Hank score the house? His Cajun queen paid a visit to old Edmond, and just like that, the Sutherlands moved out and the Hobsons moved in. That little Pinky moved faster than a bell clapper in a goose's ass. She got the place cheap. What do you think she had to do to get it?"

Tony burst into laughter. "Slim, you kid me."

"How else would she get 10,000 square feet and seven bedrooms, carriage house out back, stables and a fruit orchard? Folks 'round here say the Dupree Manor embodies the grandeur of the Old South. Up by that weeping willow, we make a left. See for yourself."

Slim steered through the stone columns down a long, winding driveway shaded by the limbs of massive oaks wreathed in streamers of Spanish moss. As he neared the loop, white patches of the mansion peeked through the greenery. Reaching the sprawling veranda, he took his foot off the gas but forgot to clutch. The jeep lurched forward, coughed twice and died.

Tony had never seen anything like the stately, black-shuttered, three-story white manor that stood amid a grove of trees that resembled the pines and magnolias of Croatia. And he had never seen anything like the short woman in high-heeled shoes and a pink-flowered cotton dress who was gazing down at them from the six-pillared veranda.

Slim wiped his forehead with the underside of his bare wrist. "Good morning, ma'am. This is Lieutenant Tony Babic. He's the new POW leader at the camp."

Tony stepped out of the open jeep and found himself at eye level with a plunging neckline and bountiful cleavage. "Good Morning, Mrs Hobson," he said. The last woman Tony had spoken to had been a broad-hipped Sicilian nurse with a shadow of a mustache. Pinky placed her hands on her hips and fashioned a lascivious smirk. At thirty-eight or forty, she was younger than her husband, a few pounds past slender and far from unattractive. She reminded him of a fading film star dressed for a society luncheon.

"Where are the others?" she drawled.

"They ain't but a couple minutes behind us, ma'am," Slim said. "Six, today – Loot's in charge of 'em."

"Well, bless Loot's heart," she said, waving at the low-hanging branches and shrubbery near the house. "I want this mess trimmed. I feel like I'm living in the Everglades. And when will the house be painted? The white's gone cream and the cream's gone flaky."

"As we speak, the duty office assembles a crew."

Tony's eyes followed the sway of Pinky's hips as she ambled into the house. How long had it been? His heart raced.

"Follow me, Loot. Joshua has tools in the barn for your crew. He's the stable boy ... Lucille Gooden's son. Lucille's the housekeeper."

Pine straw crackled beneath their feet as they rounded the house to the stables. The barn was cool and dim, the horse odor strong, though it was somehow an agreeable smell – more like damp leather than musty hay

210

and manure. Saddle blankets and tack hung on the wall, and hurricane lanterns dangled from rusty wires hooked to the rafter beams.

A young stableman in a leather apron was hammering a shoe onto a hind hoof of a big palomino. Gently, Joshua lowered the horse's hock and straightened.

"Good morning, Corporal Metcalf," he said, rubbing his arched lower back. "Yard tools are ready – rakes, scythes, sickles, clippers, mowers, bow saws, and shovels big and small. They're by the gazebo, with a stack of empty bushels for the debris." Joshua wore the face of a man eager to please. His nose was narrower and his lips thinner than the Negroes who loitered along the camp fence.

Slim introduced Tony. Joshua gave a cheerful nod.

Tony held out his hand. "Hello, Joshua. You call me Tony."

The inattentive would have missed the faint twitch in Joshua's eyes, but Tony caught the fleeting hesitation. Was Joshua taken aback by a German speaking English, or by the extended white hand of the enemy? Whatever the case, Joshua Gooden took that hand.

"Loot, I'm going out front to wait for the truck. Stay here till the guards bring your guys round."

Joshua reached for a brush and began making gentle strokes along the horse's face and thin forelock, taking care to avoid the eyes. The horse stood completely still while he brushed. Then, exchanging the smaller brush for a larger one, he began working the mane and tail with short, light strokes.

"All right, Winston, that's over with." Joshua's voice was now gentle. "Now for the part you like." He began going over the horse's coat with long, smooth strokes. Perspiration dripped from his brow. Finally, he tossed the brush aside, drew a deep breath, and put his damp cheek to the light yellow-gold sheen of the horse's neck. "There you go, big fellow." He patted the beast's shoulder with his palm. "Are you ready for the saddle?"

"Who ride?" Tony asked.

Joshua pulled out a rag protruding from his overalls hip pocket, shook some flecks of hay from it, and wiped the sweat from his face. "The lady of the house."

"Where she go?"

"Up that track through the orchard," Joshua said, laying a blanket on Winston's back. "It opens to plenty of trails beyond the peach orchard, Lieutenant."

"'Tony.' Please, you call me 'Tony.'"

Joshua flipped the girth and right stirrup over the top of the saddle and hoisted it onto the horse's back.

The question lingering in Tony's mind was sticky. He wasn't sure how he might pose it without insulting Joshua. Though he mentally rehearsed a couple of approaches, neither seemed right. Nonetheless, he decided to give it a go. "I have question. The way you talk ... the way you speak English ..."

"Winston doesn't like it when the girth is yanked tight," Joshua said. He pulled the strap through the ring and increased the pressure in increments. "See how he bloats himself. Watch this. I'm going to make him step forward." One step and Winston released a long whoosh of air, after which Joshua gave a modest tug to set the buckle. "As long as I can slide my fingers under the girth, he's happy. Now ... you were asking about my English."

"English very good ... much better than mine. How you learn so good English?"

Joshua broke into a gleaming white smile. "Why shouldn't my English be good? This is an English-speaking country."

Tony needed a moment to organize his thoughts. "But *your* English ... how you say ... very different from ... other Negro."

"I see," Joshua said. "For years, my mother worked for the Dupree's. We came here when I was three. I'm twenty-eight now. Mrs Dupree was a schoolteacher. She loved literature and enjoyed teaching grammar. She sure was a stickler for pronunciation. Mrs Dupree gave me an education. I read and write as well as college graduates. There aren't many Negro colleges in this country. I stayed here after junior school and worked as a stable boy and handyman. Before she died, she made Mr Dupree promise to keep us on."

"What of father?"

"My father volunteered for the First World War ... killed in France. Like many of our kind, he enlisted to bring dignity and respect to the Negroes for their service. Sadly, he sacrificed his life for a lost cause."

"I sorry hear this. You stay here because of mother?"

Joshua nodded.

"Joshua!"

Their heads turned to the barn doors.

"Is he ready?" Pinky had changed into a pink blouse, beige riding breeches and high leather boots. She was out of the fancy get-up but had not removed her makeup. Her eyes still had that same sultry look.

"I see you've met my stable boy," she said to Tony. "Bring him here, Joshua."

Joshua led the palomino into the heat of the day, and Pinky grabbed the reins. "Well, Shugah, how do you like this one?"

It occurred to Tony that she had forgotten his name. He studied the loose coal-black hair corralling her powdered cheeks, lined eyes and pouty, pink lips. "Look good," he said. *Horse, too.*

"Feel the luster of his hair," she said.

Tony breathed her scent while he stroked Winston's mane. When she reached for the pommel of the saddle, her left hip nudged his upper thigh. His knees weakened.

Pinky grabbed the mane unassisted, put her left foot in the stirrup and swung up into the saddle. She then pulled on the reins and trotted down the dirt path toward the peach orchard with Tony watching until she faded into the trees.

****

Usually they ate at noon, but today the prisoners had started late; in another three-and-a-half hours, their day would be over. The hot and hungry crew dropped to the grass under a sprawling oak for a meal of potato salad, roast pork and carrot sticks.

The slam of the rear screen door was loud enough for everyone to hear. "Ice tea for y'all." A pepper-haired plump woman in a white apron and billowing gray frock held a tray of glasses and an amber pitcher.

"Thank you," Tony called.

Ladders strode across the grass on the balls of his feet to retrieve the tea. He held the tray steady as he picked his way to his thirsty co-workers beneath the oak. But when the horse and rider emerged from the orchard, Ladders slowed his pace.

By the time Pinky guided Winston to the barn, his eyes were still fixed on the rider. He never saw the oak root protruding through the clumps of grass. Ladders' toe caught, and the weight in his hands threw him off balance. He dived forward like a swimmer leaping into the pool at the crack of the starter's pistol. The tray left his grip and its contents glided through the air as he belly-flopped onto the turf. Glasses crashed to the earth and tea gushed from the pitcher, splashing his mates.

"Damn it, Ladders!" Tony said.

Ladders shook his head, rolled up onto one knee and wiped dirt from his grazed chin.

Meanwhile, Pinky had reined Winston to within ten feet of the calamity. "Why, aren't *you* a clumsy clod," she said, peering down at Ladders.

"I ... I not see stick in ground."

"Root, not stick," she said. "You didn't see the root, because you were gaping at *me*. Never seen a woman before?"

Ladders' lips quivered. "Yes. I look you. You ... very beautiful." He was still on one knee, as if in a mournful bow.

"Of course I am – I'm from the South." Pinky drew the reins and guided Winston back to the barn while three others clambered to pick up the pieces. Tony chased after Pinky, but waited outside the barn.

She came out, dusting her thighs with her riding gloves.

"I am sorry, Mrs Hobson. Two glasses broken."

"That beanpole ogled me like a wolf. I've a good mind to report him to my husband."

"Please you understand. Two years, this man prisoner of war. Two years, he not see beautiful woman." Tony could see her wanton eyes needing more, so he gave it to her. "He not help himself. I think he ... how you say ... I think he hip-nut eyes?"

Pinky giggled. "This has nothing to do with that oaf's eyes. The word is 'hypnotized'."

"Yes. By you."

With that, she staged a boastful flaunt. "I have that effect on men."

Now it was Tony doing the gawking.

"You look like the cat's got your tongue," she said. "What's on your mind?"

"You say you want house painted. Man who fall ... we call him Ladders. He very good house painter."

"A painter named Ladders ... Why, that's just the funniest thing I've ever heard. Be my guest, Shugah. Bring me a team of painters."

Chapter 24

Tony had double-timed it from the postal exchange to barrack 4, knowing that Bo wouldn't be in their room. On the radio, Bing Crosby and the Andrews Sisters were singing the Hit Parade favorite, *Don't Fence Me In*. Tony and Bo hadn't been looking for a radio, but for eleven coupon dollars, they couldn't say 'no' to a Transitone. Tony lowered the volume.

Having slithered up to the headboard, he propped his head on two pillows and unfolded the letter. Halfway through the second paragraph, he was off the bed and on his feet, pacing like an expectant father. By the third read, he was back on his cot, pausing after each phrase and reflecting on what might lie between the lines. The letter fell on the blanket and his eyes closed to reveal a place where the mountain breeze swept his hair and freshened his lungs. There he heard rustling leaves and birdsong and smelled pine sap and wild rose. He had gone back to the day Sarajevo held its breath – that October Sunday when God halted the gunfire. 'This is how the world should be,' she had said.

Through the mist, her svelte figure floated toward him. Her lips curled in a delicate smile; her chestnut eyes, oval and moist, beckoned him but rendered his limbs useless. He felt the stroke of fingers on his skin, the warmth of arms pulling him close and finally, the sound of her voice, each word murmured with the sensitivity of the moment. Clasped together as one, they glided in a land of make-believe.

The twang of fingers plucking slow blues on a guitar returned him to Louisiana. Katarina's letter was as personal as it was implausible. He was about to put the letter away, when Bo burst in, dripping sweat.

"How do you work a bag in an oven? The gym smells like a hog farm on a still day ... a letter, eh? From Tata?"

"From the girl in Sarajevo."

Bo swabbed his head with a towel, and then lunged for the letter.

Tony whipped it away, immediately regretting he hadn't said the letter was from his father.

"What did she say?"

Tony wasn't going to read the letter to Bo, but he wasn't averse to talking about Katarina. "I just don't get it. Back in Zagreb, she couldn't stand the sight of me. Now she says she loves me – claims she lit a candle for me every day while I was missing."

"That's women – they can't stand you till the second you're gone."

"The question is, why now? I haven't seen her for a year. She could have written months ago. She didn't, and now this."

"Do you love her?"

"The last time we were together," Tony said in a weakened voice, "I was set to take her on a picnic blanket in the fresh air. Then I thought of her father – 1941 he died, with me trying to stop the bleeding. Ever since, his spirit is my shadow – in a good way, a very good way. Major Kirilenko got me out of some tight spots. I couldn't take his little girl for my selfish pleasure. If I'd been in love with her, it might have been different."

"Keep thinking 'bout her and you'll be as randy as a caged bitch in heat. Stay the course on Pinky. Lucky Buck's taking bets you'll nail her by month's end."

"Put your dough on Ladders. She's got a thing for string beans – why, I don't know."

"I saw him heading for the latrines when I came in," Bo said. "Bet he's giving Pinky a hand right now."

Chuckling, Tony said, "By now the applause will be over."

"Don't be so sure. Ladders is capable of two or three standing ovations."

"No doubt, he's obsessed with her. I warned him to keep his pecker in his pants or Hobson's going to troll for alligators with it. I don't think Ladders heard a word I said."

****

Four cockroach derbies attracted a barrack-full of spectators wedged along both sides of a twelve-foot section of rain gutter. Regrettably, the roaches proved ingenious and unreliable, either jumping the rails or playing dead in the stretch. Rigging the race and setting odds? Bo would have been better off taking wagers on their mating habits.

"Little critters fuck all day and eat all night," he'd said to Tony. Bo was right. Barrack 4 became so overrun with the offspring of Boney Parts, Six-Leg Winnie, and Chuck da Gull that fumigators triple-dosed

216

every corner and crevice with heavy-duty pesticide. The roaches retreated, but within twenty-four hours the other inhabitants came down with skin and eye irritations. Five guys were hospitalized for hives and blisters.

Even with the derby's collapse, Bo's entrepreneurial spirit could not be fumigated. Every second day, he'd have a new profit-making scheme. Today, he suggested they sell vodka to the locals, arguing that there was always money for hooch. "A still's easy to make. We can get sugar beets, molasses, potatoes, and all kinds of grains right here from the kitchens."

"Hooch isn't like cigarettes," Tony said. "We screw up in the distillation, someone goes blind."

"I'm not hearing any ideas from you," Bo chided.

"You're about to hear one."

Three months, and the novelty of Camp Ralston had worn thin on Tony. Perhaps it was Katarina's letter that rekindled thoughts of home and civilian life. Classes and games that had sustained him in the past, no longer pacified. He had considered escape and – even more dangerous – bedding the captain's wife. Business was safer. Business offered ample risk and reward.

Tony asked Bo if he'd lost his medals to GIs in Africa.

"They took from some of the guys," Bo said, seemingly perplexed. "What are you getting at?"

"I'm thinking war souvenirs. With coupons, we buy uniform buttons and crests from anyone who'll sell them. We replace those buttons with regular ones. Once we have enough silver and brass, we sell them to civilians." Tony opened the newspaper to the inside back page. "They call this the 'classifieds'. It's where people sell things. Anyone can advertise in the classifieds. The *Ralston News* charges twenty cents a line. People sell stoves, iceboxes, pumps, books, tools. We sell Wehrmacht mementos."

The smile on Bo's face could not have been wider.

****

The foreman of the paint crew insisted that the mansion be sanded before priming and finishing, but he refused to estimate the time it would take to sand 10,000 square feet. For a man bitten by desire, time was incidental.

"Ladders, I know what's going on," Tony said. "She's playing a cat-and-mouse game with you. "You're up there, like an eagle on the high

217

rungs of the ladder, ogling her through the windows. If she didn't know you were out there frothing at the mouth, she wouldn't be parading from room to room for hours in scanty attire."

"How do you know that, Lieutenant?"

"Never mind how I know. You're playing with fire."

The current schedule had Bo supervising the yard workers, peach pickers and painters on Mondays and Tuesdays, and Tony handling Wednesday through Saturday. Tony relished his conversations with Joshua. He'd learned that the South was its own country from 1861 to 1865 and there was a war. Joshua said the social borders hadn't moved. Was the South anything like Croatia within the Yugoslav federation before the German invasion? No, not really, Joshua had said.

Presently, the decline of cotton and mechanization was ending an unjust partnership known a sharecropping, and though Joshua seemed happy about that, he said that created another problem – unemployed field workers. To some, the opportunity was packing up and moving to the industrialized North.

Today, on hay bales in the barn, they continued that dialogue on northern migration. Tony spoke of Quaker Oats and Sycamore Preserves in Illinois. "Many jobs, and good pay if you not POW."

Though educated and capable, Tony reckoned Joshua for a man living in the South's past. By Joshua's own admission, he hadn't used his education to improve his lot in life. Tony might be able to help with that.

"I have idea to sell goods to Americans. I want to run advertising in Ralston newspaper."

Joshua's expression resembled that of a father grinning at a son's notion of becoming president of the United States.

"In Africa detention camp," Tony said. "GIs tear medals and buttons from our tunics. So I think civilians also want war souvenir. I can get a hundred metal buttons and five, maybe ten Iron Cross. Iron Cross not dime a dozen, you know. I want you to make classified for me."

Joshua frowned. "Are you asking *me* to place an ad?"

"I give you money for that."

Joshua showered Tony with questions. What was the ad to say? What would Tony charge for the souvenirs? Where would he get them? How would they be delivered?"

The queries were a good omen. "I not sure what we say. We charge fifty cents for brass button, five dollars for Iron Cross. What you think?"

Joshua shrugged his shoulders.

"We get from POWs. Don't have many. You know, low supply, high demand."

"Where do they send the money, and how do they get the buttons?"

Smirking, Tony stared at Joshua and Joshua giggled. "You want me for that too," Joshua said. "I could be thrown in jail for doing business with my country's enemy."

"This is not selling guns. Our goods harmless. Stuff people want. If trouble, we say I give you souvenirs. Gift from friendly POW is good for international relations."

Joshua had a faint smile on his face, but he was shaking his head.

"Joshua, I give you good share of profit."

"It's not that I don't appreciate the fact you want to do business with me. I just can't—"

"You think I like sharecropper, that I cheat you," Tony said. "I not cheat you. I tell you all costs first. Bo and I pay men for buttons. We pay for classified, for stamps. You get paid put classified, pack and post. I come back and explain costs."

"I'm not your man."

"Bo and I make $400 in Rockford camp. Why not here? You our man. You smart and honest."

"Sorry, Tony."

"Why Negro not want to make a buck?" Tony couldn't have posed a more piercing question.

Joshua picked up a shovel and walked out of the barn. He would change his mind, of this Tony was sure.

****

From just three barracks, Bo and Tony accumulated over a hundred buttons and six Iron Cross medals. Stoked by the accumulation of inventory, Tony presented the plan to Joshua while Bo, who happened to be with him that day, kept an eye out for Slim at the stables window.

Tony said the ad would reach 3,000 readers. "We find out how many send us money. Then we know how many souvenirs we need for *Shreveport Times*." Bo had taught him well – Tony was thinking big:

150,000 homes would receive the *Times*. Wearing a look of confidence, Tony said, "Only need one ad."

Bo turned away from the smudged and fly-specked window. "One ad and Hank the Deuce not worry," he said. "Show Josh my *Ralston News* estimate."

They had paid five cents each for the buttons and fifty cents per Iron Cross. The profit before administration was estimated at $11.50.

"Administration is you, Josh," Bo said. "Three dollars and eighty cents, your pay for ad, pick up order, pack and mail."

"You get same profit me and Bo," Tony said. "We make you equal partner."

As though unsure he had heard correctly, Joshua repeated the word 'equal'.

"Worth it to us," Tony said. "When we advertise in Shreveport, Baton Rouge and New Orleans, you need help packing. You hire others. Pay them from your share. Still much profit left for you. We have deal?"

Joshua stood in silence.

"Without you, we have no business," Tony said.

The remark seemed to break the stableman's spell, for he responded as might any businessman. "How did you come up with the sales figures?"

"Shot in the dark," Tony said, borrowing a metaphor from Hobson. "Bo and I think one or two percent of people who read *Ralston News* buy souvenir. We guess forty orders. We have deal?"

"I could be arrested, you know," Joshua said. But his right hand was extended. There was more. From his shirt pocket, he pulled out a small square of cardboard. "See if you like this: 'Authentic German Army Souvenirs. Uniform brass buttons $0.25, five for $1.00. Iron Cross medals $2.00, while they last. Send payment to Wehrmacht Souvenirs, PO Box 2120, Ralston, La.' People won't know what 'Wehrmacht' means. Doesn't matter – it creates an air of legitimacy."

Tony took a moment to make sure he understood. Then he nodded his head, smiling. "Bo, you like this?"

Bo answered in Croat. "Do you really like the ad or are you saying that to please the nigger?"

Tony glanced at Joshua and then he glared at Bo. "You're spouting Croat and suddenly that word comes out of your mouth. He knows we're talking about him. I expect better of you."

"Okay, Tony. Okay. No disrespect meant. It won't happen again. Can we talk prices? I'm thinking fifty cents on the buttons and five bucks on the Crosses."

Tony reverted to English. "Joshua, Bo and I talk price. He says we ask too little. I think he right. But we don't want to piss off POWs. We don't want them to read paper and think we cheat them. Maybe we charge higher price in newspapers they not see. For now, I say try this. Maybe no sales at all. Who knows?"

From every pocket, Tony and Bo pulled out 122 buttons, six Iron Crosses and a Yankee dollar for advertising.

****

Tony had put it off long enough. Sitting with his back against the chain-link fence in a quiet corner of the soccer field, he reread Katarina's love letter. Then he penciled "October 8, 1944" at the top of the sheet of lined paper:

'A year ago, I was wounded and swimming for my life. I didn't know an angel was praying for me. At one time I was a leper to you. I still don't know what changed your mind. I am no longer the man you think you love. The war has changed me. I cannot say how much of my old self is left. My heart is shattered by the loss of men I loved. My soul suffers from the sights I have seen. When I came to America, I thought I was done with war. I was wrong. I had to wage war against camp Nazis. Life in Ralston is better. Your confession touched me. I wish to reciprocate, but not as you might expect. The first time we met I handled the explanation of your father's death, badly. Inside, I was struggling to hold myself together. I loved your father. He died in my arms, my hands covered in his blood. He defied orders and retreated from Kraljevo to save the lives of his men, and he gave his own. Ever since, he has saved me many times. His spirit has guided me through some grave situations. I cannot say the same for Rado. My life in Croatia after the war will depend on the political situation. Goran hasn't written. You must have told him of your love for me. You asked if my desire for you at the picnic was more than male yearning. It was, but that was long ago.'

****

221

The classified ad in the *Ralston News* looked better than Tony had imagined, especially the bold newsprint heading, 'AUTHENTIC GERMAN ARMY SOUVENIRS'. He couldn't wait to show Bo, who was at the Dupree Manor with the painting crew. But, at the 1730 roll call, no one from the paint crew was back in the camp. Forty minutes later, Tony heard a jeep screech to a halt outside the barrack.

"There's trouble, Loot," Slim said. "Hank wants to see you. Your painter's misbehaved."

"Ladders?"

"More like Ladder*less*. It's bad, Loot. Good thing I'm watching your back. First we visit the infirmary."

Slim led Tony to a room guarded by two young MPs. "Bo's in there," Slim said. "Ladders is in the ward. Make it quick. Then we're off to see the Deuce."

The moment Bo saw Tony, he erupted in uncontrolled hilarity. "You won't believe it. Straight-laced Ladders." A fresh surge of laughter besieged Bo.

"Bo! I haven't the time. What happened?"

"Oh, my God. Okay, I'll try. Best story ever. He was high up the ladder—" Bo, having turned scarlet, dropped his head and wiped tears from his eyes.

"Spit it out! I have to explain to Hobson. Is Ladders hurt?"

Bo sat up. "He's … going to be okay … not hurt badly. How the hell am I to get through this? Okay, okay. He's twenty-five feet up, an arm's length to the right of the bathroom window. He's painting and gaping inside at the same time. You know why. Anyway, he sees Pinky's reflection in the big mirror behind the sink. This is where it gets good. Once he sees her in a get-up of heels, corset, garter belt and pink stockings, his dick springs to attention. She knows he's watching; pretends she doesn't and starts rubbing her arms with lotion, lifting her tits, fondling – that sort of stuff. Now, get this: she hikes one foot up on the toilet bowl, sucks her middle finger, and then … you ready for this? You know what she does?"

By now, Tony's time constraint was secondary. "Tell me."

"She goes for her bush! Her eyes are shut, she's moaning and cranking away. The window's open so he can hear her. 'Course, he's ready to fire

222

in his pants. Then, her eyes spring open, and she stares right at him. You think she hits the brakes? No fucking way!"

"Jesus Christ!"

"Oh, yeah, she was screaming for Jesus, all right!"

"Where'd you get this? You weren't there." Tony knew that Bo was not above embellishment. Ladders couldn't have furnished Bo with such minutiae. Regardless, Tony wasn't going to call him on it and diminish a glorious tale.

"I spent a half hour with him here. Made him spill the details and then had him go over it again. 'Course, he didn't like me laughing. Said he's put Pinky in a jam. I did my best to look worried ... failed miserably."

"You said Ladders was hurt."

"I'm getting to that. So what does he do when he sees her in heat? He pops his fly and gives a solid salute through the rung in the ladder. He's got a paint can and paintbrush in one hand and his dick in the other. The ladder wobbles to his tempo. Pinky sees what he's up to, and she gets even more wound up. So now you've got two of them in a frenzy."

"A fucking frenzy."

"Oh yeah. Everything's fine until Pinky arches her back and Ladders loses sight of those big eyes. He cranks that loon neck of his and loses his balance. Picture this, Tony. His dick's in his hand and the ladder slips to the side by a couple of inches. He either doesn't notice or doesn't give a shit. He sure did once the ladder came sliding down the side of the house, with him on it. White paint splatters everywhere. He would have broken his neck if not for the big hedge. Anyway, it takes his weight and he bounces off it ... ends up on his back, squirming in wet paint. The guy's on his back covered in white slop and his dick's out. By this time, Pinky's out the door, running to him, half naked. When she gets to him, he's blue."

"Figured that," Tony said through his own howls of laughter.

"His *face* is blue. He can't breathe. So she straddles him and pushes like hell on his chest. She pumps a whoosh of air out of him, and he wails like a sick cow. What with her pumping and Ladders wailing away, it looks like she's fucking him on the front lawn."

"Collapsed lung?"

"Cuts and bruises, twenty-four stitches, three busted back ribs and a fractured wrist."

Tony was laughing as hard as Bo. "Which wrist?" He couldn't help himself.

Bo relapsed into another bout of laughing fits but between the hoots, he managed to say there was more. "Brace yourself for this. Hank the Deuce left camp early and was coming up the driveway. He's driving into the circle while Pinky's pounding life back into Ladders. I got there just as Hank was dragging her into the house. I had our guys lift Ladders into the truck."

****

Hobson didn't even offer Tony a chair.

"I'm mad as a mule chewing bees," he said. "It's rape."

Tony reckoned Hobson was horrified that the story would get out and he'd be the town's laughingstock. A story like this wasn't easily suppressed. She was on top; that couldn't be rape. "Captain, please understand, Corporal Lipinski in prison camp nearly two years. Your wife a beautiful woman. Through window he see her, not able to control himself. So he … you know … Yes, better he do that in camp latrine, not on ladder." He felt the laughter coming but managed to keep a straight face. "He fall off ladder and Mrs Hobson help him breathe. She good woman do that. She—"

"Don't piss on my leg and tell me it's raining!"

"I not bullshit, Captain. People laugh at Ladders, not Pinky."

"Mrs Hobson to you! He'll pay for this – just like the last son of a bitch who got into her knickers. Two shakes of a sheep's tail, he was in Alva."

"Not Alva, Captain – Nazis kill him."

"That's Corporal Jerk-off's problem. I'm classifying him a Nazi zealot. When he's fit to travel, he's gone!"

"Not fair, Captain. Please, you reconsider."

"No chance. All POW work at the manor is cancelled."

If a moratorium on work duty continued, the link to Joshua and Wehrmacht Souvenirs would be severed, though that issue was less important. The painstaking task of changing the mind of a humiliated husband would be difficult.

Tony allowed three days to pass in the hope that Hobson's fury might subside. And perhaps it had, for Hobson granted him a ten-minute meeting. He used his time to describe the terror under Arnim and Mauer at Camp Graham. These killers knew Ladders, and for his role in the hunger strike, they would torture, maybe kill him.

"More humane you hang Corporal Lipinski here than give him to Nazis," Tony said.

"Good idea!"

****

The work stoppage at the manor was short-lived, affording Tony the opportunity to take Ladders' case directly to Pinky. He planned to see her once he got the Ladder-less paint crew working. But first, he'd talk business with Joshua.

They were barely underway when the barn door opened. Pinky stood in the sunlight. The clinging open-necked cotton dress rode up her hips as she strutted inside. For a woman with short, plumpish legs, her strides were long. Her calculated moves confirmed her love of the tease.

"Joshua, that will be all," she said. "Return when I leave."

Her big eyes and heavy fragrance had Tony tingling. If he was ever to enjoy the charms of Pinky, this would be the moment. But he was here for Ladders, not for himself. "Mrs Hobson, about Corporal Lip—"

"Your painter's behavior was lewd. Fancy a Peeping Tom doing that in the presence of a lady dressing for dinner. I heard tapping on the windowpane. I thought it was a pesky squirrel. Now everyone knows the squirrel was bald." Her lips formed into an ever-so-slight smirk.

Tony fought hard to contain his mirth. Was storytelling one of her pastimes? Though Ladders' predicament was urgent, he would let her play the game and enjoy every minute of it.

"The tapping got louder," she said. "I thought someone was hammering nails into the house. I wasn't far from the truth." Polished pink fingernails hugged the front of her thighs, lightly clawing the fabric of her dress. "The tapping came from the ladder – your man beating his drum."

Tony's gut tightened and his palms moistened.

She told her side of the story – how the ladder slid down, leaving a twelve-foot scratch on the fresh paint and how she forgot to cover herself. "I know how that looked to the workers: a Southern belle in her knickers, spread-eagled on a man with—"

"Everyone knows you try to help Ladders."

She threw Tony a scorching gaze. "Everyone 'cept my husband."

"Captain Hobson still not believe story?"

She sniggered, and said, "He's coming round."

"Mrs Hobson, Captain wants to send Ladders to Camp Alva. You can convince him to change mind. Will you do this for Ladders? Nazis *kill* Ladders there."

"Call me Pinky."

"You do this for Ladders?"

"I'm working on it. Henry needs two more nights sleeping alone. That should do it. Are *you* tired of sleeping alone?"

At that moment, Tony realized that the wetness on her upper lip was not from the mugginess in the barn. As for her eyes ... he'd seen the look before – Roza had been the first of many to summon him that way. What was he to do – disregard the possibility of a bus ticket to Alva, and certain death at the hands of the Holy Ghost, or accept her invitation?

He grabbed her by the waist and brought her close, fastening his lips to hers. Feeling her fingers clutching the hair at the back of his head, he tightened his embrace, and like a wrestler, he lifted her off the ground. Her legs came around him, and he waddled towards the hay.

"I can't breathe," she said. "You'll break me."

Gently, he lowered her onto a hay bale, hiked her dress, and yanked her panties free. Her big eyes grew bigger, and those pink polished nails dug into his back as he bucked and snorted in gluttonous abandon, mindful of the tears spilling from the corners of her eyes and streaming to her ears.

When both their gasps subsided, he rolled off her and lay on his back in the flattened hay on the floor, seconds later murmuring, "Am I tired of sleeping alone? Yes, Pinky, I'm sick and tired of sleeping alone."

She threw her head back and giggled. "Well aren't you a naughty boy. Next time, you take it slow and easy in my four-poster."

****

The ad in the *Ralston News* generated only ten orders. Eight envelopes contained paper money; two included coins taped inside folded cardboard. One person sent $6.00 for ten buttons and three medals. Another ordered twenty brass buttons. The orders generated $23.50 in sales, with a profit of $11.04 to the three partners. Tony and Bo had another moneymaker on their hands.

Their next move was to procure sufficient inventory to supply Louisiana's major population centers. By the time the offer appeared in the dailies of Shreveport, Baton Rouge and New Orleans, they had added another $280 to their treasury, but they had also canvassed every barrack in the camp. Wehrmacht Souvenirs was out of inventory. How would they supply the other thirty cities on their list, beginning with Atlanta, then Dallas and Memphis?"

Ralston's 2,000-square-foot workshop provided an assortment of woodworking tools for the men to use at any time of the day. Table saws, chisels, lathes and four jigsaws would help solve Bo and Tony's supply challenge.

POWs began carving and chiseling swastikas and Iron Crosses from two-inch squares of ¾-inch pine. The next step was sanding, applying brown shoe polish, and buffing to create an ice-smooth luster. 'POW Heinz Schultz – 1944' appeared on the back of each trinket. By the first week of January 1945, Bo and Tony had four thousand authentic POW-made souvenirs.

Chapter 25

March 1945
Zagreb, Independent State of Croatia

While Colonel Christoph Schwanitz tended to pressing, last-minute matters at the Gestapo office, Luka and the Chameleon lay naked on his bed at the Esplanade Hotel. Tonight would be Schwantiz's last night with his girl and she was damn glad of it. Tomorrow he would return to the Fatherland for good.

She heard Luka crunch on a piece of hard candy and watch him swirl the broken pieces with his tongue. "So the Russians want to be first to take Berlin," she said.

"They can have it," Luka said. "It'll keep them busy while we hunt the fascists here. Next week our army takes Sarajevo. Then it's Zagreb. By May we'll have every inch of Yugoslavia. I'm going to be a busy boy, settling scores. Your boyfriend's a warm-up."

The Chameleon eyed the trail of black undergarments strung on the floor between the window and the bed. "Old Christoph's counting on a last rumba. He's in for a shock. That pig will never touch me—"

The telephone rang twice. "That's my second costume call of the night," she said. "He's in the lobby. I've got five minutes."

"You don't want to disappoint," Luka said. "Get him hot and leave the rest to me."

****

Christoph Schwanitz inserted the key in the lock with the stealth of a burglar. The bolt released with a barely audible click, and his shoulder nudged the door just wide enough for him to pass. Inside he crept, a gift-wrapped box with a gold bow concealed behind his back.

When he looked to the window, his jaw dropped. His shapely stiletto-heeled woman, clad in a strapless, spiral-boned corset, and an SS visor cap, was peering five floors down. As his eyes raced from her nylon-stocking calves to the garter belt, to the smooth skin of her back, he stumbled back a step, his backside closing the door.

Ella turned around. Her spayed fingers gripped her hourglass waist, and for the first time since entering the room, Christoph Schwanitz blinked.

"Is this what you prescribed, Colonel?" she asked, doing a pirouette.

"I will miss you so much. I wish it were possible to take you with me. Perhaps I can put off my trip by a day." But no, he would not, having delayed twice already. He'd seen the flurry of uniforms trudging through driving snow to the train station. Each day, more left. It would only get worse.

He tossed the package onto the bed. "Open that later," he said as he fumbled with the buttons of his water-beaded trench coat.

Like a panther gaping at prey, she slinked forward. But suddenly, he felt something strike the back of his head. He tried to steady himself, but his legs crumbled.

Schwanitz shivered the moment he resumed consciousness. He felt tightness around his wrists and ankles and when he tried to move, his eyes popped. He was roped to the bedposts. Looking over the slope of his portly, bare belly to the foot of the bed, he saw the contempt on her face. Standing next to her was a snickering guy that looked like a Slav.

"Your day of reckoning," she said. "Surely you knew, or were you too stupid to see it? Why else would I fuck scum like you? I'm a whore, Christoph, but this whore sells herself for information. And you paid me well. The information in your briefcase saved thousands, including our leader. Marshal Tito thanks you for warning him of the raids on Jajce and Drvar." She moved behind Luka, put her arms around his waist, and nibbled his ear. "This is my fiancé. His name is Luka Lipovac."

Schwanitz's shivers suddenly erupted into jolting spasms.

"Guess he's heard of you," she said to Luka. Peering back at Schwanitz, she said, "I can confirm Luka's penchant for sadism. That sock in your mouth should help keep you quiet."

Schwanitz yanked on the ropes tethering his arms and legs. When his eye caught the shimmer of light on the blade in Luka's hand, he rocked the bed with such vigor that the headboard banged the wall.

Luka gave a crooked smile. "Tell him the guy next door's going to think he's up to his old tricks."

Ella translated into German and then she screamed, "Ja, Christoph! Ich will Mehr! Mehr … Mehr … Mehr!"

Her screams for more roused hearty laughter from her accomplice, who had laid the six-inch blade on Schwantiz's sweating chest. "Get me those gloves, Ella."

Luka stretched the fingers of each glove. Then he put them on, brought his hands together, and clapped once. "A dainty little worm is about to lose its skin."

Schwanitz closed his eyes, knowing what would come next. And when it did, he convulsed for the better part of a minute before falling unconscious.

"Job's done, Ella. Pack your things. If I *was* a sadist, I'd have taken my time."

While she packed her clothes and toiletries, he cleaned out the victim's billfold. "Hey Ella, there's enough money here to buy you a wedding ring." He placed the Gestapo hat on Schwanitz's head, and they slipped out, leaving the 'Do Not Disturb' sign on the doorknob.

****

The fascist retreat in Yugoslavia came as Luka had predicted. Pavelic and his top-echelon fled to Austria, where they surrendered to the British. But days before the partisans marched on Zagreb, the Austrian border was closed. Those fleeing retribution paid for their evil with their lives, and Luka participated in the slaughter, having accompanied Tito's army to the Austrian border.

Under State Security Chief Rankovic, intelligence tentacles spread to every city, town, hill and valley of the reclaimed Slavic states. They worked information lists, and rounded up dissidents, either killing them without trial or incarcerating them in the concentration camps constructed by their enemy. Rankovic's headhunters – the SDB or Sluzba drzavne bezbednosti, [State Security Service] – suppressed every attempt to thwart the 'peaceful development of socialism'. They searched homes, tapped phones, intercepted mail, jailed without trial, deported or executed whoever they pleased. The partisans had cleansed Yugoslavia of fascism, but not erased terror.

****

It had been four years. At last, it was safe for Katarina's return to Zagreb. Over the winter, her mother's hair had thinned and her skin had turned a haunting yellow. Without an appetite, Maria Kirilenko had withered and died a week after the war ended. Katarina was back in Zagreb to visit St Mark's Church and light a candle with her aunt.

But there was more. Katarina wanted to honor a promise she had made to herself – a personal meeting with Goran once the war was over. She had allowed the relationship go on too long. It could have ended so much sooner – that letter she'd ripped up. But, when she received Tony's response to her confession of love, she wrote another, asking Goran for his understanding of an amicable parting – one in which they could remain friends. Goran never responded.

Other than the absence of snow, enemy uniforms and military vehicles, Zagreb was much as Katarina had left it on that frightful day. The city's buildings remained proud and unscathed. People walked along the lanes and sidewalks, and trams screeched on the tracks. Shops looked the same, but behind their windows was a scarcity of merchandise or an overstock of non-essentials such as kerosene lamps and hand tools. Foodstuffs were in short supply. Stores rich in the right inventory were reserved for the party elite.

A graying Dr Skoda opened the front door to a young lady in a navy blue skirt and matching jacket. Even in tough times, a seamstress with ingenuity could manage to look stylish. She saw that he did not recognize her. He likely remembered a terrorized child.

"It's Katarina, Dr Skoda," she said through a guarded smile. "Katarina Kirilenko."

"Yes, of course. You look splendid. Let me look at that jaw ..." He placed his thumb and forefinger on her chin. "It's healed perfectly."

"I am grateful to you for that."

They had spoken little during her weeks of convalescence, and today's efforts at small talk were almost as awkward. She came to know him as a skilled and well-intended practitioner, but not one for conversation beyond medical matters. She told him why she had come, and he informed her that Goran no longer taught at the university, amongst other things.

"Does he still live here?"

The doctor hesitated. "You could say that. He's taken a senior job with the party. I'm not pleased by it, but when the party calls, one doesn't refuse. They want me at a hospital in Belgrade. I expect to go in the summer. Goran received a choice appointment. You know he served as a partisan, don't you?"

"Yes ..." Her eyes drifted to the portrait of Monica Skoda. "I admired that painting every day I was here. There is so much in it. The mood and expression change depending on where you are standing." A thankful type of smile preceded his sigh. Sensing his sorrow, she changed the subject and asked if Goran liked his job.

Dr Skoda shrugged. "He keeps to himself. Are you a party member?"

"As you know, I owed them, and I've paid my debt," she said with downcast eyes.

"Quid pro quo ... Have you been able to put that terrible misfortune behind you?"

She pulled on the sleeve of her blouse and fidgeted with a ringlet of hair. "I do my best."

"Goran works for the Interior Ministry as regional records director of state security. They handle citizenship, passports and cross-border traffic."

"How is he?" she asked.

"He was devastated that you called off the engagement. Still is. My son is a troubled man. He has been that way before he met you."

The engagement was Goran's fabrication, but Katarina chose not to set the record straight. The truth would only add to a father's heartache. "Will he accept me as a friend?"

"That would be a compromise. As you must surely know, Goran isn't one to compromise."

Katarina asked if she could return later when Goran was home.

Dr Skoda gave an expression of perplexity. "Goran could be here at six or at twelve. His office address is on this card. Go there. He's usually at his desk by eleven."

Smiling, she said, "Good hours."

"Not really, if you think about it."

****

Katarina had met Josip and Jelena Babic but once, at Vinograd Kralja when she was eighteen. Her troubles had started shortly after that. Would they ever end? Stomach gurgling, she steadied herself on the railing at the steps of the flat, and ascended the stairs.

Like any Croat mother, Jelena said Katarina was too thin, and insisted that she have some freshly-baked apple strudel. Over strudel and coffee, the three of them discussed the matter of mutual interest.

"The letter I sent to Rockford," Katarina said, "must have gone astray. So I posted a duplicate to Ralston. He replied to that one. I've written fifteen since. He's sent two. Now I know why – it's only right that the permitted letter a week go to you. I still worry for him."

"He's like new," Jelena said.

And the injuries you don't see? "I'm so pleased to hear that."

Notwithstanding Katarina's buoyant response, Jelena may have detected unrest because she swung her head to Josip. "He sounds happy, doesn't he?"

"You never know," Josip said. "He's a son who wouldn't worry his parents no matter the circumstance. The same is true of us – we tell him life in Croatia will be tolerable under the Communists. Tony's *current* well-being isn't the concern. It's his return that keeps me awake at night. The partisans are out for the blood of those who wore Croat uniforms. If Tony were linked to the Ustashe, he'd be dead the day he stepped on this soil. They won't like that he was a Croat lieutenant. I really don't know what to expect. We're lucky to have a friend on the inside. Having Goran high in the party no longer disappointments."

Katarina gnawed her bottom lip. She would visit Goran in the morning.

"Tony writes that he is treated with compassion," Jelena said. "And he now speaks perfect English. He's the prisoners' official spokesman."

When the Babics exhausted the contents of their son's letters, they asked about Sarajevo, how she had coped with the war, her work as a seamstress, pastimes and, finally, the nature of her relationship with their son. How would she handle that question? Hedge and say they were friends, or tell them she was madly in love with him? The test of her vow to be finished with deception had arrived.

Katarina cleared her throat. "He's the only man I have ever loved. No matter what the future holds, I know I'll never love another."

"Oh, my!" Jelena said. "I thought you and Goran—"

"It's over." Katarina lifted her cup to sip coffee. It had been empty for ten minutes. "The story is long and sad. I had a problem with the Ustashe when I lived here. I had to get out. Goran made that possible. I owe him my life."

"A *serious* problem," Josip said.

"The debt, Mr Babic, is more than paid, I assure you. I am moving back to Zagreb so that I am here when Tony returns. Did he mention me in his letters?" Her eyebrows lifted with hope.

"Katarina, you have to understand. Tony had so much to tell us about camp life, and with only so many words per letter … you know …"

****

A surly clerk-typist escorted the young lady in the stylish suit through the administration area to the boss's office. The usual workplace buzz waned as the tap of heels caused heads to turn. The clerk-typist pointed to a door, slightly ajar.

Katarina walked inside and stopped six feet from Goran's desk, awaiting acknowledgment. His shirtsleeves were rolled up to the elbows, and a cigarette dangled from his lips while he thumbed through a stack of dossiers. *Smoking?* The pallid, puffy man with a black patch covering his left eye finally looked up.

"You." He took a long drag on the cigarette and exhaled through his nose. "Why?"

"Your eye," she said. "The condition has worsened."

Goran tapped his ash to the floor. He'd yet to stand up or invite her to sit. "Why are you here? Your letter could not have been more explicit."

"In it, I asked that we be friends."

He made a muffled grunt. "Yes, so kind of you. Do you know how distressing that would be for me? I loathe the thought of you with him. What could be more hurtful than my oldest, dearest friend taking up with the woman I love?" His eye stayed on her as he stubbed the cigarette in a heaped ashtray. "Does *he* love *you*?"

Stung by the comment, she peered away.

"Shall I answer the question for you?" He struck a match and lit another smoke. "A man who loves himself cannot love another. You are his amusement to use like a toy until he tires and discards you. Anyway, it doesn't matter, because when he returns, he will never enjoy the pleasure of your charms."

She whiffed the stench of yesterday's spirits as he brushed past her to the door. He swung it open, scanned the main office, and slammed it shut. "He's on Luka's list."

"What does that mean?"

"He's an enemy of the state." Goran stalked back to his desk, pushed some folders aside, and sat on it, his thick legs dangling a foot off the floor. "Luka's the city's number one counter-intelligence agent. He is also raving mad. Years ago, your lover insulted him. Luka has a long memory. There might be more to it. I don't know, and I don't care." His face reddened. Like a frustrated child trying to jam the wrong piece into a jigsaw puzzle, he swept a stack of files to the floor. "Now you are going to hear it! That flight plan you stole? Luka had Tito call in the Spitfires. The trap you set killed three men. Does your lover know *that*?"

The room began to move around her like a carousel.

"Luka won't rest until every Croat soldier has paid dearly. He thinks your lover died in the ambush. He'll discover otherwise. Luka will watch him swing from the gallows."

"He'll discover otherwise ..." were the last words Katarina heard. When she swayed, Goran leaped from the desk. Arm around her waist, he guided her to a chair, shouting, "Get me water" at the closed door.

Her color must have returned because he rushed from the office.

The cold water he'd retrieved dispersed the remnants of her wooziness. She finally had the truth: the downing of Tony's plane wasn't coincidental. She had suspected, but hadn't been able to admit it to herself. Goran had it right: she was the Judas.

"Why did you wait so long to tell me?" she said, rubbing downcast eyes.

"I didn't want to hurt you. I kept the secret to protect *you*. Believe me when I say I take no joy in your despair."

"Please, Goran. Please help Tony. He's suffered so much."

"He stole you from me. From that I'm suffering."

"You used to be compassionate. You know the circumstances of his enlistment. He was a free spirit – you know he wasn't political. He's just one of thousands who found themselves on the wrong side of the war. He would gladly be your friend again. Please help him."

"Why should I help the one who deceived me?"

"I thought it was I who deceived you."

"You did. I should hate you as much as I hate him. But you, I love. I can't help myself."

"If you won't intervene for Tony, intervene for me." She stared at him with wet and wanting eyes. "You know that Luka forced me to steal that flight plan. You know I didn't want to harm a soul – on either side. I beg of you. If you love me as you say, you'll do this for me."

"In turbulent times, the mad are the most dangerous. I've seen what Luka can do. Only a fool would cross him." He blew a blast of smoke to the floor and stubbed out the half-finished cigarette. "I will not arouse the vipers in his snake pit."

"Not even for me?"

"Luka and his hooligans trust no one. They have spies on their spies, and more spies on those. My words would be wasted." He rose to his feet and adjusted the band of his eye patch. Then he roved the office, finally coming up behind her. "But … suppose I were able to influence Luka and the secret police … suppose I find a way to convince them to grant clemency." He placed both hands on her shoulders. "What do I get for reaching into Luka's snake pit?"

She cocked her head and gazed into his eye. "What is it you want?"

"You."

Chapter 26

October 1945
Ralston, Louisiana

Though it was autumn, the eighty-degree heat made the black tar-papered barracks uninhabitable during the day. By 16:30, Tony and Bo had downed eighteen beer garden Falstaffs between them.

"Figure that," Tony said. "I haven't been drunk since the Rockford soccer game."

Bo eased back on his chair and belched. "Never easy on three-point-two ... It's the heat. Do you think they have a garden like this at Camp Polk?"

"Polk's in the south. If they do, Ladders is as legless as us. Glad Pinky came through."

"What are we going to do back home, Tony?"

"I told you that an hour ago – good jobs go to partisans and party elite. An ambitious guy like you needn't worry. You'll make your way; you always do."

"We'll see. I've no connection to my family ... or a country that's red. Any word when we ship out?"

Tony smacked his forehead. "Like I said, Bo, when I know, you'll know. Relax."

"We still haven't figured how to move the cash. The speed bag trick's a long shot."

Tony agreed. There would be too many searches: the camp, the dock, the arrival port and who knows where else.

Bo looked over to the beer garden entrance. "Look who's here. Maybe our tubby buddy's going to buy us a Staffer."

Pink-cheeked and panting, Slim made his way to their table, dabbing his brow as he walked. "Loot, the Deuce wants to see you."

"War's over, Slim," Bo said. "Sit down and have a bottle of ice-cold piss with us." When Slim remained standing, Bo raised a scarred eyebrow. "Is Ladders back or is there a bun in Pinky's oven?"

Tony felt his head clear.

With the house painted, peaches picked and grounds manicured, workdays at Dupree were down to eight days a month. Tony had used the time constructively: discussing the thriving souvenir business with Joshua, providing new inventory, collecting money and wrestling with the captain's wife in her four-poster.

Soon every POW would be gone, and the consequences to Pinky would be life-altering – not that she couldn't live without him – she would always be able to find a willing partner to replace the last. Tony knew that the issue weighing heaviest was the certainty of Camp Ralston's closure, and the uncertainty of her husband's reassignment. As the storm neared, she'd become more demanding than ever. No one escaped the outbursts. Her discretion waned, and her liaisons with the Lagersprecher leaked to Joshua, Lucille, Slim and every POW of the manor's work crew. One word to Hobson, and Tony was in for a reunion with Mauer and Arnim.

"Is there a problem?" Tony asked Slim.

"Don't know. The Deuce is as jumpy as a frog in a dry well. If there was a problem, why would he want to meet with you tomorrow?"

****

Hobson's eyes bore into Tony. The black under those eyes suggested a restless night.

Tony felt the sweat on his upper lip. "Good morning, Captain."

"Loot, there's a wrench in the works," Hobson said, in a voice of resignation.

Tony had never heard that phrase. Was Hobson saying he was the 'wrench', and Pinky was the 'works'? If that was the case, the gig was up.

Tony certainly wasn't immune to feeling the indignity of bedding another man's wife. At the outset, he had felt the sting of self-reproach, going so far as vowing abstinence after that first tryst on the hay. Pinky had other ideas. She had made herself impossible to refuse, and eventually he'd rationalized her as a divine gift to the incarcerated man – if not him, then someone else. But even though the cracks in the logic were too wide to ignore, he had not retreated. Now Hobson had him.

"I don't know what to say, Captain."

238

"You've got no idea what the blazes I'm talking about! I've been on the blower with Widrington …" Hobson's frown deepened, but seconds later his expression shifted to perplexity. "What's wrong, Loot? The red line is barely past seventy and you're sweating like a thief in church."

Tony heaved an inaudible sigh. "Could be the flu."

His English had vastly improved. Twice a week, Tony shelled out fifteen coupon cents to watch American films. He tried to speak like the leading men. He read newspapers from cover to cover, continued with advanced English class, and attended evening lectures on subjects as diverse as American wildlife and kite-making. His grammatical errors were rare, but that American jargon – he wasn't sure he'd ever have that figured out.

"See the doc," Hobson said. "Oh, yeah, Widrington – sends his best. This glitch has to do with you. The PMG wants every camp spokesman repatriated last. You could be stuck here for another six to nine months. Sorry 'bout that, Loot."

Tony muffled a gasp of relief. But once the thought of a transfer to Camp Alva dissipated, the reality of extended incarceration sunk in.

Hobson opened his palms. "Same goes for me. I'm stuck here with you."

Pinky too. Tony hadn't seen her in weeks.

****

No one knew when their time would come. By Christmas 1945, 550 prisoners had departed Ralston. In January, another 934 boarded trains for Northeastern ports. Production of war mementos for Wehrmacht Souvenirs came to an end in February – the last of the inventory smuggled in bags tied to the undercarriages of transport trucks and Slim's jeep. Six townspeople continued distributing the goods from their shanties. Joshua packed in the barn loft while assessing reader demographics and modifying newspaper choices. For his role in the operation, he had earned twenty times his annual stable boy's salary. And two Negro families had stepped up from destitution to self-sufficiency.

The partners' three-line classified ad had reached markets representing thirty percent of the United States, and that was without New York or Chicago. The *New York Daily News* boasted a circulation of two million. Using average response rates, Tony, Bo and Joshua would need 5,000 carvings to supply this massive metropolis. With a final tally of 412 swastikas and 630 Iron Crosses, they had nowhere near enough for that jackpot.

In preparation for Tony and Bo's repatriation, Joshua exchanged small notes for large bills at the town bank. Initially, the bankers viewed him with suspicion, assuming the notes were counterfeit since no Negro had ever walked in with that much money. But their skepticism dissipated when Joshua opened his own account and fed it regularly and abundantly. How the black man earned the money was inconsequential; Joshua Gooden became a valued customer. As fifties and hundreds materialized, Bo sutured them into his jacket linings. If the remaining inventory sold before his time to go, the big bruiser would leave Camp Ralston in a beat-up army jacket worth a little over $2,000 – enough cash to buy two brand-new cars.

Bo drew a circle around April 2, 1946 on the girlie wall calendar. In the week leading up to his release, he put in for external supervisory duty. Camp Ralston held less than half its capacity of POWs. Nonetheless, cane and cotton farmers remained eager to employ low-cost labor.

On the morning of April 1, Bo laid out his belongings neatly on his cot. Rather than stuff them in his rucksack, he moved them about, exchanging their positions as though they were pieces of a large puzzle or a work of modern art. He moved a shirt from near the headboard to the foot of the bed and replaced it with three auto magazines. Then he roamed the room, eyeing the rafters and Tony who was at the window peering out to a passive laneway.

"Are you going to tell me," Tony said, "or are you going to take your troubles with you?" He turned from the window, and suddenly Bo had him in a bear hug. Two-and-a-half years they'd known each other. There had been plenty to celebrate, but this was their first embrace.

Tony wheezed, "What the ...?"

"Thanks, man. Thanks for everything." Bo tightened his grip and lifted Tony off the floor. "I've finally got you where I want you. Now I'm going to slam you to the mat and knock some sense into that curly blond head of yours." He hiked Tony higher and dropped him horizontally on the bed, severing the leg cleats supporting the springs. The bedspring, the mattress and Tony slammed the floorboards.

When their laughter subsided into awkward silence, Bo said, "Except for those bastards at Graham, I've had the time of my life in America. Today I'm working the Desjardin fields." He tapped his watch. "I can't be late. Goodbye, Tony."

****

As it turned out, there was good reason why Bo's 'goodbye' came off with an air of finality.

Tony found Hobson scampering back and forth between his office window and the shelves jammed with books and trophies.

"Seems your bunkmate likes America better than Yugoslavia," Hobson said, glaring at Tony, but continuing to pace. "Start talking."

"I'm surprised as you, Captain. I thought he'd be on tomorrow's train to New York."

"Oh, he'll be on that train all right – we're already out there with dogs. The FBI's been called in to help. A big cue ball like that won't be hard to find. He's either on his way to Shreveport or Baton Rouge. He must have said something."

"Not one word. Captain, the war's over. Bo's no danger to anyone. What harm can come of an escape?"

Hobson came to an abrupt halt. "My reputation is a good place to start. Wherever the hell they're sending me, I don't want to arrive as Private Hobson."

Tony didn't care about that. If they caught Bo, Tony would have his own problems. They would find the money and a wide-scale search of the camp would follow. Tony might as well say goodbye to his dough. Still, once he thought it through, he understood Bo's motive. There was the money but also the prospect of partisan reprisal and Communist rule in the new Yugoslavia. The choice between that and democratic America had been an easy one.

****

Bo had planned the escape the moment the war ended. In the loft of one of three Desjardin barns, he had constructed a two-foot-deep false wall with old barn wood, running the length of the shortest wall. The compartment was roomy enough for him to hide upright or lying down. Currently, the loft served as storage for discarded tools and machine parts. Bo had never seen anyone climb the ladder to retrieve a piece of hardware or add to the collection.

241

He had enough food and water to last ten days – two weeks in a pinch. The biggest risk was the dogs. Thankfully, they didn't climb ladders. They would smell him in the barn, but then again, they would smell him all over the plantation. He had made sure of that by pissing in every corner and leaving snot rags here and there.

Bo's second concern was a heatwave and ventilation within his constricted hiding place. The *Ralston News* forecast called for highs of 74° – uncomfortable with the humidity but not unbearable. Regardless, he would be able to hear the searchers, and when their day was done he could remove two boards, secured from the inside, for fresh air and a stretch.

It wasn't long before the roar of engines fractured the supper hour calm. Doors slammed, dogs barked and men shouted. Bo heard someone yell, "Start with the houses, huts and barns. Those with dogs – let them smell Zick's undershirt and shorts. Then spread out and search every inch with a fine-tooth comb."

Below Bo, the barn door squeaked open. "Go, boy! Spike's onto something. Zick's been here. Check under the wagon and then see what's up there."

Bo heard the ladder thump against the lip of the loft's square opening. *Don't move and don't sweat.*

"Just a bunch of parts," the guy yelled down. "Couple of broken axles, rusty saw blades, old scythes, some rope … a Desjardin sign on the wall, a portable—"

"Anywhere a big guy can hide?" said a voice from below. "Spike's at the ladder, standing on his hind legs. Maybe we should haul him up by a rope."

"There's nothing up here but rafters and junk. Suit yourself."

"No offense, Tim, but I'm coming up just to be sure. Walk the perimeters with your eyes peeled to the floor. He might have dropped or left something behind – a cigarette butt or a candy wrapper."

Bo felt his right leg cramp. His heartbeat quickened. Perspiration trickled down his brow into his eyes, but he was used to the sting. *Stay still. Relax.*

The two on the loft agreed that Bo had been there, but had nowhere to hide.

FBI agents arrived at daybreak, retracing the sweep. By midday, Bo reckoned the temperature in his dark cubby had risen past eighty. He had layered tar paper between the boards and the two-by-fours to make a seal, hoping it would retain his odor. If they didn't hoist a dog up, he was safe. He would stay for as long as his food lasted; by then the search party would be miles away.

****

A week passed without word of capture. Another week and Bo could be in any of forty-eight states. Tony knew he was safe when a 'Greetings from California' postcard arrived. *'How you? You need me you write JG of WSC. He knows how to find me.'* Tony grinned at the image of a muscle-bound baldy lying on a sunny California beach.

Camp Ralston was down to 950 POWs. Soon there would be no one left to trim the Dupree hedges and tend the orchard. A simple nod from Slim and the sentries waved the jeep through the gates. Tony was off to the Dupree Manor for the last time. As the jeep sputtered into the roundabout, he scanned the second-story windows. A drape waved in one of the guest rooms, though there was no breeze.

"Slim, can I have five minutes alone with Joshua?"

"You ain't gonna fly the coop like Bo, are you? Because if you do that, I'll be ass deep in—"

"No, Slim. I have family in Croatia that I must see. After that, who knows? Perhaps I'll make America home."

Slim nodded, chewing his toothpick thoughtfully and Tony headed for the barn.

Tony found Joshua stacking bales of hay. "Joshua, I'm here to say goodbye. Thanks for being my partner and my good friend. One day, we will meet again."

Joshua wiped his brow. "I should be the one thanking you. You made me feel like an equal. You have no idea what that means to a black man. My life is forever changed, all because of you."

"That's pushing it, don't you think?"

"You taught me how to make money for myself. I'm going to keep the business going by finding other souvenirs to sell through the mail. I've already thought of a name: 'Unique Wares of America'. I've got responsibilities – six packers who want to keep their jobs."

"I like hearing that. Joshua, before I go I need a favor."

"Anything."

Tony loosened his belt and unbuttoned his fly.

Joshua's eyes whitened, and he staggered back a step. He added another when Tony dropped his trousers and whipped down his undershorts.

Tony chuckled. "Don't worry; I've got someone else for that." He raised his shorts to the light and picked the thread binding the paper. "There's $2,200 here. I want you to mind it until I come back to America."

"You want to leave all that money with *me*? How do you know I won't steal it or spend it?"

"I know, just like *you* know. If you need the money for your business, use it. Just give me a bonus when the business thrives. If it fails, well, that's my tough luck. Put the money in the bank or bury it in a can. I don't care. I get a $600 captivity check from Uncle Sam when I leave. In Croatia, that's a fortune."

He knew enough of Joshua to understand the anxiety created by the incomprehensible proposition. Here was a white man – a foreigner – entrusting his entire fortune to a black man.

"I can't," Joshua said.

"You said no to the business and changed your mind. Bo and I made the products. *You* ran the business. *You* made yourself more than a thousand bucks. Not bad in a country with a minimum wage of forty cents an hour. I am asking for help. I need *you* to help *me*."

"If I never hear from you again, what do I do?"

"Let's agree on this: if you don't hear from me within ten years, the money's yours. I can't say what lies ahead for me. Tito could line me up before a firing squad. I might spend five years in a jail, being on the wrong side. Do we have a deal?"

"I'll hold your money for twenty years. I'm going to change the post box from Wehrmacht Souvenirs to UWA, short for Unique Wares of America. Write to me."

"Letters from a Communist country could be a problem. Don't expect one. My friend, it is time I go."

Joshua looked at Tony like a man bidding his brother goodbye. Tony held out his hand and Joshua took it, firmly, but he didn't seem interested in a short handshake.

"It's all right, Joshua," Tony wheezed. "You can let go." Joshua's arm dropped to his side, and Tony walked away, never looking back.

He heard the idling of the Jeep's engine – Slim would be tinkering under the hood. This presented the perfect opportunity to enter Lucille's kitchen from the back porch and dash up the winding staircase. He hiked the stairs two at a time, coming to the bedroom with the fluttering drape.

The fully clothed woman with smeared makeup and red eyes lay curled on the double bed.

"What's wrong, Pinky?" Tony widened his eyes and pointed to himself.

"Well, aren't *you* pretentious? I'm not in the mood. I'm moving to a dump called Fort Benning in Georgia."

Her snivels of self-pity didn't subside until she mistook his soothing palms for suggestion – and she took her comfort from him in the only way she knew how.

****

Finally, it was Tony's time to pack. The War Department issued two blankets, a first aid kit, cup, fork and spoon, and a rucksack. Radios, cameras, currency, knives, lighters and tools were prohibited.

He had saved the first of Katarina's thirty-four letters. He'd use that one to bookmark the pages of *Treasure Island* and *Journey to the Center of the Earth*. By scanning the library editions, he knew they'd be great novels of escape. Both would help him through the monotony and the angst of the long journey home.

He stowed the books, toothbrush, soap and a recently purchased camera at the bottom of his duffel with the first aid kit. If they searched the bag and confiscated the camera, so be it. He added a change of clothes, some chocolate bars, a carton of Lucky Strikes, an assortment of souvenirs, a large envelope of Bobby Rose's newspaper articles, six certificates of academic achievement, photographs, and one suicide note. As Corporal Vogler's commanding officer, he owed the widow a personal explanation of the truth.

In an open wool overcoat draped over a repaired German uniform, he stood in the doorway and looked into the vacant barrack for the last time. His years in America would make for some good stories. He carried his duffel and rucksack to the porch, lowered himself to the step, and dropped his head between his knees. His reverie was brief. The howl of

Slim's engine and the clatter of gravel wrenched him from his melancholy.

"Set to go, Loot?"

Tony gathered his gear and walked to the jeep. "I'll miss my American confidant."

Slim cranked his hand as if it were a pump handle.

"Surely, you can't be *that* happy to see me go."

"God, no! You made life interesting 'round here."

Tony glanced at the nearest tower and the slothful guard leaning on the rail. "Got something for you, Slim," he said. He pulled a $100 bill from his baggy trouser pocket.

Wide-eyed, Slim almost choked on his toothpick. "What the ...?"

"It's a token of my thanks."

"Ain't ever had my hands on one of these ... Now, doesn't that take the cake? How the hell does a prisoner of war—"

"Don't ask. Buy that '36 Dodge. You said you'd buy it if you had the money. The Transitone in my room is a gift from me and Bo."

Tony was the last prisoner to pass through the gates of Camp Ralston and board a train for New York. By August, the camp would be pastureland.

Chapter 27

May 1946
New York, New York

At the blast of the foghorn, dockworkers unhooked the gangways so the tugs could maneuver the ship into the harbor. When it was far enough from the wharves, the tugs disengaged and motored back to shore. The Statue of Liberty faded into the distance. In the wind, Tony strained his eyes to keep the coast in sight. As the land of opportunity receded, he felt the jab of trepidation in the pit of his stomach. Had he erred by not vanishing into America as Bo had? Quartered in the ship's hold with almost a thousand other POWs, he kept to himself over the tedious voyage, pondering a gamut of emotions that pinched and poked a spirit already sapped by apprehension. Inactivity had a way of calling out the demons that lurked in every shadow along the long road he had traveled.

The sighting of the English Channel came on the port side. The shores to the left were Britain's. Soon the majestic, weather-etched white cliffs of Normandy appeared to starboard. The ship cruised into the Bay of the Seine and docked at the cape of bombed-out Le Havre in northwest France.

Baleful eyes of French soldiers and civilians, filled with indignation over the German occupation, gawked at the prisoners as they crammed the deck rails. Sixteen hundred filed from the ship to boxcars destined for the coal mines of Nord-Pas-de-Calais, where they would labor. Three hundred more squeezed onto wooden benches of rickety passenger carriages built before the Great War of 1914-18. Steam hissed and iron wheels lumbered. Four hundred fifty miles down the track was the rubble of Babenhausen, in the Frankfurt district of the American-occupied zone. Here Tony would eat his first meal in Europe – a ladleful of canned pork and beans and a slice of stale bread.

**** ****

A former stockade for Russian prisoners, Babenhausen's barracks matched the square footage of those at Ralston and Graham, but they were filthy, dark and dingy, and jammed with almost three hundred instead of fifty. No one was tall enough to peer out the four tiny windows at the higher roofline. Internees slept on three levels of wall-to-wall planks layered with straw, three to a rack. For security reasons, it was difficult to approach the American guards, though Tony sought every opportunity to do so.

Eventually, a compassionate sergeant named O'Hara responded to his persistent advances. O'Hara said the situation might worsen before it got better. "You have no idea how difficult it is to deal with millions of DPs in four zones," O'Hara said. He pointed to the sea of mud that covered most of the site. "The rains haven't helped."

Rainwater from the leaky roof in Tony's barrack had overflowed every pail and ration tin; everyone and everything was soaked.

They were getting seventy-five to a hundred former slave workers and POWs a day – supposedly to be fed, clothed and medically treated. With the barracks at capacity, the extras dwelled in shanties, pup tents, and stalls that had once housed German horses. Hideous conditions, malnutrition, desperation and despondency did not make for a harmonious mix. The resourceful made clubs or sharpened soup spoons to defend themselves or intimidate others. Tony drew on the weapons of diplomacy and his command of English.

"Next month, we're getting 1,000 Russian Jews," O'Hara said. "How we're going to feed them is anyone's guess. They'll be skin and bone to start with. If something doesn't change in a jiffy, we'll have a mass graveyard on our hands."

"Then release us," Tony said. "We're no danger to anyone."

"Inadequate troops for escort."

"I can go with a commissar, no? I'm waiting for one from Croatia."

"You mean a *Yugoslav* commissar."

Tony had seen the commissars – officials of the Communist bloc – who came to the camps to 'educate' and pressure POWs into accompanying them to their homeland. If a POW chose the custody of a 'sanctioned' emissary, the US Army was free to discharge him.

O'Hara urged Tony to be patient. "How long have you been here?"

"Two weeks."

"Then you've heard their bullshit. These guys come for your trinkets and your checks from Uncle Sam. When you leave, you're fleeced. We hear of beatings and murder. Most are hooligans preying on the weak. Yugoslav commissars come every week to ten days. To a hungry man, they're especially convincing."

"Do the others know this?"

"Those who know, hiss and spit at them – the Russians in particular. We send extra guards to protect the Soviet commissars ... I have to go." Before trotting off, O'Hara slipped a small pouch of peanuts into Tony's hip pocket.

A week later, 500 emaciated Jews arrived. Tony gaped in horror as they shuffled off to a wired area of horse stalls reserved for displaced families. He couldn't help noticing a waiflike little girl in a dirty checkered dress, clutching her mother's hand. The child was one of the youngest in the camp, perhaps three or four. It wasn't her matted hair, knobby knees and spindly, scabby legs that jerked his heartstrings – he was accustomed to seeing people in this condition – it was the blankness in the little girl's eyes. As she hobbled past, she stared ahead, never blinking or glancing at the squalor around her. She disappeared into the gloom of the stables.

The chow at Algiers had been despicable, but a prisoner survived if he kept it down. Here, everyone but the flies lost weight. Contaminated food and water brought dysentery or typhoid. In their straw cots, dysentery sufferers discharged greenish soup and red blood. Feverish typhoid victims fared no better. Men grew cunning, fighting for a place in the food line, robbing and killing those too weak or too trusting. The wise slept with one eye open.

Tony managed to scavenge scraps of food, but a month of famine cut his well-fed frame by thirty pounds. Weeks ago, he had traded his camera for half a can of C-ration meat-and-potato hash. Where the Reaper lurked, possessions were cheap.

On a cloudy afternoon after a downpour, Tony found a safe place on a damp plank by his barrack from which to view the area where a Soviet commissar would preach his drivel. Today's food rations, scheduled for morning delivery, had not arrived. That might explain why the commissar's cold and hungry audience of Slavic refugees was double the usual numbers.

Three armed GIs stood near the well-fed Soviet official. The customary escort was six to eight. Tony figured the Yanks were also stretched –

249

hopefully, unloading incoming crates of chow. The commissar scanned the shivering lot.

"I see the same sad faces," he said in Russian. "Stay here, you die. Come with me, you live. Those who left last month are warm and dry and stuffing themselves with hot bowls of pirozhki and shashlyk. What they can't finish, they give to the dogs. Follow me to prosperity."

As the commissar baited them with promises of food and mistruths about the good life under Uncle Joe, Tony measured their sentiment. One didn't have to understand Russian to feel the commissar's contempt for this wasted lot. Placid at first, the refugees began shifting their weight from one foot to the other. Some kicked at the mud; others scratched at the nits in their hair or wiped their runny noses with the back of their hands. A jaundiced elder hawked up a mouthful of phlegm and spat at the emissary, the greenish glob landing on his pant leg. The commissar backed away but not far enough to dodge a second missile. The wad stuck to the toe of his boot.

Enraged, the commissar dug into his pocket – for a gun, Tony reckoned.

But no, he withdrew a clenched fist. "You're nothing but a herd of monkeys in a filthy zoo. Here, monkeys." He flung a handful of nuts, and like a flock of pigeons descending on breadcrumbs, the starving men kicked, gouged and shoved as they sifted through the grime. On hands and knees, the lucky ones scooped up a prize, cracked the shell and devoured the morsel.

When the last scavenger rose, the commissar laughed. "I thought so ... a bunch of filthy monkeys."

Suddenly, like mob of skeletal rugby players, they charged, knocking two guards to the ground. Outstretched arms clawed for the chunky Russian in the long coat. One of the guards ran for help while the other two who had jumped to their feet, raised their rifles, retreated a few paces and watched in bewilderment as the internees slammed their tormentor to the muck. They had him by the arms and the legs and he writhed like a wolf in a jaw trap.

"No-o-o-o. Let go! Help me!"

Eight had a hold, two per limb. They heaved in opposing directions, lifting him from the sludge as he howled.

"Lower his ass to the ground!" one said. They dropped him into the mud without letting go. "I count to three. On three, pull with all your strength."

Though they looked weak individually, it occurred to Tony that eight enraged men working in concert might do some damage.

"Ready? One ..."

Mutely, the commissar mouthed, "No ..."

"Two ... Three!" They yanked in unison. With a nauseating pop, one arm ripped from the shoulder socket followed by a gush of vomit from the victim's mouth. The fellow holding the severed arm swung it around him as if he were an Olympian doing the hammer throw, and hurled it over the barbed wire, where it landed on the hood of a parked Army truck. The mob then worked on the other limbs, though by now there was little point.

When it ended, few remained at the scene. From the sidelines some retched, though nothing came from their empty stomachs. Others, like Tony, turned to stone. A severed arm lay near the still twitching two-legged head and torso. The man who had led the butchery broke the commissar's neck while another scoured his pockets for more nuts. The mayhem had lasted less than a minute.

The astonished eyes of the dead man looked up into the horror-struck faces of converging GIs.

Tony crossed himself. This time he did not pray for the dead; he prayed for the living.

****

The Communist Serb commissar, known as Novak, worked his targets individually. He asked of Tony's war background, and despite O'Hara's warnings of Novak's purpose, Tony responded willingly. This commissar might be needed.

Novak had said that Tony's 3rd Bomber Wing of the 8th Squadron was executed when the partisans reclaimed Sarajevo. As the army made their way to the Austrian border, they spared no one in uniform. Novak was prepared to offer proof, but that might take a month. He'd grinned as he appraised Tony's withered body, and then asked if Tony had that much time.

A week short of a month, Novak returned with the official obituary of the 3rd Wing. "These men were hanged in Sarajevo," he said, handing

Tony the list. "It is now safe to come home. Marshal Tito has promised to heal past hatreds in Yugoslavia. Other than Nazis and Ustashe, who will forever be guilty of war crimes, the retribution is over. Those of the party, who are proponents of revenge, face the same punishments they inflict. Rebuild your life. Don't die in this hell."

Slowly, Tony opened the paper, taking his time to flatten the creases. Then he began reading the names of those with whom he had raised hell, hoofed a ball, dealt cards, played practical jokes and flown combat missions – Housek, Vinny Rukavina and many more. Novak talked on, but Tony heard nothing. His mind was in another place, another time. He could hear Major Kirilenko reading *The Ode to the Dead Soldier* in honor of the 1941 brigade that evaporated like dew in the hot sun.

By failing to evade the Spitfires and return to Sarajevo, Tony had kept his name off Novak's death list. Would his life, spared back then, now sputter out in the Babenhausen quicksand? Might this camp's departures ever exceed the arrivals? He could stay another week. Another month would leave him too weak to ward off the specters of starvation, disease and anarchy.

The human soul was a complex mosaic – of precisely what, he couldn't say. Though his soul had been slashed, torn and scalded, he had retained his sense of survival. If that instinct should finally give up the ghost, so would he.

"Next week, Commissar Novak … next week I go with you."

****

He left with four Slovenes under the guard of ten partisan soldiers, traveling by rail to the border of Austria and into Slovenia, one of six states of the new Yugoslavia. Novak had promised a warm shower at the first stop. The gaunt POWs stepped onto the rail dock, and Commissar Novak pointed to the far end. The guards had already pulled their pistols.

"Empty your rucksacks. Remove shirts, trousers, shoes and socks."

The fleecing was right on cue. Tony had little to give except a three-by-six-inch piece of paper issued by the United States Army. A couple of years' pay for each former prisoner they escorted would net the bandits a heap of money.

The tip of a rifle barrel gouged Tony's ribs. He dumped his bag and sat with the other four, shivering in their skivvies, legs crossed, belongings spread in front of them: clothing, blankets, toothbrushes, combs, playing

252

cards, pencils, notepaper, a chess set, a harmonica, four books, five first-aid kits, and one pine carving of a war medal, signed by a Heinz Schultz.

"Nothing but a pile of fucking rubbish" Novak said. "I want those Army checks. Give them up or be shot. Who's first to die?"

The Slovenes relinquished the checks. With four checks between his thumb and fingers, Novak squatted in front of the motionless holdout and let the fire in his eyes do the talking. Tony was about to say that he didn't have the check when Novak winced as though shot by a gun with a silencer.

"Damn knee!" he said, hopping to his feet and kicking at the air as if shaking an uninvited lodger from a nest in his pants. Holding the knee, he then bent over Tony. "Take everything off! Give me the wristwatch and the check!"

Tony blinked under the blast of spittle. "I can't give you a check I don't have. It was stolen while I slept. Here … a beautiful Omega – twenty dollars I paid."

Novak snatched the watch. "Give over the check or I'll put a slug in your head. Is your life worth a few hundred dollars?" The gun came out of its holster. "To me, your life means nothing." He jabbed the barrel against Tony's shaved head, making it bob with each prod. Until this point, Tony had kept his fear hidden. Now, though, his entire body shook.

"Aha, we are there, are we? This is your last chance. Comrades, come and see. Any second, this guy's gonna piss himself. Expect a check or our first casualty."

"I c-c-can't give you w-w-what I d-d-don't have. Ch-ch-check was stolen."

An accomplice held a Luger to Tony's head while Novak searched the pockets and linings of two pairs of trousers. He came up empty and scavenged through the shirts, jacket and overcoat. No check. Novak's eyes rested on the balled wool socks by Tony's feet. Dozens of tiny vermin scuttled and hopped about in the wool.

"Check his boots, Vlad. And you, Babic, unroll those socks."

Though his hands were shaking, Tony managed to pull the socks open.

"Flip them over," Novak said.

Tony complied and laid them side by side like a couple of dead perch on a wharf.

"Now turn them inside out."

Tony stuck his trembling fingers inside each sock, pinched the wool at the toe, and peeled it back as if drawing the skin from a snake. Then he shook the fleas from his hands.

"Get up and spread your legs," Novak said, "and you, Vlad, look up his ass."

Tony widened his stance. With Vlad behind him, Tony closed his eyes and braced for a kick in the balls, but all he felt was the tickle of cold steel on his testicles.

The reluctant inspector inhaled, held his breath, and spread Tony's cheeks. "This guy's filthy. Nothing sticking out that I can see."

"Goose him!"

Vlad flinched. "Do I have to?"

"Tell you what, Vlad. Just supervise his next shit. The check could be way up there, wrapped in cigarette foil."

"Everyone dress. Bag the stuff you want." Novak walked from the platform into the town. Tony boarded the train, minus a wristwatch but still in possession of a $650 Army check stowed between two layers of socks that appeared as one.

Their next stop was Ljubljana, Slovenia's capital, where everyone disembarked except Tony and two partisan soldiers of Serb descent.

The soldiers said they were taking him to Belgrade for trial. "State Security Service pays fifty dinars a head," one of them said. "Hold out your hands." He wrapped Tony's wrists with two loops of twine." The ends of the twine were poorly knotted but up to the task.

The other passengers must have known that the skinny man in the German jacket was destined for a meeting with the secret police, because they looked everywhere but at the threesome. Whenever the SDB was involved, the wise looked the other way.

If Tony could steal ten minutes to gnaw the twine, he might spring free. His refusal to engage in conversation added to the monotony of guarding a weak and docile prisoner on a milk run they had made numerous times. When one of them left his seat for a stroll down the carriage aisle, Tony knew that their attention was waning. The other, on the bench facing Tony, gazed out the window.

Tony brought his bound wrists to his head and began scratching, prompting the guard to shift his eyes from the scenery, but not for long.

He was likely used to seeing men claw at lice and pick at scabs. Tony lowered his wrist and locked his front teeth onto one of the knots, nibbling on it until the wandering Serb made a turn at the door to the adjoining car.

An hour later, the fellow passed through to the forward carriage. Still in Slovenia, some fifty miles from Zagreb, they were passing small meadows in a valley bordered by forest and subalpine hills. The windowpane was now the guard's pillow.

Close your eyes. Patiently, Tony eyed the door and his drowsy chaperone, whose eyelids flickered. Finally they closed. Back and forth Tony ran the twine over the sharp edge of a chipped bicuspid. The twine snapped.

Wrists free, he lunged from his seat. He felt the mash of bone on his knuckles as his fist flattened the guard's nose. Before the guard could cry out or raise his hands to stop the gushing blood, Tony gave him another, square in the forehead, certain he had broken a finger.

The guy rolled from the bench to the floor, and Tony seized his billfold and the gun, stuffing them in his coat. He leaped from the moving train. Landing as he had been tutored in parachute school, he rolled up unharmed but for bruised bones and scrapes, hopped to his feet, slung his duffel over his shoulder, and made for the nearby meadow and the forest beyond. From there he followed the winding Sava River and the miles of tracks joining Ljubljana to Zagreb.

An hour and a half into the trek, emerging from the woods, he came upon rows of rustic Slovenian farmhouses at the rear of little ten- to twenty-acre plots. He craved food, and he needed inconspicuous clothing to blend in with the citizenry at the outskirts of Zagreb. From the seclusion of the woods, he would enter a house. Most of them looked vacant. He picked the one with drawn drapes on the tiny back window.

He wasn't twenty feet out of the woods when a woman came around the side of the house, carrying a basket of laundry. She walked to the clothesline and began pegging clothes, having missed him. Into the woods he dashed with all the stealth of a charging bear, rustling dry leaves and snapping twigs beneath his feet.

Migrating southward behind a dozen more parcels of land, he re-emerged at a red-roofed stucco dwelling. Four workers, who likely lived there, tended their beet field near the road connecting the acreages. Two wore dresses, so it stood to reason that the house was empty. Tony crept to the rear and slid along the plastered exterior until his hand touched the doorknob. He opened the door to glorious smells. On a woodstove still warm from the night rested a pot of sausage and sauerkraut. Using the wooden ladle as a shovel, he gobbled down what he could, then stashed a freshly baked loaf of bread and four carrots in his rucksack.

A pine armoire in the bedroom yielded a soiled pageboy cap, a plaid shirt and a pair of trousers sewn for a much thicker waistline. Happily, there was also a belt. From the billfold he stole from the guard, he removed twelve dinars in Tito's new currency – about three dollars – and left it on the kitchen table. It would more than compensate the family for the inconvenience.

His stomach rebelled from the shock of so much food, but he kept it all down and pushed on. After two or three hours walking the bank of the Sava, taking care to stay out of sight where it periodically converged with the rail lines, he dropped to his knees and let his buttocks rest on his heels, like a Zen monk in meditation. His chin fell to his chest, and perhaps a minute passed before he scanned the mountainous horizon.

Alone in Croatia's wilds, he thrust his head back and howled to the heavens, "Aaaahhh! I am home ... home!" Then he collapsed to the earth and rolled onto his back, his damp eyes blinking madly at the racing clouds in the sky.

****

From a vantage point in the hills, he viewed a cityscape frozen in time. Later, though, along the roads and laneways, he could see that much had changed: littered curbs, discolored monuments, soot-blemished buildings, half-empty shops and, in the parkways, dandelions and dry weeds instead of flowers. Townsfolk went about their business as always, seemingly indifferent to the regression, though surely they couldn't ignore the mutation of the country's political landscape. He had yet to see Jurisic Street, and already the winds of change had swept away the elation of his homecoming.

An hour after dark, with the pageboy's cap pulled low, he followed the graveled trail across the Zrinjevac Park. To avoid crossing paths with someone who might recognize him in the fading bustle of Ban Jelacic Square, he chose a circuitous route toward the rail station, then veered east and, three blocks later, walked north to Jurisic without meeting a soul.

He spotted a fellow hunched on the top step of the entryway to the tenement across the road and one down from the Babic flat. A tenant enjoying a smoke in the night air wasn't peculiar – indeed, on many a night in the steamy American South, he had done the same. It was the regularity of the man's movements that seemed off. They reminded him of the orderly sentry in Ralston's north tower – the one with the habit of looking left, then straight ahead, and then right; left, ahead, and right, at three-second intervals.

Tony crossed the road and waited a half hour in another laneway, then set off on a wide two-block loop to Jelacic Square. Hoping the 'smoker' had retired, he neared the quiet square a second time, approaching from the west and exiting at the police station on the corner of Jurisic and Petrinjska. But rising smoke from the doorway on Jurisic confirmed his earlier suspicions. He made a casual diversion into the nearest apartment house and went through the main corridor to the alley behind his parents' flat. Crouching against the brick of the adjacent building, he waited.

One by one, the tenement lights dimmed. It was safe enough to crack the padlock on the coal hatch. He went down a ladder, and with his hands extended in front of him in the pitch blackness, he stumbled forward over loose chunks of coal, groping for the main wood support in the center of the basement. This would put him halfway to the exit. His shoulder grazed rough timber, and four steps later he felt the damp stone wall. *Almost there ...*

Sidestepping and brushing the fieldstones with his palms, he ran his fingertips against a finished wood edge – the door casing? A key to the flat had always hung on a nail to the right of a joist above the door. He slid his fingers along the dusty surface, finding nothing but splinters.

Maybe it was on the left. But no, it had hung on the right. He stretched higher and felt his way back toward the door ... There it was. He slipped it into his pocket and trotted up the basement stairs to the vestibule, pausing to peek out the high window of the main door. The watcher was still there.

Up two flights of stairs, he came to the door with the ornate brass nameplate. He inserted the key and turned.

****

Tony inhaled half a loaf of bread and two bowls of chicken soup while Josip and Jelena did the talking. But too soon the clouds of worry descended, casting a shroud over their elation. Josip warned of the SDB, and the dangers facing soldiers of the former independent Croat state. The SDB had come yesterday and today, questioning, searching the flat for Tony.

"The man across the street?" Tony asked Josip.

"Across the street, in the hallways – agents everywhere. We no longer know who to trust."

"Someone reported my escape. They knew I'd come here."

"They'll be at our door in the morning," Josip said. "Go to Vinograd Kralja. Wait for us there. We must decide whether you should turn yourself in or flee the country."

"I can't—"

"Tony, this isn't the Croatia you left. I will confer with Goran. He's high up in state security. He went with the Communists. Men make choices in turbulent times. I suspect he measured the probabilities and put personal well-being over political ideals. Whatever the case, he remains a friend of this family. Right now we need friends in high places. I will seek his guidance."

"He never wrote," Tony said. "It's because of Katarina. You see, she doesn't love him, and ... I still haven't got this part figured ... she loves me. Goran blames me for the split."

After a long pause, Josip said it couldn't hurt to hear Goran's thoughts on the matter. "If I like what I hear, it might be wise to have him speak on your behalf. He doesn't have to know you're back. Go to the vineyard and hide there until you hear from us."

Chapter 28

A half hour past sunrise, and Katarina was at the sewing machine. In four days, Aunt Adela would return from her vacation at the coast. She had left a list of alterations, a pattern and the material for the princess gown that Katarina was to make for a child actress of the Croatian National Theater. At this rate, Katarina would be finished the day after tomorrow.

By mid-morning a firm rap on her door silenced the whirr of her machine. The weary eyes of the caller suggested ominous news.

Josip Babic apologized for the intrusion. "I've come to seek your guidance. It's Tony – he's home. The SDB is after him. Like hawks, they watch our flat. An agent was on me the second I left." Josip fell silent, and a shaky hand came to his temples as though he needed a moment to compose himself. When he resumed, he spoke much slower, seemingly calmer. "I lost him at the market, and to be safe, I walked to the rail station to lose myself in the crowd. Don't worry; I wasn't followed here." He paused once more. "When you came to see us, you confessed your love for Tony. Am I correct in assuming devout loyalty?"

Blushing, Katarina nodded. She briefly looked away but then her eyes came back to this father in distress. "For your son," she said, "I would give my life."

"I see," Josip said, looking like he'd suddenly lost his breath. "Then we are birds of a feather. I've contemplated seeking Goran's help, but Tony thinks Goran blames him for the break-up. True?"

"Tony had nothing to do with it. It wasn't until he went missing did I realize my love for him. But yes, Goran blames Tony." She looked away, her thoughts on the condition Goran placed on his assistance. "That doesn't mean he won't help."

Josip's expression conveyed doubt, so she added, "I'm fully aware that Goran should be handled with extreme caution." But then, her downcast eyes elevated. "What if I were to tell him that Tony is expected in the country in a week or two? He could take that information to the secret police."

"The SDB already know that Tony is here."

"Yes. But they don't know that *we* know. If they're unaware of Vinograd Kralja, they'll keep watching your flat."

Shaking his head, Josip said, "Not sure if they know we have the vineyard. Goran does, of course. Jelena and I won't go near the place in case we are followed. *You* could go. Will you?"

Her heart skipped a beat.

"Katarina, we can't involve Goran without Tony's consent. Discuss the situation with him. He may prefer to escape over the Alps. He shouldn't feel he has to stay here because of us."

****

Katarina's last hour of fine embroidery was riddled with errors – unusual for an accomplished dressmaker who had begun her craft as a child. By ten minutes to midnight, she worked with the clumsiness of a novice. Whatever had possessed her to think she could cope with the minutiae of tiny hearts and sequins while in such a mental fog? Why rush a job that calmer hands could finish in three or four hours? Her foot slid off the pedal.

She needed rest, but sleep would be as difficult as the intricate embroidery. In the morning, she would see the man she had loved from afar – the man on whom she had inflicted countless pain. The thought made her palms damp and her head light. Would he be the man she remembered?

'I'm not the man you think you love,' Tony had written. 'The war has changed me.' Stranger or not, she had no doubt that the man hiding out at Vinograd Kralja was the man she would always love.

With love, there was no middle ground: a woman was in love or she was not. One didn't fall in love an inch at a time. Love was quick, stealthy: all of a sudden it was upon you. For Katarina, it struck the moment she realized Tony was late for Sunday dinner in Sarajevo. Though she considered herself a woman of prudence and common sense, she was madly in love with a man she barely knew. The day they met, he was aloof and mechanical. Several weeks later, at the Esplanade Hotel, he was a glib, irreverent soldier nursing his coffee. The faux St Martin's Day celebration disclosed yet another Tony Babic – a jester, a caring soul, a thoughtful son … a rogue. At the soccer pitch, she had encountered the brash, cocky show-off. And on that glorious day in the

Dinaric hills, she had peeled back the veneer to discover compassion and tenderness.

Tony had referred to her as an angel and confessed a yearning beyond mere physical desire. True, those words had been spoken long ago. His scars were deep. How deep and how long they would take to heal, she could not speculate. She would be a fool to build hope on four letters in a year-and-a-half. She had waited six months for a second letter after posting seventeen, telling him of the Bosnian orphans and her dying mother, reiterating her devotion, and vowing never to go back to Goran. But none of those seventeen letters addressed his query of how she came to love him so suddenly and so unconditionally. She knew of the sacrifices he had made, and she was prepared to accept his right to go his own way without her. Yes, he was free to do that, but until he made that choice, she was his.

In her Christmas letter, she had taken a stab at his question of how she had come to love him. Bystanders of war also grew old fast, she had said. By the time she reconnected with him in Sarajevo, the schoolgirl he had met in Zagreb had become a woman. Katarina the woman felt differently about Tony the soldier. When he went missing she knew. The feeling was love. Three years of separation hadn't altered her conviction. That was enduring love.

She rose early, bathed, curled her hair, and dressed in three outfits before deciding on the beige tweed jacket, off-white blouse, sleek brown trousers and hiking shoes. Katarina dabbed each side of her neck with a drop of perfume, brushed out her thick mane into a wavy sheen and repainted her nails with a calmer hand than last night's. Her reflection, she checked a final time, noticing the snugness of the trousers. Of course they were snug; she had made them with him in mind.

By seven forty-five, she was at Dolac market exchanging ration coupons to buy a small portion of meat and cheese, and some bread. Lunch basket on her arm, she waited on the curb outside Adela's flat, appearing as though she had missed her train to Sarajevo.

Yesterday, she had gone to the textile warehouse to ask if the deliveryman might give her a lift to the countryside. He had five deliveries before nine thirty, but if she would pay for his petrol and an extra dinar for his trouble, he'd pick her up at quarter to ten. At twenty before ten, Katarina felt the stirrings of panic. How would she ever compose herself when she met him? Let him speak first? Throwing her arms around his neck and smothering him with kisses might not be a good idea. Many times she had visualized that very thing, and once even mentioned it to her mother. Maria Kirilenko had said she would know what to do when the time came.

****

They motored down the dusty road of a vineyard in disrepair. One of the gates was off its top hinge, blocking the driveway. The driver stopped the truck and she opened her door.

Katarina stood at the top of the driveway and looked about. The fertile hillside and rich vines had gone to seed, overrun with wild berry brambles and tangled creepers. There wasn't a worker to be seen.

Through the clumps of weeds on the driveway, she made her way to the little stucco house with the red door. Chipped and cracked white plaster had dimmed to creamy yellow. Tiles, some broken, cluttered the ground, and the gaps they left in the roof stood out like missing teeth. A broken latch hung on the door weathered to dull pink by harsh winds and scorching sun.

She stepped onto the porch. The boards creaked.

"Tony? Are you here?"

A bird chirped in reply. Katarina put her ear to the door and knocked again. Then she jiggled the damaged latch. The door screeched ajar, and she craned her neck inside. "Tony?"

Cigarette smoke and the faint smell of coffee lingered in the air. Stale ersatz, she assumed. From her position in the doorway, she saw the kitchen sideboard, cluttered with a cup, knife, spoon, side plate, preserves jar, water pail and ladle. Stepping over to the cast-iron woodstove, she touched the stovepipe. Cold. A chair had been pulled back from the table – this was where he had eaten breakfast and smoked the cigarette that was now a butt in the ashtray.

He had been reading. Katarina never got past the *Drahtpost* headline. Her peripheral vision caught a familiar face on one of the clippings: a headshot and an action photo of Tony scoring a goal. She shook her head and grinned. English literacy was unnecessary to get the gist of the captions. Another article suggested some sort of trouble in the prisoner-of-war camp. It appeared that Tony was involved in a revolt against some Nazis. The situation must have been serious if American

262

newspapers covered the story. She had him pegged as politically indifferent. Wrong again.

After perusing every article, she ventured outside. Her shout for Tony flushed two swallows from a vine. He must be in the barn.

On the way, she noticed healthy grapes clustered on rows of well-pruned vines. Not all was in decay. Josip had been here. He'd done what he could. Perhaps his son would find time to persuade the berries to grow, swell and sweeten.

Near the barn, hearing the grate of steel on steel, she swept back her hair and buttoned her blazer. Then she slipped through a gap between the heavy doors. A scrawny, bald worker in a loose under-vest arched over a workbench by a window. Though his back was to her, she could see him pushing a file over an ax head secured in a vise. Drawing nearer, she realized that the worker was not bald. He had sandy-colored hair trimmed to a quarter inch of his scalp.

"Excuse me ..."

The filing stopped, but the worker did not turn around. Rather, he lifted his nearly bare noggin to the cobwebbed window in front of him, as if some bird outside had caught his attention.

"I'm looking for Tony Babic. Do you know where I can find him?"

He put the file down and wiped his hands and arms on a rag from an old shirt. Again he raised his head to the window panes.

Louder, she said, "Is Tony Babic here?"

"So you've come," he said.

"I ... I beg your pardon."

He tossed the rag on the workbench and swiveled to face her. His smile couldn't mask the hollowness in his cheeks and the dullness in his eyes. Katarina shivered like a frightened child caught on a sheet of ice, arms crisscrossed over her bosom, fingertips clasping her shoulders. The lines on his thin, drawn face told of more anguish than she could bear. Her eyes welled, and a sob fought to breach the knot in her throat.

By the time her whimper escaped he was inches away. She fell into his arms and buried her face in the sunken chest that had once been hardened muscle. The more she breathed in his scent through the loose vest, the more she whimpered.

"There's no need to cry," he said.

"You ... can't possibly know ... how much I love you."

"Why wouldn't I? Thirty letters told me so."

She recognized his wit, but it failed to console. "You can't know ..." she sniffled, "my pain."

"Why such pain?"

Because I'm the reason for your suffering. She couldn't find the courage to say it.

"Come to the cottage," he said. "We shall celebrate my homecoming with a glass of Grasevina. You'll feel better."

In the kitchen, she asked for a minute to freshen up the mess she had made of herself. Away from his gaze, she poured water from a bucket into a basin and wiped the mascara smears from her cheeks and chin. Her pinkish swollen eyes weren't as easy to repair. There was little choice but to enter the sitting room still wearing the traces of her distress. She didn't get far, for a skeletal man with two glasses of wine in his hands blocked the doorway from the kitchen.

"This should help," he said, smiling.

Katarina paused for a heartbeat, and then accepted the wine. They sank onto the musty settee cushions and clinked glasses, he with eyes that took her in, she with peripheral vision.

"Welcome home," she whispered. When her lips touched the glass, she downed half the wine in two gulps. Heat seeped into her cheeks from the obvious indiscretion. "Oh my ... I am so nervous ... I so seldom drink. Honest, I don't."

"I often drink, and *I'm* nervous," he said, chuckling. "I know I look like a slave camp survivor. And in a way, I am – thin as a broomstick – lost nearly fifty pounds in two months." He brushed his scalp with the palm of his hand. "This shave was my eviction notice to the lice living in my hair. I've been scrubbing with mother's soap concoction. She promised it would kill the eggs, and it must have; the smell was so bad it almost killed *me*."

She managed a smile.

"Give me a month; I'll be my old self," he said, gesturing at her glass with the spout of the bottle. "Want another splash of Josip's best?"

"Tiny bit," she said, knowing she could use more.

He poured, and this time she sipped sparingly.

"I've brought us lunch." To be this thin, he must be famished.

"Splendid – I have to eat every chance I get."

The lightheadedness struck the moment she sprang to her feet. Afraid he would notice, she scuttled to the kitchen where she grasped the counter-top, pausing to catch her breath. Her trembling fingers reached for the handle of the top drawer. "Are the knives in the—"

She felt hands on her hips and stiffened. He couldn't have been dissuaded because his palms slid up to her waist and tightened while his nose burrowed into the hair at the side of her neck. She closed her eyes and her head rolled to the opposite shoulder, whereupon he brushed away strands of hair with his chin and gently pecked the dampened skin of her neck.

Not since the attack by the Ustasha had Katarina felt a man's breath so close to her throat. Goran had tried many advances, to be sure, but she had always fended him off. But no, the bony frame who caressed her from behind awakened a long-dormant desire.

She turned, not to slip away but to meet his eager eyes.

"My God," he said. "You are so much more than I remembered. There's not a woman on earth as beautiful as you."

As their lips met, she clung to his neck, and his arms wrapped around her in a tight embrace.

When their kiss broke, Tony gasped and then in a whisper he said, "I want you."

Katarina had lived this scene in her dreams. She had even played out the fairytale in the light of day. And yet, she could not summon the response she had practiced so many times. Stunned by his admission and aroused by his touch, a timid nod was all she could manage.

****

She had fallen asleep in his arms, and he had clung to her, getting up an hour later to fix something for dinner – a combination of delights from her lunch basket, potatoes from the cold room in the cellar and garden beans. He cleared the table of newspaper clippings and found the only clean tablecloth in the house – the one with the navy blue pattern. He laid it diagonally, arranged a place setting for two and stepped back to judge its effect.

Was this how Jelena might set a table for his father's birthday? No, the decor was too sparse. He slapped his forehead and darted out the door like a spooked rabbit. At the end of the driveway along the property line, hundreds of tall white daisies waved in the breeze.

Minutes later, he had arranged the stems just so in the clay vase his mother had baked and painted when he was a boy. It would make a wonderful centerpiece between two candles. But would candles make sense in the daylight? Yes – perfect sense.

While she slept, he sat on the side of the bed next to her, studying her, watching her every breath. For the first time in months, he breathed easy. The woman in his bed had managed to banish the worry of being in a land where he was the enemy.

After three hours of sleep, he woke her with a long, wet kiss. "Can I interest you in an early dinner?"

Eyes half closed, Katarina yawned. "What time is it?"

"Five minutes to five … Was it the exercise that tired you?"

She blinked a half dozen times. "You'd like to think that, wouldn't you? I didn't sleep at all last night."

"So it wasn't our love-making." He cupped her head in his hands and planted another kiss. "It isn't dark till nine. There's no reason to get up unless you're hungry."

"If that's the case, why did you wake me?"

****

They lay breathless in each other's arms, the bed sheets pushed into a heap at their feet. She ran her finger along the jagged scar on his knee. "Was this wound the worst?"

"This zipper has the most interesting history, but that story's for another time."

Her face grew serious. "We must talk about your predicament."

"You mean my future in the land of the commissars. My father thinks Goran can be of help. Do you?"

Her eyes dulled. Goran would help if she paid his price. Even then, she couldn't say whether he would succeed in securing outright clemency.

"Katarina?"

She blinked several times to break the trance. "He's so jealous of you."

"He despises me. All that time away, he didn't write a line." Tony slid out of bed, exposing the back of a withered old man.

"Did you *eat* in that detention camp?"

"A can of C-rations a day, maybe. I would have wasted away if I hadn't got out of there. To be honest, I was in worse shape when they sent me to Africa. I needed a crutch to walk. The food you brought will

266

add a pound. I can tell you this another time. Back to my problem. Does Goran have the power to influence the secret police, and even if he could, *would he?*"

"He has the connections to find out what's in store for you. A friend of his runs the secret police. As far as I know, they still hunt Croat soldiers, but not with the same viciousness when the war ended."

"They executed my friends in Sarajevo," he said. "I'm the sole survivor."

"The war was still on when that happened," she said.

"A long time ago, a good soldier told me to plan for the worst. I don't like putting my head in Goran's hands. I'd better figure out how to get the hell out of here. I can get to the Slovenian Alps and hike into the English or American zones of Austria. Will you find out how the Allies divided it? I don't want to find myself in the Russian zone. If they catch me, I'm dead."

"That's easy to get."

"I need to know if the SDB want me in a dungeon. As I see it, I've been in jail since 1941. I loathe another day of incarceration. I suppose there's no harm in your asking Goran if I'm looking at jail time. If he can't get me off, the decision's easy. If he says he can, I've got some soul-searching to do. Make sense?"

"It's not for me to say."

"Does Goran resent you?"

"He still loves me. That's a powerful weapon. I'm prepared to use it for you."

Tony sucked in a whistling breath. "I don't like the sound of that."

"Emotionally."

"You think he knows I'm back?"

"If the SDB knows, he knows."

"Then, he'll know I'm here. They'll come for me."

"Other than going to Goran," she said, "is there anything else I can do for you in Zagreb?"

"Be careful. You've become a collaborator. Don't let him know you've been here, and don't let on you know I'm home." He looked away and scratched his head. "Oh, yes. There is one other thing you can do for me."

Katarina waited, and he said, "Stay the night."

She stayed two nights. Like a loyal mate, she worked alongside him during the day, trimming vines, weeding the vegetable garden, helping restore the inside and outside of the cottage. As they toiled, they shared tales of their youth – light, comical anecdotes. Neither dared tread on the broken glass scattered across the terrain of their late adolescence.

Food was plentiful, thanks to Josip's foresight. Fearing harsh times, in the fall he had slaughtered a two-hundred-pound hog and cured the meat as hams, sausages, bacon and salt pork. What he couldn't cure or smoke, they had preserved in jars and in cans of lard laced with salt. The root cellar also housed an abundance of potatoes, beets, turnips, cabbages and apples, which Katarina turned into soups and strudels to last Tony a week.

****

Katarina held the spindly arms that wrapped around her from behind. They swayed gently in the warm breeze, their eyes cast to the once-lush vines.

"Will it always be this way for us?" she said.

"What do you mean?"

"When our skin is loose and our hair white, will we feel like this – feel this way about each other?"

Though Katarina had yet to consent to the terms of Goran's proposition, she had no doubt that she would sacrifice herself to save Tony. Anyway, Tony wasn't the kind of man to forgive her past treachery. Her lucid mind said he was already lost, but her bewildered heart held out for a miraculous twist of fate.

"White hair's a long way off," he said. "I can't think that far ahead. With those savages on my tail, I can't even predict where I'll be next year. I've got a world to see. I'm going to make up for losing the best years of my life. I want to get back in the cockpit, swim the California surf, climb Kilimanjaro, hike the canyons of—"

"And me …?" She whipped around and glared into his eyes. He held her gaze for a moment, and then looked away, taking a step back.

"Is there a seat on the plane or a towel on the beach for me?" she asked.

"Katarina … I'm sorry if you misconstrued my intentions. I thought my letters were clear. I told you not to wait for me. I need some time. By God, I've earned it."

She knew he was right. He should be able to do whatever he pleased, whenever he pleased. She had been foolish to step into the future.

"Try to understand," he said. "I've been living day to day for so long, my mind is mush. If not for my parents and a few unfinished responsibilities, I'd have escaped Camp Ralston and stayed in America."

"These two days and nights," she said. "What was that? I thought it was love. Did I misconstrue that, too?"

In the height of passion, Katarina had screamed out her love for him. Heavy panting had been his only reply.

"Love to me, sex to you," she sighed, turning away.

She felt his hand on her shoulder and she brushed it aside but remained on the porch, peering up the entry lane to the road.

"Come here," he said. "Let me try to explain. This isn't easy for me, either. You don't know what I've been through."

Unknowingly, he had doused her with ice water reality. Whatever had made her think she could have it all?

"I've never felt about any other woman the way I feel about you. It's not that I don't love you. I'm not sure I even know what love is. Be certain, these days were more than sex. Trust me, I know."

She could see that he was squelching a grin.

"Don't worry, I won't explain. I need your patience and understanding. Please, Katarina. Give it to me."

It wasn't much to ask. The end was imminent. She should be grateful for these days with him.

"I'll promise more than that," she said. "No matter what the future holds, no matter what happens between you and me, whether we are joined in bed or separated by oceans or another man, I will always love you. That is a promise I will keep all the way to my grave."

His mouth opened, and he blinked as if his eyes stung.

Chapter 29

Goran did not hold a royal flush, but he held a secret so lethal that when he played his hand, the union of Tony and Katarina would be as dead as a fossil. Those cards he would hold until his marital pact with Katarina was ratified. But there was a possible snag – Luka. Goran's bond with the brute had never been strong, but the glue that connected them weakened the instant Ustasha bullets tore into the professor's chest. With Milic gone, Luka emerged as a driver of party doctrine, with Goran a mere passenger.

Aware that new constitutions decreed after bloody wars seldom erased centuries of hatred, Tito sought to silence Yugoslavian unrest by unleashing the power of the police and the propaganda of brotherly love. Any lingering doubts Goran had about Tito's resolve to divide and conquer vanished with the guilty sentences of the Chetnik leader and Zagreb's Archbishop. Archbishop Stepinac received a fifteen-year jail sentence for dissidence during the war; the Chetnik was publicly executed.

The SDB suppressed nationalistic expression, particularly in Croatia. Informing became the Communist regime's obsession – agents recruited tattlers and arrested innocents, whom they pressured into ratting on others. Friends informed on friends; brothers turned on brothers; children snitched on the mothers that bore them. A rat would eventually crawl out from its hole and inform the SDB of Vinograd Kralja and its whereabouts. If Tony was in Croatia, they would find him there.

Goran understood Luka's ways and means. During the war, Luka had operated like a spiteful cat, careful not to kill forthwith but to paw, toss about and maim. The fun ended when the mouse fell still. Hordes of enemies had fed Luka's thirst for pursuit and conquest. But a year after the war's end, Tito's own thirst for fleeing Nazis, Ustashe, Chetniks and their collaborators had waned. With the world watching, Tito's strategy shifted to clandestine measures rather than street justice. By the summer of 1946, the ripest of the low-hanging fruit had been plucked and the buds of peaceful opposition to single party rule were on the high branches of the tree. And though Luka remained eager to shear any and all who would not fall into lockstep with the party, Tito denied him his prey. This only amplified Luka's angst and volatility.

Though Goran had kept his distance, he would have to engage Luka to enact his scheme. For now, he was content to work indirectly and let events unfold – let the cat apprehend Tony – let it have its fun. When the interrogations were underway, Goran would observe Katarina's growing desperation. He had considered her lost forever – until this promising turn.

As for Tony's penance, Goran favored incarceration hundreds of miles from Zagreb. All he had to do was effect a substantial reduction in the sentence to ingratiate himself to Katarina – ten years in prison instead of death, eight years rather than twenty. Reduce the punishment, banish the threat and play the hand.

****

The SDB converged on Vinograd Kralja the Monday morning following Katarina's weekend visit. They handcuffed Tony and threw him in a paddy wagon while they searched for evidence linking him to anti-Communist activity. By noon he was in the Petrinjska jailhouse, a Zagreb holding tank for prisoners destined for military court, or would-be informers requiring SDB persuasion.

An SDB cop furnished him with a carbon copy of the charges, signed by Secretary Luka Lipovac. He was accused of enemy collaboration and violations against the people.

The jailhouse, erected as a temporary lock-up for petty thieves and disorderly drunks, now included post-war objectors – peaceful men who dared oppose the Communist dogma. Demanding repentance and setting an example as a deterrent, the SDB seldom detained them for long. Repeat offenders were shipped to camps in the country or the islands, never to be seen again.

At first, the questioning had been civil and straightforward. Tony corroborated the account contained in the SDB's dossier, concluding with his Babenhausen internment but avoiding the aftermath.

"You jumped a train in Slovenia, Babic," the interrogator said, "and you assaulted a soldier of the People's Army. You illegally entered Zagreb, and you failed to report to the ministry. Why the assault? Why the refusal to report? A man with nothing to hide does not commit such infractions."

"Your thugs stole from me and bound me like I was a criminal. Was that necessary?"

"We ask the questions. Expect a personal visit from Secretary Lipovac. I recommend you answer honestly and without hesitation. Denounce your war service and pledge to support Marshal Tito's socialism. We know much more than you think. Shall we start again?

"When will the secretary come?"

"You're a stubborn one. Answer my questions satisfactorily or I shall report your insolence to the secretary."

"When will he come?"

"When he's damn well ready."

****

Days passed and no one arrived. Then, on Tony's sixth day in jail, a turnkey delivered a book and a note.

"Looks like someone gives a damn for you," the jailer said. "We don't." In addition to the book and the note, he slipped a pencil and some note paper between the bars.

Once Tony was alone, be read the note:

'I have been pestering the desk superintendent for the right to exchange letters with you. They've granted permission every Tuesday and Saturday, providing we avoid political commentary. Bear in mind that my letters will be read by others before they reach you. The same is true of your letters to me.

I bought The Count of Monte Cristo *from a friend who teaches at the university. This is a wonderful story about the wrongful trial and imprisonment of a young man who escapes and vows vengeance upon his conspirators. The book is long. It will help pass the time.*

I joined your mother and father for dinner on Sunday. They shared your escapades as a young boy. Your father laughs when he says you were either just getting into trouble or just getting out of it.

I haven't heard from Goran, although I am sure he is concerned for you. I think he must be on the coast for a holiday because he didn't bring me the tonic from his cousin. You remember meeting his cousin, don't you? He was the big fellow. I think you called him scruffy. I might have

272

to travel to his cousin myself. I'm not really sure I should go. I don't want to aggravate Goran or my sore back.'

Tony read that paragraph a second time. 'Cousin' must be the pseudonym for Luka. Katarina was asking whether she should circumvent Goran and make a personal plea to Luka. Seemingly, Goran hadn't made any progress. Tony continued reading:

'Those few days with you at Vinograd Kralja were the happiest of my life. I know we will be together again, and when we are, every day will be like that. How is the food? Do you ...'

He examined the rest of the letter for other clues but found none. What to do and where to go? He scribbled a brief reply:

'Thanks for Monte Cristo. *I saw the movie at Camp Ralston. I can't help but see myself as the wrongly accused Edmond Dantes. You, of course, are the beautiful Mercedes, who longs for his return. Seeing you as Mercedes makes the story much more realistic. I am treated well. The food is okay, and I've gained weight. Of course, I have a long way to go.*

I am sorry that nasty backache still bothers you. A long train ride won't help. Be patient. I think it is better that you wait for Goran to bring the tonic.'

When the turnkey returned, he would give him the letter. In the meantime, he lost himself as *The Count of Monte Cristo.*

****

Like a wounded bull, Luka charged into the house that once belonged to the professor. "Fucking waste of time," he said. "I should have known better." He flopped down onto the armchair and glared at a charred log in the fireplace.

"And it's nice to see you, too," said his wife, who had dressed to the nines to please him. "Pissing away Rankovic's money means you've got explaining to do."

"Damn it, Ella, that's for me to worry about! It could be worse. I could have spent every last dinar looking for a phantom."

"Don't take your screw-up out on me!"

"Don't call it a screw-up!"

He and an Italian-speaking assassin had been in Rome chasing down a rumor that had Ante Pavelic in the protection of the Catholic Church and ready to spring from his hovel to Argentina via the Nazi ratline. Though such matters lay with Yugoslav foreign intelligence, Luka had pestered Rankovic for permission to hunt their arch-enemy. Rankovic had told him it was a long shot. Nevertheless, he had approved an exit visa and five thousand dinars for expenses and informant 'incentives'.

Luka told Ella that a third of the funds had gone to pay-offs, when he finally discovered that Pavelic was already in Argentina. The fact that Pavelic had been gone for a month had not deterred Italian scam artists from proclaiming the contrary and extracting the push money.

She knew that Luka needed a diversion when he was in one of these moods. The usual remedy was a good brawl. She'd given him some whopping spats herself, yet no matter how heated or vile the argument, he had never laid a hand on her. Only once had she goaded him beyond the breaking point. She'd never seen the punch, but it came within an inch from her ear with such force that it bashed right through the thick plaster to the next room. She shuddered at the recollection.

"Maybe a punching bag is in order," she said. "Do you remember a Croat airman by the name of Tony Babic?"

"You know I do. He'd dead."

"We have him at Petrinjska."

****

The instant Tony saw the swagger, the broad shoulders and the sneer, he remembered. The ruts in the big man's face had deepened, and his cheekbones seemed higher and sharper, but this was the same contemptuous lout Tony had angered at Zagreb University.

"Where would you like him?" one of the turnkeys asked the secretary.

"Six feet deep. For now, room 2. You can carry him out when I'm done."

The jailers marched Tony through a windowless door near the holding area. But for a small table and two chairs in the middle, the room was empty. By the time the lock clicked open, Tony had studied the shape and size of every stone in the wall facing him. Aware of Luka's gaze, Tony stared straight ahead at a jagged crack in the wall while the secretary circled. Suddenly, a powerful right hook to the jaw thrust Tony sideways, his chair toppled and his head bounced off the concrete floor.

"That's a shot from long ago, you traitorous shit. Now, get back in that chair before I land another!"

Tony returned to consciousness coughing, spitting and gasping for air. Two teeth lay amid the splatters of blood. He labored to one knee.

"Oh, what the fuck," Luka said, landing a low blow to the mid-section.

Air whooshed from Tony's lungs. As he lay bent and winded, Luka kicked his ribs and kidneys.

"Be sitting at that table when I get back or I'll boot you to death."

Tony heard the door slam. His only thought was the sharp pain in his ribs – the slightest move was torture – it even hurt to breathe. But if he didn't get into that chair, a kick or two to the head would make certain he never got up. He tried to uncurl from the fetal position and almost fainted. Holding his breath, he barrel-rolled onto his back and let out a cry. Perhaps he could drag himself to the overturned chair.

A minute later, he had the chair upright. He reached for the edge of the tabletop, intending to haul his backside high enough to slide onto the chair. Twice his hand slipped away.

Somehow in his weakened state, he managed to roll onto his stomach and get to one knee, still spitting blood. He hugged his waist for a minute and forced himself upright. When his tormentor returned, the prisoner was in the chair.

Luka tossed a satchel on the table. "I'm going to ask some questions. Lie, and you'll rot in here for a year awaiting trial. I'll start easy: you're a fascist sympathizer, aren't you?"

Tony shook his head, and Luka's fist struck his shoulder.

"Talk!"

"I'm no more fascist than you."

"Then why'd you join Hitler's heathens?"

"No choice."

"They all say that. I remember you prancing like a fucking peacock in your fancy uniform, proud as shit to wear the colors of the *fascist* State of Croatia." Luka dug into the bag and pulled out a lacquered-wood replica of an Iron Cross. He wielded it in front of Tony's nose. "A keepsake of your Nazi service?"

Though Tony's panting had begun to ease, the sight of the carving made his breath catch in his throat. "A friend ... in the prison camp made it."

Luka turned it over. "What's your Nazi pal's name?"

"Heinz Shultz was not a Nazi."

Luka unfolded several newspaper articles. "What about these? Look at your mug – proud as shit to play for the Nazis."

"The team was German." Tony had worked out how to move his split lip over the gap in his teeth to reduce the lisp. "SS officers ordered me to smile. They threatened to kill me if I didn't play. I know how this looks. If you will give—"

"Just following orders, right? Right now, the world's hearing a lot of that bullshit in Nuremburg."

Tony didn't know what this meant, nor would he ask. Luka's grimy fingers pushed a piece of notepaper across the table. "I don't read German, but I sure as hell recognize *Mein Kampf.* Your favorite book? Translate, and don't lie, 'cause the wife speaks German. I'll show her it."

Tony hadn't looked at Hermann Vogler's suicide note since sealing the envelope. But for some very strange reason, he now saw what he, Bo and Ladders had not seen. The revelation hit him like another boot to the solar plexus. Tony and his barrack mates had viewed individual ears of corn and peeled back the husks, scrutinizing words and phrases in pursuit of an explanation. Back at Graham, they had missed the cornfield:

'*Mein Kampf mit der Aufsicht ist zu unerträglich geworden. Mein Alternative ist eine Flucht. Ich kann nicht fliehen, Tod ist mein Überleben. Männer warten auf den Frieden, wenn der Krieg enden. Ich werde darauf nicht warten. Die Zeit meiner Ruhe ist in meiner Wahl. Heute ist das. Hermann Vogler*'

"Get on with it, Babic! Translate!"

"This is a suicide note written by a POW who's used 'Mein Kampf' literally. 'Mein Kampf' represents Hermann's struggle and his failure to cope with prison."

"Why'd you save it?"

"To give it to his widow."

"She's gonna have to wait a long time."

"The words ... mean nothing," Tony said. "There's a code in there. Hermann was telling us who killed him. Reading down, the first letter of each line gives the name of the killer: *M-A-U-E-R*. A ruthless Nazi murdered this man. Helmut Mauer forced Hermann to write the suicide note." He pointed to the non-soccer articles. "Those prove my hatred of fascism."

Tony translated each of them, adding graphic vignettes of the Nazis' tyranny in Rockford. And slowly, Luka's inquisition of Tony migrated to questions about Camp Graham and the Nazis. Detecting his interrogator's curiosity, Tony embellished scenes and sketched vivid depictions of the villains.

"Colonel Wolfgang von Arnim and Major Helmut Mauer, eh?" Luka jotted down the names. "Nasty bastards. Camp Graham and then Camp Alva, you say."

"Camp Alva, Oklahoma."

"They must be back in Germany," Luka said, picking at his yellowed teeth with the pencil lead. "I'd love to bring 'em in. You know, Babic, being anti-fascist is only half the battle here in Yugoslavia. The court won't see these. I'm keeping them for you. Next subject: why'd you assault our comrade in Slovenia?"

"They were taking me to Belgrade. They had robbed me, threatened to kill me and tied me up."

"Handcuffing or tying up is what police do when transporting convicts."

"If I'm to go to court, I'd prefer Zagreb to Belgrade."

"Why didn't you report to the Zagreb Ministry?"

"I was going to. I wanted some time with my family."

"Did you spend time with your girlfriend?"

"I don't have a girlfriend."

Luka's lips parted into a sly grin. "Me and Katarina are old friends. Met her in Zagreb. We worked together for the partisans in Sarajevo." He smacked his tongue three times. "Got into her in Split."

"You're a liar!" Tony braced for another punch.

Luka rose from his chair and cocked his fist, but the blow never came. Instead, he sat down, clasped his hands together, and rested them on the table. "Smashing looker –five foot six, brown eyes, black hair to the shoulders, luscious lips, long legs, firm ass, torpedo tits, nipples like—"

"You're describing thousands."

"How 'bout the beauty dot on her right cheek. You knew she was a partisan, didn't you? Been with us since '42."

Below the table, Tony's knuckles were white. Was this psychological warfare or something else? "You feed tidbits of truth and invent the rest."

"That so, eh? I'll skip the birthmarks between her neck and knees and get to October 8, 1943. That date mean anything to you?"

"You know it does. It's in my file."

"The day you met up with four Spitfires, right?"

How the hell ...? Tony had never mentioned four Spitfires to the interrogator in Africa, America, or here in Europe.

"Monday to Thursday, you bombed mountain hideouts. Friday and Saturday you were supposed to fly sea reconnaissance. We couldn't let you do that because we needed those guns, so we ordered the Spitfires. Now, how did we know all that? I'm going to let you think about that for a—"

"Tell me!"

"Sure you wanna know?"

"Yes."

"Your girlfriend told us. Can't say how she weaseled that flight plan from you, but she did. I sure know she can be convincing ... especially when she uses her fem—"

"If you had it, you got it from a mole at the base."

"Wrong. She gave me a copy of the original in a Sarajevo chapel. Ask Skoda if you don't believe me."

What's Goran ...? "How can I do that? You don't allow visitors."

"I can do whatever the fuck I like. And what I'm going to do right now is let you stew on this. You won't see me until you're ready to hand over a written apology for your war service, and a promise to support the socialist ideals of the Federal People's Republic of Yugoslavia. Give me that and you *might* avoid the gallows."

Chapter 30

Tony's head pounded from a migraine, but finding sleep to relieve it wasn't nearly as important as holding on to the fragments from Luka's allegations. In the still of the night, Tony gazed through the bars of his cell to the shadows of the hallway, revisiting every detail of the interrogation, and rummaging for inconsistencies that might explain the lies.

A man did not forget the beauty of a woman like Katarina. Possibly, Luka had met her in the early months of the war, through Goran. If Luka had kept tabs on her, he would know she had returned from Sarajevo.

Four days of mountain bombing ... four Spitfires ... two days of Adriatic surveillance. Did someone supply that information to the partisans or did it come from the Allies in a report? His mind, like his body, ached.

A half hour before sunrise, the most comforting and the most plausible of the explanations brought sleep. But an hour later he woke – the original logic in tatters and his bruises throbbing. A report by the Allies would have itemized three downed fighter planes, three lost British pilots, and two enemy parachutes. Luka hadn't mentioned any of that. Could it be conspicuous avoidance? This reasoning led him back to the mole theory. Everyone he could think of from the Sarajevo airbase was on Commissar Novak's death list. The partisans rewarded early turncoats; they wouldn't kill one of their own. If the spy was Katarina, there had to be anomalies, inconsistencies, coincidences.

He thought back to the steps of St Mark's and embarked on a gradual and deliberate five-year journey from there to Vinograd Kralja. The list of peculiarities was short – collectively, they raised doubt. He penciled a list:

She leaves Zagreb in haste. Details vague.
She spends two years with Goran, an unlikely suitor.
Two years she doesn't see me. Then she's at the soccer game.
She asks where I fly.
She waits a year to write and confesses her love.

He underlined 'asks where I fly'. She had posed that question only once. It was the night of the Sarajevo soccer match, and he would have forgotten all about it if not for her displeasure at his refusal to confide. A spy wouldn't give up so easily. A spy would pester the mark in the days and weeks to follow. She hadn't. He scratched out line four.

What of her hurried exit from Zagreb? She had said there was an altercation at the tailor shop with an Ustasha trooper whom she had slapped. She had not offered any details, the reason for the altercation, what the Ustasha had said, or how she escaped. Had the Ustashe been onto a beautiful partisan agent?

He had felt the attraction on her first visit to the vineyard. Dancing, they had clung to each other. Yet, she had selected his romantically inept friend. Was that a relationship of convenience or a liaison for the good of the revolution?

Only Katarina could provide the answers:

'Dear Katarina, Luka Lipovac came yesterday. He said he knows you. Is this true? He told a tale that began with you and me in Sarajevo and ended on October 8, 1943. Set my mind at ease.'

A jailor took the letter on a Tuesday. In four days, Tony would have his answer. But Saturday passed without reply. So did the following Tuesday. On Wednesday, they moved him to the military prison, where he would languish for more than a month in a damp cell. In this prison his cracked ribs knitted and he regained most of his weight but none of his spirit – strange for a man who had endured far worse for far longer. He must have been in love with Katarina. If not, he couldn't possibly hurt this much.

****

Tony woke to the tapping on the bars of his cell. Someone from the Ministry of the Interior had come to see him – Luka, he supposed. Yet it was a bloated, pasty man with a patch over his left eye that peered through the bars of his cell.

"I know I have some explaining to do," Goran said.

Tony shrugged. Other than the missing teeth, he showed no sign of Luka's beating.

Goran fumbled with the latch of his cigarette case. "Damn thing. I'm in need of a new one ... ah, got it. Smoke?"

Tony took one and leaned over the lighter in Goran's trembling fingers.

"I should have written," Goran said, "but the situation ... well, you know ... I joined the partisans and the party ... then this business with Katarina and you. It took some courage to come here."

"Yes," Tony said. "I can smell it."

"Suppose you could use a nip yourself. Look Tony, twenty minutes is all I have."

"Then, start with Katarina."

Goran sucked air through his teeth. "So Luka's told you."

"Told me what?"

"That she was a partisan agent."

Fist cocked, Tony lunged forward. "I ought to break your fucking neck!"

"Hear me out," Goran said, cowering behind raised palms and extended fingers.

"Why would I listen? You'd lie, cheat, or kill to get her back."

"I'm here to tell you the truth. If you don't want it, I'll be gone."

They had been standing throughout the exchange. Tony lowered himself to his cot, leaned back and supported one bent knee with meshed fingers.

They had given Goran a stool. He flicked the ash to the floor. "Yes, I was jealous of you, and yes, I'm still in love with her. But, I'm resigned to losing her. I thought the Allies would wear Hitler down, and she said it was better we join the partisans early than late. I didn't know she was already one of them. She deceived me as well. I knew nothing of the sting Milic set up with her and Luka. They kept it from me. She gave them your flight itinerary." He showed Tony the back of his hand. "Broken fingers – still fat and crooked. I was in such a rage when I found out, that I wrestled Luka to the ground. One of my punches hit the floor."

"There's a hole in your story. I didn't give her the schedule."

"Well, she got it. Perhaps she copied it while you slept."

"I didn't sleep with her. She was your girl. That schedule was safely tucked inside my tunic." He couldn't recall if he removed his jacket that night in Sarajevo.

They sat in silence for the better part of a minute.

"The news gets better, Tony. It will cost me some money, but there is a deal in the making. Your jail term will be four months, less your two months of time served, if you agree to permanent exile."

"Will they give me a passport?"

"Only party members have passports."

"That means the Alps. I could die up there."

"You can do it. The Americans will grant refugee immunity."

****

Another two months slipped by without contact from Katarina, Luka or Goran. But within days of his fourth month of captivity, the clatter of a nightstick on iron had Tony on his feet.

Luka peered between the bars. "You've got a forty-eight-hour head start. Then, I come looking." He tossed a small manila envelope to the floor of the cell.

Tony tore it open. "A passport and a travel visa ... Goran said this wasn't—"

"You can thank the wife for this," Luka said. "You've got two days to use it."

"*Whose* wife? I don't understand."

"You don't have to." Luka smacked his lips. "You might want to check on your girlfriend before you go. Like you, she's also put on weight."

****

Adela gestured to the closed bedroom door. "She's in there, Tony. She isn't feeling well."

Drawn drapes darkened the bedroom where Katarina lay in a robe. The moment he walked in, Katarina loosened the fabric hugging her slightly rounded midriff. Tears filled her eyes. "Will you ever forgive me?"

"So it is true. But ... why?"

"It's a long and painful story," she said.

"Then you'd better get started." He lowered himself to the bottom corner of her bed as Katarina opened the drawer of the night table.

"It started in the store where I worked. The truth is here." She held out the letter she had written but never mailed. He would not take it.

As she read, she stuttered and stammered, stopping several times to dab her eyes and clear her nose. At the most painful passages, she choked on her words and gagged as though she might vomit. Then her quivering lips fell silent as she gathered up the pages and offered them to him again, her puffy eyes pleading that he read the evidence of her guilt for himself.

But Tony remained stoical, his hands clenched into a ball on his lap. Did she really think he would help with a task that was hers alone to bear?

She continued reading. The night she stole the flight itinerary they had been sitting across from a freshly lit fire. The blaze soon over-heated the room and once Tony had shed his tunic she'd asked him to mend a slow leak in the drainpipe of the kitchen sink. While he made the repairs, she had pilfered his pocket and copied the contents.

After twenty minutes of halting speech, with tears streaming her cheeks, she acknowledged that the terrible deception would torment her for the rest of her life. "I accept my penance. I know I have lost you forever. I only pray that you will find the compassion ... to forgive. I know I will never see you again, but you will always be in my heart. I am so sorry."

Beneath his cold façade, he was stunned by the revelation. She owed the partisans, not for killing the rapist but for saving her life.

"Luka said you slept with him. True?"

"No. He was respectful ... he lied about that flight plan, leading me to believe that intelligence would be used to save innocent lives from bombs."

"Why didn't you tell me?"

"Would it have mattered?"

He thought on that. "You wouldn't be pregnant! Now you're in a hell of a bind. What are you going to do?"

"See that my child has a father who will provide for us. Goran and I will marry."

Tony sneered. "That's ridiculous! Even Goran wouldn't want you like this."

She folded her wet hankie and blew her nose. "That's where you're wrong. Yes, he called me a good-for-nothing whore when he saw me this way. The next day he was over it, promising to love the child as his own. I have to think of the baby. Goran's insanely jealous, but with you gone, he will have what he's always wanted."

"And you'll have a liar, a snake and a pathetic drunk for a husband!"

****

283

Later that evening, Adela shook Katarina awake, handing her a wet facecloth and a brush. "He's back," she said.

When Tony entered her bedroom, Katarina asked why he'd come and why so late.

"Tomorrow, the priest who christened me will marry us. Then I leave."

"You want to marry *me*?"

Tony gave a sardonic laugh. "No, I don't want to marry you. This is a marriage of necessity. Goran will not be the father of my child." He gave his reasons, most of which she could not deny.

"Goran negotiated for your freedom," she said, "in return for my hand in marriage."

"Maybe he did; maybe he didn't. If it wasn't my child in your womb, you could marry Hitler's brother, for all I care."

It was all so sudden. How could she possibly marry a man who despised her? But as her mind raced to uncover and appraise the ramifications and their impact, she kept returning to the enigma's reality. Tony was the victim of her treachery.

Finally, she broke the silence. "All right, I won't marry him. That doesn't mean I should marry you."

"You want to raise a bastard? What kind of mother thinks like that? A marriage makes certain the scheming degenerate won't pull a fast one later."

He hadn't mentioned that in his earlier rationale. "Could you get me water?" she asked in a weak voice.

He must have seen her sudden pallor, for he rushed from the room and returned with a full glass. "Here ... this should help."

Though she had yet to agree to the shocking proposal, Tony continued as if consent was given. "There are two conditions," he said. "I want your promise to leave Croatia when it is safe to do so. You will move near me, where I can be a part of the child's life. I will settle in Salzburg for the time being."

"Am I to understand we shall not live as husband and wife?"

"We shall not."

"I cannot travel with a baby."

"I said *when* it is safe to do so. You will need a travel visa."

"Goran's department is in charge of that."

"Where there's corruption, there's ways. My second condition is that you and the child live with my mother and father. They want you to move in with them. Do you have my Army check?"

She did.

"I'll leave half for the baby. Now listen carefully. It is critical that you remain on good terms with Goran. You don't want him for an enemy. Wait until I'm in Austria before telling him we've married. Say I gave you no choice. Stay close to my mother and father – they'll love the child and give you support. Despite the torture you've caused their son, they are fond of you."

****

Katarina gave Goran the news by letter, concerned that that he might go into uncontrollable rage. She might as well have delivered the bombshell in person. Shouting profanities, he pounded on Adela's door, late one evening.

"Don't answer it," Katarina said to Adela. "He might think we're out."

But Goran wasn't dissuaded. He splintered the lock in a drunken fury.

"Get out of my way!" he said, knocking Adela aside as he thundered through the apartment waving a pistol. "I'll kill him!"

Katarina watched from the doorway of the bedroom.

"And you!" he said, glaring at her. "Why do you punish me so? You tricked me!"

"I carry his child. I killed his friends. He suffered because of me. He insisted I marry him for the baby's sake."

"I won't rest until he's dead. When he's in his grave, you will be mine." He fired the gun at the window, shattering the pane, and ran off.

Aware that Goran would use the next morning to sleep off the hangover, Katarina went to the ministry in the afternoon. Without waiting to be announced, she stormed into his office, and slapped his face so hard that her palm stung.

"If you ever do that again," she screamed. "If you ever lose control and threaten me or my family, I will kill *you*. Don't think I won't do it, Goran. I've already buried a blade in one man's back. Don't think this office makes you immune."

She stared at his astonished look and the blood line between his nose and upper lip for two or three seconds. Rather than stomp from the office, she walked away with calmness of a woman who had enjoyed an afternoon tea.

Chapter 31

May 1947
Salzburg, Austria

Eight months had passed since Tony had left Yugoslavia. For a while, Tony had lived off Uncle Sam's prisoner-of-war check, and found his way into the city's soccer community, working as a game-to-game mercenary for clubs in need of scoring punch. The part-time vocation connected him with the owner of the Austria-Salzburg Soccer Club, and in the spring, Tony joined Herr Voorman's team as a forward and his Mirabel Chocolate Company as a maintenance mechanic. With steady employment, he would continue making up for his lost years in this exciting city of beauty and culture.

His skills as a nimble player soon won the praise of fans and afforded the life of a carefree bachelor. He worked regular shifts at Mirabel, traveled with the team to nearby towns, and closed the nightclubs and taverns three or four times a week with a pretty fraülein on his arm. Mirabel wages and under-the-table performance bonuses from the boss, who wished to maintain the team's amateur status, sustained his indulgences.

He thought of Katarina when he wrote her monthly allowance check and when a snapshot of their daughter, Janica, arrived in the mail. Katarina and Janica's exit visas had yet to materialize – something Tony chalked up to Communist bureaucracy. But by the early months of 1950, he accepted that there had to be more to it.

That's when the dreams began – at first once every week or so, then more often. The content varied, but the ending that jostled him conscious was always the same: a tearful woman sitting up in bed, pleading forgiveness. Seldom did he get back to sleep. After hours of twisting and turning, he would switch on the nightlight to study the snapshots of his little girl, and consider her life and future in a Communist country.

Awakened by a pre-dawn May thundershower, he raised a photo to the light. On the back, the little girl's mother described what a black-and-white photograph could not: the place, the time and sometimes the circumstance, such as a birthday or a Sunday outing. Katarina had written that Janica's eyes gleamed copper-green, an extraordinary combination of the father's blue and the mother's brown. Her hair, which appeared white, was actually platinum, like Tony's at that age, and curly, too.

The photo collection numbered ten. He had framed his favorites and displayed them on the dresser. Janica had to be the prettiest little girl he had ever seen. The most recent snapshot, the one he now held under the lamp, captured Janica in a short knit dress and white knee socks. She stood by a bust of a bronzed harvest woman at Republic Square. The Communists had renamed Jelacic Square and removed the famous warrior monument.

For Tony, the photograph was bittersweet: here was his angelic daughter with one hand on her hip, a tiny purse held in the other – a grinning angel in the shadow of a morose figure of repression. On the back of the photo, beneath 'Janica at three', the little girl had penciled a heart.

Days later, Tony charged down the soccer pitch, looking for a pass, when his legs went rubbery and he crashed to the turf. By the time the trainers reached him, he felt like he was going to vomit. They raised his arms over their shoulders and dragged him to the bench, and for the rest of the game his head hung low in his hands and he stared at his muddy boots.

He had never considered himself a coward – from 1941 to 1946, he had bloody well proved his courage. But today, for the first time in ten years, he thought otherwise. Luka had given him the ticket out, and he had taken it, saving his own skin, running from the Communists as fast as he could – leaving Katarina and the unborn in the lurch. At the time, it all made sense. He had earned the right to be free, and he had lived up to his responsibility by marrying the pregnant woman, leaving her money and vowing to provide for her in the future.

Yes, she had betrayed him. But he had also betrayed her. Katarina and Janica were the captives. He was free. No longer could he duck from the blame or the guilt.

Oddly enough, that night, he found dreamless sleep. And in the weeks to follow, the tearful woman pleading for absolution never reappeared.

Yet, his shame lingered. Nothing could numb it – not the cold booze in the bars or the warm flesh in his bed.

Two lines in a letter were all that were needed: '*You asked if I would ever forgive you. It has taken me a long time – more than three years. Yes, Katarina, I forgive you. Now I ask you to forgive me.*'

In the envelope, he included a picture of the Austria-Salzburg team and a news clipping. She must have written back the day she received the exoneration. Her response was also brief: '*I do not know what you want me to forgive. Whatever it is you have done, you have my unconditional forgiveness. Know that my love for you has never wavered. I hope you like this photograph.*'

The three-by-five-inch snapshot of Katarina was his first picture of her. It slipped from his grasp, and he picked it up from his lap and balanced it against the stem of the bedside lamp. He would give it until the end of the year; if his wife and daughter didn't have visas by Christmas, he would return to Yugoslavia and do his time as an enemy of the state.

****

The resurrection of their relationship began slowly, first with letters, then with the sound of voices over the telephone on the second Sunday of every month. The conversations, guarded at first, grew animated, and then became tender and loving in the moments before the receivers went down. At Tony's urging, Katarina kept things cordial with Goran, who, as a senior party member, enjoyed the privilege of a home telephone.

On those Sundays when she spoke with Tony, Katarina and Janica spent the remainder of the day with their host. Goran's love for Katarina had overflowed to Janica. He treated her as a niece, showering her with gifts and taking her to the zoo, the children's theater and the amusement parks.

Nonetheless, Katarina grew adept at separating lies from truth. Goran said he had accepted that they would never be a couple. This, she knew, was a fabrication. She also suspected that he was not helping with the exit papers. The drunken tantrum, in which Goran said he wished Tony had drowned in the sea, stayed fresh in her mind. She was certain that Goran would see to Tony's execution should he ever return to Yugoslavia.

****

Knowing of Herr Voorman's government connections and considerable influence, Tony decided to invite him to a fancy restaurant, supposedly out of appreciation for his kindness. And now Voorman, who always sought insight into the motivations of others, peered into the aging striker's eyes as they raised their wineglasses.

"To you, Herr Voorman," Tony said. Their goblets clanked. "Thank you for opening so many doors for me."

"You've opened plenty yourself," Voorman quipped with a roguish wink.

Sheepishly, Tony said, "Not lately."

"Yes, you've seemed a bit off. You haven't once looked over at that luscious thing sitting by the wine rack. What's happened to that spark?"

"I don't wish to burden you with—"

"*Burden?* We are friends, Tony. Your problems are my problems."

"I appreciate that, Herr Voorman. The problem is that the Yugoslav Communists continue to punish me for my war service. They kicked my parents out of their Zagreb flat and forced them into a dilapidated country vineyard where they struggle to make a living. Winemakers and fruit growers who resist Tito's scheme of socialist madness are soon without customers."

Tony said that customer loyalty in the new Yugoslavia had vanished like a fart in a windstorm, another of Hobson's idioms, translated into German. "The worst is this: the Communists won't permit my wife and child to leave the country. They lived with my mother and father. Now they share a small room in a flat."

Voorman struck a match and lit a cigar, but remained silent.

"You have friends in high places," Tony said. "Could something be done to get them out? Something diplomatic or ...?"

Voorman gently clasped Tony's forearm. "Perhaps it is friends in *low* places you need. I have those, too."

Weeks later, Voorman came with a plan. If Tony could raise the bribe money, Voorman would see that it reached the right people in Zagreb's Interior Ministry. But Tony would have to be patient – these things took time.

Tony supplied the cash and Voorman dispatched it. But the months flew by and the visas failed to appear. Voorman found out why. A top Yugoslav official had vetoed Katarina and Janica's release at the last stage of authorization. Voorman's connection had tried another insider with more of Tony's money. The recipient was sacked and banished to a work camp on an Adriatic island of rock.

"Two separate hundred-mark sweeteners," Voorman said. "Tony, someone has it in for you."

"There are two possibilities. Neither can be bribed. One is in love with my wife. He doesn't need money because his grandfather made a fortune producing fountain pens. The other is a Communist zealot who loathes me for my political leanings."

Voorman grinned. "Your past life must have been very interesting."

"With respect, Herr Voorman, I am sick of telling that story. If we can't get my family out, I will go back to them."

"There is always a way. But you will need a lot more than 200 deutschmarks."

Tony had a lot more than 200 deutschmarks, but it was in America under the care of Joshua Gooden.

****

Tony had reinstated his relationship with Joshua soon after he came to terms with his love for Katarina. The former partners had traded letters and Tony had learned that Joshua's days in Ralston were now down to just one week a month. The rest of Joshua's time was spent in Atlanta at the thriving headquarters of UWA Distributors. He had moved the business in 1949 after an odious but rewarding exchange at one of the South's biggest food companies.

The food manufacturer's vice president had noticed mail-order advertising for Unique Wares of America in the *Atlanta Journal* and had called the company to speak with the president. Joshua had asked how he might be of assistance. The executive said he was interested in striking a deal to fill promotional orders for box-top premiums and money-saving coupons. Excited by the possibility of landing such a large and reputable customer, Joshua had driven 500 miles to Atlanta to personally present UWA's credentials. And he had met with a startled vice president, an old Southerner whose office displayed Civil War artifacts, including a Confederate flag and an oil portrait of Robert E. Lee. The rebel loyalist never even offered Joshua a chair, let alone five minutes to make a case for UWA's capabilities. He said he had changed his mind, deciding to fill promotional orders in-house for security reasons.

In one of the letters, Joshua had said that he should have known better than to think a Negro could waltz into the office of a Dixie blueblood and expect to be welcomed as an equal. But his angst had dissipated on the drive home – the fellow had given him a brilliant idea.

The USA had entered the age of post-war coupons and promotional incentives. American housewives bought products for box tops that could be redeemed for all sorts of gimmicks: cents-off coupons, cookbooks, notepads, recipe cards, measuring spoons, figurines, key chains and baseball cards. Joshua reckoned a company wouldn't want to use trained production workers to sort, pack and ship promotional goods. One pack-and-ship enterprise could do it all, and if enough companies came on board, the cost would be less than the hourly factory wage. UWA had the experience and the infrastructure to fill the orders faster and cheaper. There was only one problem: Joshua Gooden could not be the face of the company.

Joshua needed a personable white man to sell the service. The right white man lived in Pasadena, California. Joshua had contacted Bo and made an offer the big bruiser could not refuse. And so 'Bob Smith' moved to Atlanta. It wasn't long before UWA had more business than it could handle.

In Ralston, the Dupree Manor had gone up for sale shortly after Edmond Dupree's passing. Joshua didn't need a house that big, and the purchase didn't make much sense, what with him spending so much time in Atlanta. But he had to have it – partly because of its history, partly because the manor embodied the grandeur of the Old South, but mostly because of what the estate represented. The Dupree Manor had housed the most successful, most respected family in the entire county. Although Joshua's name was on the deed, he had bought the house for the Southern Negro. The manor would become an icon of black achievement.

Chapter 32

April 1952
Hamburg, West Germany

The call came into the switchboard of the Hamburg Bundeskriminalamt, or BKA, West Germany's version of the FBI. The man on the line calmly asked to speak to Officer Mauer. The operator put him through.

"Hello."

"Are you late?" the caller asked.

Mauer stiffened, covered the mouthpiece with his hand, and hunched over his desk. "By twenty-two minutes."

"Then I have the correct policeman. I have an assignment for you. Midnight tomorrow, we meet at the Luxor."

Mauer had not heard from the former SS colonel for almost a year, having assumed his value to Arnim and the Odessa may have diminished with his last assassination. He relished the activities of the covert Organisation Der Ehjemaligen SS-Angehorigen (ex-members of the SS), which had flourished in the final days of war and the first years of peace. Odessa was now waning, but there was still work to do – Nazis on the run needed new identities and safe ratlines to South American havens. The network consisted of forgers, bankers, businessmen and assassins. Mauer was Arnim's man in situations requiring suicide or accidental death. In four years, he had completed five assignments, unfettered.

Unlike those connected to the death camps, Mauer wasn't under siege by the bloodhounds – a false identity was unnecessary. Yes, he loved Odessa work, but he despised the compensation. Honor and fifty deutsche marks per hit would not buy a poorly paid cop an automobile. He yearned for the power and privilege afforded Arnim by the riches of dead Jews. With Arnim almost sixty years old and plagued by emphysema, the job of Hamburg Odessa chief was no longer a speck on the horizon. He considered himself a possible heir. After Hamburg, there would be more for him. He was still young. Notwithstanding his paltry pay, Odessa fed other needs. Had they known about his fetish for the choke, they would expect him to hang a victim free of charge.

A post-war year of hard labor in the French coal mines, and Mauer had returned to the Fatherland bitter and penniless. The money he had stolen from Tony Babic would have made a substantial difference in his life back in Germany. Also, by refusing to hide his relationship with the SS, he had sabotaged any chance of returning to police work.

****

Arnim had never met a brighter, more disciplined soldier than Helmut Mauer. After repatriation, he had lost track of him. But two years later, an Odessa agent found Mauer working as a night security guard. Out of uniform, Mauer was thin and drawn, apathetic. Arnim wanted him rehabilitated, for he could be useful to Odessa.

Reclusive industrialist Klaus Weiskopf had purchased Sea Eagle Shipbuilding with Odessa's Zurich deposits. If Weiskopf had returned to Germany as Wolfgang von Arnim, someone would have asked how a former SS colonel had amassed two-and-a-half million marks to buy one of Hamburg's esteemed shipbuilders.

At a private dinner with Mauer, Arnim had alluded to the *role* of Odessa but stopped short of admitting its existence. Mauer's eyes had glowed with excitement. Arnim offered employment at Sea Eagle and Mauer accepted, moving to Hamburg.

By 1951, the parliament had ratified the Bundeskriminalamt federal police force. Recruitment rested with those who held similar roles in Hitler's fascist police; no longer were former Nazis and SS men *verboten*. Those with police experience submitted applications and signed on. Knowing Mauer wasn't suited to a clerical position in Sea Eagle's purchasing department, Klaus Weiskopf suggested he resign and sign on with the BKA where he would have license to threaten, beat and steal.

****

Mauer headed for a narrow side street in the heart of the portside district of Hamburg's Reeperbahn. At twenty minutes to twelve, he slipped through the thin facade of the brothel and went up the stairs to the smoky cocktail lounge of lush red walls, velour curtains and bust portraits illuminated by dim lamps. On the bar stool nearest the door, a makeup-caked blonde woman nursed a tall drink. Her fishnet-stocking legs were crossed, and her skirt hiked high. Mauer saw Vreni's apprehension the instant she set eyes on him.

"Evening, Officer. I didn't expect you back so soon."

He could see that her smile was forced. "Tonight I am not here for you," he said, coldly.

"You like Johnny Ray, officer?"

"Is that a drink?"

"A singer. That's him singing *Cry*."

Mauer hadn't noticed. Already he was intoxicated by the black choker around the prostitute's neck, and the mental image of her bulging eyes as she gagged for air. The last time they were together he had choked her stupid in the red room at the end of the corridor. He had fooled with Vreni long enough to know that she was aware of the dangers. Oh yes, she played his game for the money but like her client, she understood the delicate threshold between carelessness and control.

As he gawked at her cleavage, a rush of heat flushed his pallid skin. He moved closer. "Next week I come for you," he said, expecting Vreni to pull back in fright. This time she showed no fear – for that, he would have to pay. He expected the Luxor's services for free, but no, if word spread, too many cops would hang around expecting a handout. All he could wheedle from the madam was a small discount, adequate to keep the BKA out of the brothel's affairs.

"Tonight I meet a business man," he said. "None of the whores are to know me."

Vreni nodded agreement. "I will treat you like a complete stranger until next week." She tugged on her choker, slanted her head, and stuck her tongue out the side of her mouth.

Mauer glanced out over the room of sailors from the cargo ships in port. Eager to drink, smoke and romp with the girls, they knocked back their brews and crooned with Johnny Ray. With no one looking his way, he wrenched Vreni by her wrist, yanking her close. "Tease me again and you'll have an accident." This time he saw the fright. "Be very careful with men like me."

He picked up the schnapps he had ordered but wouldn't pay for, and meandered through the maze of patrons to a padded crescent-shaped bench behind an oval table in a secluded corner.

A panting man with a mustache and Vandyke beard lowered his portly frame and slid into the booth next to Mauer.

"What would you like to drink, Herr Weiskopf?" Mauer asked.

Arnim loosened his necktie. "Beck's," he said, wheezing. "Good … good to see you, Helmut."

The stairs would have taken their toll. Mauer found Arnim's disrespect for his own body disgusting. Arnim was two sizes larger than a year ago and seventy-five pounds heavier than the man Mauer knew in Casablanca. At least the facial hair, broad backside and vast belly provided outstanding camouflage.

Still the subordinate, Mauer endured the useless preamble. Tonight it went longer than their last meeting.

"You are a frequent visitor, Helmut?"

Arnim liked to ask questions whose answers he knew, but Mauer was wise to the trap. "Every two weeks I'm here on police affairs – once a month on personal affairs."

Arnim coughed into a handkerchief and wiped his mouth. "I am pleased that you are back in good form. Be sure you do not kill. That would conclude your work with the organization."

Mauer showed no emotion. Yes, there were certain constraints.

Not until Arnim's second beer was in his fist did he advance the discussion. "The assignment I have for you … is not the usual business." He glanced left and right, seemingly content that no one was close enough to overhear.

Mauer leaned forward. "Is the organization displeased with my work?"

"Why do you say this? Your record is impeccable. Currently, the ratlines are quiet. At present, the organization undergoes a phase of surveillance and intelligence. This does not mean your services will not be called upon. At last month's conference, we reviewed a request from our man in Salzburg. He tabled a low-priority assignment, one that's been on the D-list for some time. When I saw the name on the docket, I nearly choked. I thought of you, Helmut – though not because I choked …" He peered at Mauer, expecting a grin.

He wouldn't get one. Mauer loathed jokes about his perversions.

"This goes back to Camp Graham," Arnim said. "We have an opportunity to settle an old score. And you, Helmut … you can earn a stack of deutschmarks in the process."

"Who is this person?"

"The assignment is called Operation Zagreb. The name on the docket is a Slav by the name of Babic."

Mauer cracked his knuckles. His face had already turned into a demonic mask.

That might explain Arnim's snicker. "Babic has been living in Austria since '46. Salzburg says he's Ustasha. That entitles him to organization support."

"Did you set Salzburg straight?"

"Think beyond your repugnance, Helmut. I accepted the assignment – said I had just the right man to get Babic's family out of Yugoslavia. Those on the D-list pay for assistance. The incentive is lucrative. All will go to you, Helmut … a token of appreciation for past service."

"How much?"

"Five thousand marks."

Mauer felt his heartbeat race. His annual Bundeskriminalamt wage was half that.

Arnim chuckled. "You can thank Salzburg. Well, no, you can't actually – you don't know his identity. One day, perhaps."

****

Herr Voorman's latest plan was time-consuming, complicated and precarious. That explained the high cost of the operation. An Odessa man would have to travel to a Communist country and usher out the wife and child of an exiled Ustasha lieutenant. Entry into Yugoslavia was no simple matter. The undercover agent would need a bona fide reason to get in and out. Voorman estimated 250 deutschmarks for the passport forger, 250 for travel and accommodation expenses, and 5,000 to compensate the skilled escort.

He sat with Tony in his office, its walls adorned with pictures of Voorman with famous people ranging from politicians to opera singers and, of course, soccer players. Tony had agreed to the scheme in principle and had asked for a short-term loan.

"Tony, Tony, Tony." Voorman rested his folded hands on his oversized desk. "I am not in the loan business. I am just a confectioner with an expensive sports sideline."

At thirty-one years old, his star forward had passed the speed baton to players ten years his junior. Demoted from forward to the midfield, Tony had managed to get the job done on experience, but the injured leg took a beating and Voorman knew it. The fans' adulation receded, and with it Tony's equity with the team owner. Indeed, had Voorman not already sponsored a fascist Ustasha officer's case to the Odessa, he would have ended it. But now, he was obliged to see it through.

"I am afraid you will have to raise the money elsewhere," Voorman said. "The moment you have the funds, I'll get it under way."

"You can start now."

Voorman raised his brow. "Come, now, Tony. If you had the money, you would not be in here asking for financing."

"The money is in America. It might take a month to get here. I can't waste another day. This has gone on for too long."

"You're not shitting me, are you?"

"I'd never lie to you, Herr Voorman."

"I'll need 500 to get us started, another 1,000 in six weeks. That's a good-faith disbursement to the professional who will risk his neck for you. You pay him the remaining 4,000 when your wife and child are in Austria. You *will* have the money, won't you? These people I have commissioned are not ones to double-cross."

"Never would I put my wife and child in peril."

"Four thousand marks when he delivers?" Voorman asked.

"Yes. When will that be?"

"Patience, Tony. Operation Zagreb is not a kindergarten field trip. The undertaking must be researched, planned and rehearsed. We do not want mistakes. Now, this is what I want your wife to do ..."

Chapter 33

With the Stalin union rancid, Tito needed new markets and technologies to advance Yugoslavia beyond its dependency on agriculture. Opening the borders for heavy-industry expositions for short periods seemed a way to stimulate the economy. Some of the visitors were even allowed to bring their families and make a holiday of it.

Once Mauer completed the refresher course in Serbo-Croatian, he moved on to the basics of German shipbuilding. It wasn't as if he was expected to be an expert at Zagreb's September International Trade Fair. All he had to do was know enough to handle questions from border guards, Yugoslav cops and trade delegates. Mauer would attend the trade fair as the representative of Sea Eagle Shipbuilders.

While he studied shipbuilding, Katarina attended German classes and read travel and history books on the port of Hamburg. She didn't know why. Tony said it was better this way; he would fill her in when he had permission to do so. In the meantime, she was to visit a photo studio and get passport photographs of herself and Janica. The photos had to look as if they were snapped by the same camera that captured the mugs of those in the samples he had sent – the same paper stock, the same size, the same lighting, the same sober pose.

****

Four weeks ahead of the trade fair, he gave her the final details. The funding was in place courtesy of Joshua who had airmailed a money order for $2,250. Tony had converted half of that into deutschmarks and placed the remainder in a bank account for US funds.

"A businessman will come for you and Janica during the trade fair," he told her. "I don't know his name. They insist I respect the secrecy of the operation. When the fair is over, you and Janica are to leave with him by train and clear Slovenian customs as a family. He's a German living in Hamburg. This is why they want you to know the city. The Yugoslavian Ministry authorized three one-week visitation visas – one for him, the others for his wife and daughter. He'll enter Yugoslavia alone and bring passports for you and Janica. You'll need them at the border. Say 'yes' if you understand. Say 'not really' if you need an explanation."

"It is safe, Tony. I heard the door close. Goran's outside with Janica."

"These people have thought of everything. Klagenfurt's a half day by rail. Your job is to converse with this fellow in German whenever necessary. He'll contact you in Zagreb. He's getting 5,000 marks for this. I'd have paid ten times that."

****

Arnim counted out 1,250 deutschmarks. "Put 1,000 in the bank, Helmut. Two-fifty is for your expenses. Don't go cheap and pocket the leftovers – an executive of Sea Eagle stays at the best hotels. Your reservation is at the Zagreb Palace." He handed Mauer the rail tickets. "You will go through Villach and cross into Slovenia north of Jesenice. Your return will be at the Dravograd crossing – we do not want you meeting the same customs agent, do we? The ticket is first class. Travel in a well-tailored suit. You have one, don't you?"

Mauer bristled at the condescension. "Of course I do." It was already Wednesday. He had two days to coerce a tailor into making one.

"Buy a better one," Arnim said. "You can now afford it. Remember, Helmut, your assignment is to escort Babic's family to Austria ... unharmed. Do not intimidate or traumatize. Once they are out and you have your money, do whatever you like. I am certain you've given plenty of thought to Babic's retribution."

"Indeed, Herr Weiskopf. I've been admiring the photo of the Russian bitch. He shall watch me deal with her."

"Deliver them to Klagenfurt. If Babic is not at the station, he will be at the Sandwirth Hotel. You get 4,000 marks when you hand them over. Unfortunately, I will miss the look on his face when he sees her on your arm. But, Helmut, Salzburg has to know you have delivered them safely. Do not allow vindictive emotions to interfere. Get your money; let a month pass. Then punish. Dispose of the bodies, and leave no trace. Odessa does not excuse lose ends."

****

"The escort is in Zagreb without complications," Voorman said to Tony by telephone. "Tell your wife to be ready."

"She's expecting a call from me at six tomorrow. Can it wait till then?"

"Of course. He will not make contact until the fair opens on Monday. She is to be home the entire day."

"Any other instructions?"

"She is to act like a wife."

"And my daughter? She's too young to—"

"Your wife will tell her that he is a family friend. Forty minutes before the Austrian border, he will give her a sweet laced with a sedative. This will make her sleep during the inspection."

"I'm not sure I like that. Is he a doctor?"

"The candy is doctor-prescribed. Don't worry, Tony. This man is a professional."

****

The organization that masterminded the escapes of Ante Pavelic, Adolf Eichmann and Josef Mengele left nothing to chance. Large or small, Odessa's methods were meticulous. For Operation Zagreb, they gave Mauer dossiers on the two Croats he was to avoid – Luka Lipovac, a rabid hunter of Nazis and Ustashe, and Goran Skoda, the director of state security records. Skoda was educated and fluent in German. He was also madly in love with Babic's wife and known to take any measure to confine her to Zagreb.

From his room at the Palace, Mauer retraced another agenda – this one deviated from Odessa's. At Camp Graham he had put his interests above those of the Reich, but his plan to steal the Croats' money had ended in disaster. He now had a glorious opportunity to right that wrong. A steady hand reached for the telephone. He asked for Herr Skoda, in German.

"This is he. With whom am I speaking?"

"My name is Helmut Mauer. I am a Hamburg businessman in Zagreb for the International Trade Fair."

"Why do you call *me*, Herr Mauer? My ministry is not involved in trade and commerce."

"This, I know. This is not why I call. You and I share a mutual interest: Tony Babic." Mauer heard a gasp and then silence. He extended the pause, then added, "Be assured, this man is not a friend of mine. The issue I wish to bring to your attention is important – too important to discuss on the telephone. Might I come by your residence, tomorrow or the next day?"

"Tomorrow I have guests for dinner. Come earlier … at three. I live at—"

"I know where you live."

The exchange had gone better than expected. The Croat's clipped speech confirmed the inner turmoil. Mauer liked that. He would do business with Goran, then Katarina. Odessa mandated that he spend an hour with Katarina so that they would not appear as strangers on the train or at the border. He had information for her to memorize, as well as travel visas and a weathered German passport with date stamps and places visited. Odessa had prepared a complete history of her life since leaving Yugoslavia in 1945: where she had lived; how she met her husband; the place of their daughter's birth. The details might prove useful in an awkward situation. After the meeting, Mauer was not to see her again until they boarded the Friday train. They would clear customs in Dravograd and travel another thirty-five miles to Klagenfurt, Austria.

Mauer couldn't wait to see her in living color. He had played out the fantasy countless times. In a month, his dream would come true. Katarina would be first to die, with Tony Babic watching. Then he would take his time with Babic, pardoning the daughter. A pretty five-year-old would command a high price on the black market, and until a buyer paid his price, he would raise Janica as his own. He had the papers to do it, though not Arnim's consent. That didn't matter – Arnim would be dead.

****

Goran greeted a pale, gaunt, well-dressed man with a package under his arm: a bottle of premium schnapps.

"A gift for you, Herr Skoda," Mauer said.

"Come – come in. We can talk in the parlor. I'll open this. I assume you like schnapps."

"I am German. Of course I do." The eye patch had taken Mauer by surprise, but he acted like it wasn't there. He walked through the entryway as though oblivious of the spectacular art and furnishings. But his peripheral vision hadn't missed them, nor had he overlooked the value of a two-story flat in the heart of Zagreb, surely an inheritance, though that was a question he wouldn't dream of asking.

Goran uncorked the schnapps and poured two shots, handing one to Mauer, who had settled on the couch behind the coffee table. Then he sat in his father's desk armchair and swiveled it around toward his guest.

"I am intrigued by your telephone call, Herr Mauer – I am wondering how you got my name ... and what you wish to discuss."

"The world shrinks as we speak, Herr Skoda. I shall be candid, assuming you will keep this conversation to yourself."

"Until I know your purpose, I cannot make that promise. On the other hand, be assured that I am a person of discretion."

"And wisdom. I would not have come had I not been prepared to share my story. You shall see that you have much to gain. In addition to my role as an executive of Sea Eagle Shipbuilding, I am involved in an organization engaged in clandestine activity throughout Europe. Months ago, a colleague informed me that bribes were issued to people in your ministry. You discovered the violation and reprimanded the wrongdoers."

"If you were involved in some way, it was most unwise to come here. I can have you imprisoned."

"Herr Skoda, my interest isn't in bribing people. The compensation for such work is measly. I am above that. Babic is pursuing a new strategy to bring his wife and child to Austria. He has yet to make a contract with my organization, but he is in discussions."

"How will they get out?"

"That would be a betrayal of trust. He has the money to pay, and this time you shall not be able to stop him – unless I help you."

"Why would you help a complete stranger?"

"I am an unabashed mercenary. I take care of problems for people with money." Mauer shifted on the couch and leaned forward. "I command a healthy reward for discretion, professionalism and results. But you must be aware that if Babic's deal is consummated, I am powerless to assist you. That would conflict with the interests of other members of the organization." His eyes remained riveted on Goran. Mauer hadn't blinked for the better part of a minute.

Goran adjusted the patch over his eye. "I see. And what services, may I ask, do you offer?"

"I need to know I can trust you." Mauer blinked as he eased back and gently tapped the arm of the couch with the skeletal fingers of his right hand. "If you are interested in pursuing this discussion, I suggest you explain to me your relationship with Katarina. Tell me how you met. Describe the current situation."

Goran got out of his chair and walked to the window. "You are extremely presumptuous."

"In my business, I have to be. It is not as personal as you think. I know most of your story. I seek corroboration."

Goran cast his eyes on the grounds of Tomislav Square. "The leaves are beginning to fall," he said. "Summer was short this year. Perhaps nature is making us pay for the mild winter."

He turned from the window. "The story is upsetting. The moment you feel that I have verified the account, please stop me."

Two schnapps later, Mauer had what he was looking for. Goran couldn't hide his hatred or his obsession.

"So if I understand you correctly, Herr Skoda, you will do whatever is necessary to keep Katarina here."

"And the little girl."

"One matter isn't clear: how will you convince a Catholic woman in love with her husband to divorce him. And if she did, would she marry you?"

"A moot point. Never will Katarina divorce Tony. The best I can hope for is keeping Katarina and Janica in Zagreb. Strange as it seems, I have grown to love her daughter – a precious child – so happy and so loving. Often they come for Sunday dinner. I'm thankful for that. Katarina is indebted to me – in hindsight, a mistake; he'd be in a work camp, and still be there – or, better yet, dead."

"If he were dead, would she marry you?"

"She pacifies me because of my influence. In this country, life is harsh for those without ties to the upper echelons of power. Katarina agreed to marry me years ago when Tony impregnated her. That story is incidental to our discussion. I will not share it." He poured himself another shot.

"Your troubles might end if she were widowed."

Goran threw the schnapps down his throat. "Are you a mercenary assassin?"

Mauer's lips crinkled into a thin a smile. He hadn't planned on going for it so soon. "My victims are never murdered. They suffer accidental death or perish by their own hand. I am very clean and very convincing."

Goran's expression turned stony. "I must ask you to leave."

"Your reaction is typical of new clients. Even a grievously wronged man seldom agrees to rid himself of his enemy in a conversation of minutes. "Think on it, Herr Skoda. Consider the outcome and the consequences for yourself." He considered adding, *she'll be with you forever,* but decided to let Goran draw that inference on his own. "I'm at the Palace. If you wish to pursue this further, contact me there. I'm on the floor of the fair during the day but free most evenings. If I do not hear from you, this conversation never happened. No harm done. Herr Skoda, it has been a pleasure. I shall see myself out."

****

After Monday's trade fair, Mauer checked the front desk for messages. There was one: '*I wish to discuss further. I will be home this evening.*'

Mauer arrived at eight. The instant he was inside, Goran said, "How would you do it?"

"First, Herr Skoda, you must be certain you wish to proceed."

Goran ran his finger under the eye patch and adjusted the string. "There can be no suffering. It must be quick."

Mauer followed him to the parlor, but rather than sit, Goran went to the window and yanked the drapes together. When he returned, his cheeks were red and his chin, wet.

Mauer's senses told him that Goran wasn't fully committed. Nonetheless, he pressed on. "An auto accident is popular, but the target does not own a car. Suicide is better and more controllable. However, you are ahead of yourself. My terms may not please you."

Goran, who had remained standing, finally settled into an armchair across from Mauer. "How much?" he asked.

"In Germany, I am paid half down, the rest when the job is done. This I cannot do for you – not that I don't trust you – getting money from debtors in Communist countries is problematic. I am prepared to offer a preferred rate if you settle in advance. I shall execute this contract for 5,000 deutschmarks in cash."

"How do I know you won't take my money and run?"

"How do you think I know so much about you, Babic and Katarina? I am equally familiar with Secretary Lipovac and his crazed post-war antics. Herr Skoda, my organization is not in the business of double-crossing clients. If I tell you Babic will die by his own hand, then so it will be. If you choose to pass on this opportunity, I guarantee that Katarina and her daughter will find their way to Austria. It matters not to me. I am a businessman. If Babic paid me enough, I would have his family out of Yugoslavia by next week. Take another night to think on it. If you still wish to proceed, come to the hotel with 5,000 deutschmarks. Bring a suicide note handwritten in Croatian. I will have it typed when I get to Salzburg.

Mauer gave him a piece of paper. In German, he had written: '*I cannot bear living without Katarina and Janica. God forgive me for this sin.*' "Write that in Croat. Do not sign the note."

"That's it?" Goran said, back on his feet and pacing. "No more?"

"Brevity gives the authorities less to interpret. Babic has been away from his loved ones for years. Whatever the reasons – loneliness, despair, guilt, frustration – the rationale is plausible. The police would rather the note be in his handwriting, but that is impossible. I don't like using forgers in these situations."

"How ... will he die?"

"A spiked drink. The rest falls into place. Shall I inform my organization of a contract?"

"Our contract will halt Tony's?"

"With us, yes. From what I know of Babic, he will look to others."

"When will you do it?"

"I leave on Friday. I shall make a diversion to Salzburg, and Babic will be dead by Sunday."

****

The business with Goran delayed Mauer's meeting with Katarina. On Tuesday, Goran gave Mauer the cash and the hand-written note. But a few minutes before seven the following morning, Mauer woke to hammering on his door. In a dressing gown, hair uncombed, and still unshaven, he peeked through the tiny crack in the door. Goran looked as though he had drunk the night away.

"We need to talk," Goran said.

"Get in here and make it quick!"

"I've changed my mind," Goran said. "I cannot live with it."

"Yesterday you consummated the contract. Twelve hours later, you break it?"

"There is no harm, Herr Mauer. The conversation never happened. Give me my money back."

"Ah, but the conversation did happen. My associates have been notified. You expect me to rescind and tarnish my reputation?"

"Yes. I do not want him murdered."

"You are relinquishing control of the situation." Mauer wiped sleep from his eyes. If he refused to return the money, Goran could alert the SDB. An ex-SS officer did not wish to meet Luka Lipovac.

Without observable emotion, Mauer said, "Obviously I have made an error in judgment. The contract shall be rescinded. The money is in the hotel safe and I am now running late for a meeting. I am on the trade floor at eleven, and tonight an Italian exhibitor joins me for dinner. Shall I come by ..." he looked at his watch, "... three hours from now?" Goran's expression inferred that he would rather have the money now. "Ten o'clock I shall bring you the money. I assume only you will be home. I do not want eavesdroppers or a second unpleasant surprise. Please leave me to dress. I am very rushed."

Mauer slammed the door behind Goran louder than he intended, and then walked to the desk, where he scribbled a note on Palace stationery:

'Dear Mrs Babic,

I planned to contact you earlier. I have been busy with the trade fair. I would like an hour of your time, today. I have materials for you to study, and matters to discuss. I shall come for you at one o'clock. Please leave your daughter with another while we walk in the park.

Hamburg'

He slipped the note under the door of Adela's flat. Then he went shopping.

Chapter 34

Mauer arrived early, but didn't knock until ten minutes past the hour. His host looked no better than he had in the morning.

"What is wrong, Herr Skoda? Afraid I would not show?"

"I saw your displeasure at the hotel," Goran said, adjusting the eye patch. "Is everything all right now? You know … between us?"

"I am over my misjudgment. If that is coffee I smell, I have a tonic to spice it up. You would not be averse to a drop of Irish whiskey would you? Or is it too early to drink to the deal never made? You were quite right, Herr Skoda; no harm was done. You haven't changed your mind again, have you?"

"Heavens no," Goran said, scooting to the kitchen. He returned to the parlor with the coffee. Using one hand to steady the other, he poured two steaming cups to within an inch of the brim.

Mauer dispensed an ounce of whiskey into each, noticing no sugar or milk. Perfect. "Might I trouble you for a dollop of milk?"

The moment Goran departed, Mauer added three drops from a vial into his host's cup.

Within ten minutes, Goran found the slumber that had eluded him the night before. Holding him under the arms, Mauer dragged his limp body to the entrance hall and hauled him up onto a chair he had placed directly below the second-floor landing. In a sitting position, Goran's head lolled backward but was stable for the time being.

From his convention satchel, Mauer retrieved a half-inch rope that he looped over the banister at the top of the stairs. The ends fell to the ground floor. He then made a hangman's noose and slipped it over Goran's head. Around his own waist he tied the loose end and gently tugged on the rope to raise Goran's head, though not enough to cut off the air supply. When the time came for Mauer to drop down onto the floor from the second stair, the rope would pull taut over the upper banister and lift Goran high enough that his toes would barely touch the floor. Mauer quivered in anticipation.

Goran moaned, thirty seconds later, stirring. His instinct would be to tear at the rope around his neck, to relieve the tension. But his fingers would never get under the rope, for by that time, it would be tight, and deep in soft tissue.

Goran opened his eye. "What the … Where am I? What is—"

"You are at the scaffold of your execution." Mauer pulled on the rope and cried out. "Oh, mein Gott! Look at him squirm! Fight, you bastard! Show me fight."

Crimson face aghast, Goran clawed for his life. Then, realizing he could not loosen the knot, he grasped at the line above his head, but it slipped through his fingers – the rope too thin, and Goran too weak.

Blinking wildly, Mauer was now howling. "Do not surrender! Fight to the end!" But, as always, the kicking and the thrashing slowed to a stop, and arms flopped to the sides.

"Oh, I love a popping eye. Yours is the size of a golf ball! Now for the finale: the tongue. Come, give it to me – show it." Goran's mouth opened. "Ja, there it is."

Mauer admired the sight for thirty seconds and then he lowered the body and wiped the tears from his own eyes. It was a good kill. Unknotting the rope from his waist, he hauled the body up five stairs and returned to the second-floor landing, where he wrapped the rope around the banister, knotted it and cut off the excess line. Then he lifted Goran's body and pushed it over the side banister. It swing outward and back, like a pendulum, finally coming to a stop a foot above the scatter rug. The chair lay on its side, just as it would if kicked by a man determined to hang himself.

Mauer rinsed, dried and put away the cups, then combed the kitchen and sitting room for any evidence of a visitor. He stuffed the personally handwritten note into the dead man's breast pocket, packed the surplus rope in the satchel and slipped away.

****

At the sound of a knock, Katarina fluffed her hair and put a smile on her lips, yet the smile vanished once she opened the door to a piercing stare that would send a shiver up any woman's spine.

Had he noticed? Collecting herself, she said, "Guten Tag. Sie müssen der Mann von Hamburg sein."

Mauer's thin lips lifted, but his riveting stare persisted. "Your German is good, Frau Babic. I am the man from Hamburg."

Cold eyes migrated all over her, as though they couldn't find a resting place. His lack of propriety made her ill at ease, though she dared not show it.

"Please," she said. "You excuse my pronunciation ... It isn't as good as I want it to be."

"The passport picture I have of you," her visitor said. "I tried to imagine the color of your eyes. You are more beautiful in the flesh."

His leer left little doubt of the remark's intent, and when he told her his name, Katarina's chest contracted and her breath caught as she made a frantic attempt to maintain the slightest sign of joy. Tony had told her of the Nazis of Camp Graham; that Helmut Mauer was the only man he truly feared. He had called Mauer 'the most evil creature on the face of the earth'. Was the unnerving creature now peering into her eyes *that* Helmut Mauer?

"At last I know your name," she said as she whisked past him into the hallway. "For a long time, you were 'the man from Hamburg'." She closed the door, and began walking down the hall. She didn't get far.

"Before we go," Mauer said. "I have a question for you. I saw your fright when I introduced myself. Have you heard my name before?"

"Nein, Herr Mauer."

"Don't call me that. To you I am Helmut. Get used to that. Did your husband mention my name?"

"Tony does not know your name. He said your name was secret."

"You lost your color. Why?"

The answer was easy: she was scared out of her wits. *Yes, exactly.* "I was frightened, Herr Mau ... um, Helmut. I have been frightened all week long. I still am ... They might catch us."

"You have nothing to fear," he said, opening his arms as though to bestow a loving embrace. But his fingers beckoned like the white claws of a cunning predator. "Come to me."

Katarina's weakened knees wouldn't budge. So he stepped toward her, pulled her close, and held her there for an unseemly long moment. She would tolerate him if this was what it took to reunite her and Janica with Tony. But when his bloodless lips brushed her cheek, her body went rigid. Finally, she tried to wriggle free. But he would not release his hold.

"A wife must never resist a husband. This is a test to see how you react under stressful conditions. If you cannot relax, they will not believe you are my wife." He kissed her on the cheek and let go. Three minutes with this ghoulish creature, and already she had lost the ability to force the feeblest of smiles.

On a bench in Zrinjevac Park he gave her a docket of papers. "This is the history of your six years in Hamburg. We met when you asked for directions near the docks. Three months later, we married." He showed her the page of dates, places and times, then handed her Janica Mauer's German birth certificate. "See? Same date, but the place of birth is Hamburg. This is your passport. I've replicated the Slovenian entry stamps."

She leafed through the well-used passport, checking the visa stamps from border cities in the countries they had visited together.

"Memorize the crossings and the dates. Here are your identity papers and transit visas. Keep everything together. Meet me at the train station on Friday at eleven thirty, not a second later. Bring the passport, visas and identity papers. Burn everything else. Travel with one suitcase large enough to carry the clothes you brought from Hamburg to Zagreb. Should they search your bag, you don't want them thinking you are moving from one country to another."

"And if I need to contact you beforehand?" she asked.

"Why would you?"

"I don't know. But if I should …?"

"Call the Palace Hotel."

****

Katarina needed a telephone. Hopefully, Goran was home. The matter was important – one that could not possibly wait until Sunday. He would, of course, listen from the adjoining room, but she had a plan to avert that.

After rapping several times, she jotted a note. She folded it, ready to jam it between the door and the frame, then, on a whim, tried the latch. How strange that the door was unlocked.

"Goran? Are you home?"

If not for the urgency, she would never have gone inside. She entered, and turned toward the parlor … and gave a little cry, staggered to the staircase, and collapsed on the bottom step, ten feet from the motionless, dangling body.

Why would he? Why now? The first question was perhaps not as difficult as the second. Goran could not have known of the latest plot to get her out of Yugoslavia.

Using the banister for support, she hoisted herself upright and made her way to the telephone. At first, her trembling hands were disobliging. But, she managed to reach the operator. *Please, Tony, be there.*

He answered. "It's gone wrong," she said.

"I can't hear you," Tony said from Salzburg.

"I'm at Goran's. He's ... hanged himself."

"Hanged himself? Right there in the house? Jesus!"

They spoke of their shock and disbelief, and then Katarina brought the conversation to the possible ramifications. "Why now?" she said. "Do you think he knew?"

"Impossible."

She raked her hand through her hair. "It's too dangerous for us to leave."

"Everything's in place, Katarina. Has the Hamburg man contacted you?"

"The Hamburg man is Helmut Mauer." From the other end of the line, she heard a pattern of short breaths. "It's him, Tony. He looks inhuman – tall, thin, cunning, repulsive—"

In a whisper, Tony said, "What the hell is going on? After all these years ... he wants his revenge." A few seconds of stillness passed.

"Get Janica and Adela out of the flat. Go to the coast, right away, the instant you get home. Make sure he's not watching the building. I'm useless to you here. Don't waste another minute on the phone. No. Don't hang up. How could they? I need a moment – I have to think."

She had never heard such panic in his voice. "Should I report the suicide?"

"Say nothing. Just get out of there. Fast. Find another phone. I might have ... Wait a minute. Did Goran leave a suicide note?"

"I don't know. I couldn't stand to look at him."

"Oh, Katarina, this is so important. I hate to ask this of you ... I need you to look for a note ... and check the noose around his neck."

"For what?"

"I want to know if the knot's a hangman's noose. If it is, count the number of coils. I'm sorry. I wouldn't ask if it weren't so ... Please do it."

She laid the receiver on the table and returned to a face that was bruised and grotesque. The corner of a piece of paper jutted from Goran's vest pocket. She counted the coils, snatched the note, and ran back to the parlor.

"He knew we were going, Tony. That's why he took his life." She read him the note.

"Did the knot have five coils?"

"How did you know?"

"Mauer didn't touch you, did he?"

"No. I did my best to stay calm, but he saw my fright. I said I was afraid we'd be caught. I think he believed me because he gave me the passport and some things to study."

"You have the passport?"

"And the travel visas."

"This is our chance, Katarina. He was to provide the cover and do the talking. You speak enough German to get by on your own. Leave today. There should still be a seven o'clock train to Ljubljana. Spend the night there and leave for Dravograd and Klagenfurt in the morning. I'll be at the Klagenfurt station waiting for you. If you make a change or there's a problem, leave a message at my hotel in Klagenfurt, the Sandwirth."

"Won't it look suspicious, a young woman without a husband traveling with her little girl?"

"Not necessarily. Tell the border guard you decided to leave Zagreb a day earlier than your husband. This is our opportunity. We have to take it. Mauer was going to drug Janica before the border."

"You didn't tell me that."

"They said a mild sedative to make her sleep. I didn't like it, either, but there was no turning back. If you can get her to stay quiet ..."

"She's never quiet, nor is she shy talking with strangers. I could tell her we're playing a game of quiet. That might work. A sedative ... I'm not so sure that's a—"

"You don't want her correcting a customs guy who's called you 'Mrs Mauer'."

"It's too risky" she said. "I have to think of—"

313

"You have to do it. How about a mild sedative? Take Adela with you as far as Ljubljana. She can return to Zagreb on Saturday. Mauer will be gone by then. Call me the minute you check into the hotel. I need to know you're safe. Promise me you'll be on that train."

"What of Goran and the note?"

"Destroy the note. I'll take care of the rest from here. Tomorrow, we will be together."

Chapter 35

By twenty minutes to eleven, Tony was a wreck. The bell of the telephone remained passive. If it didn't ring by eleven, they had not made it to Ljubljana. Surely she would have called if she had missed the train or changed her mind. Had Mauer been watching? Had he seen them leave the tenement with travel bags? Had he apprehended them? Or, worse, had he hopped the same train?

Tony had to admit to himself that it was a slapdash plan – a few-minute conversation under nerve-racking conditions.

Five minutes past the hour, Katarina called to say they were in Ljubljana. "The train was twenty minutes late," she said. "By the time we checked in and were in our room, we—"

"I was afraid that ..." Tony caught himself before uttering Mauer's name. "May I speak with Janica for a second?" He heard the call to their daughter.

"Hello, Tata. I've been on a train – a *big* train. So fast and noisy! It hissed when it started. I couldn't hear Mama. I've seen many trains, Tata. It's fun to be inside one."

"I'm so happy you enjoyed the ride. Are you going on another train tomorrow?"

"I don't know ... Mama, are we going on another train?" After a moment's pause, she said, "Mama says yes."

Katarina came on the line. "She's a real little chatterbox, isn't she?"

"I'm going to let her talk all day and all night if she wants to."

"If the train's on time," Katarina said, "we're in Dravograd at eleven thirty. We go through passport control and board the Villach line. All going well, we will meet you on the platform at one thirty. What do I do if you aren't there?"

"I'll be there. You're right, though – better to be safe. Check into the Crown Hotel and wait for my call."

"And if you don't call?"

Tony didn't have an answer for that one. "I can't wait to see you both," he said. "By the way, do you know Mauer's Zagreb hotel?"

"The Palace. Why do you ask?"

"To make sure he hasn't checked out."

Tony packed a large suitcase with clothes and his most prized possessions. In his pocket he would carry the US immigration visas sponsored by Bobby Rose. If Katarina and Janica were on the Klagenfurt train, all of them would spend a night at the Sandwirth and, in the morning, depart for the German port of Bremerhaven, on the North Sea. The only formality left in the US immigration process was a medical examination confirming the family's good health.

From New York, they would travel to Chicago and stay two or three weeks, depending on the literary needs of Bobby Rose, who wanted to publish a series of articles on the war's 'circumstantial enemies' – the good guys on the bad side. Tony wondered if anyone cared. The war ended seven years ago. Nonetheless, he would fulfill his commitment, after which the three of them would veer south to Atlanta for a reunion with Joshua and Bo. That was the plan – as long as Katarina and Janica made it to Austria.

Tony rose early, packed, mailed his notice of moving to his Salzburg landlord, and emptied his bank account. He was in his Klagenfurt hotel room at noon. If all went as it should, a half hour from now Katarina would clear customs. An hour later, he dialed the Zagreb SDB.

"I must speak with Secretary Lipovac. The matter is urgent to the security of the Yugoslav state."

"The secretary is not in the office," the clerk said. "May I put you through to his assistant?"

"That won't do. Is Secretary Lipovac at his home?"

"I am not at liberty to divulge that—"

Tony hung up and redialed. This time he asked to be connected to Luka's residence. A husky-voiced woman answered.

"Is this Mrs Lipovac?" Tony asked.

"Sure is."

"I'm calling from Austria for your husband."

"Who's this?"

"My name is Tony Babic. He knows me."

"This is Ella Roza Lipovac – don't suppose you remember me?"

"I'm afraid we've never met."

"We sure have – between the vines at Vinograd Kralja ... or should I say, between the sheets? You knew me as Roza."

Tony lowered himself to the bed. "No man could forget you. Now ... it's starting to make sense." His head was spinning with the complications and coincidences of the past twenty-four hours. "Is it you I should thank for that visa back in '46. Luka's change of heart was hard to figure. I wasn't one of his favorites."

"No," she said. "But, you didn't call to thank me for a visa. What is it you want?"

"I've a present for Luka. But he'll have to move quickly to claim it. I have a heartless war criminal for him – an SS Major." Without divulging the name, he gave Ella most of the story, including Mauer's history, his crimes in America and his sick obsessions. "He's been in Zagreb less than a week and he's already killed a man. I'm prepared to make a trade with Luka. I'll trade the Nazi for four exit visas from Yugoslavia. I want the visas for my mother, father, wife and daughter. The visas are to be issued by the end of next week. My wife is in Croatia against her will. I haven't seen her in six years. I'm not sure my parents will want to leave. In any case, I'd like them to have the choice. Do you think Luka will make that trade?"

"I'm a senior member of the party," Ella said. "If I make a deal, Luka will go along with it. He goes off, sometimes for days. I'm not sure I can locate him. Don't underestimate my skills at apprehending criminals. During the war, they called me 'the Chameleon'. You wouldn't know of that. Doesn't matter – give me the rest of the story."

"Do you agree to the deal?"

"Give me his name and location. If we take him, it's a deal."

For Tony, the pact was a back-up should Katarina and Janica not pass border inspection. "The Nazi is Helmut Mauer. He still goes by that name. The man he murdered in Zagreb is Goran Skoda."

"My God! I know Goran."

Another coincidence. Was there more? At this point, did it matter?

"He's hanging by the neck in his flat," Tony said. "The knot is a five-coil hangman's noose. That's Mauer's trademark. I've no idea why he murdered Goran or how they knew each other."

317

"We'll find out," Ella said. "You say Mauer's checking out of the Palace tomorrow. We'll take him tonight. If I can't reach Luka, I'll do it myself."

"You must not. Mauer's a monster. The hairs on my neck are standing up, just thinking about him. Have a gang of agents with you. When you have him, ask the whereabouts of his SS colonel, Wolfgang von Arnim. He's the bigger fish, the one who ran the war court. Be careful. Mauer is extremely dangerous."

"So am I," she said.

****

Though Ella had led Tony to believe Luka was incognito, she knew that he'd be at his favorite café, on Ilica Street, holding court with a band of cohorts.

"Here comes Ella," Luka said to his pals as she approached his table. "What's on her mind?"

Ella asked the others for privacy, then filled him in – everything but the name of the Nazi and Goran's murder. "Can you agree to four visas?"

"For an SS major and a live lead on an SS colonel? You bet. Skoda's gonna go off his fucking rocker." He motioned for two more coffees.

"Goran's dead. The murderer is SS-Major Helmut Mauer."

"Holy Shit! I'll get Babic *eight* visas – get on with it."

"He's here in Zagreb until Friday morning." Ella gave the details and offered thoughts on how they might apprehend Mauer. As she spoke, his eyes clouded, and under the table his knee bobbed up and down like the needle of a hardworking sewing machine. "What a fucking strike! But, Ella, what's Mauer's connection to Skoda?"

"Tony doesn't know."

"What the hell would Skoda have to do with the *trade fair*? Oh, what the hell – Mauer will sing by morning anyway. He better not tell us Arnim's dead or in Argentina."

Walking to Tomislav Square, they homed in on the most promising options. None were conventional or foolproof – they never were. The fun was tiptoeing through the hazards. As with Christoph Schwanitz and the Ustasha sergeant who murdered Professor Milic, Luka and Ella decided to do it their own, appropriately ironic way.

****

At the dinner hour, a thin, steely-eyed man in a black suit marched past the hotel doorman to the front desk. Nearby, in a lounge chair, Luka peered over the newspaper. The man looked impatient. A dumpy Italian at the counter was struggling to communicate with the desk clerk. In Serbo-Croatian, with a strong German accent, the edgy one said, "Give me my key. Then you deal with him."

The clerk, seemingly not wanting to annoy either guest, plucked a key, a message and an envelope from pigeonhole 211. "Two messages, Herr Mauer," he said before returning his attention to the Italian.

Mauer read the message taken by the hotel switchboard. Then he tore open the envelope and read as he ascended the stairs to the second floor.

Luka left the hotel, satisfied that Mauer would meet the mysterious woman who had left him a note.

****

A less strenuous life had added a few pounds since the war, but at thirty-four, Ella was still striking. Tonight, she would corral the pig and bring it to the spit. She painted her face, stepped into a scandalously short dress, and slipped on a pair of heels.

On the arm of a big man in a three-piece suit, she entered the hotel. Alone, she sauntered into the cocktail lounge while her escort plopped himself into a lobby armchair and tucked his head into the newspaper he had read hours ago.

She saw the target enter the lounge, his hair slicked back and eagerness in his hollow black eyes. Waving him over would be unnecessary.

When the small talk ended, he asked how long he had with her.

She planned to tease him for fifteen minutes, and then get him to the room. "Your benefactor paid for an hour." His demeanor had told her that he would be nasty behind closed doors. In the prelude, astute ladies of the evening exploited such a man's needs and proclivities to increase his lust, to boost the stakes. Though such foreplay was unnecessary in a pre-paid liaison, Ella relished the art of masquerade. She wanted to egg him on, augment his anger, and stimulate his need to inflict pain and God knows whatever else. "You won't need half as long," she said, dismissively.

"Why do you say this?"

"I know your type. You think I can't see your desperation?"

"You are wasting my time," he said, wringing his hands.

319

"The hour starts in the room," she said. "Can you keep your pants on till I finish my drink?"

"Finish it!"

"Oh my, I've a feeling you're going to give me a thrashing I won't forget."

"You have no idea."

"Oh, but I do. That's why I command the highest price in Zagreb."

"How much, and who paid you?"

"That would be telling." His wry grin indicated that he'd know soon enough. "Do you play the breath game?"

"You couldn't have asked a better question." She finished her drink, dabbed her luscious lips, and said, "Till I'm fucking blue."

Mauer's eyes followed the sway of her backside as she mounted the staircase. He would beat some respect into that luscious ass. Whatever her price, she would earn every dinar. At the landing, he clipped the back of her head with an open hand and shoved her down the hall to room 211. Near the door, he sped past her, inserted the key and pushed the door open, hitting the light switch.

But the room remained dark. Muttering an oath, Mauer charged inside, hands reaching toward the lamp on the night table. He never got there. The door slammed, and the room illuminated. His hands came to his mouth and he dropped to his knees.

The bedspring, mattress and night tables had been removed, and the walls were draped in blue, white and red striped banners with a yellow-bordered red star at the center. Three armed men in uniform stepped up behind him. Two more flanked a well-dressed burly man who sat at the writing desk in front of the window. The big man rhythmically tapped a gavel into his palm. But it was the five-coiled noose hanging from the chandelier that had Mauer cowering.

In German, Ella said, "Major Mauer, you are charged with war crimes from 1939 to 1945, which include the murder of Hermann Vogler. You are also charged with the murder of Goran Skoda. Now, get up and sit in that chair, facing Judge Luka Lipovac."

When Mauer didn't move, the SDB cops dragged him to the chair and threw him upon it.

"How do you plead?" Ella asked.

"Not guilty," he said in a quiet snivel.

Ella grabbed the rope, and Mauer recoiled as she gave him several lashes to the head and neck. Holding the rope to his eyes, she said, "This was found in your room – it matches the rope around Goran Skoda's neck. Shall I join the ends, or do you wish to reconsider your plea?"

When Mauer didn't answer, Luka motioned Ella forward with his pseudo gavel, a farmer's mallet. In her ear he whispered, "Get to Arnim."

She turned back to Mauer. "In the lounge, you asked who paid me. Still want to know?"

Mauer's eyes were downcast to the floor.

"She grabbed him by the hair to hike his chin. "Show respect for this court, or that noose goes around your neck. Do you want to know?"

Mauer nodded rapidly and a few drops of sweat dripped from his chin to the floor.

"An old friend of yours paid me. His name is Tony Babic."

"Impossible," Mauer said, his eyes still fixed on the floor boards.

"If it weren't possible, you wouldn't be here. Or are you here because of Wolfgang von Arnim? Do you know him?"

Ella winked at Luka, but Mauer remained silent.

Luka slammed the mallet to the table. "I want Wolfgang von Arnim! Talk or I cut your nuts off!" Luka pulled a knife, walked over to Mauer and held the blade at his crotch. "Understand, Nazi pig?"

"What happens to me if I tell you?" Mauer asked.

"Cough up Arnim, you avoid the noose and the knife – you'll go to an island prison."

"How do I know I can trust you?"

Luka laughed. "These SS porkers are all the same. They want to keep calling the shots. Nick and Vlado! Pull his pants down." Luka offered Ella the knife. "Here, have a go at him."

Mauer began trembling all over. "I ... talk," he stuttered.

When there was nothing left for Mauer to give, Luka ordered his cops from the room.

****

On the platform, Tony waited, clutching the life-size doll adorned in a red and white print dress and shiny red shoes. Gisela wore a blond wig of human hair. She had been the most expensive doll in the store. The other gift, for Katarina, he had bought a year ago. *Dear God, let them be on that train.* The last possible snag would be the Yugoslav border guards.

Earlier, he had called the Lipovac home. Ella confirmed Mauer's arrest. When Tony asked what they did with him, she said he wouldn't want to know. Mauer was out of his life forever, and they would use their connections in Germany to seize Arnim. The visas would be delivered at the end of the week, all to Vinograd Kralja.

Finally, Tony heard the squeal of the train's brakes. It slowed to a stop and the tide of passengers descended from the coaches. Within minutes, the flow eased to a trickle and his spirits sank. Frantic, he trotted down the platform, peering through the windows into the compartments.

Two cars from the end, a little girl in blond ringlets jumped from the doorstep to the dock. Tony dropped to one knee and rocked the mannequin from side to side like a pendulum. Janica's eyes darted between her father and the doll.

"Come and meet Gisela," he said to her. "She is for you."

Janica ran into his arms. "Thank you, Tata. She is beautiful, and tall as me!"

"Yes. And hair and eyes like yours."

He glanced beyond his little girl to the woman several paces back and tears filled his eyes. Katarina bent over him, and in the silence she wiped his anguish aside with her thumb, and ran her fingers though his curls.

Finally, Tony managed to say, "She's wonderful," and Katarina nodded as she dabbed her own eyes with a handkerchief.

Still on one knee, he handed her a tiny box.

Katarina's lips quivered, and when she opened the box, she uttered a gasp.

"You married me so I could be Janica's father," he said. "Now I'm asking you to be my wife."

About the author

John Richard Bell was born in Chigwell, UK and now resides in Vancouver, Canada. Before becoming an author of business books and historical fiction, he was the CEO of a Fortune 500 company and a global strategy consultant. A prolific blogger, John's musings on strategy, leadership and branding have appeared in various journals such as Fortune, Forbes and ceoafterlife.com.

58056941R00200

Made in the USA
San Bernardino, CA
25 November 2017